PRAISE FOR
THE YOUNG OF OTHER ANIMALS

"*The Young of Other Animals* is an addictively moving and suspenseful novel with family secrets fueling the narrative. Cander presents a complex study of the ways in which women respond to trauma, and how those scars can be passed down from mother to daughter. Cander excels in writing richly drawn women characters and complicated family relationships. Paula and Mayree are characters that will stay with me for a long time."

—Lara Prescott, *New York Times* bestselling author of
The Secrets We Kept

"Love and loss, in Cander's powerfully addictive new novel, unearth dark secrets and a shared trauma that threaten to earthquake an already shaky bond between a mother and daughter. Cander's usual cloquence with characters is in full force here, as is her understanding that feelings are not facts, love is persistent, and what we think might kill us can be the very thing to save us."

—Caroline Leavitt, *New York Times* bestselling author of
With or Without You

"Several dark and twisty rivers run through Chris Cander's latest engrossing novel—a compelling crime mystery, a deft exploration of flawed mother-daughter relationships, and an intimate view of violent childhood trauma. *The Young of Other Animals* delivers as a suspense novel and as an homage to the resilience of female relationships."

—Julia Heaberlin, international bestselling author of
Night Will Find You

"*The Young of Other Animals* is unlike any book I've read before—an intense, distinctive novel about mothers and daughters, generational trauma, and redemption. Part family drama, part mystery, and part dark comedy, this book is gutting in the way only the best literature, written by an author with immense skill, wisdom, and compassion, can be. What a knockout."

—Ashley Winstead, author of *Midnight Is the Darkest Hour*

"*The Young of Other Animals* is a gut punch of a novel—a deeply suspenseful, profoundly moving exploration of the aftermath of trauma, set in an atmospheric Austin of years past and featuring an unforgettable mother-daughter duo. I couldn't turn pages fast enough, though I wanted to savor every line. Chris Cander is a true talent."

—Katie Gutierrez, national bestselling author of *More Than You'll Ever Know*

"*The Young of Other Animals* is chilling, moving, and urgent, one of those books that demands your full attention until you've finished the very last page. Chris Cander's propulsive, beautifully layered prose tackles cycles of violence and the complicated shame of survival, but this is also a story full of hope—a novel about resiliency, growing up, mothers and daughters, and above all, the way women love and care for one another."

—Kimberly King Parsons, National Book Award–nominated author of *Black Light*

"Chris Cander made my heart pound in this gripping tale of womanhood, trust, friendship, consent, fear, and, at its core, a woman's enduring strength."

—Zibby Owens, author of *Blank*

"Chris Cander's blazing and beautifully written novel *The Young of Other Animals* opens with an astonishing attack on a young woman. What follows is a meditation on the trauma of violence—the push and pull of vulnerability and resilience—a mind-bending whodunit, and a thrilling conclusion. Superbly crafted, the story grabbed me from the start, carried me deep into the hearts of its characters, and by the last page, I didn't want to let go. I'll be unpacking this one for a long while."

—C. J. Washington, author of *The Intangible* and *Imperfect Lives*

"Mother-daughter relationships can be fraught with tension, and these mother-daughter duos are ready to ignite. Chris Cander crafts a fascinating novel about family dynamics, true friendship, and intergenerational trauma. A young woman in jeopardy is just the start of this sizzling work of suspense. *The Young of Other Animals* is poised to ignite a fire in every reader who picks it up."

—Pamela Klinger-Horn, event coordinator at Valley Bookseller

The
Young
of
Other
Animals

ALSO BY CHRIS CANDER

The Young of Other Animals

A Novel

CHRIS CANDER

x

Little
a

Published by Little A, New York

www.apub.com

Amazon, the Amazon logo, and Little A are trademarks of Amazon.com, Inc., or its affiliates.

ISBN-13: 9781662514999 (hardcover)
ISBN-13: 9781662515002 (paperback)
ISBN-13: 9781662515019 (digital)

Cover design by Faceout Studio, Amanda Hudson
Cover image: © Giulio_Fornasar / Shutterstock; © Khosrork / Getty

Printed in the United States of America

First edition

For my mom,
who has always believed
and believed in me

You do not have to be good.

You do not have to walk on your knees

for a hundred miles through the desert, repenting.

You only have to let the soft animal of your body

love what it loves.

Tell me about despair, yours, and I will tell you mine.

—*Mary Oliver, "Wild Geese"*

Paula

*F*ind the road. Paula looked up, checked the position of the moon, then turned around. She ran in the direction she assumed she'd come from, keeping the thick, bright crescent on her left—this shred of logic and her gut being all she had to navigate by.

The woods seemed thicker. Had they been this dense before? There was nothing familiar, nothing to indicate she was going the right way. She stopped, bent forward to catch her breath. Her right arm hurt; her mouth tasted like copper. She spat on the dirt.

A moment later, there was a soft, muffled sound behind her: the crunch of leaves. She yelped and spun around, fists balled, ready to fight him off again. But it was only a large armadillo, standing on its hind legs about three yards behind her, sniffing at the air for danger. Her ability to smell its foul odor meant that it was upwind and likely couldn't smell her, even though the seat of her pants was soaked through with urine. In spite of her drunken panic, Paula's thoughts briefly fixated on the animal, which, for some reason, she assumed was female. Why was she out of her burrow in the middle of the night? March was birthing season. Where were her pups? Didn't they need their mama?

Suddenly, in a way that had become totally uncharacteristic, Paula desperately wanted her own mother. She wanted to run into Mayree's open arms, curl into a small heap on her lap, and cling to her neck like she had as a child, letting her mother rock her, shushing softly, assuring her that everything was going to be all right.

But how would it be all right? The guy had seemed so nice at the party; she'd never have gone willingly with him otherwise. Now, over and over, she could hear him screaming in her ear, could feel the blade against her neck and the blinding pain in her jaw from his fist. She didn't know if he'd started chasing her again or if she'd killed him—oh god, what if she'd killed him?

She should've found the road by now. She'd probably been running in circles around the woods; underneath the canopy of trees, the moon had been difficult to follow. By the time she saw the car's interior light in the distance, her ankles were raw from where her new shoes had rubbed them, and the bloody gash on her arm had crusted over. She couldn't believe it—not only was his car still there, but it sounded like the engine was running. She dropped onto all fours in case he'd beaten her back to it. In the abrupt stillness, his voice filled her mind: *you asked for this.*

No, she hadn't. All she'd wanted was to make a phone call.

Crouched low, she moved forward, expecting the guy to jump out from somewhere at her. What had he said his name was? Patrick? Michael? Had she forgotten? Had he even told her? She picked up a stick to use as a weapon, then dashed from tree to tree, pressing herself into the darkness until she was confident enough that nobody else was there, and made a run for the car. After a quick glance into the back seat, she closed the passenger door, then ran around to the driver's side and locked herself in, imagining she'd only barely escaped. The light dimmed to off. If not for her fear, her shock, she'd have wept for this small miracle. Instead, she jammed the accelerator and peeled out onto the paved road, hardly caring where she was going as long as it was away.

The road came to a T and she stopped. A sign for Grisham Trail pointed to the left. That was the road she and Kelly had used to enter the park earlier that night. She turned the wheel, her forearm aching with the effort. There were no other cars anywhere, which only added to her surreal sense of being utterly alone in the world. She had no idea what time it was or how long she'd been gone. An hour? Three? Would Kelly still be at the party? Would anyone?

She sped down Grisham Trail, passing signs for boat ramps and camping areas. Then she saw a sign for Baldwin Cove and felt a pang of sorrow. That was where she and Kelly used to go camping and fishing with their fathers when they were younger, and it was where the frat party Paula hadn't even wanted to attend had been earlier tonight. Her sorrow flashed to anger—practically as soon as they'd arrived, Kelly had gone off with some guy and left her to drink alone among a bunch of strangers. It wasn't the first time she'd abandoned Paula at a party, assuming Paula would find someone to hang out with, find another ride, and later, forgive her, which she always did.

She wished her father were here, alive, to help her.

Paula slowed down as she neared the turnoff, her grip fierce on the steering wheel. As she scanned the parking area, her anger morphed into anticipation; right now, she needed her best friend. Also, although she felt weirdly, drunkenly alert, she didn't want to drive herself all the way back to Austin. There were only a dozen or so cars left and, thank god, Kelly's was one of them. Paula pulled up as close as she could get to the beach, where two guys shielded their eyes and yelled at her to turn off the headlights. Their harsh voices made her cower. Scared to leave the car, she leaned forward to search for Kelly in the dying light of the bonfire through the windshield. There! Paula leaped out of the car and ran.

"Kelly!" Paula's voice was trapped in her throat, the way it sometimes happened in nightmares, her scream only a whisper that nobody could hear. "Kelly!" Paula flung herself onto the sandy gravel next to Kelly, who was lying on a towel, up close against another body.

"Jesus, Paul! You scared the shit out of me."

Kelly was still there, making out with the same guy, like everything was normal, like nothing had happened. The relief Paula felt surged through her with such vigor that she hunched forward and gagged.

Kelly scrabbled away from her and made a noise of disgust. "She's wasted," she said to the guy. "Can you get her some water?" He nodded and meandered off.

Then she turned to Paula. "What have you been doing? I thought you'd gone home or something."

Paula sputtered, unable to speak. She began to shake, suddenly cold. She didn't know what was happening to her body. She couldn't reconcile what had happened over the past hour or more with the fact that she was now physically back where they'd started the evening, when she'd been merely unhappy. When she was unaware that she was about to be violently attacked.

Kelly looked at Paula's arm, the blood caked through her sweater sleeve, all the way to her hand. "You're bleeding. What the fuck happened to you? Did you fall down?" She leaned down and sniffed dramatically near Paula's lower half. "Did you pee yourself?"

Paula moaned quietly and began to cry held-back tears that dragged what was left of her makeup down her cheeks.

Kelly shook out the towel she'd been on and wrapped it around Paula's shoulders. "Okay, okay, let's get you home. I stopped drinking a while ago, so I'm okay to drive. We can stop at Whataburger if you want. You should probably eat something to soak up all the alcohol. I just want to get my new guy's phone number—and his name—then we can go." She looked around to see where he'd gone. The last few partygoers were packing up to leave. Someone emptied their cup onto the bonfire with a splash and a sizzle.

"No," Paula said, finally able to form words. "We need to go home now."

"He'll be back. What's another couple minutes?"

Minutes? Paula couldn't bear being there another second. "Now. Come on." She gave the car she'd escaped in a wide berth, pulling Kelly toward hers, making desperate, guttural sounds.

Kelly yanked her arm away. "For fuck's sake, Paula. You can't just get shit-faced and expect me to drop everything to take you home when you get sick. That's hardly fair."

But Paula kept dragging her friend, despite Kelly's protestations as she looked for the guy she'd been making out with, and then they were at her car and Paula was riffling through Kelly's purse, searching for her keys. She needed to get away from there, to get the screaming voice out of her head.

"What is *with* you?" Kelly swatted Paula's hand, pulled out the keys, and unlocked the car. "Make sure you put the towel down first. I don't want my seat to stink like piss."

Paula scrambled inside, locked her door, tried to make herself small. She peered out at the road. Would he have had time to walk all the way back to the cove? What if someone else had come along and given him a ride so he could look for her? What if he was hiding, preparing to ambush the car? "Hurry," she said.

Kelly stood on the sill of her open door and called out with great drama, "Goodbye, whoever you are. May we meet again!" When nobody called back, she sighed and let herself drop into her seat. "I hope you're happy. He was a really good kisser."

"Just go."

"Is this about Will? I told you, Paul—that wastoid isn't worth getting drunk over. Tonight was supposed to be your fresh start."

"It's not about Will," Paula said, although in part, it was. If she hadn't been pining for him, if she hadn't wanted to find a phone so she could call him, she wouldn't have been lured away from the party.

Kelly pulled out onto the road, fishtailing a little in the loose gravel. "Hang on! I might actually still be a little drunk after all." She laughed.

Paula was still shaking. Her jaw ached so much that her ears were ringing. Her body hurt all over. She angled the air vent away from her face, hugged herself tightly, and said nothing.

"Okay, what's going on with you? I've seen you drunk plenty of times but I've never seen you act like this. You mixed, didn't you? You should've stuck with the wine coolers. You know if you switch fuel in the middle of a flight, you're in for a crash landing." Kelly patted her on the arm that wasn't covered in blood. "Did you have that trash can punch? I bet that shit was nasty. Remember what I told you about only drinking from a bottle or can you open yourself? You never know if somebody spiked it with something bad."

"Someone tried to kill me," Paula said in barely a whisper. Saying it aloud had a literal sobering effect.

"That's right. That's why you have to be careful. From now on, bottles and cans only."

Paula shook her head and started to cry again. Kelly sighed dramatically, her forbearance so fake that it made Paula want to either hit her or cry harder or both.

"It wasn't the punch!" She shoved her bloodied arm in front of Kelly. "Someone actually tried to kill me!"

They were still on the road out of the park, not quite to the highway that would take them back to town. Kelly pulled over to the shoulder and turned to Paula. "What the fuck are you talking about?"

Nearly hysterical, alternately gasping and hiccuping in between phrases, Paula sketched out the story: she did drink the trash can punch, in fact, and it had made her drunk and weepy. The details were fuzzy. She must've been talking about her ex-boyfriend, Will, and some nice guy had overheard and offered to take her to a pay phone so she could call him. She accepted and he drove her somewhere—to the middle of nowhere, it seemed—and when she realized that he wasn't being nice, that he was going to hurt her for some reason, she got scared and threw up inside the car. He hit her in the jaw and body; then he pulled a knife and pressed it against her throat. She fought him off—she had no idea how—cutting her arm in the process, and then he chased her through the woods. He fell, hard, maybe hard enough to knock him out, or even kill him. She didn't stay to check. She ran away, back to his car, which she drove to find Kelly, who was now staring at her with her mouth open. When Paula finished speaking, she sucked in as much air as she could and held it, trying to stop the hiccups.

"You're shitting me."

"I'm not! It happened! Look at me." Paula held up her arm again, as if Kelly could see underneath the blood-caked sweater and into the knife gash and beyond to all the parts inside her body that would, for the rest of her life, she assumed, carry the evidence of her terror.

"I am looking, okay?" Kelly seemed both aghast and doubtful. "He really had a knife? And you fought him off? You're saying the keys to his car were still in the ignition?" Yes, yes, yes. "Jesus, why didn't you tell me in the first place? I thought you were just drunk. Should we go to the police?"

She hadn't thought that far. When the guy had been chasing her and grabbed her shirt from behind, she'd stopped running. Still going fast, he'd tripped over her left foot and gone down hard in front of her. For a moment she hadn't moved. Neither had he. Arms and legs splayed, he'd lain face down in the dirt. He could've broken his neck when he fell. She'd felt first an instinct to check him for signs of life, then another, stronger impulse: to run. She should've made sure he was alive before she did. A good person would've done that. What if she'd really killed him? Didn't she have an obligation to tell the authorities about a possible death? "Maybe?"

"If we go to the police, we'll get in huge trouble," Kelly said, shaking her head. "We were drinking. You were drunk. We're still underage. And I may have done a line or two of cocaine earlier. How's that going to look on our law school applications?"

"You did cocaine?"

"Just a little. Don't worry, it's worn off." Then she asked more rapid-fire questions Paula couldn't answer: "What was his name?" And "What did he look like?" And "What kind of car was it?"

She wasn't sure, wasn't sure, wasn't sure. She hadn't paid attention to the car; she could only recall that it was dark. Black or gray. Maybe even green. The guy's face was a total blank. His hair was dark, too, but she couldn't remember his features. He'd seemed friendly. The more she concentrated, the less certain about everything she became. A sense of shame and culpability began to work its way into her thoughts. *You asked for this.* Maybe she did. "I just wanted to call Will."

"Why would you go off with a stranger like that?" Kelly looked at her with what appeared to be genuine horror.

Paula glared at her. "What do you mean? You went off with a stranger, too. You were making out with some random guy whose name you didn't even know!" Paula banged her fist on the dash so hard the glove compartment door fell open. Until that moment, she'd never wondered—not seriously—why she and Kelly were still friends.

Kelly looked at her hard, then reached over and slammed the glove box door shut. Without a word, she threw the car into drive and took off, whipping up a cloud of dust behind them.

They drove in silence for a moment. Paula cradled her hurt arm with the other. Again, her mind went back to the woods. She remembered her body, strung out from all the adrenaline, running over rocks and roots, crashing through mesquite trees, her small purse banging against her hip, the guy right behind her. She heard again the rustle of underbrush and their panting breaths—from the vantage of her disembodied consciousness it was almost peaceful—then felt his hand grabbing her shirt, jolting her back to fear. *Stop.* She'd heard it out loud, a female voice, maybe her own, and she had. She'd come to a dead stop, legs planted on the dry ground, and he'd tripped over her. Then she'd started running again.

Her purse. Where was it? "Oh my god," Paula said, patting herself down.

"What?"

"I can't find my purse." Frantic, she searched the floor with her hands. "It's not here!"

Kelly slowed the car. "Are you sure?"

"My license is in there. My keys." She'd had it in the woods. Had she dropped it? No, she remembered it hanging across her body when she got back to his car. Had she somehow left it inside?

"You have an extra set of keys. We'll get you a new license."

"No." She felt light-headed. The fear of returning to the car back at the cove was overpowered by the fear of the guy finding her purse, and in it her name and address and the keys to her house—if he hadn't already. "We have to go back."

Kelly sighed, then turned around and headed toward Baldwin Cove.

Back at the parking area, there were no cars anywhere in sight. None. Kelly leaned forward with her arms draped around the steering wheel. "Well?"

Paula got out and looked around in disbelief. There was some trash strewn around the parking lot—but no people and no cars. She'd parked it right there. Had she turned the ignition off? Had he returned for it? If so, then he was alive. And if he was alive, then she wasn't guilty of murdering him. But also, he might now know who she was and where she lived. At that moment, she wasn't sure which was worse.

Maybe someone else had taken it. Could the car have slipped into gear and rolled away? She jogged to the edge of the lake and looked in, trying to see beneath the moonlit surface. There! A flash of some-thing between waves—a fender? Desperate to confirm its presence, she waded in, kicking around to make contact with the sunken car. Then a fish broke the surface and skittered away. Of course it was a fish, not a fender. Fish were nocturnal feeders, she knew. Her father used to take her night fishing for just that reason. How could she be so stupid? She stood knee-deep in the water, letting the cold sting her as punishment.

She turned around and surveyed the beach, the parking area, the road beyond it. The car really was gone. Either the guy had come back for it or someone else had taken it. Would he try to find her? Would the police?

What if they found his body? Wouldn't they find it hard to believe she was innocent if she hadn't reported the assault? *You asked for this.* She'd peed her pants in the car. Could it be traced back to her, like a fingerprint? She looked around again. How could she prove that she'd been taken against her will, that she'd fought for her life and won? The cut alone wasn't enough; it could've been from a fall, like Kelly had thought, or a stray nail, or even self-inflicted. She had nothing but her own story, with its missing details and paltry descriptions. She hadn't even thought to memorize the license plate number. And Kelly was right: she was drunk. Paula felt like she would be sick again, but there was nothing in her stomach to let go of.

She slogged back across the narrow stretch of beach where the party had taken place. The fire was out, the pit soaked with lake water. She kicked one of the plastic cups that had been left behind. Then she saw her purse lying in the gravel near where she'd found Kelly. The strap was broken; she must've torn it when she'd landed on the ground. She unzipped it and checked the contents. Her keys, wallet, driver's license, college ID, lip gloss—everything was there.

"You found it," Kelly said when Paula slid back into her seat. She sounded like she was talking to a small child who'd lost a toy.

"You don't believe me, do you?" Paula asked.

After a too-long pause, Kelly said, "I'm not saying that."

"I swear it happened," she said, hopelessness cracking her voice. "I wouldn't make that up."

"What do you want to do?"

Paula considered whether or not they should go to the police. Fear and panic still shimmered beneath her skin, but more than anything she wanted to go home. "Let's just get out of here."

"Okay," Kelly said.

Soon they turned onto the state highway. At that hour they shared the road with only a few long-haul trucks. The silence between them felt like a wall. Paula wanted Kelly to believe her, to be on her side, to make her feel better. She'd never experienced anything as terrifying as what had happened tonight. She didn't want to carry the memory of it around alone. She felt too alone already.

"You remember when we were little and we used to go to the barbershop on Saturdays with our dads?" Paula asked. "There was that canister of lollipops by the cash register. Then they'd take us for ice cream after."

"Yeah."

Paula closed her eyes and saw her late father sitting down, cape over his broad shoulders, the barber in his apron standing behind him. His best friend—Kelly's father, Stan—in the chair next to his. "Remember how it smelled in there? Kind of musky and powdery at the same time? Aftershave, or whatever it was."

"Aftershave, I think," Kelly said.

"I have such strong memories of my dad smelling like that. I never smelled it again after they stopped going to the barbershop. But it was so weird, because tonight this guy smelled just like it. I know I was drunk, but I swear, it was like stepping back in time." Paula leaned her head back against the seat. She was exhausted. Her body ached. Her heart ached worse.

"It's going to be okay, Paul."

Paula wasn't so sure. All the way to her house and after Kelly dropped her off and as she lay mostly awake waiting for the sun to come up, Paula replayed the evening over and over in her mind, searching her memory for forgotten details. Each time, the experience seemed to slip further and further away. P⋯⋯ ⋯new it had happened; ⋯⋯ of it, not only because she w⋯ ⋯rt but because she felt ch⋯⋯⋯ ⋯⋯ just didn't know by how much.

Mayree

Mayree woke to the sound of her late husband, Frank, tiptoeing up the staircase, not even bothering to avoid the creaky treads. *You scoundrel,* she thought. *You scamp.* She rolled over and checked the clock on her nightstand: 1:46 a.m. She sat up, indignant even before she was fully awake, and glowered in the dark at his untouched side of the bed. It took her a moment to remember that the reason it was empty was because he was dead.

"Oh, Frank," she said aloud. "There you go, screwing around on me even from the grave."

I'm free to do whatever I want to now, Mayree, she could imagine him saying, laying extra heavy on the second syllable of her name like he always did when he was irritated. May-*REE.* She punched her pillow into submission and lay back down. It must've been Paula coming home from whatever she'd been up to. Well, at least Mayree had made good on her promise to her daughter: she hadn't waited up for her. She'd gone to bed at ten after spending yet another anxious Saturday night all alone in her oversize, well-decorated brick Colonial in Austin's desirable Old Enfield neighborhood, smoking cigarettes and crocheting lap blankets, for god's sake. Someone—she didn't remember who—had given her a basket filled with a dozen skeins of polyester yarn, some crochet hooks, and instructions for a simple pattern, along with a card that suggested such an activity "might be therapeutic during this difficult time." Mayree didn't know if it was therapeutic, but it was something to do with her hands during the endless hours she spent worrying about how to live penniless and alone and being furious with herself for having become so dependent in the first place. In the five months since Frank had died, she'd already made half a dozen fifty-two-by-forty-two-inch throws, and had called the craft store to order more yarn.

She stared up at the ceiling, counting the slow rotations of the ceiling fan. But instead of calming her, the repetitive motion made her irritable. The problem was that she was a forty-nine-year-old widow with no income, no career, no interesting hobbies, no social life. She'd even had a falling-out with her best friend, Sissy. Mayree reluctantly volunteered at the animal shelter once a week, but otherwise her life now was nothing but a series of empty calendar squares and a gaping hole where a sense of purpose should've been.

Especially over the last decade, even when they could hardly stand the sight of each other, she and Frank had always done things as a couple: bridge parties, country club socials, formal events. Frank said it was part and parcel of his status as a commercial real estate developer, but even though she trained herself to look and act like she belonged with them, Mayree felt like she was playing dress-up. Once, while preparing dinner, she'd overheard one of their guests tell Frank that Mayree was a tough cookie, which she took as a compliment until Frank replied that he'd gotten the girl out of Blanco but couldn't get the Blanco out of the girl.

Most of her female acquaintances were married to Frank's partners or clients, including Sissy, who was married to Frank's best friend and personal attorney, Stan. They fussed over her at the funeral—all except for Sissy—begging her to let them know what they could do as they knit their brows and pressed their hands to their chests. But after an initial surge of attention—which upon reflection was probably just pity—they gradually stopped calling to check on her, stopped inviting her out for shopping or meals, which she couldn't afford to do anymore anyway. There was something about her kind of loss that seemed to repulse people, like it was a foul odor or a contagion. There was also the problem of her sudden singularity; it was awkward for a couple to dine with her alone, especially for the man. In group settings, it complicated seating arrangements, unbalanced teams on game nights, introduced the uncertainty of who might be her plus-one—not that she could envision having one now. Frank hadn't been dead a month when their bridge club replaced them with a perky couple who'd been the group's alternate for years.

Mayree and Frank had been married since she was twenty-four. When they'd met, Mayree Lada had been only a few miserable months into her job teaching kindergarten, inexplicably homesick for her family's cattle ranch back in Blanco, which she'd been desperate to escape since she was seventeen years and seven months old, and questioning whether moving the fifty miles east to Austin had been such a great idea after all. Her roommate, Judy, sensing that Mayree was close to fleeing for home, asked her beau to fix Mayree up with somebody charming who would keep her put, at least until the end of their lease.

Despite Mayree's insistence that she didn't want a blind date, much less a husband, Judy introduced her to the strapping, smooth-talking entrepreneur Francis Gordon Baker III. He blew into her life like a tornado a week after her twenty-third birthday, shaking her tenuous hold on adulthood and kicking up the dust around her. He wasn't even particularly handsome, with his padded heft, prematurely thinning hair, and eyeteeth that flared slightly forward. If he was aware of his physical imperfections, he didn't acknowledge them. Never before had she met someone with as much swagger, with so much ambition, and with such charm. She assumed he'd blow out of her life just as hard and quickly as he'd entered, and she was looking forward to it. Even when he was physically still, which he was most of the time, the energy coming off him was like being drunk and having the record player turned up to full volume and slapping away a swarm of mosquitoes all at the same time.

As exciting as he was, she'd been ready for a respite, anxious for some quiet time to put the pieces of her life back into their proper order. But he didn't leave. He stayed until she fell completely in love with and then married him, until she bore his child and learned to tolerate his moods, until she hated him for his infidelities, and still longer— until her hatred subsided into resentment and then into resignation. She stayed until his financial success distracted her from his disloyalty, until her unhappiness became a personality trait, until she lost her own identity. They were finally settling into a truculent companionship that might've gotten them through their golden years together, until, finally and unexpectedly at the age of fifty-one, he'd died of a likely preventable heart attack in his secretary's bed. As Mayree tossed her handful of dirt onto his coffin, she merely whispered, "Fuck you, Frank," instead of shouting it, because she didn't want his secretary turned mistress, who'd always been suspiciously nice to her, to feel smug at her outburst.

She wondered now if she should've stepped out on Frank during those years when he was doing it to her, back when she had a reasonable chance of attracting that kind of attention. At least she'd have something interesting to think about on sleepless nights like these. She'd felt pretty then, her body strong and supple, her auburn hair thick and glossy. How exciting it might've been to meet an alluring man at a bar, say, and go with him to a hotel for an afternoon of champagne cocktails and illicit sex. Maybe a traveling salesman or—even better—someone young and athletic, like a bull rider. She could've been a southern Mrs. Robinson, Anne Bancroft in a pair of handmade Luccheses.

Oh, what the hell was she thinking about that nonsense for? She'd no sooner have gone to bed with someone other than her husband than saddle a stranger's mount. She barely wanted to sleep with *him*. Well, not after she realized he didn't actually love her like she did him. Not like he'd promised to and convinced her he would. It was humiliating how easily he'd forsaken her. Of course, she of all people should've known not to trust someone who'd decided to put himself in charge of her body, her heart.

No, Frank's deplorable sexual conduct never rubbed off on her, though she'd certainly have been justified if it had. It would've been nice to know what it felt like to be cherished. Now it was too late; she'd shriveled over the past few years, like a cut apple left out for too long. She was scrawny instead of slim, her skin dry as crepe paper and translucent in a sickly-looking way, her hair thinning and dull. It was all that endless dieting and smoking, no doubt. She wondered if she could even attract a man now if she wanted to, which she didn't. Not even if he promised to cherish and take care of her, which would be nice but would also be total horseshit because he'd only say that to get into her pants. Men were such dogs. She released a heavy sigh.

Mayree flung back the covers and reached through the dark for her pack of Virginia Slims. *You've come a long way, baby*, indeed. She patted the knife she kept on her nightstand—an antique switchblade with an abalone handle that she'd stolen from her father after she'd learned firsthand how vulnerable she was—and grabbed the lighter next to it. After a deep, appreciative inhale, she took her time blowing the smoke toward Frank's side of the bed.

She wondered what Paula had been up to that night and why she'd come home so late. Mayree had always believed that nothing good ever happened after midnight, so she'd been strict about Paula's curfew, even into her freshman year of college, when she came home from the dorm for holidays. These days, it was nearly impossible to govern her daughter's schedule, not only because she was a nineteen-year-old sophomore with a waitressing job, but because the increased tension between them made all their interactions harder.

There was just enough light from the streetlamp outside for her to see the family portrait hanging on the wall. It was several years old, taken when Mayree was nearing forty and Paula was almost ten. They looked happy together, a benefit of hiring a professional photographer who could make the three of them all laugh at the same time. To Mayree's chagrin, Paula looked almost exactly like her father—although a thousand dollars' worth of orthodontia kept her from having to go through life with his snaggleteeth. Now she worried Paula may have inherited his carnal tendencies, too.

Ever since she'd met that boy at work last November, Paula had been acting like a dog in heat, chasing him around, whining about his inattentiveness. Several weeks ago, Mayree had picked up the phone in the kitchen to call the handyman about changing some light bulbs and had been shocked to hear Paula on the line, breathily describing her alleged scanty attire—though Mayree had seen her only moments before bundled up in sweatpants and heavy socks—and Will making urgent-sounding groans in response. As disgusting as it was, Mayree hadn't hung up right away; it had been quite some time since she'd heard a man moan in pleasure.

She didn't confront Paula about Will until she found birth control pills hidden inside an empty pack of Marlboro Lights in her night-stand drawer. Paula bellowed about Mayree not having the right to go through her things, that she was only at home because her dorm had flooded, to which Mayree replied that regardless of the reason, as long as Paula was living under her roof, she had every right, and furthermore, as bad as her taste in cigarettes was, did Paula not understand that if she spent all her energy on a pointless romance, then she might as well kiss her law school aspirations goodbye? To that, Paula responded that the cigarettes weren't even hers; she'd found the empty pack in a restaurant parking lot.

"Listen up, missy," Mayree had said, circling her finger in the direction of her daughter's reproductive area. "You'd better not get yourself knocked up, especially by that hayseed."

"That's why I'm on birth control, Mom."

"Well, just make sure you don't forget to take it or else you'll be saddled with his bastard for the rest of your life. Or worse, you'll go off to law school and saddle *me* with it. I'm not ready for grandchildren."

Truth was, she didn't think she'd ever be ready to be a grandmother. She still hadn't recovered from being a mother. Just like she hadn't planned on getting married, she hadn't planned on having children. She had two much-older brothers and only older cousins, so she'd never had any experience with children until she had her own. Even when she was young, her classmates annoyed her with their incessant movement and boisterous voices. The only reason she got her teaching certificate was because her daddy had restricted her to three options: become either a nurse or a teacher or find a suitable husband. At that time, she would've rather been hunted down by a wild animal than allow a man to touch her intimately. And since she didn't care for the sight of blood and wasn't particularly patient with people whining about their ailments, that left teaching. But lord, was she appalled by the amount of blood and whining that went on in a kindergarten classroom, not to mention all sorts of other bodily fluids and emotions: snot, tears, pee, vomit, and a god-awful amount of crying. Children screamed at each other or for their mothers, got in fights, fell off jungle gym equipment, fidgeted, picked their noses, stuck their hands down their pants, fell asleep. It wasn't so much a teaching position as a long, unfulfilling babysitting job. That was part of why she agreed to marry Frank: so he could rescue her from her deplorable employment.

Shortly after they married, Mayree told Frank that she needed to go visit her ailing aunt Linda in Fort Worth. That the aunt was ailing wasn't a lie, and Mayree did stop by her house with a tin of pecan pralines she picked up from the Kandarr General Store on the way. But her true errand was to get fitted for a diaphragm so that there would be no little Bakers running around. They hadn't discussed having children, but if Frank expected to have a brood of his own, she had a plan to get out of it. She'd seen a recruiting advertisement for Pan Am in a magazine seeking applications for stewardesses. Stewardesses could be married, but they shouldn't have children, and definitely couldn't be pregnant. See the world? Yes, please. She and Frank could fly anywhere they wanted for free. That sounded better than anything she could've imagined. That sounded perfect. She wasn't accepted the first or second time she tried, but she remained hopeful. She was still young. She went on a diet, determined to stay well under the airline's weight limit.

Then one unusually warm Tuesday night a few months after their third wedding anniversary, Frank had come home from a night out with the boys, eager for some attention. "I got ahold of some bad ice, honey," he'd told her. *Bad ice* was what he always blamed for getting sloppy drunk. "But I need a little loving from my beautiful bride." He'd been so inebriated, Mayree didn't bother with the diaphragm, thinking he was too sauced to even get it up. The whole episode was over practically before it started, and Mayree rolled back onto her side of the bed, mildly annoyed and thoroughly unsatisfied.

Paula Lee Baker was born the following September. A busy, serious child who took up all Mayree's time and energy, she cried damn near her entire first year of life, refusing to be put down for a minute, and even when held and swaddled was difficult to console. She walked and talked early, was fussy about what she ate and wore, demanded answers to an inexhaustible mess of questions. She required constant supervision, attention, and cleaning. Mayree was so completely exhausted by Paula's very existence that she could hardly keep her head on straight—and she never again let Frank have his way with her unless she had protection. He didn't seem to mind. He loved Paula—more than he loved Mayree, that was for sure—and one child was apparently enough for him.

Mayree shook her head at her younger self, smashed out her cigarette, and tiptoed down the hall to Paula's room. She cracked the door just enough to see that she was tucked safely under her covers.

Though by then she was wide awake, she forced herself to lie back down and close her eyes. It was a relief that Paula was home; she had plenty of other things to fret about, but at least her daughter wasn't one of them. Mayree patted Frank's empty spot beside her and hoped she'd be able to get back to sleep after all.

Paula

Paula crept up the stairs, trying to avoid the creaky treads so she wouldn't awaken her mother. Whatever fleeting thought she'd had earlier about wanting Mayree's comfort was long gone now. Instead, she wished her father, whose death was still so new, were there. He would have hugged her and—she imagined—promised to find and murder the guy who'd hurt her. If not him then Felicia, their longtime housekeeper, who'd hold her hand and sing her hymns until she fell asleep. But Paula didn't want to talk about what had happened. She just wanted to get out of her filthy, stinking clothes and into bed.

She closed the door to her room quietly and stood for a moment in the dark. She'd left the window open earlier, and now the breeze animated the curtains in an unpredictable, disconcerting fashion. In middle and high school, Paula used to climb through this window and down the trellis whenever she wanted to sneak out of the house. Before, it had seemed like a portal to freedom: at first to Kelly's house or parties, later to boys and bars. Facing it now, she felt exposed. She closed and locked it, and pulled first the gauzy inner curtains together and then the heavy chintz ones that had only ever been used for decoration. With all light and outside air closed off, Paula felt, if not safe, then at least enshrouded.

Paula took off her leggings and underwear and shoved them into a small old duffel bag she'd used when she was on the high school swim team. That smell from earlier returned to her: that musky, powdery scent. The familiarity of it made her shiver.

She pulled her sweater over her head and, sucking air through clenched teeth, slowly peeled it off her left arm. The wound opened and started to bleed. She limped to her bathroom and pressed a washcloth against it. If it didn't stop soon, she might have to get stitches. Could she do it without telling her mother? She released pressure briefly to put a towel around her waist, then sank down onto the bath mat to wait for the bleeding to stop.

She heard the guy's voice as distinctly as if he were in the bathroom next to her. *You asked for this.* The clarity of it was so alarming she jerked away from the tub and flung back the curtain, thinking he was there. He wasn't, but the adrenaline surge was overwhelming. Then she remembered something else he'd said: *I was being nice and you fucked it up.* What had she fucked up? Yes, she'd gotten drunk—she felt drunk still, even though she'd sobered up—and wanted to call Will, the boy she'd fallen in love with four and a half months ago, two weeks after her father died. The guy from last night didn't know anything about her or Will. What had made him want to hurt her after she got in the car with him? What did he think she'd done wrong?

Paula hadn't even wanted to go out. She'd wanted to stay near the phone in case Will called, maybe let herself cry a little while she studied. Everyone was sick of her blubbering about him, so she had to do it in private. "He's just a stupid guy," Kelly had said. "Get over him." Her mother had said, "Good riddance," and flicked the cigarette she held between her manicured fingers in a gesture of dismissal. Now, after hardly any time to heal such a soul-wound, they made her feel like she was being ridiculous and needy and weak. "Even if he was worth crying over," Mayree said, "you wouldn't get him back by moping around and sniveling about how heartbroken you are. It's undignified. And anyway, you don't want him back, believe me."

But Paula did want him back. She'd lost so much already; she couldn't bear the loss of Will, too.

A few days after her father's death, her mother revealed that not only had he been sleeping with his secretary, but he'd also left them with an uncertain amount of debt. The abrupt loss of her beloved father was traumatic on its own, but learning the shocking news about his affair and his money problems was so jarring, Paula's soul rattled with confusion. It seemed impossible to reconcile such behavior with the loving, devoted father she knew him to be.

Mayree didn't know exactly how bad their financial situation was yet, but she'd worried out loud about paying for Paula's college tuition plus room and board. Paula didn't want to add more to her mother's obvious anxiety—and also didn't want to move back home—so she immediately got a job waiting tables at a Tex-Mex place called Mamacita's.

Will Davis, as headwaiter, was assigned to train her. She shadowed him for her first shift, following him around all night, listening carefully to his instructions, her nervousness receding under his care. He held her gaze when he spoke to her, his attention undivided even by the busyness around them. He encouraged and complimented her, never made her feel stupid when she asked questions or made mistakes. As they worked, he asked her about herself and seemed intently interested in her responses. He told her he was the fourth of six kids from a strict, lower-middle-class Catholic family in Missouri. He had bigger dreams than his siblings, several of whom were adults still working their same after-school jobs at McDonald's. He wanted to do something important with his life. She was impressed that he'd managed to get out from under his parents' authority, that he was living on his own terms, without their support. By the end of that first shift, Paula felt an attraction to Will that bordered on desperation.

Although he seemed interested in her, too, he teased her for requesting that their manager, Pete, give her all the same shifts as his. He mentioned once that he didn't deal well with distractions, so she'd tried not to be one. She'd been careful not to overwhelm him with phone calls or invitations, and limited their "accidental" encounters between classes on campus to as few as she could bear. He'd warmed to her quickly, though. He teased her and flirted with her and let her chase him. She caught him long enough to fall truly in love with him and imagine him as a permanent fixture in her life. She'd thought he felt the same way.

Over Thanksgiving break, the dorm room she'd shared with Kelly had flooded, and so they had to relocate while the facilities department replaced the burst pipe and repaired the damage. They wouldn't be able to get back in until late in the spring semester—if at all. Mayree had said, "I see no need to pay for housing when you've got your own room right here for free." Moving back home now wasn't just a step backward toward childhood or a more immediate reminder of the loss of her father; it meant she couldn't spend as much private time with Will as she wanted. Mayree would lose her mind if Paula took a man upstairs to her room, even if they were in love and exclusive. And although she'd occasionally spent the night at Will's house, she sensed he wasn't open to her being there every night.

Paula started putting aside some of her waitressing income for an apartment. If she had her own place, Will could come over whenever it was convenient, night or day. She'd give him a drawer and some closet space. A toothbrush to keep next to hers. She'd learn to cook so she could make him fancy dinners. In turn, he would bring her breakfast in bed and wrap himself around her when she fell asleep at night. And maybe it would become a regular thing for them to relax and eat and fall sleep together, so regular that at some point he might even move in. Then maybe she wouldn't feel so lonesome and miserable all the time, wondering what he was doing or when he was going to call.

Then, without warning or, apparently, remorse, he dumped her. Just a few days after he'd finally told her he loved her too, he called to announce that he'd saved up enough money to quit his job at Mamacita's. He was going to Cancún for spring break, but when he got back, he needed to focus on finishing his degree. No distractions. He was supposed to have graduated in 1986, he reminded her, but now, three years later, he was still only a junior. She was a great gal, he said. He hoped she understood.

She didn't understand. He'd been so tender, so attentive when they were together. Even now, after this horrible night, her body registered his absence as a sickness. Thinking of him was like swallowing a stone and feeling it drop into the vast empty space inside her. She thought if he knew how much she truly loved him, he'd give her another chance. But she hadn't had the opportunity to convince him, because he hadn't returned any of her calls.

Sitting on the bathroom floor, the guy's disembodied voice spoke to her again: *Hey, I'm the one doing you a favor here. You don't want to use the phone? Fine.*

She felt like she was going crazy with these previously unremembered snatches of conversation popping into her mind. After lifting the washcloth off her arm carefully, she saw that the bleeding had finally stopped. Naked, she walked back into her bedroom and stuffed the washcloth along with her sweater and bra into her swim bag. Even if she could wash out the blood and urine and vomit and dirt, she'd never be able to rid those clothes of the fear she'd felt while wearing them. Maybe she should burn them. Not tonight—she was too tired. But soon. She and Kelly used to write down the names of people they didn't like, rip them out of their spiral notebooks, and burn them in "witch pyres" in one of their backyards. Well, Kelly was the one who did it. Paula just provided the matches. She tossed the bag into her closet and closed the door.

She wrapped her arms around herself, feeling her ribs sheltering this new hollowness inside. She was so, so tired, but there was no way she could sleep with this stench, this filth on her skin. The shower might wake her mother, though. What would Paula say to Mayree if Mayree came in, storming mad? Or more likely, quietly disappointed. After a moment, Paula decided: nothing. She would say nothing.

She turned on the shower as hot as it would go, and stepped in.

Mayree

Mayree blinked her eyes against the assault of morning light. "Coffee," she said, and flung her right arm across the span of the bed. When it landed against the bedspread, she groaned and rolled over, and peered at the digital clock: 10:29 a.m. The one thing Frank had been consistently thoughtful about was making coffee. She wasn't yet used to weekends without him.

She tucked under the covers again. Having a dead husband and a nearly grown child meant time no longer mattered like it used to.

Eyes closed, she listened for movement about the house. Nothing, and no wonder: Paula hadn't come home until half past one. It was now Sunday, right? The days slid together so easily into unbroken, dull stretches of time now. She thought about it: yes, it was Sunday. She tapped out a cigarette.

As Paula was leaving last night, she'd made a snide remark: "You don't have to wait up for me, Mom. If I were in school somewhere else, you wouldn't even know what I was doing. Or if I was living in my own apartment or still in the dorm, I might be there studying or I might be out walking the streets turning tricks for all you knew." She'd stood there, defiant, ready for a fight.

Mayree recognized that moxie. She'd had some, too, once upon a time, before it was stolen from her. "Have a nice time, then. I won't wait up."

At that, Paula had seemed to relax. Her shoulders dropped and her voice softened. "Thank you. I'll see you in the morning." Outside, Kelly honked. Paula paused, then turned back to her mother. "Maybe we can make pancakes tomorrow. Like we used to."

Mayree had looked at her, at the red lipstick that accentuated her youthful pout, the blue eyeliner that made her eyes look sultry, like she was trying too hard to attract the kind of attention she didn't need. "Maybe so," she'd said.

Paula nodded, then patted the doorframe before stepping out, a gesture of finality she'd picked up from her father.

Once upon a time, when her daughter asked for pancakes on a Sunday morning, Mayree most likely would've said, *Yes, why not*, even if she wasn't in the mood to cook. Pancakes were so simple, and for some reason Paula thought they were a real treat, especially when Mayree made smiley faces with chocolate chips. A pancake breakfast would buy her a whole day of grace, so easy it was like cheating at parenting. But last night, for reasons she didn't fully understand until this moment, even plain pancakes had seemed too generous.

Now, with the nicotine kicking in, she realized she didn't want to make pancakes for Paula because of Frank. More specifically because of how much Paula had been acting like Frank. Going out when she should've been studying, all made up and ready for trouble. Why should she reward such behavior? She knew what happened when girls—when people—presented themselves to fate like that. Mayree should've stood up to her husband when she'd had the chance, before his unruly habits and her tacit acceptance of them became so ingrained that there'd been no point in trying to change him. But it wasn't too late for her daughter. Paula was still young, her principles and practices still evolving. They could be disrupted and reformed while Mayree still had at least a little power left over her. Would it serve Paula for Mayree to get up and prepare a special breakfast and act like everything was just fine and dandy?

It would've been so much easier raising a child who didn't remind her so much of the worst parts of them both.

"Fuck no," Mayree said aloud. She liked the way her new vernacular sounded in the otherwise empty bedroom. Long ago, Mayree's daddy had slapped her silly the one time she'd said *fuck* loud enough for him to hear, and Frank thought it was crass when women swore, but now that there was absolutely nobody to give a damn, she'd started cussing like a cowboy. "Fuck that," she blew out in a whisper, along with an exhale of smoke. The words felt good leaving her mouth.

Mayree smoked until the cigarette burned to the filter. The sun was offensively bright outside the window. *Fuck,* she thought, and flung off the covers. She'd make the damn pancakes. What else did she have to do on a Sunday morning at the ass end of winter?

She set the table with her wedding china, a fussy, floral pattern that her mother had helped her pick out. Would she someday do the same with Paula? She'd hoped her daughter would focus on her future as an attorney, not as somebody's wife. But the way she'd mooned over Will, Mayree figured she probably wouldn't. It was a new world out there; women had all kinds of choices these days. She wondered what kind of life she might've led if instead of being born in 1940, she'd been born in 1969 like Paula. If she'd grown up in a city instead of on a cattle ranch smack-dab in the middle of nowhere. If she'd had a forward-thinking mother or at least a father who wasn't so iron-handed, so cruel. If the little bit of fire she did have inside her hadn't been stamped out before she'd even reached adulthood. She could've been a stewardess, like she'd once wanted to be. Or a pilot, for that matter, or a journalist or even a businesswoman. A banker. Something.

Oh, who was she kidding? What did she know about being a modern woman? About living a life of adventure? Nothing. She'd missed her chance.

The quiet in the house started to get to her as she arranged the cutlery. She'd like at least to be able to call her recently former best friend, Sissy, and invite her over for dinner or a game of cards. But Sissy wasn't speaking to her. Or she wasn't speaking to Sissy. Either way, it was now a matter of pride.

She paused, watching dust motes floating on a beam of light. Was that a normal amount of dust in the air, or had Felicia, who'd worked for them since Paula was a toddler, not gotten around to dusting? There'd been a time when Mayree was too busy to notice such lonesome things as motes; a long stretch of years with a child running around while Mayree hosted parties and made up from fights with Frank. There'd been noise and chaos and a sense of purpose, and even when she'd hated every minute of it, she'd have to admit she'd loved it, too. She swatted at the air and stood up to gather ingredients for the pancakes.

She beat an egg with a whisk, perhaps harder than she needed to, then added the other items. After half a damn lifetime, she knew the recipe backward and no longer bothered to measure anything exactly. When the batter on the griddle started to bubble, she sighed. Then she kicked the step stool in the pantry over to the side where she could reach the bag of chocolate chips, and dropped them in one by one to make a smiley face. She made a whole stack of pancakes, enough for the two of them plus a friend. Mayree still wasn't used to cooking for only two. If not Sissy, maybe she should call Sissy's daughter and invite her over. Kelly had been a fixture at the Bakers' house for so long she even had her own usual chair.

"Paula!" she called. "Paw-laaaaa!"

Nothing.

She flicked her lighter, smelling the sweetness of the fuel before the burn. Inhaled. She turned the television to channel seven for company and sat down.

A reporter was standing in front of a stately-looking home speaking into his microphone with a grave expression: *Austin residents are dealing with the trauma of being part of a growing statistic: burglaries in affluent neighborhoods are on the rise. The latest victim, a Tarrytown homeowner who did not want to give her name or show her face on camera, expressed regret that she'd forgotten to lock her back door. "Losing precious family heirlooms was bad enough," she said. "But I'm feeling disturbed and violated that people were inside our house, touching everything. It's disgusting."*

"Idiot," Mayree said on an exhale. She clicked off the television. "How hard is it to lock your damn doors?" The rash of thefts gave her something else to worry about. She already had it on her list to call their accountant. It had become increasingly clear that Frank wasn't nearly as good at managing money as he'd let her believe. Adding injury to the insult of his dying in another woman's bed, creditors including credit card companies, the IRS, and at least one shady business partner had started sending bills to the house. It pissed her off to no end that she had to figure out what he'd owed whom and how she was going to pay them, not to mention how she was supposed to finish raising their daughter and live out her own miserable years. She'd never planned on going broke, but here she was. Now she also needed to check with the insurance agent to see if they were covered in case their house was burgled.

She wondered whether Paula had been drunk when she came home, and if she'd forgotten to lock their door on her way in. It wouldn't surprise her if she had; Frank used to do it all the time.

She checked the bolt and, satisfied, turned off the front porch light before trudging up the stairs. Knocking twice, not for permission but in announcement, Mayree let herself into Paula's bedroom. It took her a moment for her eyes to adjust to the darkness.

"I made you pancakes like you wanted. Chocolate chips and everything. Get up and wash your face and come downstairs."

Paula grunted and hauled herself over onto the other side of her bed.

Mayree responded by marching over to the window and yanking back the heavy curtains, launching another explosion of dust motes into the air, which she dramatically swatted away. "Jesus, Felicia better up her game," she said. "This house is filthy. Of course, if your father had been as good with money as he claimed, I wouldn't have had to cut her back to once a week."

At the onslaught of light, Paula leaped out of bed and drew the curtains back closed. "Don't," she said.

"Don't what?" Mayree stepped back.

"Just don't." Paula staggered back to the bed and yanked her covers up over her head.

Plunged back into the darkness, Mayree stood there, quiet. As challenging as Paula had been as a baby and toddler, she'd grown into a good, mostly obedient girl. When Sissy and Mayree used to go shopping and brought home bags of clothes for their kids to try, Kelly had been the one to fling them into a corner. *No.* And *ugly.* And *I'd never wear that.* Mayree never understood how Sissy could let her get away with such behavior. It shot her through with pride that, in contrast, Paula had always thanked Mayree and incorporated whatever new items of clothing her mother had brought home into her wardrobe. Furthermore, Paula never asked to return an unwanted birthday or Christmas gift, never complained about what Mayree did or didn't cook for dinner, didn't wait until ten o'clock the night before a project was due to ask for help or demand a trip to the drugstore for markers or poster board. She did her homework, cleaned her plate, kept her room tidy, told the truth—or at least Mayree assumed she did. What had happened to *that* little girl?

"You okay?"

Silence.

"Paula?" Mayree stepped tentatively toward the bed. She wasn't a natural caregiver, even to her own child, mostly because she'd never been taught how to be. She came from hardy stock; if anyone in her immediate family became ill, they were expected to push through it. On the ranch, complaining wasn't tolerated. There was no such thing as food on trays or TV in the bedroom for a head cold. She didn't even know her mother had high blood pressure until she died of an aneurysm, or that her father had had a heart condition until his funeral. And her in-laws were already dead before she met Frank. Growing up, hired hands tended to the sick animals. She couldn't stand the sight of a dying cow—wild-eyed, panting. Death was too ugly to confront face-on. At least Frank had the decency to go quickly, albeit under disgraceful circumstances. "You okay?"

"I'm fine. Just tired."

"Well, according to you, you have an exam tomorrow morning."

"I know."

"So you need to get up and study. You worked Friday and were out late last night. Too late, I might add."

"I know."

"And you've had plenty of sleep to recover, so come on now."

Paula shifted deeper into her bedding. "I'm fine, okay? I'll get up in a minute."

"You need to study if you want to get a decent grade. It's your future, you know. Waste not, want not."

"I studied yesterday."

Mayree huffed. "Well, the pancakes are getting cold."

"You eat them."

It was a comment that wouldn't have surprised or even bothered Mayree if Frank had tossed it off, but coming from Paula, it sounded so dismissive that her feelings were actually hurt. She stood there quietly, not knowing what to say, watching the steady rise and fall of the comforter, under which Paula lay otherwise still. After a moment, Mayree backed out of the room and closed the door. Her own parents would've had no time for that kind of insolence. No matter what, they'd have expected her to pull her boots up and get on with it. And she had always gotten on with it—even at the worst of times, even when nobody had any idea what she was enduring. It was hard not to expect Paula to do the same.

At the kitchen table, she stared at the tall stack of pancakes. She'd put the one with the most cheerful chocolate chip face on top. She couldn't decide whether to stab it with a fork or toss the whole thing into the garbage.

"Fuck that," she said aloud. She sat down at Paula's seat and dragged the serving plate over. Slowly, she poured half a bottle of maple syrup all over the pancakes and, as she watched dust particles collide against one another, ate every last bite.

Paula

Paula stayed in her darkened room all Sunday morning and into the afternoon, getting up only to pee and drink water from her bathroom sink before returning to bed.

When she was very young, she often had nightmares that would awaken her, trembling, unable to scream or even speak. Craving her mother's comfort, she would go into her parents' room and slip into bed beside her. But Mayree tended to thrash in bed, and besides that, didn't really like to share her space with anyone. Even her father tended to sleep on the far edge of their bed. Once, in her sleep, Mayree had shoved Paula to the floor. After that, anytime Paula needed asylum from her bad dreams, she crawled in next to her father. Snuggled against his soft, warm bulk, listening to the rhythm of his breathing, she could force away the memory of whatever monster had been chasing her. Unlike Mayree, her father always seemed delighted by her presence. He worked a lot, but when he was home, he listened, taught, comforted, charmed. She never doubted his love for her. She disliked the acrid stink of alcohol on his breath and skin—her sense of smell had always been unusually sharp—but enduring it was worth it for those few hours of peaceful, protected sleep. If only he were still alive, that odor would be like perfume.

Instead, she held on to her old stuffed dog with the droopy ears and sad-looking plastic eyes that had been a meager substitute for the real dog Mayree never let her have. She buried her face in its threadbare neck, willing away the intrusive, fragmented memories that were returning to her from the night before, sometimes with terrifying new details, like when the guy had pressed the knife to her throat and told her, *I'm gonna cut your throat and then I'm gonna fuck you in it. You hear me? I'm gonna fuck you in the neck.* He'd smiled as he said it, his lips curling back like an animal baring its teeth.

Even as detached and unreal as it sounded now, her body felt primed to fight, a surging feeling that made her woozy until it passed.

When the pounding inside her skull subsided, she slid down against the side of her bed with her knees drawn up, considered the telephone on her nightstand, then dialed Will's number. The thick receiver felt like a weight in her hand. Finally, his answering machine picked up: "You know what to do." Will's outgoing message sounded deep and throaty, like it belonged to a giant. To Paula, that he was only a few inches taller than she, with a build made wiry from years of rock climbing, made the incongruity of his tone that much more powerful.

"Hi. It's me," she said quietly so her mother wouldn't hear. "I . . ." Too late, she realized she called before she'd thought about what she was going to say. Tell him she missed him like she was running out of the air she needed to breathe? Ask him to meet? "I guess I just . . ." She wanted to tell him about last night so he would comfort her. Who else did she have who would wrap her in their arms and make her feel loved and safe? "I just wanted to say hi. Call me back if you can. I mean, if you want to. Okay. Bye." She hung up and clutched the stuffed dog against her aching chest.

Her gaze fell to the hem of the white ruffled bed skirt. A stray thread was hanging down, a few stitches having come loose. Paula hooked it with her fingernail and slowly, with just a bit of tension, pulled. The skirt lifted, revealing the trove of forgotten items beneath Paula's bed:

the intricately folded notes she and Kelly used to pass in school; the mum she'd received from her homecoming date her senior year; her diploma; her second-favorite stuffed animal, because at her age, two on her bed was too many; the birthday cards her father had given her every year from birth, signed with a short note about how much she'd grown over the past year and *I love you the most. Love, Daddy.*

Maybe it was the narcissism of youth, but she had actually believed that her father loved her the most. Or maybe it was that she had no reason to doubt it. Didn't most daddies adore their little girls? Certainly, he was far more patient and attentive to her than he had been with her mother. Was that because Mayree always seemed coiled up tight as a rattlesnake ready to strike? Or was Mayree like that because she knew about his affair—or affairs? Paula pushed away the thought of him kissing someone besides her mother. It bothered her that she couldn't remember him even doing that.

She dropped the thread and the bed skirt fluttered back into place. The white cast-iron bed frame dug into her spine where she leaned against it. *You asked for this.*

How?

For Christmas when they were fifteen, she and Kelly asked their mothers to decorate their rooms in preppy pink-and-green motifs. Pink walls, pink-and-green bedspreads, pink phones and green gingham lampshades on their matching nightstands. The way Kelly always took the lead with Paula, Kelly's mother did the same with Mayree. Sissy had a knack for interior decoration, and so she told Mayree exactly what to do so they could create identical rooms in houses a block apart.

But last July, without telling Mayree in advance, even before they fell out, Sissy had redone Kelly's room for her nineteenth birthday: everything white and cream, lots of plants. Kelly was defensive when Paula came over. "Don't be mad. She just wanted to make sure it would turn out," Kelly said. "Ask your mom to do yours for your birthday. Tell her you want shades of ecru."

Paula hadn't been mad. It still hadn't occurred to her then that she and Kelly were separate beings. That they might be, or eventually would be, moving in different directions. That Kelly might not always have Paula's best interests in mind.

When Paula mentioned it, Mayree had sighed and said the paint was practically still wet from the last time, but maybe for Christmas. Then her father died in October, right between her birthday and the holidays, and there'd been no talk of redoing her room. Her spring tuition check bounced before Mayree transferred money from their savings, proof of the unraveling of their safety net. They hadn't even put up a tree.

Now her childish-looking room made her angry. She didn't want to be trapped there in the room she grew up in, afraid of the danger beyond the stupid pink walls, abandoned by the two men she loved in spite of their failings, disbelieved by her best friend, and disregarded by her always-angry mother. Paula gathered up her bedspread and pink thermal blanket and light green sheets and the stupid gingham lamp, careful of her bandaged arm, and carried them down the hall to the never-used guest room. She stripped that bed of its neutral-colored bedding and took it to her own room. It was hardly subversive, this tiny act of rebellion, but she didn't know what else to do. She didn't know if she was still in danger. She didn't know if she was in trouble. Although she resented being at home, there was no place else for her to go. These thoughts spinning in her mind were exhausting. Sleep was the only way to escape. Before burying herself beneath the guest room comforter, she reached down and pulled the cord out of the phone jack—she didn't want to hear the sound of nobody calling.

~

Around three o'clock, Paula woke to the sound of a lawn mower going back and forth beneath her window. The light around the perimeter of the curtains had shifted, and she was disoriented for a few moments. For years they'd hired teenagers from the neighborhood to do the lawn, but as soon as her father died, Herb Walker, the retired actuary next door, insisted on doing it himself. "The missus and I wouldn't think of letting you worry about yet another thing," he'd told Mayree when she'd gone out to stop him the first time, smoothing what was left of his hair over to the opposite side of his sweating brow and ignoring Paula's scowl. He was far too out of shape to be doing even his own yard, much less the Bakers', and the missus in question was obviously furious that her husband, who'd been ogling Mayree for going on two decades, had finally resorted to overt solicitousness. The idea of creepy old Mr. Walker lurching up and down their property in perfectly neat rows was unnerving—the idea of anyone being that close to her house right now was unnerving—and she burrowed deeper into bed. She pictured Mrs. Walker, eyes narrowed and fists pressed hard against her ample hips, and under that imagined guardianship she fell back asleep again.

Careful your step.

Such a strange warning.

You hear me?

Paula stirred.

I'm gonna fuck you in the neck.

Paula flung her covers off and sat up. "No!" she said.

Mayree backed away. "Settle," she said, using her rancher voice, like Paula was an unbroken horse.

"What?" Paula said, her heart racing. The lights were off and the curtains still closed. It was dark outside, the way it had been as she was running through the dark woods, the guy right behind her.

Mayree put a tray of food down on Paula's desk. "I just said that Kelly called. She wanted to know if you were feeling okay."

Paula closed her eyes, fighting off the memory of the nightmare. "I'm okay." But she wasn't. She felt like she was losing her mind. A moment ago she'd been running in the light of the moon, faint beneath the canopy of trees. What was that mama armadillo doing right now? Maybe she was tucked in with her babies, all of them in a curl, safe in their burrow. She'd brought home a pair of orphaned skunks one time, so new they didn't even have fur on their delicate pink skin. She hated the pink walls of her bedroom. She'd paint them white. Or maybe ecru. Kelly hadn't believed her, but it had happened. Right? Or had she just been so terribly, miserably drunk that she'd only imagined it all? She felt so strange, like she couldn't trust her own racing thoughts.

"You look terrible. Are you sick?" Mayree asked.

Paula pushed herself back against the headboard, ran her fingers through her hair. "What time is it?"

Mayree went to her and tried to press the back of her hand against Paula's forehead, the way she'd always done when she suspected a fever. But Paula, flinching, leaned away before Mayree could make contact. As much as she craved physical touch, her mother's wasn't it. Her jaw still ached, and the inside of her cheek had been cut. She hoped there wasn't a bruise she'd have to explain.

"I'm fine."

"Suit yourself," Mayree said, then pointed to the tray. "I made enchiladas." As she was closing the door behind her, she paused. "I don't know if you're hungover or heartbroken or what, but you've got to pull yourself together. Staying out all night and then sleeping all day is simply undignified."

~

At nine thirty the next morning, Kelly rang the doorbell instead of honking from the driveway as she typically did when picking Paula up. "Hi, Mama B!" Kelly's bright voice carried all the way upstairs, where Paula was reluctantly pulling on her boots.

"Hi, sweetie," Mayree said. "Come on in. Have you had breakfast? I have some eggs ready. You and Paula can share."

"I ate already, but thank you. My mom wanted me to return this to you. She said she meant to give it back a while ago, but . . ."

Paula reached the bottom of the stairs as Kelly held out a book. "Hey, Paul," she said.

"Hey."

Mayree smoothed down a small rip on the cover. "Did she like it, at least?"

Kelly gave her an apologetic smile. "I don't think so."

Paula saw Mayree wince and then immediately try to recover a placid expression on her drawn, sleep-creased face as she clutched the collar of her old bathrobe and pushed her shoulders back. But with her hair still rolled in spongy pink curlers, and leftover mascara smudged beneath her eyes, she looked more pitiful than prim. "We'll be late," Paula said, pushing past her mother to the door.

"What about breakfast?"

"I'm not hungry," she said with a wave. Her arm hurt when she lifted it. "I'll see you later."

"Good luck on your test," Mayree called out.

Kelly turned and blew her a kiss. "Thanks, Mama B."

In the car, Kelly turned to Paula. "What's with you today? You still hungover?"

"No," Paula said, not looking at her.

"Well, you sure are grumpy."

"I'm not grumpy." She laid on the last word like a car horn in traffic. She unzipped her backpack and dug around for something she might've left in there to eat. Nothing. She didn't want to go to class today; but even more than that, she didn't want to stay home with Mayree, who'd no doubt give her hell for missing her exam.

"Hungry, then. Or pissed off. From the way your eyebrows are practically touching, I'm thinking pissed. Who is it? Will? Or your mom?" She poked Paula in the ribs.

Paula wrenched herself sideways away from her. "Jesus, Kelly."

"What!"

"You seriously don't know?" Paula asked.

"What? No. I called you twice yesterday and your mom said you were holed up in your room. I figured you were mad at somebody."

"Yeah, I am mad. And freaked out and confused and scared."

"Is this about Saturday night?"

"Oh my god. Are you kidding? Yes, it's about Saturday night."

"I know I was drinking, too, and did that tiny bit of coke, but, Paul, you were really drunk. Like really, really drunk. You were barely making any sense. Do you even remember anything?"

"I remember everything!"

"Like falling asleep by the fire?"

"I did not fall asleep." Paula stared at the cup holder, frantically scanning her memory.

"You sure did. Twice. The first time, I woke you up to move you farther away because I was worried a spark was going to land on you. Remember that?" Paula remained silent. She didn't, and it was unnerving. "Then you passed out again and I came to check on you and you said Will was coming to pick you up and that you had to pee. I offered to take you, but you said you were just going to go behind the bushes across the road. Remember that? No? And that girl you'd been talking to said she had to go, too, so you went with her. Before you came back, I honestly figured you'd asked her to take you home."

"What girl?"

Kelly shot her a look. "You're getting all pissy with me and you don't even remember who you were talking to? I don't know, some girl I've never seen before."

"It wasn't a girl. It was a guy." *The* guy. Paula could hear the uncertainty in her own voice. None of this was making sense.

"Not unless he had huge boobs and dangly earrings."

"But—" Paula pressed the heels of her hands against her eyes until she saw flickers of light behind her lids. She rolled back the tape in her mind, trying to reconcile what Kelly was saying with what she could recall.

~

"Come on," Kelly had said Saturday afternoon, using her begging voice. "Just for an hour. Two, max."

"I can't. I have to study for the government test." Paula twisted the phone cord around her index finger.

"Bullshit. You've never had to study for anything. You just want to sit by the phone in case Will calls."

"No, I don't." Though she most certainly did.

"Liar. I can see you blushing through the phone line." Kelly sighed. "Look, it'll be good for you to get out. You're getting moldy. Besides, I don't want to go alone."

"You should be studying, too."

"I'll be fine. I'm going to cheat off you on the LSAT anyway, so all I have to do is pass. So get dressed. It's Saturday night; Will's not going to call."

"I hate you," Paula said, sighing. "Where's this stupid party anyway?"

"Yay! I hate you, too. Lake Travis. Near where we used to go camping."

"Fine. But you have to drive." She'd inherited her mother's hideous powder-blue Pontiac Bonneville after Mayree upgraded to her father's newer Audi sedan. Of course it made sense that her mother would get the better car, but Paula would've loved sliding into the seat that had been her father's, that feeling of closeness it would've provided. Then she imagined some strange woman sitting in the passenger seat and it made her resentful; she didn't know how Mayree could bear it.

Kelly squealed and said she'd pick Paula up in an hour. "Wear something cute. Oh, I know! Wear your new outfit. And do your eyes like I showed you, with the teal eyeliner. There'll be tons of guys there." She hung up before Paula could protest.

On her way out, her mother had looked over her glasses at Paula, scanning her up and down. "I thought you were studying for a government exam." She was sitting in her wingback chair, crocheting a blanket identical to the one draped over her lap.

"I did."

"That's quite a paint job you've got on."

Paula looked at her reflection in the mirror above the mantel. Kelly had given her a blue eyeliner pencil to try, saying it would make her aqua-colored irises look lavender. The effect wasn't quite as dramatic as that, but Paula liked it. She'd paired it with neutral shadow and a strong red lipstick. "What's wrong with it?"

"Depends on what you're selling," Mayree said, one eyebrow arched.

That's what her father always used to ask: "What are you selling?" He'd once told her that he approached every business deal, social engagement, and poker game with the attitude that everybody was selling something whether they realized it or not: their desires, self-image, trustworthiness, availability. He only needed to figure out how badly someone wanted to sell whatever they had—and whether or not he wanted to buy it. He'd probably used that technique with women, too.

"I'm not selling myself if that's what you mean," Paula said, crossing her arms defensively. She was wearing stretch pants and an oversize sweater that nearly covered her rear end; nothing was showing except maybe the suggestion of breasts where the strap of her purse divided them. She wondered what her father's mistress—or mistresses—wore, and shuddered.

"Well." Mayree went back to her crocheting. "Don't be too late. I'm tired and don't want to have to wait up half the night."

"You don't have to wait up for me, Mom." Paula sighed. She'd been living in the dorms since freshman year, and would be still if the pipes hadn't broken, assuming they could pay for it. Mayree made her feel like she was back in high school.

With the windows down and music loud, they'd driven to Pace Bend Park, a teardrop-shaped jut of land northwest of Austin, so named for the bend of deep lake water that curved around it. On the east side were sloping shorelines and gravel beaches where the girls occasionally camped with their fathers when they were younger. Passing those familiar spots made her even more wistful than she already was. Maybe that was why her mother seemed irritated that she was going to a party out there; it reminded her of the time her father spent with Paula.

Kelly pulled up to the north end of a shallow cove and parked alongside the dozen or more other cars already there. Beach towels and cooler in hand, they walked toward the group of people gathered around a small bonfire.

"How many of these people do you know?" Paula whispered.

Kelly looked around, then back to Paula. "One," she said. She touched her finger to Paula's nose and laughed. "So far."

"You're kidding me. What are we doing here then?"

"A girl from my English class told me about it. It'll be fun, I promise."

Someone showed up with a boom box and turned it on. Someone else handed out plastic cups and invited everyone to help themselves to a cooler filled with trash can punch. Kelly pulled Paula closer to the bonfire and goaded her into dancing among the group of strangers. She was already tipsy from the wine coolers they'd had on the drive. The sunset slid below the horizon, and a chorus of spring peepers started up. It was warm even for late March, too warm for her sweater, and being so close to the fire was becoming uncomfortable. Her shoes were uncomfortable. Paula wanted to sit down for a while and cool off.

They sat down on their towels, which had been dragged into a circle of other towels and chairs. Kelly handed Paula a wine cooler, blessedly cold, and offered some to those sitting nearby. Even though

Paula knew how to work a table of customers at the restaurant—flirting with the men, complimenting the women, encouraging them to order another round of drinks or dessert to increase their final tab and therefore her tip—she knew she'd never be as slick as Kelly in social situations. Watching her friend's composure had always made her slightly uncomfortable and more than a little envious. Why couldn't she be like Kelly and enjoy the moment? It was a beautiful night by the lake; she was a straight-A student with a clear future; she was smack-dab in the midst of music and laughter and camaraderie. She should be having fun, but for many reasons, she was miserable.

"My heart is actually sick," she said.

"What?"

"I want to call Will." She picked at the label on the sweaty bottle. For a while, he'd been the best thing in her life. The way he'd sometimes look at her, like she was also the best thing in his, made her feel like everything else was going to be okay.

"No, you don't," Kelly said.

"I do. I just want to hear his voice." A rise of panic. "I don't understand why he broke up with me. I want him to tell me once and for all, and then I'll be able to get over it."

Kelly reached for her hand. "He did tell you, Paul. He told you and then he showed you by not calling for two weeks. Why do you want to pick that scab?"

"I miss him."

"Only because you're tipsy." She squeezed Paula's hand before letting it go and reaching into the cooler again. "You're worth so much more. You deserve a guy who'll appreciate you."

"He did appreciate me." She could hear the whine in her own voice.

Kelly handed her another bottle. "This is probably the only time I'm going to totally agree with your mother, bless her heart—besides the time she told us not to play outside wearing circle bandages as bikini tops when we were eight—but he was stringing you along. If he was

such a great guy, then why did he dump you? You've got to let it go."
Kelly dusted her hands together as if that were all it would take to put
Will out of Paula's mind for good. "And tonight is the perfect time to
get started." She looked over Paula's shoulder and smiled.

"I think I'd rather just go home."

"No way. We just got here!"

A moment later, a good-looking guy approached Paula and Kelly and
offered them each a Lone Star. Kelly took the beer and, winking at Paula,
reached into her pocket for her keys. Paula let out a short groan. Kelly
was going to do her one reliable party trick, indicating that she liked the
Lone Star guy, and soon Paula was going to be on her own. Kelly stabbed
her car key into the top of the can, then popped the tab, tilted her head
back, and drained all twelve ounces in mere seconds. Then she released a
tiny belch into her fist and grinned.

"Wow," Lone Star said.

"The trick is to relax your throat," Kelly told him seductively. Paula
rolled her eyes. "Want me to teach you?"

"Sure," he said, dragging out the word as if to convey his enthusiasm.

Kelly tossed her thick auburn hair off her shoulders and winked at
him. She had freckles and curves that other girls might be self-conscious
about, but not her. She loved that she stood out. Without even trying,
Kelly had always been able to get any guy she wanted. Nobody was out
of her league. She had her first boyfriend in fifth grade. When they were
freshmen in high school, three seniors asked her to the prom. She never
slept with any of them to make them like her, either; she didn't even lose
her virginity until the summer before they started college.

In contrast, Paula lacked everything that Kelly had: confidence,
charm, ease. The guys she'd dated before weren't the cool, good-looking
types; her first real boyfriend was the only male member of the Future
Homemakers of America club at her high school. Even though Will
had flirted with her at work and made her feel special when he focused
his attention on her, she'd seen him do it with other waitresses and

customers, too. She initially resigned herself to the idea that he was out of her league; when he finally asked her out one night after a shift, she'd been so flattered that she'd replied, "Really?" When Will kissed her after that first dinner, she'd been so hungry for more of his affection that it was she who proposed they go back to his apartment.

"Actually," Paula said to Kelly, "I'm not feeling all that great. I think we should go."

"Have another drink. You'll be fine." Kelly winked at her and took Lone Star's hand.

Paula watched them go off toward the lake. She finished her beer, then got up to help herself to a full cup of the trash can punch, half of which she chugged while standing at the cooler. She topped it off, weaved her way back to her towel, and plopped down. Kelly and Lone Star were nowhere to be seen.

Mayree

T hat you?" Mayree called from the other room.

She could hear Felicia Johnson, the Bakers' housekeeper of almost eighteen years, let herself in the back door, hang her purse and sweater on a hook in the utility room, then immediately start cleaning up her employer's uneaten breakfast.

"It's me," Felicia called back over the running water. "Want me to make you some fresh coffee?"

Mayree wandered in and sat down, already weary from the day even before *Good Morning America* was over. "Thank you. That would be lovely." She tapped out a cigarette and lit it.

"You didn't eat your eggs again," Felicia said as she set down a clean ashtray. "You keep skipping meals and pretty soon some strong wind's gonna come along and carry you right off."

"That's rude."

"It's the truth." Felicia looked at Mayree with a set mouth and an arched eyebrow. "Not to mention wasteful."

Mayree nodded in assent and after Felicia returned to the sink, flicked her ashes mostly into the tray, making sure some landed on the kitchen table. Then she felt guilty about it and scooped them back up. "Paula's acting strange."

"Is it that boy?"

"Isn't it always about a boy?"

"Mm-hmm."

They were quiet for a while, the smell of coffee brewing and the sound of dishes being washed by competent hands a comfort to Mayree, whose mind flipped between Paula's worthless ex-boyfriend and Frank, the two most troublesome males in her recent history. Felicia was likely thinking of her wayward nephew, Curtis—her husband's brother's only child—who'd gotten caught up in some mischief the year prior and had spent the past nine or so months in juvenile detention. He was set to be released that very week. Felicia had never had her own children, but had stepped in to care for Curtis the times his parents had either split town or landed in prison. If Mayree was being honest, Felicia had also been like a mother to Paula over the years, especially when Mayree was having what Felicia called one of "her spells." If she was being *really* honest, Felicia had practically been like a mother to Mayree, too. That was one of the reasons she hadn't been able to let her go, in spite of her money worries.

Mayree had cut Felicia's time back to Mondays only, and to try to offset the abrupt hit to Felicia's income, doubled what she normally paid her and wrote a lengthy letter of recommendation. She didn't know what else to do, and she hated herself—and Frank—for having to do it.

"You worried about Curtis?" Mayree asked.

Felicia wiped her hands on the dishrag and sighed. "I'm trying not to, but you know how it is. We worry about the people we love."

Mayree nodded. "Paula stayed in her room all day yesterday."

"Sleeping?"

"I think so. Mostly."

"She'll be all right. Heartache takes time, especially when you're young."

Mayree tried to think back to the first time she'd had her heart broken. Not her spirit—her spirit had been broken in a single afternoon the week after she graduated high school—but her heart. Her first heartbreak came a few days before Paula's first birthday.

The first nine months or so after Paula was born, Frank had moved through the motions of parenting, helpless, hapless. Then, when Mayree didn't "take to motherhood" like he thought she should, he became distant and frustrated. To be fair, she was all of those things, too. But she remembered distinctly the Fourth of July weekend of that year. She'd spent the day trying to get ready for a party, nursing Paula every hour it seemed, crying each of the three times she spit up on Mayree's newly changed outfit. Frank had swooped in, hair freshly cut, smelling of aftershave, and picked Paula up and spun her around like he was dancing at her future wedding. She'd been so grateful for that moment of joy. For weeks after, he seemed happier than he had in a long time, and she'd thought that they'd turned a corner together, that they were going to be okay. It didn't necessarily make parenting easier, but she was starting to feel hopeful again. Then there was the Saturday about two months after that when he'd come in, showered and expectant, announcing that he was off to get his monthly haircut and shave—a week after he'd gotten his last one.

"Why do you have to go again so soon?" she'd asked him. His face had gone red, the idiot—people were never as subtle as they thought they were—and she'd thrown a full bottle of formula at his head. He'd denied he was really going to see some other woman, of course, but she'd known. To tell the truth, it was his lying about it that hurt worse than the act itself. He'd broken her heart so many times after that over the years that by the time he died, it was hardly more than a lump of scar tissue.

"I'll give her room some extra love today," Felicia said as she poured the coffee. "If she's gonna be spending all her time up there, it ought to be kept up."

Mayree accepted the mug and sighed. She could never replicate the strength and flavor of Felicia's coffee, even though she used the same grounds, the same machine. In fact, just about everything Felicia prepared tasted better than Mayree's. The day she'd shown up at the house for an interview after responding to Mayree's ad in the local paper—Seeking immediate household help five days/week for family with a wild toddler, mostly cleaning but would appreciate some childcare and cooking as I've just about had it—Felicia had taken one look at the bags under Mayree's eyes, the unfolded laundry on the kitchen table, the unwashed dishes in the sink, and a naked Paula streaking up and down the hallway, jammed her fists against her hips, and said, "Lord have mercy, I didn't get here a minute too soon." She scooped Paula up as she ran by and passed a hand over her wispy baby hair. Paula responded by giggling and plunging her chubby fingers into Felicia's curls. "Get yourself back to bed for an hour," she said to Mayree, who'd have cried with gratitude if she was the type to cry at all. "I'm gonna go ahead and start today." That was almost eighteen years ago. Monday through Friday, Felicia worked alongside Mayree on nearly every aspect of home management and child-rearing. Felicia brought her own lunch and took a break every afternoon to watch *One Life to Live*, her favorite soap opera. Within the first week, though, Mayree had invited Felicia eat from the Bakers' fridge so she wouldn't have to bring anything, and Felicia reciprocated the kindness by keeping Mayree apprised of the daytime drama of the Lord and Gray families. By the second week, they were eating lunch together and sitting down at three thirty each afternoon to watch their "stories." After Frank died, it took Mayree a month to find the courage to tell Felicia that he'd left her with an alarming amount of debt, which meant she'd have to cut back on everything, including Felicia, until she figured out how deep in the hole they actually were.

"You know I hate not having you here every day."

"And you know I'd like to be here. I've still got to earn a living, too, you know. Besides, once a week is hardly time enough to set this place right, much less keep it that way." She made a show of restacking the mugs in the cupboard, which Mayree had shoved haphazardly in the last time she emptied the dishwasher.

"I'm sorry." Mayree felt her gut catch. Letting Felicia down was just one more in a list of things she felt guilty about. "For everything."

"I know," Felicia said.

"Not just that." Mayree stubbed out her cigarette, blew the steam off the lip of the mug. "It gets lonesome."

As hurt as she'd been by Frank when he was alive, and angry at him now that he was dead, the absoluteness of his being gone made her feel like she'd just left a loud and clamorous party. There was some relief in it, but also a disturbing sense of missing out on something. Even Paula being back home didn't offer much relief from her isolation; they'd become even more distant from each other since Frank died and Will showed up. Added to that, Mayree didn't have Sissy at all anymore, and now she saw Felicia only on Mondays.

"Aww, you saying you miss me?" Felicia flashed a wry smile.

"You're going to make me say it?"

Felicia shook her head. "I know it costs you more than money to tell somebody you care for them. But I also know how you feel without you saying it, so we'll just leave it at that."

"Thank you kindly," Mayree said, dipping her head with mock appreciation. "Now if this soap opera is over, I'm going to get my shower and go to Safeway before all the produce is picked over."

"I'll write you out a list."

Mayree put her mug in the sink and patted Felicia on the arm. Felicia covered Mayree's hand with her own for just a moment, then went back to work.

～

Mayree knew it was pathetic how much time she spent getting herself ready for a trip to the grocery store, but she also knew that to be seen in public without her face on and hair done would be akin to admitting defeat. Her own mother died at age fifty-three, and assuming Mayree would live at least that long, that meant she had four years left to keep herself looking presentable. Not that anyone cared. Still, it was Monday, and after being in her bathrobe all weekend, even she was disgusted by her slovenliness. She pulled at the bags beneath her eyes, made darker by the fluorescent bulbs above her bathroom mirror. She lifted the skin by her jowls, turned her head side to side.

"Pah," she said, and gave her reflection the middle finger.

~

Mayree tottered behind her shopping cart on heels too high for midday, wearing a silk dress and the short mink coat Frank had given her for Christmas three years ago. She'd discovered the receipt from Saks Fifth Avenue in his attaché case when he asked her to bring him a file—for not one but two black sable furs. She never asked him who the recipient of the other one was.

Though there was a steady wind, it wasn't cool enough for a fur today, not that it was ever very cold in Austin. The air-conditioning inside the store was on, and anyway, it made her look more glamorous than she felt. Good thing, too: down the cereal aisle, she spotted her old friend, Sissy, wearing a pair of jeans and a Polo shirt. She looked okay. Fine, she looked good. Dammit. Sissy always could pull off a simple outfit. And she must've frosted her hair recently. Sissy tucked a blonde lock behind her ear as she examined the rows and rows of options. Mayree glanced at herself in the glass doors of the frozen foods and was disappointed. She wished now that she'd worn something less fussy, like a plain skirt and espadrilles.

Well, that's enough of that, she thought. She straightened her back and pushed her cart forward, walking slowly to appear nonchalant if not downright elegant. Why shouldn't she dress up for the day? She opened a random door just so that she could see Sissy's reflection in the glass before it fogged up. There was no mistake, Sissy was definitely looking at her. Mayree reached in and grabbed two bags of frozen something-or-other, and dropped them into the cart before moving on.

~

She knew it was stupid, this falling-out between them after fifteen years of friendship. Nearly six months ago, a month before he died, Frank took Paula and Kelly to a Kenny G concert at the Austin Opera house. Sissy was home with Kelly's older brother, Dean, who was about to leave for basic training. Sissy's husband, Stan, who'd moved out for a trial separation the month before—he needed "a break," he'd said—was allegedly out with colleagues, and Mayree was, if she was being honest, having a spell, one of those times when she was too tired, too depressed to do anything but smoke and watch TV. Even if Frank had invited her to go with them, which he didn't, she'd have said no; she detested smooth jazz.

At eleven thirty, Sissy called Mayree. "Kelly's not home yet. Did they go to your house?"

Mayree, awakened from a dead sleep, said, "I don't know. Maybe." And hung up.

Twenty minutes later, Sissy called again. "She's still not home."

"Lord have mercy, Sissy. It's not like they're on the moon. They're probably back at the dorm."

"You think it's funny? There's all kind of crazy going on these days. And they're not at the dorm because they're fumigating this weekend, remember? Where do you think they are?"

"Frank's got them. They probably stopped for ice cream or something."

"You sure?"

"Sure enough." Mayree knew Frank loved Paula too much to let anything happen to her on his watch.

There was a huffy exhale on the line. "Mayree, I have to tell you something."

"Sissy, it's o-dark-thirty. Can't this wait?" Mayree leaned over, patted around the nightstand for a cigarette and lighter.

"I don't think so." Sissy paused. "Frank is having an affair."

Mayree sat up in her dark bedroom. "What the hell are you talking about?"

"It's true. Stan told me. Before he left. Frank's probably with her now. That could be why the girls aren't home. Maybe he didn't actually go to the concert. Maybe he dropped them off and forgot to pick them up."

Mayree considered Sissy her very best friend. In fact, because they'd spent so much time together over the years, she was practically Mayree's only friend. The wives of Frank's associates didn't count. She'd told Sissy many, many personal things over the years. They'd raised their girls like sisters, her son Dean like Paula's older brother, traveled and spent holidays together, spent weekends alone while their husbands went away on hunting and fishing trips. But Mayree had never, ever let Sissy—or anybody else—know that Frank was unfaithful to her. It was bad enough that she knew; she'd be absolutely mortified if other people did, too. It hadn't occurred to her before that Frank might not have been as discreet. Even though Sissy wasn't wrong about Frank, Mayree was as mad at her for saying it aloud as if she'd been lying. She heard those words out of Sissy's mouth all the way down in her soul.

"Sissy, you are a jealous, awful cunt. You hear me? You mind your own damned business. I'm not the one whose husband left."

There was a gasp, then a huff, then, "Screw you, Mayree!"

Mayree heard Sissy smash down the phone, the after-ring echoing in her ears. She lay there, heart pounding, desperate to call Sissy back and equally determined not to. A few minutes later, the front door opened and slammed, Paula and Kelly bantering with Frank as they clomped up the stairs. Mayree stubbed out her cigarette and flapped at the air to dispel the odor. Then she rolled over, squeezed her eyes closed, and pretended to be asleep.

~

Mayree finished the shopping, peeking around aisle corners before venturing down any to be sure she wouldn't run into Sissy, and being extra cheerful to the few acquaintances she saw. Even though her feet were killing her and she was now uncomfortably warm in her fur coat, she gave the cashier a big smile as she handed him the check, tipped the bagger an extra dollar, and exited the store like a celebrity on a float in a parade.

The wind had picked up while she was inside the store, and now her hair, which she'd worked on so carefully, was flying around in hairsprayed clumps and getting stuck in her lipstick. She tried to walk faster, but was severely limited by her ridiculous heels, which had looked and felt just fine when she was standing still in front of her full-length mirror in her bathroom but not while crossing pockmarked asphalt in a gale. She vowed to toss them in the trash the minute she got home, if she could even manage to get to the damn car.

Just as she finally made it and was unlocking the trunk of her sedan, she heard a woman farther down the row scream, "Look out!" Mayree swiveled toward the voice to see what the matter was, and just then, an empty shopping cart careening across the lot rammed right into Mayree from behind and knocked her to the ground.

"Oh, I'm so sorry," a young man said, crouching down and peering into her face. "I was just finishing unloading my cart and it got away from me. I didn't even realize it until it was too late. Are you hurt? Can I help you up?"

A small throng of people gathered around her, offering help. Someone tried to pull her up, while someone else wondered if she needed an ambulance. "I'm fine," she said, even as she struggled to stand. How absolutely mortifying. "Really, please go," she said to the group, not looking at anyone directly. Her pantyhose had torn and there was gravel stuck into the flesh of her kneecaps and palms. But there was only a little stream of blood running down her shin, and nothing felt broken or sprained. "Please," she said again, and everyone but the young man wandered off.

He held her gently by the arm and dusted a bit of gravel or something off her sleeve, like she was either a little girl or an old woman. "Are you sure you're okay?" he asked, looking her over.

Holding on to her own shopping cart for support, she glanced around to be sure nobody was still looking at her. And of course, just then Sissy came out of the store in her sensible flats and pushed her groceries confidently into the headwind. Mayree pivoted so that her back was toward her and hissed at the young man, who upon closer inspection was probably still a teenager, "Oh for heaven's sake, I'm fine."

"Your leg's bleeding."

"It's hardly the worst of my concerns. Now thank you and please run along. This is embarrassing enough."

"I'll put your groceries in the trunk for you." Maybe he was angling for a tip.

Mayree could see Sissy heading toward them. The parking lot wasn't very large; it was entirely possible that she'd parked on the same row. "Oh fine," she said, and hurried into the car so Sissy couldn't bear witness to her humiliation.

She hadn't had to worry; Sissy went down another row, and if she'd noticed Mayree at all it didn't show on her face. In fact, she looked distracted by the wind, tucking frosted strands of hair behind her ears in a futile attempt to keep it out of her eyes. Mayree wondered if she planned to go to the nail salon after she took her groceries home, the way they always used to do together on Mondays.

The trunk slammed and the young man appeared at her window. He made a hand crank motion to get her to roll it down. She did, and he handed her one of her shoes. She hadn't even realized she didn't have it on.

"I'm really sorry," he said, pushing his dark hair off his face. "It's like a tornado out here."

Now that Sissy and the likelihood of further humiliation had passed her by, Mayree sighed. "What's your name?" she asked him.

"Michael."

"Well, Michael, I accept your apology, though it isn't necessary."

He placed his hand on his heart. "Thank you."

Something about the gesture moved her. "Have we met before?" she asked as she dug in her purse for a few bills. "You look a little bit familiar." He smiled so brightly it surprised her. She snapped her fingers. "I think I know. Did you use to cut our lawn?"

His smile faded as quickly as it came, turning into something like a sneer. She had no idea why he looked so offended. "Probably," he said, then patted the roof before walking away.

Mayree shrugged and rolled the window up. She couldn't wait to get home and put her bathrobe back on.

February 19, 1989

Dear Mama,

Sundays are the worst in here, even though pretty much every day is the same. I don't know if I ever told you what it's like. I guess that's because I hate thinking about it. Wake-up call is at 6:30 in the morning, even on holidays and weekends. We get fifteen minutes to do hygiene, then go to breakfast where we get two mini bags of cereal, a carton of milk, two waffles, a mini packet of syrup, and an orange. They call it "Continental Style," like that makes it better, but it's the same thing every single day. Right after that they do pat downs for contraband and then give us fifteen more minutes for Restroom Break. At first it was hard to take a crap on command like that but now I can. They don't like it if you ask to use the toilet other times. On school days, we go from 8:30 to 4:30 with a lunch break in the middle. We get hot lunch on Tuesdays and Thursdays, which is lasagna, a carton of milk, a roll, and a salad with croutons. Cold tray days we get bologna sandwiches, milk, Jell-O, fruit, and macaroni salad. After school we get an hour of PE and then five minutes to take a shower. Well, really only three minutes in the shower and then two to get dressed. We change underwear every day but our clothes every other day. Dinner is at 5:30. That's the only meal that ever changes. It's hamburgers, meatballs, chicken potpie, tacos, or burritos. No milk at night but we can have fruit punch powder to mix in water if we want. After dinner we go to group or back to our cells to read or write letters or if we had a Disciplinary Action that day then we have to go to bed, no lights. One reason I hate Sundays is because we have to do more cleanup than on school days, but mostly it's because we have mandatory church service (even the Jews and Muslims have to go) and the pastor says the same thing every week. I don't mean just the same stuff about God and being good and all that. I mean, he reuses the same exact sermon word for word. I think it's because most of the people in here only stay for a few days before they get released or else sent to jail so he figures he can get away with it. I could probably take his place by now after a year and a half of Sundays, except I'd never do that because I don't believe in God. I know you do or at least you used to and so I'm sorry if it hurts your feelings for me to say I don't, but I just can't see how so much bad stuff can happen if there was really a God. Just thinking about all the bad stuff you've had to go through makes me so mad I could punch that pastor in the face. I won't, I promise. I'm trying to be better about controlling my anger, which still gets hot when I think too much about things, but at least I know better than to knock out a preacher or even say I was thinking about it to anyone but you. Especially since I'm about to get out of here soon. I hope.

I love you, Mama.

Your son

Paula

Paula and Kelly didn't speak at all the rest of the short drive to the University of Texas campus. They parked in the garage and walked together to the white stone building on the South Mall of campus where their American Government class was held. It was Paula's least favorite class, which was problematic because she was majoring in government. She'd really enjoyed the Intro to Oceanography they'd taken their first semester to fulfill one of the natural science and technology require-ments, even began to secretly imagine shifting to a science degree, but Kelly had read somewhere that 13 percent of successful law school applicants majored in government and so that's what they both did.

Paula couldn't even remember when she and Kelly first talked about becoming lawyers, but it seemed like it had been written in stone some-where along the journey from elementary school to college. Over a joint family dinner one night in high school, they announced they were going to practice criminal defense at their own firm, Cagle and Baker, PC. Both their fathers roared in approval, lifting their refilled glasses and saying the world needed more good women to stick up for the bad guys. Uncle Stan, drunk enough to slur, had thumbed his hand toward her father and said, "Especially this one." He and Frank had laughed again. Paula remembered both her mother and Aunt Sissy rolling their eyes.

As they passed the Presbyterian church near the parking garage, a man lurched down the entrance steps onto the sidewalk just in front of them, grumbling loudly. Paula yelped and froze midstride. The man, barefoot, filthy, and reeking of body odor and alcohol, stumbled into the street. A passing car honked and swerved, and the man lifted his middle finger and swayed as he peered into the oncoming traffic. "Fuck you!" the man yelled. "You hear me? Fuck you!"

Paula's heart pounded like a bird trapped in a cage as she watched another car go by, and then the man zigzagged across the crosswalk.

Kelly took her hand. "Jeez, you're white as a sheet. Are you okay?"

I'm gonna cut your throat and then I'm gonna fuck you in it. You hear me? I'm gonna fuck you in the neck. Paula shook her head.

"Come on," Kelly said, pulling her. "It was just some drunk dude keeping Austin weird. You're fine."

Paula didn't feel fine. These terrorizing moments kept randomly playing in her mind like scenes from a horror movie. Each time, the blood drained from her head and pooled in her gut, leaving her breathless and paralyzed. If she thought too much about them, the memories faded so quickly it was hard to believe they'd been there at all.

And Kelly had told her she'd been talking to some girl, not a guy like she remembered. She was so disoriented. Of course it was a guy. And where did such horrible scenes and words come from if not from actual events? And if not from a knife, how did she get the gash on her arm?

"We're going to be late to class if we don't get a move on," Kelly said. She started walking, and reluctantly, slowly Paula followed, eventually matching Kelly's pace, but remaining several steps behind her. Everything heightened her apprehension: a barking dog, the screech of a car's brakes, bursts of laughter or shouts of greeting, even the wind crashing through the tall canopy of oak trees lining the sidewalk. Paula turned toward each new noise, gauging its threat.

"Did you hear me?" Kelly asked. She'd stopped walking and was standing in Paula's path with one hand on her hip.

"What? No."

"Forget it."

"I'm sorry," Paula said. "I guess I'm not feeling all that great."

Kelly reached into her purse and handed Paula a candy bar. "Told ya you were hungry," she said with a smirk. "Come on. You can eat while we walk."

A dark-haired guy walking toward them waved. Paula thought he looked familiar. Kelly waved back and said, "Hey, I thought you were going to call me after spring break," with a faux pout. Paula moved to the edge of the sidewalk as he approached, searching his face and her memory to come up with a match. Nothing. He said something to Kelly as he passed, and she spun around and took a few backward steps as she blew him a kiss.

"Who was that?" Paula shrank into herself. The fact that she couldn't remember what her attacker looked like only added to her sense of confusion.

"I actually have no idea," Kelly said with a laugh. "But he's cute, huh?" Then she sighed. "I really need to get better at asking guys' names before I try to make out with them." She laughed again and poked Paula in the ribs.

Paula bent herself over to get out of the way. "Be careful—my arm still hurts where it was cut." She looked at Kelly. "With a knife."

Kelly winced but said nothing.

The idea of flirting with a random stranger, something she and Kelly used to spend entire weekends doing in high school, now seemed like a very dangerous risk. That guy could've been a pervert, a rapist, a murderer. Even bad guys can look nice on the outside. The bird of her heart resumed beating its wings against its cage of her ribs.

They took their seats in the classroom, and at exactly ten o'clock the teaching assistant, who'd been staring at her watch, began passing out the blue test booklets. "Professor Wright is out today, so I'll be proctoring the exam. We'd like at least three pages discussing the features of the Intermediate-Range Nuclear Forces Treaty, which, as Professor Wright has explained, is one of the most important arms control agreements between Washington and Moscow in recent history." There were quite a few groans from around the room. This was one of several topics they'd been told to be prepared to write an essay about. "Settle down, please," she said, clearly enjoying her authority. "You should discuss in detail the issues that inspired the negotiations between Reagan and Gorbachev, what geopolitical regions were affected and how, and what the results of the INF Treaty have been so far." She checked her watch. "You have fifty-nine minutes. Go."

Kelly looked over at Paula with an exaggerated expression and mouthed the word *shit.*

Paula glanced around the room and saw that most of the twenty or so students had opened their booklets and already started writing. She'd attended all of Dr. Wright's lectures on the Cold War and Soviet politics, taken notes, done the supplemental reading. But right now, she could hardly remember any of it. In spite of her supposed panic, Kelly was bent over her booklet, writing furiously. From within her benumbed daze, Paula watched Kelly fill the page with her big, looping script: *In the early '80s, the USSR deployed a missile in Europe called the SS-20. The US responded by sending their own intermediate-range missiles. It was like moving pawns in a chess game, except if it kept going, it could have triggered a nuclear apocalypse instead of a checkmate.*

The teaching assistant stood between their two desks. "Keep your eyes on your own paper," she said, stabbing her finger at Paula's blank booklet.

"Sorry," Paula said. "I wasn't trying to—"

"Save it."

Feeling the heat of two dozen pairs of eyes on her, Paula sank down in her seat, heat rising to her face. Her pen hovered at the first line, but she couldn't think of anything to write except for what Kelly had already put down. She stared at the empty page, willing herself to remember something her Soviet-obsessed professor had said, but she simply couldn't concentrate on anything long enough. Her mind drifted from one tangential thought to another, eventually snagging on the lyrics of that annoyingly catchy Billy Ocean song from last year about getting out of his mind and into his car. Into his car. *Into his car.*

Paula turned and whispered to Kelly in a register somewhere between grief and desperation, "I know I was drunk, but I swear—"

"Miss Baker! It *is* Miss Baker, isn't it?"

Paula felt the unmistakable stinging that always preceded tears.

"You are dismissed."

"But—" She looked at Kelly, whose eyes were wide, but whose mouth remained closed.

"You can take it up with Professor Wright, but I'll warn you: as a long-practicing prosecutor, he has a low opinion of cheaters."

Someone in the back of the classroom snickered, but Paula didn't bother to turn around. She grabbed her backpack and fled. She ran out of the building, down the Mall, past the fountain, and stopped when she reached the Drag only because she'd run completely out of breath. At the corner of Twenty-First and Guadalupe, she leaned against a light pole covered in flyers announcing live blues at Threadgill's and Antone's and other venues, messages by people seeking roommates and bandmates, missing cat and dog posters, offers for tutoring and house-cleaning. The wind gusted, riffling the papers and flinging dust in her face. She tried to think of a time—a single time—she'd ever cheated on a test or a paper. She couldn't. She'd lied in the past—of course she'd lied—but they were mostly innocent, or at least not grave, not hurtful or destructive. She'd stolen stuff before, too, but again it wasn't anything serious: small amounts of money from her mother's purse here and there, candy from the 7-Eleven, a pair of cheap earrings from a display case on a dare. But she'd never once cheated. She'd never needed to.

After catching her breath, she became aware of the goose bumps on her arms and the rumbling in her stomach, as much from hunger as nerves. She decided to walk to Snack's for a cup of coffee and something to eat; if she went home now, her mother would demand to know why she wasn't in class taking her exam. No way was she going to tell her the truth. She could make up some excuse about being sick, but then Mayree would blame it on Will and give her a lecture about pulling herself up by her bootstraps and hound her about scheduling a makeup test. Still on edge from Saturday night, fearful of more than just a stupid test, she didn't have the energy to deal with all that. Instead, she'd wait at the coffee shop until the class was nearly over and then walk back to the fountain to meet Kelly for Spanish.

She walked alone against the wind, frequently checking behind her to make sure she wasn't being followed, and glancing at the people she passed, assessing danger. At Snack's, Paula settled at a table in the back, facing the door in case she had to make a quick exit, but avoiding making eye contact with anyone. As she picked at her sandwich, feeling the ache in her jaw as she chewed, she tried to make sense of the discrepancies between her and Kelly's versions of the party. She thought of Kelly's dismissal of her fears, and her silence in class, her failure to defend Paula to the teaching assistant. If it turned out Paula had killed that guy in the park, would Kelly defend her to the authorities? Apparently Kelly cared more about her stupid law career than she did her best friend. Paula abandoned the idea of going back to campus that day, not even for their economics class later that evening; she didn't want to see Kelly again after all. She tried to study but couldn't concentrate; her mind raced from one uncomfortable thought to another. An hour passed, then two. Finally, after she'd have been finished with her INF Treaty test and then their eleven o'clock Spanish class, she hooked her thumbs behind the straps of her backpack and trudged out of the coffee shop and through the wind and traffic toward home, looking over her shoulder and scanning her surroundings as she walked.

As she rounded the corner onto her street, she saw Felicia's ancient maroon Thunderbird parked in front of her house and immediately felt a sense of relief. For as long as she could remember, she usually went to Felicia when she needed a Band-Aid, a hug, a snack. Her father was her protector, her mentor, and when he was home, sometimes even her playmate. But for the small, daily moments of comfort that a daughter normally would seek from her mother, she figured out early on that Felicia was more emotionally reliable than Mayree. When Paula got her first period, it was Felicia she told, and Felicia who taught her how to affix and properly dispose of a sanitary pad, then welcomed her to womanhood by baking her red velvet cupcakes. If Mayree was out or shut up in her room, Felicia was the one who picked her up from swim team practice or took her to the mall or gave advice on whatever she was struggling with. More than a few times, since she played the role so well, Paula had wished that Felicia actually was her mother, especially when Mayree was in one of her moods. The one time she'd said that out loud, Felicia had admonished her: "Now don't you go saying that in front of your mama or you'll break her heart." But she'd pulled Paula into a hug and held her close anyway.

Paula quickened her step as she approached her front yard, anticipating Felicia's calm presence, her unconditional understanding. Paula wouldn't even have to explain anything; Felicia would just *know*. With any luck, Mayree would be out shopping or getting her hair done or something. She didn't want to sit across from her mother over dinner enduring an interrogation about Saturday night or her staying in bed yesterday or her exam. No matter what she might say in her own defense, Mayree would find some reason to blame Paula for her own misfortunes and give her some variation of her favorite lecture on personal responsibility. Maybe she could just slip inside and hide out in her room forever.

"Shit," she said when she saw Mayree's car parked in the driveway next to her own. For a moment she considered turning around. But where would she go? Not Kelly's. Definitely not Will's. Not back to campus or to work. Or anywhere she might feel unsafe or embarrassed or both. She just hoped Mayree was busy in some other part of the house.

When she went inside, closing the door extra quietly behind her, she found both her mother and their housekeeper sitting at the kitchen table—and her old swim bag with her soiled and bloody clothing from Saturday night spilling out between them.

"Paula," Mayree said, exhaling a cloud of cigarette smoke. "What in god's name is this?"

Mayree

Earlier that afternoon, Mayree had carefully driven home from the supermarket, worried the wind might hurl another shopping cart, or something worse, at her. By the time she got there, her knees had begun to ache and stiffen. She pulled into the driveway, popped the trunk, and hobbled inside through the back door.

"Felicia!" she called, dropping her purse on a chair and peeling off her fur coat, which she now loathed. "I'm home! Groceries are in the trunk!" No answer but the sound of the vacuum running. Mayree could tell by the sound that she was in Frank's study—why Felicia insisted on cleaning it every week when nobody ever went in there was beyond her. "Dammit," she said. The ice cream would melt and the vegetables would thaw if she left them in the car until Felicia got around to it. She brought all the bags inside in two limping, barefoot trips, the pebbled walkway shredding what was left of her pantyhose, shoved the frozen and perishable items into their repositories wherever they would fit, then checked the answering machine for messages.

"Mrs. Baker, this is Ernie Duncan from Texas Commerce Bank returning your calls. I wish I had more definitive news for you. I know how frustrating it must be, but we're still working on—"

Mayree hit the delete button, then hauled herself upstairs to her bathroom, grumbling all the way.

"Christ Almighty," she said aloud as she approached herself in the full-length mirror, her hands flying up to pat down her tumbleweed of hair. "Look at this god-awful mess." She held out the hem of her silk dress, aware now that the delicate fabric had been torn where she'd fallen on it. With some difficulty, which made her even angrier, she yanked it off, balled it up, and threw it in the corner. She huffed at her gaunt figure, the deflated cups of her bra that used to hold up a pair of full breasts, the slack paunch of middle age behind the waistband of her underpants, her skinned and bloodied knees. Closing her eyes against the sight of herself, she went to the medicine cabinet for antiseptic and bandages.

After taking off her hose, she sat on the edge of the bathtub and scrubbed the blood off her shins. She could tell Felicia had already cleaned in there, and though she'd never say anything, Mayree knew that Felicia liked something to stay unsullied for at least a few hours before it was subjected again to the exploitation of daily use. Too bad. She dropped her used towel onto the floor. Then, remembering that Felicia wouldn't be back until next week, she picked it up again.

Mayree was stoic as she tended to her wounds. She'd been taught: pain was for animals.

Her outrage at the day brimmed as she surveyed her closet, which was full of dresses and separates that she'd once thought were elegant and stylish but that now all looked pretentious or garish or tacky. She wondered what Frank's secretary had been wearing the night he died. Not much, obviously. One by one, she snatched various items out, glared at them, passed judgment aloud in a disgusted tone—"What was I thinking?" Or "What do I need gowns for if nobody invites me to anything anymore?" Or "Sissy would never wear something as hideous as this"—and hurled them into an astonishingly large pile on the floor.

When she was finished, there was hardly anything left hanging up. She splashed some water on her face to cool it down. Pulling again at her cheeks and eyelids and neck, she stuck her tongue out at her reflection, then reached into her bathrobe pocket for her cigarettes. She sucked in a long breath and held it, waiting for the nicotine to kick in as she stared down the pile of clothes and wondered what she was supposed to wear. It wasn't like she could afford to replace it all. Not now, anyway. Until Stan figured out who all Frank owed money to and their banker finished doing his *forensic accounting* as he called it, then she had to assume that she and Paula were paupers. Maybe they'd get a windfall in the form of life insurance or some property she didn't know about, but if not, Mayree didn't know how long they'd be able to keep the house. To her dismay, she actually didn't know shit about their finances; she'd assumed that if he couldn't keep his dick in his pants, then Frank was at least doing the only other thing she'd expected of him: making money.

For now, the days of impulse buys at the department store and phone calls to catalog companies to order all the things she'd circled were gone. Maybe she could take some of her things to a consignment store. Frank's, too, come to think of it. Their formal wear, at least. Five months since he died and Frank's clothes were still hanging in his closet. She'd get rid of them immediately. She'd probably only be able to sell the more casual pieces at a garage sale, but there was no way in hell she'd ever advertise her new financial situation to her neighbors by putting their wardrobes on the lawn. She'd rather wear what she had, gaudy or unfashionable as it might be.

"Frank, you asshole," she said, flicking her cigarette butt into the sink. "This is your fault." She kicked the pile of clothes, which made her knee ache worse, then limped downstairs to his study to ask Felicia to help her hang everything back up.

But Felicia wasn't there. She must've gone upstairs while Mayree was in her closet. Sighing at the profound shittiness of her day, she plopped down in Frank's desk chair and put her head in her hands. Some minutes later, just after she'd started to relax, Felicia called out from the kitchen.

"Mayree, where are you? Can you come in here a minute?"

"Sweet Jesus, what is it now?" Mayree said under her breath. After everything she'd been through today, her housekeeper was yelling at her like *she* was the employer. She pushed herself up and ambled out of Frank's office. "Hold your horses, I'm coming!"

Felicia pointed at a green duffel bag on the kitchen table.

"What's this?" Mayree asked. She leaned close for a better look, then reared back with a look of revulsion. "That smells like a gas station toilet. Don't tell me there's a dead animal in there covered in its own piss."

"I wish." Felicia unzipped the bag and pulled out Paula's reeking outfit. "I was taking special care in her room, like I said I would, and I found this in the back of her closet. I figured there's a story behind it—and probably not a good one."

Mayree lifted the sleeve of Paula's sweater, alarmed by the amount of dried blood on it. "She was wearing this when she went out Saturday night."

"You think that boy had something to do with it?"

"He'd better not have." Mayree dropped the sleeve, then sat down. She thought back to how Paula had spent Sunday in her room like she was sick. She'd gone out, gotten drunk, and come home—just like her father used to do. Mayree had assumed her daughter was either hungover or wallowing over Will. She hadn't worried until now that there was something actually the matter. "Did you find anything else?"

Felicia pulled out a chair and sat down, too. "Only that she'd swapped out her comforter for the one in the guest room. Lamp, too. Everything else was like it usually is."

"I saw she'd done that when I checked on her yesterday, but she was in a mood so I didn't ask her about it." Mayree thought uneasily about how little she knew about Paula's state of mind. Even including her dramatic infatuation with Will, Paula hadn't ever exhibited anything other than normal teenage behavior. A bag of bloody clothes was definitely not normal.

Felicia gestured at the sleeve hanging out of the bag. "Did you see a cut on her? Or you think that's somebody else's blood?"

Mayree shook her head. "I don't know." She picked up and examined each article of clothing, even the underwear. It felt like a violation of her daughter's privacy, but she needed to know what other bodily fluids might be on them.

"This is making me real nervous," Felicia said. She clasped her hands together as though in prayer.

"Me too," Mayree said. "Whatever it is can't be good, not if she's hiding it." Mayree was all too familiar with that phenomenon.

"She ought to be home soon," Felicia said. "Right?"

Mayree looked at the clock and nodded. "Her Spanish class ended at noon." She was glad she knew that about her daughter, at least. She lit a cigarette and paced the length of the kitchen, willing the minutes to pass more quickly as she thought about all the ways a young woman was vulnerable in this world.

Then the back door was very quietly opened and shut, and Paula emerged from the utility room. She came to an abrupt and panicked-looking stop as soon as she saw them.

"Paula," Mayree said, exhaling a cloud of cigarette smoke. "What in god's name is this? Whose blood is this?"

Paula looked from Mayree to Felicia and back again. "It's nothing," she said, moving to grab the bag.

But Mayree was faster, and slapped her own hand down on it first. "The hell it is. You want to tell me what happened?"

"No," Paula said, her face flashing from panicked to angry. "I don't."

Mayree felt a rise of anger in response to Paula's that temporarily overwhelmed her feelings of concern. "Don't sass me. You stash a bag

73

of reeking, bloody clothes under my roof; you owe me an explanation as to why."

"If I wanted you to know, I wouldn't have stashed it."

Mayree smashed her cigarette into the ashtray and took a long, audible inhale that made her nostrils flare. She turned to Felicia. "Don't worry about finishing up today. We'll see you next week."

"I don't mind. There's not too much left to do." Felicia glanced at Paula, who was now gnawing at her fingernail.

Mayree touched her housekeeper's hand. "Felicia, it's time to go. I'll take care of it."

Felicia nodded, and none of them spoke as she brushed her hand gently down Paula's back, collected her sweater and purse from their place in the utility room, and let herself out the back.

Mayree didn't even wait for her to walk down the driveway to her car before she launched her interrogation.

"Start talking, missy. Now!"

Paula took the seat Felicia had vacated and put her head down on top of her crossed arms. Mayree gave her a moment to settle in. But the longer her daughter remained still, the more unsettled Mayree became. She worried what that stillness could mean. "What? Did you wrestle a steer?" No response. "Hold up a blood bank?" Paula's silence thickened the air in the kitchen.

"Did that pissant Will do something to you?" Paula very subtly rolled her forehead back and forth on her arm. "Did you do something to *him*?" Another head roll no. "Then what, Paula? Did you drink bad ice and piss yourself? Are you embarrassed? Is that all?" Another silent roll.

Scared, Mayree slammed her palm down flat on the table, shocking Paula into a military-straight posture and back into the conversation. "Then what in the hell kind of trouble did you get into?" she yelled.

"I got attacked, okay?" Paula yelled back. "I was at a party with Kelly at Pace Bend and someone attacked me."

Mayree's insides seized up. "What do you mean, *attacked* you? Who?"

"I don't know, an attacker! Why are you being such a bitch?"

Bitch. The word was as sharply intoned as a knife. She didn't even stop to think; she reached across the table and smacked Paula hard across her left cheek. "I will not suffer your smart-ass right now!"

Paula pressed her hand against the pinking skin and looked at her mother with a mixture of shock and fear that would've made someone like Sissy Cagle jump up and gather her daughter into her arms and smother her with apologies. Oh, who was she kidding—Sissy would never even think of slapping her children across the face. Instead, Mayree doubled down on her fury, angry as much at Paula as at anyone who'd hurt her. "WHO AND WHY! NOW!"

Obviously fighting tears, Paula told her she couldn't remember everything, but that she'd gone with some guy to make a phone call. He'd become violent, and she'd fought him and run away. Mayree could tell by the swaths of missing detail and illogical sequencing of events that she was not getting the whole truth.

"So let me get this straight," she said. "You went to a party in the middle of nowhere all made up, got yourself blind drunk, asked a stranger to take you to a pay phone, then got into a car with him—*willingly*—and he hit you? Cut you? Is that correct?"

Paula dug the heels of her hands into her eye sockets and swiped off the tears as though she was angry at them for being there. "Something like that," Paula said, her eyes red but expressionless, the emotion gone from her voice.

"Why you? What were you doing?"

"Nothing! Just forget about it, okay?"

"Look at me," Mayree said. Paula turned her head and stared at nothing, which infuriated rather than softened Mayree, rendering her unable to muster the empathy she knew she should have. "Look at me! What have I always, always said to you about men? I warned you for precisely this reason, and you went and did the exact opposite of everything I have ever told you." Starting with her index finger pointed at the ceiling, she counted them off on her hand. "One: don't dress up like a hooker. You want to be sexy and cute, I get it. It's normal to want boys to notice you. But guess what? They see a girl who's trying too hard and they think she's desperate. They think she's easy. They'll pick you up, use you, then throw you away like an empty beer can. Two: do not get drunk. You especially, with a daddy like yours who probably passed down the genes for being totally asinine under the influence of alcohol. Men see a drunk girl and think, *Giddyup.* Three: never, ever, ever get into a stranger's car, I don't care if he's a thousand years old. You let someone take you somewhere—*especially* if you're alone—and you're basically giving him an engraved invitation to take advantage of you." Mayree stabbed her extended fingers into the air. Her voice caught as she spoke, her heart pounded. "I've told you these things, have I not? I warned you what could happen, didn't I? And now you've seen for yourself. Maybe now you'll pay attention when I tell you something for your own good." Mayree, half-spent, leaned back in her chair and lit a cigarette. Fear and rage felt like two sides of the same coin.

"I didn't ask for it," Paula said quietly.

Mayree felt like her throat was being squeezed. How had she, who knew better, failed to keep Paula safe from men like Will and whoever this attacker was, who feasted themselves on good girls, claiming their innocence and virtue? She was supposed to be her guide. Mayree should've been tougher, to show Paula how to be.

Well, she would be tough now. She would point at and name the dangers, the way she'd done when Paula was little. *The stove is hot. It can burn you.* How else would she ensure that her daughter realized the importance of personal responsibility and protection? Nobody had taught Paula; she'd had to learn it the hard way.

"You're a pretty girl. You can't help that," Mayree said.

"So it's my fault?"

Mayree blew smoke toward the ceiling. "Like it or not, you have to be careful. We all do." She tapped her cigarette forcefully against the ashtray. "Now," she said after a moment, looking her over. "Your arm's okay, right?"

Paula nodded, but she drew her arm in close to her torso, as if to hide it.

"And nobody knows about this but Kelly?"

"And the guy who did it," Paula said in a flat voice.

"I assume he was drunk, too?"

Paula shrugged. "Maybe."

"Maybe," Mayree said. "I'm going to take that as a yes. So there's a chance he doesn't even remember you. If you're lucky, he won't remember you from Adam and that'll be the last of it. I'm sure your father didn't remember half the things he said or did when he was shit-faced. Makes it easier to put things behind you." She took a hard drag, then squinted through an exhale at Paula. "Anything else you need to tell me while we're here?"

Paula shook her head.

"You're not pregnant by any chance, are you?"

Paula snapped her head up. "Jesus, Mom, no. Of course not."

Mayree exhaled. "Then here's what we're going to do." She gestured at the bag with her cigarette. "You're going to take this out and put it in the trash can, then roll it to the curb. Tomorrow is trash pickup. Then it'll be gone, out of our lives, and we're never going to speak of it again. You hear me? You're going to have to pull yourself up by your bootstraps and put this behind you. As a woman, this is how you survive." Mayree nodded, hoping the gesture would reassure them both. "You got a good scare, but you learned a good lesson. You're lucky, you know. This could've been a lot worse. It could've been bad." When Paula didn't move, Mayree pushed the bag toward her. "Go on."

Paula did as she was told.

~

The next morning, after a nearly sleepless night, Mayree stood at the kitchen sink with a cup of mediocre coffee. She'd gone into Paula's room each time she'd gotten up to pee and peered over her sleeping form as she had when Paula was a baby, as helpless now as she had been back then, the only comfort being the breath entering and leaving her daughter's vulnerable body. She hovered a hand over Paula's chest, not quite able to touch it, but wanting to feel the rise and fall all the same.

She watched the garbage truck approach their house. A burly-looking man in a soiled uniform jumped off the back, heaved their can up, and shook the contents into the hopper. She'd hoped to catch a glimpse of green as the bag was dropped in with the rest of the trash, but her view was slightly off angle. It didn't matter. Just knowing it was gone was a relief. Paula had experienced something unpleasant, but it was mild by comparison and now it was over. Her daughter wouldn't be scarred, just better prepared for the future. She'd be fine.

Mayree poured the remnants of her coffee down the sink, then flipped on the television to find out what was happening elsewhere in the world; she didn't care where, just any place but here.

Paula

Last night, after they'd eaten dinner together in silence except for the clink of their forks, Mayree left the table without a word and heaved herself into her wingback chair like she weighed twice what she actually did. Paula had done the dishes and, as she walked past the living room, glanced inside at her mother. She was crocheting another one of her ugly lap blankets with a scowl on her face, and didn't even bother to look up.

The next morning, Paula left a note on the kitchen table—*Drove myself to class*—and slipped out of the house before her mother woke up. She couldn't bear the thought of dealing with her after yesterday. If Mayree was awake, she'd demand to know how Paula had slept and if she wanted breakfast and what time she'd be home, an undercurrent of tension running between them even as Mayree pretended that everything was normal. It wasn't the tension Paula wanted to avoid by leaving early that morning, it was the normalcy—the simultaneously distracted and overbearing normalcy that typified her interactions with Mayree—that would make Paula feel worse than she already did, because right now, nothing felt normal at all.

Instinctively, Paula had known her mother wouldn't offer her the comfort she needed after Saturday night, but what she couldn't understand was why Mayree had gotten so angry at her, blaming her for being hurt because she'd been drunk—and pretty—as if the guy hadn't been responsible at all.

And Mayree had been so adamant about Paula getting past it immediately. How was she supposed to do that? What about the horrific invectives that punctuated her thoughts, reminding her what the guy had threatened to do to her? Just ignore them? Maybe she should. But until she figured out how to do that, she would try to avoid everyone.

~

Her English class didn't start until nine, so she had some time to kill, if she even ended up going. She hadn't decided. It wasn't like anyone would notice; core classes like that one had several hundred students and were mostly taught by graduate students who probably didn't care if anyone showed up or not. Just imagining sitting there in an auditorium full of people made her shudder. If the guy hadn't died where he'd fallen—and so far there'd been nothing in the news about a dead body in Pace Bend Park—he could be looking for her. He could be anywhere, even in one of her classes.

She drove the less than half a mile to Kelly's—shorter on foot if they jumped the fence and cut across the three-acre property halfway between their houses where the old governor's mansion was, like they did when they were younger—to leave a note on her windshield. She hadn't wanted to call, because she was still upset about Kelly's treasonous silence yesterday as the teaching assistant threw her out of class, and that she hadn't called to check on her later, even though Paula had also missed their next two classes. But she had to let Kelly know that she wasn't going to class again today and therefore didn't need a ride to campus. She didn't want to risk her encountering Mayree and talking about the exam that Paula hadn't taken.

She parked in front of the sprawling live oak that was so big its branches extended all the way across the street and provided shade to nearly half the neighbor's front yard. Looking up, she could see the "desks" that Kelly's father had built when they were nine, nailing two planks onto a scaffold bough just above and parallel to the big branch they liked to sit on. Paula wouldn't have been able to count the number of hours they spent up there talking, drawing, doing homework, and trying to befriend jittery squirrels. She didn't want to endure normalcy with Kelly today either. Sighing, she pulled a pen and spiral notebook out of her backpack.

Hey. I'm making up the gov test this morning then going to the dentist so don't need a ride today. See you tomorrow. She was about to sign it the way they always did—*LYLAS*, for *love you like a sister*—but stopped. Right now, it would've been a lie. She ripped out the page, jogged up the drive to Kelly's car, and stuck the note underneath her windshield wiper. She'd worry later about her skipped classes and the exam she didn't and wasn't planning to take.

Instead, she let the Bonneville wander, simply wanting to get away from anything that reminded her of Saturday night. Kelly didn't believe anything had happened, and her own memory was sketchy; it would be easy enough to bury it somewhere in her mind. Once the cut on her arm healed, it would be like it'd never happened. She should've burned the fucking bag of clothes that night. Then Felicia wouldn't have found it, and Mayree never would have known anything had gone wrong beyond her having too much to drink, which was bad enough. Furious with herself, she banged her fist on the steering wheel.

She cruised several blocks south of the campus, not wanting anyone to recognize her ugly blue car. Ahead of her, the recently installed Goddess of Liberty statue on top of the capitol dome gleamed in the morning light, like a signal directing her forward. Without actually deciding to, she crossed over I-35 and continued east on the alley-size street bordering the old city-owned cemetery, which made her think of her father, his body cremated and buried, his spirit—if there was such a thing—unavailable to provide her any comfort.

A new current of grief ran through her as she found herself turning onto the street where Will and his roommate rented a tiny, gable-roofed house that had definitely seen better days. The yellow paint would've been cheerful if it wasn't peeling so badly. The porch and the sidewalk leading up to it were both cracked and listing; the screen door was ripped from the previous tenant's dog; and the curtains were nothing but old, mismatched sheets that Will had thumbtacked above the windows on the inside. The interior wasn't much better; Will didn't bother much with housekeeping. There were usually dishes piled in and around the sink, clothes were strewn illogically (she'd once found a T-shirt behind a box of cereal in a cabinet), and the furniture smelled vaguely of spilled beer and mold. Mayree would've been appalled. Yet even now, Paula could see past the grubby facade. Inside—presumably—Will would be showering or getting dressed for class. The Dead would be playing on his stereo, incense burning, books splayed out on his bed and coffee table. He'd be running a comb through his sandy hair as he considered interesting thoughts.

She still couldn't fathom why he'd so abruptly broken up with her. It wasn't like she kept him from studying or insisted he spend money on her that he didn't have. She was happy to sit next to him while he listened to music, paying careful attention as he sang along with the lyrics he found meaningful. Content to enjoy simple meals or leftovers from the restaurant. Whatever. She just liked being around him, inspired by the ease and informality with which he maneuvered through the world. She missed the way he'd kiss her on the forehead sometimes, for no apparent reason. And how he used to read aloud to her in bed until she fell asleep. Even if she only slept a few minutes, it was always the most peaceful sort of rest. Especially without her father around to lean on, she worried that she'd never find someone else who made her feel as loved as Will had.

For the second time that morning, she stared wistfully at a house. In this case, she parked on the other side of his driveway, just up the hill. There were some garbage cans, a fence, and a row of enormous agave plants that would give her a little cover while she still had a clear view of his front door. She just wanted to see him. She wouldn't even say hello. Well, maybe she would. Or maybe he'd notice her hard-to-miss car after all, come jogging over, tell her how happy he was to see her, that he'd meant to call her back but had been busy, so busy, he regretted the way things ended, would she like to go to dinner or breakfast, would she like to come inside and crawl under the covers?

Paula became aware of a dull ache in her legs from sitting still. She looked at her watch. Why hadn't Will come out of the house by now? She leaned forward, squinting at the windows, the screen door, looking for any indication of movement inside. He didn't own a car, and kept his bike inside the house after the last one was stolen off his porch, so she couldn't tell if he was even home. His roommate had a day job, so it was unlikely Will would be anywhere with him. Maybe he was still asleep; he wasn't generally a morning person. He had astronomy at nine, though, and since he'd said he was going to focus more diligently on his academic work, she expected him to emerge soon. But she'd been there for almost an hour. Diligent or not, he wasn't the type to leave for class an hour before it started. In fact, she'd gotten used to him startling from some reverie, checking the time, then saying, "Oh shit, I'm late!" Any moment, he'd probably wheel his bike out the front door and take off at a sprint for campus.

When he didn't, her thoughts began to curl around the dark, unpleasant visions she could hardly bear to imagine: that Will was inside with another girl—kissing her, looking into her eyes, telling her he loved her. Maybe that's why he hadn't returned her call from Sunday night. He'd already moved on. Her hand shook as she turned the key in the ignition.

She drove off, not wanting to look at his house and disappointing herself by doing it anyway. She wanted to be disgusted by the shabbiness of the tiny structure and the falling-down neighborhood around it, filled as it was with littered, unkempt yards and grubby children, but she couldn't. It still felt like a hallowed place because—for a brief time, anyway—she'd been wanted there.

She sped up to the next intersection and made an abrupt left turn, anxious to get away, then had to slam her brakes to avoid hitting a bent old woman pushing a laundry cart across the street. Paula gasped, her heart pounding; she'd come so close to running her over, going too fast, thinking about the wrong things. The woman didn't even look up, just kept slowly moving across the asphalt. Once she'd made it across, Paula, who couldn't catch her breath, pulled into a storefront parking spot and closed her eyes, berating herself for being so stupid and willing herself to calm down.

After several minutes, Paula lifted her head off the steering wheel and sat back. "Now what?" she asked herself aloud. She'd actually let herself imagine that Will would welcome her inside his shitty little house and keep her safe and hidden for the day or maybe forever. Where was she going to go now? She didn't want to go to class or to a café or back home. She didn't feel like walking along Town Lake and it was too cold to go swimming at Barton Springs—not that she wanted to be exposed and alone outside anyway.

She looked at the shop in front of her. She hadn't noticed the red, white, and blue barber pole out front when she pulled in or the faded CHAPO'S BARBER SHOP painted in the same colors on the big picture window. This was where her father used to get his hair cut, long ago. In fact, he'd once owned the strip center and leased the three shops to their various tenants. It was so close to Will's house, yet she deliberately hadn't driven past it any of the times she'd gone there. It was too painful and strange to see it out of context, without him. She looked across the street, and there it was, the ice cream place. She and Kelly would accompany their fathers on their monthly trips to Chapo's just so they could get helados afterward. Mayree would never let Paula eat so much sugar at once, but Frank always let her get a triple scoop with her favorites: cinnamon churro and horchata strawberry and piña loca. She could taste the flavors even now. She perked up at the idea of having ice cream for breakfast, but the CLOSED sign hung on the door. Too early. But Chapo's was already open; the lights were on and the ceiling fan was spinning. It was familiar again after however many years since she'd last been there. Through the window, she could see they still had a candy jar full of lollipops on the counter.

A bell tinkled above her when she pushed the door open.

"Morning, señorita." A white-haired man in an apron pulled a pair of scissors from a canister of blue liquid and wiped them off. "What can I do for you?"

Paula looked around, taking in the row of chairs, the padded bench along the back wall, the well-worn black-and-white linoleum floor. She was gripped by a fantasy of her father swinging wide the door, bellowing out a deep *hello* to everyone in the shop, heaving himself into the seat by the window, then, as the barber swung a smock over Frank's belly and snapped it behind his neck, asking, "How's it hanging, Chapo?" Chapo. He didn't recognize her. But why would he? It had been years.

"Um," she said. There were no other customers there. She couldn't very well leave now. "I guess I'll get a trim?"

"You don't want to go to a beauty salon? Para las mujeres?" She shook her head and he shrugged. "Wash first?"

"No, thank you." She'd showered and shampooed before she left home that morning. He gestured to a chair, the same one her father would've taken. When he closed the gown snaps at the nape of her neck, she flinched. "Just a trim," she reminded him.

"Sí, señorita." He spritzed her hair with a spray bottle until it was wet, then combed it gently. "I won't take too much. You want to look pretty for the boys, yes?" He smiled at her in the mirror. Chapo seemed more like a kindly grandfather than a lecher, but her stomach clenched anyway. Mayree's commandments from yesterday returned: "I know you want to look sexy and cute. You want boys to notice you." She thought of the guy who'd wanted to kill her. *You asked for this.* She'd never thought she was beautiful, but she knew she was pretty in her own way. People often complimented her on her thick, dark-blonde hair. Mayree, in particular, expressed jealousy about that genetic blessing that had apparently come from Frank's side of the family. "Be damn grateful you didn't get my sad little head feathers," Mayree often said. Will used to lift chunks of it up and let it cascade out of his fingers, claiming to be mesmerized by its thickness, its texture. She'd been flattered by his attention, even though she had no more control over her hair than she did her eye color or surname. Had the guy chosen her Saturday night because of her hair?

"I changed my mind," Paula said. "Cut it all off."

"What do you mean *all*?"

Paula flicked her hand out from under the smock and pointed at the electric hair clippers. "Buzz it. All of it."

Chapo shook his head and tsk-tsked. "No, you don't mean it. You don't want to look like a marimacha, do you?" Paula looked at his reflection, not understanding. "A dyke."

She glared at him, disgusted both by his use of that word and his presumption. What she wanted to look like was none of his business.

The bell tinkled and, in a brief respite from the tension between them, they both watched a paunchy man amble in, tip the brim of his cattleman's hat in their direction, and take a seat in the chair next to Paula's. Another barber emerged from the back and greeted him, took his hat and placed it crown down on a cart, and covered him with a smock.

"Do it," Paula said in a low whisper.

Chapo heaved a sigh. "You're sure?" The other customer glanced in their direction just before his barber leaned him back to nearly horizontal in his chair.

Paula nodded, and Chapo combed a section of bra strap–length hair near her temple and held it out, a pair of open scissors hovering around it. They stared at each other in the mirror for a moment, a strange, silent game of chicken, until finally, Chapo made the first cut and the liberated clump slid down the front of her smock and onto the floor. There was no going back now, and so no point in watching. Instead, she shifted her attention to what was happening in the other chair.

The barber lathered the man's face and neck, then wrapped him like a mummy with two steaming towels. Paula remembered her father undergoing the same ritual, could even remember him groaning as the barber pressed the towels into place. At the time, she didn't think much of what her father was experiencing physically, just registered it as a ritual for and among men. She knew her and Kelly's presence was unnecessary but not unwelcome, and that their stillness would be rewarded with helados. Sometimes, if time seemed to pass too slowly, or if she and Kelly were antsy, they'd go next door to the washateria and play hide and seek among the big machines. The lady who worked there never minded, as long as they didn't disturb any customers. Sometimes she even let them push each other around in the big rolling metal baskets until their fathers came looking for them. Now, from her chair, she watched the man next to her visibly relax, the rise and fall of his barrel chest slowing. She wondered if those minutes her restless, boisterous father spent lying with his face covered were a similar reprieve from her mother, possibly, or whatever else complicated his days—because the other three Saturdays a month, he shaved himself at home with an electric razor.

She stole a glance at herself and was surprisingly dispassionate about the fact that it looked like she'd let a toddler cut her hair. Chapo raised a single eyebrow; he seemed disappointed by her lack of reaction. Next to her, the barber held taut a cowhide strop and began stroking a straight-edge razor back and forth across it. Back and forth, back and forth, the blade catching and throwing off reflected light. Chapo turned on the clippers and held her head still with his fingertips. She could feel the vibration in her skull as he raked the clippers up her scalp, starting at the nape of her neck. The other barber removed the towels, lathered the man's cheeks, jaw, and neck again with quick, tight circles of a brush. Shards of dark-blonde hair rained down on her shoulders, her chest. She could see the man's pulse in his neck. When the barber touched the blade to the man's exposed throat, Paula flinched—*I'm gonna cut your throat and then I'm gonna fuck you in it*—and Chapo nicked her behind the ear.

"Ay," he said, holding a towel there. "This is why you shouldn't cut your hair like a boy." He showed her a minuscule drop of red. "Not much blood, you'll be fine. But hold still this time, okay?"

She held still.

The barber scraped the man's skin, gently, carefully, wiping the foam and stubble onto a towel after each stroke. Chapo finished clipping her hair to a quarter-inch, then neatened the edges of her hairline with another attachment. The barber wiped the man's face and neck with another steaming towel. When he lifted it away, his skin looked pink and raw beneath the sun spots and wrinkles. Chapo took a soft brush and drew it down her face, her ears, her neck, dusting away the fine hairs left behind.

"Well?" he asked, offering her a hand mirror so she could see the back of her shorn head.

The barber opened a bottle of greenish liquid and splashed some into his palm, and as he slapped it onto the man's face, the distinctive musky, powdery odor traveled into and overpowered Paula's lungs and mind.

She yanked the smock away from her neck, popping open the snaps and sending tiny hairs flying. Air, she needed fresh air. The smell was too strong. The two barbers and the customer stared at her as she grabbed her purse off the cart and fumbled inside for some money.

"What can I tell you, señorita?" Chapo said, shrugging. "You asked for this."

You asked for this.

She found a twenty-dollar bill and thrust it at Chapo, then sprinted across the shop. Her pulse was so loud inside her head she didn't even hear the tinkling of the bell when she yanked open the door and ran out.

February 26, 1989

Dear Mama,

The only way to get through this is to try not to think. I focus on doing my hygiene and chores and school and stuff. If I'm cleaning, I think about you and I focus on the splatters and stains and scrub extra hard like you always did. But thinking about you makes me miss you bad, so I switch and concentrate on the smell of soap and the feeling of holding the sponge and the dirty warm water on my hands. I think about moving like Bruce Lee, real slow like water. I don't talk to the guards unless they talk to me. I keep it simple and low if I talk to any of the other guys cuz I don't want to start a fight. I tell myself that being stealthy like that is my superpower. Not thinking is hard, though, because there's nothing else to do. Pretty soon the stuff that makes me mad starts creeping in again and makes me want to fucking smash somebody in the face and watch them bleed. Sometimes that's all I can think about. It makes me laugh. I know you'd be upset with me if I did it, though, so I don't. But it's real hard to do nothing but exist.

Love,
Your son

Mayree

Mayree was still in her bathrobe watching *The Price Is Right* when the doorbell rang. Her nerves were still a little fried from thinking about Paula's situation, because she bounced a little in her chair. The show announcer had just said the name of the first contestant and told her to *come on down*, and Mayree's heart pounded as she wondered who might be at her door. She calmed herself with the thought that robbers and attackers probably didn't ring the bell. She waited a moment with her ear cocked toward the door. She wasn't expecting anybody. No guests, no repair personnel, no deliveries. And sure as shit, nobody was going to be standing there holding a bouquet of flowers for her. If anything, it was the mailman, wanting to be sure she saw the two or three envelopes marked "past due" that she'd been receiving on a regular basis lately. Lord knew why he took such an interest in her personal business. Maybe pointing out her misfortunes made him feel better about having chosen a career path that required him to walk house to house in all manner of weather and listen to people's dogs barking at him all day.

The bell rang again. "Jesus Christ on a stick, Roger! Just leave it. You keep bothering me like this, I'm going to rethink leaving you any Christmas money this year!" she yelled at the door as the TV audience cheered.

The third time she heard the chime—a ridiculous, tinny rendering of "Big Ben" that she'd always loathed and now swore she'd get replaced if she had to rip it out of the ceiling herself—she jumped up. Roger wouldn't ring three times. Even if attackers were unlikely to use a doorbell, Paula's story had awakened an old fear. She grabbed a crochet hook and yanked the door open, ready for a brawl. She was completely unprepared, however, to greet Sissy, who was standing on Mayree's unswept porch wearing a hot-pink sweater and carrying a foil-covered offering that was unmistakably her famous King Ranch chicken casserole. Clutching the glass dish with her favorite oven mitts, the tips scorched from use, Sissy smiled through the mouthwatering steam rising off the top. It brought Mayree's guard to the verge of collapse, knowing that since it took her almost two hours to make this particular recipe, with homemade corn tortillas and jalapeños that she'd pickled herself, it meant that Sissy had spent the morning thinking about her.

"Well?" Sissy said, still smiling. "You going to invite me in?"

Mayree stepped aside, and as Sissy sauntered past her toward the kitchen like she'd done hundreds of times in the past, Mayree ran her fingers through her hair and straightened the collar of her bathrobe, as if that would do a bit of good. Surely Sissy had seen her yesterday at the market, all dolled up and ridiculous looking in her heels and fur, and now here Mayree was with morning breath and a rat's nest on her head.

"I made it how you like it," Sissy said over her shoulder. "No mushrooms. I have to say, I've gotten to where I prefer it without them, too. It was Stan who insisted I put them in, but now that he's gone"—she took off her mitts and dropped them on the table—"the mushrooms are, too." She pulled out a chair and sat down, as though everything were normal between them. As if almost six months hadn't passed since their last conversation, unless their brief exchange at Frank's funeral counted. "You got any coffee left?"

"I do," Mayree said, and went to the fridge to get the heavy cream. Even after all these months apart, she was still in the habit of keeping a pint of it on hand for Sissy, who thought drinking unsweetened coffee was practically a sin. She'd just picked up a fresh container yesterday, as a matter of fact, which meant that Sissy would know she'd been thinking about her, too.

To be fair, they probably would've reconciled after Frank died if Sissy hadn't shown up at his funeral. Mayree hated funerals. *Hated* them. All the pomp, the solicitous, hollow condolences, the stupid hymns and readings from the Gospels, the overwhelming quantity of flowers—whoever thought flowers at a funeral were a good idea?—that people sent to the church or the house that would die their own stinking deaths in a few days and had to be endured and dealt with, like aftershocks following an earthquake. Her mother's graveside ceremony was short and private, as Irene had requested, and planned entirely by the mortician in Blanco. Her father, Ray, didn't help at all, either because he'd just shelled out for Mayree and Frank's wedding, or because he couldn't be bothered. But Ray, who moved his new lady friend, Joan, into his home not two weeks after Irene died and then opened up his own worm farm three years later, had prearranged an elaborate memorial service and burial for himself. Mayree, who was five months pregnant when he died and therefore already pissed off, couldn't believe the utter horseshit coming out of everyone's mouths as they took their assigned turns at the pulpit to talk about what a good, honorable, God-fearing man Ray was. All these years later, she didn't know if it was the morning sickness, or the flowers, or the blue-sky eulogies that made her double over during her would-be stepmother's rendering of "How Great Thou Art." She just knew that was the last funeral she'd ever attend if she could help it.

She couldn't very well get out of her own husband's service—though she seriously considered coming down with a bug—but why Sissy had to show up was beyond Mayree. It'd have been good to have her best friend by her side, but she still hadn't forgiven her for speaking about Frank's infidelity aloud. It might've been okay if she'd just stayed in the back and minded her own business, but Sissy had the gall not only to come through the receiving line like a regular mourner, knowing full well that her last words just a month before had been *Screw you, Mayree*, but she'd actually sat in the same pew as Frank's mistress. For all Mayree knew, Sissy might've even told that hideous woman, who was infuriatingly attractive, that she was sorry for her loss. Probably everybody there—including Paula, unfortunately—knew who the platinum blonde in the black veil was, which only made the whole event worse.

Even thinking of it now made Mayree's pulse tick up a notch, and cooled the warmth she'd only a moment ago started to feel toward her former friend. She hoped this visit wasn't about Paula. Although part of her would like to confide in Sissy, ask her if she'd done the right thing by telling Paula to put the whole nasty business out of her mind, she also didn't want to invite criticism. She didn't think she could handle any more negativity at the moment. "So, what brings you by?" she said after setting down Sissy's coffee and pulling out a chair for herself.

"It's been a while, hasn't it?"

"That it has." Mayree tapped out a cigarette, even though Sissy didn't care for the smell.

"First, I want to apologize." Sissy ran her thumb around the rim of her mug. Apparently, she'd gone to the nail salon after grocery shopping yesterday after all.

"Oh?"

"Well, don't act so surprised."

Mayree blew a tiny thread of smoke in Sissy's direction. "I'm not acting."

"I shouldn't have said what I did about Frank. It was too personal." She fanned the smoke away from her face.

"I can't say I disagree."

"But, Mayree." She softened her voice. "Stan told me that you knew about her. And . . . the others. All that time, why didn't you tell me?"

She'd thought about it, for sure. Frequently, in fact. It would've made things so much easier, letting Sissy know why Frank was always home late and why sometimes they didn't speak to one another at dinner, instead of forever coming up with excuses. But she didn't grow up like Paula and Kelly, telling friends every single personal thing that happened to them, every thought that popped into their heads. Maybe these girls were lucky that way. Even though she often wished she could open up all the way, especially with Sissy, Mayree didn't like seeming needy or pathetic. She had to be strong. And to do so, there were certain shameful truths in her life that needed to stay private, particularly the worst ones.

"Especially after I told you Stan left. That's why I knew when you called me a *jealous, awful, C-word* you didn't really mean it. Why would I be jealous if I knew that you knew? We were in the same boat by then," Sissy said. "Didn't you trust me?"

Mayree looked at her hard. "You be truthful now, Sissy Cagle. If I'd told you about Frank's women back when you and Stan were still living happily ever after, what would you have thought?"

"What do you mean?"

"I'm not speaking Spanish. I mean exactly what I asked. What would you have thought?"

"I don't know. I'd have been mad at him. For you. With you. I'd have told Stan to talk to him. I'd have helped you plan and carry out his murder. I'd have made you King Ranch casserole. I don't know."

"Those are all things you'd have *done*. But what would you have *thought*? What would you have thought about *me*?"

Sissy sat back in her chair and said nothing, just looked at Mayree with an inscrutable expression.

"I'll tell you what you'd have thought. You'd have wondered whether I still put out. Or if I was any good in bed. You'd have thought I should've been nicer to my husband, shown him more appreciation, behaved like a lady, stopped smoking, made a better effort." Like the models on *The Price Is Right*, she swept her arm grandly from the hem of her bathrobe to the top of her tousled head. "You'd have felt sorry for me. And you'd have thought that, for whatever reason, Frank's being unfaithful was somehow my fault. Everybody else probably thinks that."

Sissy put her hand out, but Mayree pulled hers away. "I wouldn't have thought any of those things. I swear. It wasn't your fault. Even when Stan told me, I didn't think it was your fault, not for a second. Just like I don't think it's my fault that Stan left. I think men are wonderful, filthy animals who think with their small heads most of the time and it usually has very little to do with us."

Mayree raised a resentful eyebrow. Right or wrong, she'd been raised to assume that behind every good man were more men, and behind every bad one was a worse woman. It pissed her off to no end when she thought about it, but all the men she'd known, from her daddy to her husband, seemed to think that whenever something went sideways, it was somehow a woman's fault. She'd lived with that idea for so long, it was hard not to believe it. "Actually, I think it probably does."

Now it was Sissy's turn to glare across the table. "What are you saying? Do you know something about Stan and me that I don't?"

"I don't know shit about Stan. I'm speaking in general. But if you ask me, you're better off without him. The mushrooms were the least of it."

"How dare you make light of what I'm going through? We've been married more than half my life, and I'm supposed to be grateful now that he's gone?" Sissy's eyes pinked at the rims and her bottom lip twitched.

"You get used to it." Mayree stamped out her cigarette and folded her hands on the table. She knew she was being unkind, but she couldn't seem to stop herself. The more vulnerable Sissy was, the meaner Mayree felt.

Sissy opened her mouth to speak, then closed it. Took a deep breath and blew it slowly out. "I'm not going to get upset with you, Mayree. I know you're hurting and when people hurt, they take it out on the ones they're closest to."

"Is that something you read in one of your self-help books?" Even if she *was* hurting—which she wasn't because she was too strong for that—she didn't like the feeling she got when Sissy pried into her character, like she was peering into Mayree's mind with a flashlight.

Sissy scraped the chair back and stood up. "Why do you insist on being so ugly to me? I brought you a fucking casserole! I came over here to offer to take you shopping, my treat, and to get your hair done, and to talk to you about whatever's going on with Paula, since according to Kelly, she's been acting strangely the past few days. Now I'm wondering if there's something in the tap over here affecting both of y'all."

Mayree stood. There it was. Sissy implying Paula was screwed up meant, therefore, so was she. "First of all, I don't need your charity. I am perfectly capable of taking myself shopping and to the hairdresser if that's what I want, and for your information, Paula is on her period, not that it's any business of yours, and aside from that is doing perfectly well and acting as normal as any teenager does, regardless of whatever Kelly says. And since you seem so intent on knowing everything, Kelly got very drunk on Saturday night and is probably still hungover, so her views on Paula's mood are most likely clouded by the beer goggles she had on. Whatever went on with Paula involved Kelly, too."

Sissy snatched up her oven mitts and strode out of the kitchen. "Don't worry about returning that dish," she said over her shoulder. "It's old and dinged up—just like someone else I know." She slammed the door behind her, which Mayree could feel all the way through the kitchen floor.

"Fuck you!" Mayree shouted in the direction Sissy'd gone while looking at her own reflection in the oven door. Gripping the chair back, her knuckles were pale. Her whole body was vibrating with emotion— anger or grief or some cocktail of fervor she didn't even have a name for.

She didn't know why she couldn't just accept Sissy's apology and go back to how things used to be between them: doing their errands together, swapping and discussing books, complaining about how hard it could be raising spirited girls, passing peaceful afternoons and evenings exchanging ideas, recipes, gossip, or just comfortable silence. Sissy was the closest thing she'd ever had to a sister, and now she'd probably never speak to her again. Sissy was right; Mayree was already old and dinged up. She would likely spend the rest of her miserable life with nobody but the cruel ghosts of her past, her housekeeper, and her mysterious, self-destructive daughter, slowly burying herself under piles of the stupid lap blankets she crocheted.

She looked at the casserole still sitting on the table where Sissy'd left it. Underneath the foil, she knew, the flavors would be meticulously combined and the cheese on top would be a perfect, bubbling, golden brown. If she were a better, happier person, she'd have sat down with a fork and eaten her fill straight out of the dish. But because she was not, she picked it up, held it high above her head, letting the hot glass scorch her fingers, then slammed it down onto the Saltillo tile as hard as she could.

"Fuck you, Mayree," she whispered.

Paula

Paula ran out of the barbershop and toward the parking lot. As she passed an overgrown patch of wild rosemary, she grabbed a stem, stripped it of its needles, and clutched them in her fist. She got to her car and locked herself inside. The outside air was cool enough, but she'd parked in the sun, which was now almost directly overhead, and the inside of the Bonneville was uncomfortably hot and stank like burned vinyl. But even the interior's familiar funk wasn't strong enough to counter the powerful scent of aftershave that clung relentlessly to her nostrils. She rubbed her hands together, crushing the rosemary leaves to release their fragrance, and held them to her face as she breathed in and out, in and out, forcing herself to think of something pleasant.

Bank fishing on Lady Bird Lake with her father. He always pretended that her fish were bigger. No, that made her miss him too much. *Summer camp. Learning to sail and water ski on Lake LBJ. Earning a merit for bravery after doing a double flip off the high dive. Getting picked for the coveted breakfast ride, eating a cowboy skillet while the sun rose over the arroyo.* But then her horse had gotten spooked by a snake and bucked her off right into a cactus patch. It had taken two nurses and the camp director several hours to pluck all the quills out with tweezers. Forget that. *Seeing Willie Nelson in concert.* No, no. She'd gone with Kelly, singing along with "Mammas Don't Let Your Babies Grow Up to Be Cowboys" and all their other favorites. She didn't want to think about Kelly. Something else. *Felicia's hugs. The sound of her singing hymns while she cleaned.* But that brought to mind her finding the bag of clothes in Paula's closet, and Mayree's anger, and what she'd blamed her for, and the party she hadn't wanted to go to—none of this would've happened if she hadn't let Kelly twist her arm into going—and Will, who was still breaking her heart even then. She dropped the crumbles of rosemary and wiped her hands on her jeans. Angled the rearview mirror, paused, glanced at her nearly bald head before quickly looking away. And now this. Everyone would think she was crazy. Maybe they'd be right.

Judging by the undisturbed yellow-green film of pollen on her mother's windshield in their driveway, Paula could tell that Mayree hadn't left the house. Because Mayree didn't take walks or do any gardening, that meant she was inside, either smoking at the kitchen table or watching television or making one of her stupid blankets. If Paula was lucky, she might be in her bedroom. Eventually Mayree was going to see her hair and go ballistic, but Paula wasn't ready to deal with it yet. She popped the trunk, remembering the few items of Will's she'd stashed back there after they'd broken up—not wanting to get rid of them but not wanting to look at them all the time, either—including his Texas Proud Sesquicentennial trucker cap.

She put it on and went to the back of the house, took a deep breath, and let herself in, prepared to sprint through the kitchen to the stairs if Mayree was there. She wasn't, but Paula hurried anyway, almost taking a fall when she hit a greasy spot on the tile. There was a time when she'd have stopped and cleaned up a mess like that, even if it wasn't hers, more to help Felicia than Mayree, but still. That felt like a long, long time ago. Regaining her balance, she crept up to her room and closed the door behind her.

On the floor was a note in her mother's shaky script: *Your manager called to remind you you're working the 4 p.m. shift tonight. -M*

Shit. She'd forgotten all about it, of course. The week before, she'd agreed to work several early shifts. Now she could barely remember what day it was. Tuesday. Jesus, it was only Tuesday. It felt like she'd lived a lifetime in the span of three days. She balled up the note and threw it in the trash can.

In the bathroom, she took off Will's hat and touched what was left of her hair. Under her palm, it felt like soft grass. She looked at herself in the mirror, slowly turning her head from side to side, examining a scratch she hadn't noticed before, the shape of her skull, the surprisingly graceful curve of her neckline. Without a frame of hair around them, her features looked austere and exaggerated: the dark circles under her eyes, the pimple on her forehead, the blonde fuzz on her upper lip. It hadn't occurred to her before how much a person could hide behind a hairstyle. She took a step back and stared into her own eyes, wanting to see, if not beauty, then strength and confidence. But instead there was fear, grief, and shame. And now no way to conceal it.

~

There were only a few customers at Mamacita's when she arrived, but all the employees were, as usual, moving with alacrity and purpose like a well-caffeinated colony of ants even without Will, who'd been a maestro of a headwaiter before he'd quit. Her manager, Pete, used a motto that had been handed down to him from the time he was a baby waiter, and he had a perverse affinity for enforcing it on others: *If you've got time to lean, you've got time to clean.* "Leaning" included anything other than work—resting, chatting, using the bathroom when all the tables in one's station were full—and would result in a stern warning, a reduction or rescheduling of shifts, or dismissal. Paula had gotten her first warning just two weeks after she'd started. Pete called her to his office in the kitchen and told her that he didn't care if she followed Will around looking like a lost dog when she wasn't at the restaurant, but that it wouldn't fly when she was. When she'd called in sick to work the day after the breakup two and a half weeks ago, Pete told her it was okay this once, but to get her shit together and show up for her next shift. He admitted she was otherwise good at her job, and they were already down too many waiters to let her go, but he gave her a final warning for being distracted and careless, forgetting to refill water glasses or drop checks, and showing up late after promising to take an early shift. He then suggested that she hadn't been truly in love with Will anyway, but the idea of him: a strong, confident, elusive male figure that would take the metaphorical place of her dead father. "Gross," she'd said defensively. "I never slept with my father." But sex aside, maybe Pete had been right.

"What the hell did you do to yourself?" Pete said when he saw her. "Man, I think you're taking that breakup a little too seriously."

She forced a laugh, but felt her cheeks burn.

"Listen, I need you sharp tonight. We have a sixteen-top coming in at seven, including Lieutenant Governor Hobby and a bunch of senators. It'll be you, Nicole, and Juan as headwaiter, so I need y'all to set up as soon as the tables in the party room start clearing out. Do you know why they're here?"

"What do you mean?"

"I mean, the legislature's in session. Are they celebrating something or doing business?"

"How would I know?"

"Didn't you say you're studying government? Don't you political science nerds get off on knowing that kind of shit?"

"Oh." Paula shrugged. She didn't know the first thing about local politics. "Yeah, I guess. But no, I have no idea."

Pete rolled his eyes. "Well, don't fuck anything up."

A month ago, she might have flipped him off, or made a retort, or rolled her eyes back at him. But now, his warning felt like a curse.

She served two tables, then four, then seven. She was polite, attentive without being overbearing—prescient, even. Customers thanked her for anticipating their needs, for the extra tortillas they didn't know they wanted, the napkin to replace the one that had fallen on the floor. Her tips were better than usual, and she, lost in a fast-paced sense of purpose, started to feel better. The few people who commented on her hair were complimentary, suggesting she was a badass or a rebel. An older woman with a frosted perm said she was inspired to cut all her hair off after seeing Paula's buzz. Maybe this was what she'd needed—a return to something normal after all. Interaction with regular people. Busyness. She felt herself smiling for the first time since she and Kelly were on their way to the party last weekend.

But during a lull in activity, as she stood in the kitchen waiting for the line cooks to load her tray with an order, she made the mistake of letting her thoughts drift back to the drive that took her to Pace Bend Park, a place from which she still hadn't permanently returned.

~

"See? I told you that eyeliner would look cool on you," Kelly had said once Paula was in the car, a brand-new white Ford Probe GT that her father bought for its four-star safety rating and whose model name made Kelly and Paula giggle every time they said it.

"My mother thinks I look like a slut."

"She said that?"

Paula flipped down the visor and checked her lipstick in the mirror as Kelly squealed away from the curb. It would take more than half an hour to get to Pace Bend Park, where the party was probably already underway. "She implied it."

"She's just still pissed that your dad was screwing his secretary." Paula swatted Kelly's shoulder lightly with the back of her hand. "What?" Kelly said. "I'm only quoting you."

"I know. I try not to think about it because it makes me mad when I do." Paula slumped in her seat. When Mayree told her about her father's infidelity, Paula could hardly believe it. His death was shocking enough, but learning how and with whom he'd died made it exponentially worse. Mayree had said, "Get used to it, all men do it." She'd sounded cavalier, as usual, but Paula knew that she was deeply wounded underneath. If Paula was hurt and disgusted by her father being in this particular category of "all men," she could only imagine how it made her mother feel.

"What if that's why Will broke up with me? What if he was fucking around and just didn't want to tell me? Oh god," she said, moaning as if in physical pain. "What if he's in love with someone else?"

"Settle down, cowgirl. You're going to mess up your makeup if you start crying over that idiot now."

"He's not an idiot," Paula said, swiping at the damp beneath her eyes.

"He's kind of an idiot. He broke up with you, didn't he?" Kelly reached over and poked Paula in the ribs, causing her to both flinch and smile in spite of herself. Kelly had figured out that trick by accident when they were in second grade and had been using it ever since. "Reach back and grab us some wine coolers. You'll feel better."

"We can't drink while we're driving."

"Says who?"

"Says the law? We have like forty more minutes. You'll be wasted before we get there if you start now."

"Now I don't want to be the one to break up the future Cagle and Baker, PC, but damn if you wouldn't make *such* a great prosecutor, you know that? Such a little rule follower. And of course, I'll be the best defense attorney in Texas. We just have to promise we'll never be on opposite sides of the same case. Now hand me a peach one."

Paula sighed, then unscrewed the top before giving it to her friend. "Just one," she said.

Kelly winked at her and took a long slug. Kelly always teased her for being such a conformist, while her mother chided her for not being conformist enough. *What the hell,* Paula thought, and opened one for herself. A few sips in and she could already feel herself relax. Kelly rolled down the windows and turned up the music. They laughed and sang along with the radio and drank two more each and before they knew it, they'd arrived.

~

"Order up," the cook said again, louder the second time.

"Sorry," Paula said, shaking off the memory. She grabbed the tray and pushed through the swinging doors, grabbing a folding stand on her way out, then strode through the restaurant to deliver the customers' food.

As the last of the patrons in the back cleared out, she and her coworkers rushed to push five tables together and arrange the chairs so the senators could sit comfortably. They started to arrive just before seven, and as they were seated by the hostess, Paula or the other two servers greeted each group and took their drink order.

"Must be celebrating something," Paula said to Pete as he passed her at the bar. "They're having margaritas."

"Good. Get them drunk and tell them to lower the drinking age back to nineteen. We'll make more money that way."

"You mean we'll make more *legally*," she said, even though he was already out of earshot. "Half the kids who come in here have fake IDs." Paula's first night training at Mamacita's, she'd followed Will to a table of pretty, giggling young women who were probably still in high school. When Will introduced himself as their server and asked what they were drinking, one of them nervously offered what was clearly a fake ID.

"No need," Will had said with a wink. "I'm sure you ladies are legit."

Now she wondered if his flirting had always been about the tips—or if he'd been cheating on her the whole time they were together.

As her mind wandered to and from uncomfortable thoughts, her earlier efficiency languished. Paula delivered the margaritas, nearly spilling one, and took orders from the senators who'd arrived while she was at the bar, forgetting them almost immediately. Normally she could memorize any number of special requests; now she took out her pad and pen. "Sorry," she said to a woman whose shoulder pads made her look like a linebacker. "Did you say *with* salt?"

"No, I said with*out*—twice," the woman said before turning her attention to the man next to her.

The headwaiter, Juan, flared his eyes at her, and Paula mouthed back, *Sorry*. After she returned with the next round, she reached between two people engaged in conversation to swap an empty bowl of salsa for a fresh one and bumped someone's arm, sloshing salsa onto the tablecloth. She cleaned it up as quickly as she could, apologizing the entire time even though that further interrupted their dialogue. Such small flubs shouldn't have been a big deal, but it shook her confidence, perhaps because she was already on Pete's radar, and he'd specifically told her not to fuck anything up with this group. She asked Nicole to cover for her so she could use the restroom. She just needed to splash some water on her face and take a minute to reset.

Pete was standing by the door when she came out. "What the fuck, Paula? Are you five years old? Couldn't you wait until after you took their orders?"

"It was an emergency."

"Nicole and Juan are over there busting their asses."

She glanced into the party room and saw them both scribbling in their black plastic notebooks on opposite sides of the table. "I know, I'm sorry."

"Run some food." He flicked his hand toward the kitchen, and she speed-walked through the swinging doors. She loaded appetizers for her table on the large oval tray: two sizzling platters of shrimp brochette, two quesadillas, a goblet of ceviche, a large bowl of guacamole. Juan rushed in and loaded an identical order for the other end of their table.

"You got it?" Juan asked her as she slid the tray off the line shelf and onto her shoulder. Her time on the high school swim team had made her upper body strong; she took pride in being able to carry extra-heavy trays.

"Got it," she said with a grunt.

"Right behind you," Juan said, shouldering his own tray.

It wasn't far from the kitchen to the party room, maybe thirty yards across the polished concrete floor and underneath a colorful canopy of picado banners strung from one side of the restaurant to the other. She moved quickly, hardly needing to look where she was going except to be sure nobody was in her path. She moved out of the way of someone heading to the table, a dark-haired man who said, "Careful your step" as she passed him. That phrase was eerily familiar, yet so unexpected as to cause her to literally stop in her tracks.

It was the guy from Saturday night. He'd said that to her as she stumbled on their way to his car. *Careful your step.* She remembered how he'd grabbed her arm.

She didn't even have time to steady her tray before she was hit from behind and knocked to the ground. Juan landed nearby as both trays and their contents crashed around them. Normally, when someone dropped something, people clapped as if to cheer up the person who did the dropping. But this was so calamitous that the response was silence. For a long, strange moment, there was no din of conversation, no cutlery against ceramic plates, just the conjunto music that played in a loop over the loudspeakers. Then all at once, Pete and a swarm of other servers were helping her and Juan up, gathering the shattered dishes and ruined food, assuring other patrons that *everyone was fine, we apologize for the disruption, the kitchen will remake the appetizers right away, the next round of drinks is on us, we're so sorry.*

Pete held her by the upper arm and pulled her into the kitchen to get her cleaned up. "What happened?" he asked, his voice full of concern. He was always worried about liability. "Did you slip?"

She shook her head and pointed at the guy, who was now seated at her table. "It's him," she said, loud enough for him to hear. "He attacked me."

"What?" Pete said. "Who?"

Paula pointed again. "Him." Slowly, the man stood up, buttoned his suit jacket, and walked toward them. Most of the customers had resumed talking and dining, but the ones at the long table were still quiet, watching. As he approached, Paula let her hand drop to her side. She was wrong. For one thing, he was easily two decades older than the guy who'd abducted her; his dark hair was shot through with silver. He was definitely taller. Well, maybe taller. She couldn't conjure her attacker's face, but this man didn't look familiar. The only similarity she was reasonably certain of was that he had said, *Careful your step.* But as the seconds ticked by, she wasn't even sure of that.

"I'm Senator Huribe," he said. "Can I help?"

Paula looked at him and, with parted lips, said nothing. Pete jumped in. "I'm so very sorry, Senator. There seems to be a misunderstanding. I think Paula here has bumped her head."

"Did you say that I attacked you?" he said to Paula.

"I . . . I thought you were somebody else," she said, looking down at her shoes, the ugly orthopedic ones the restaurant required them to wear, which were now splattered with guacamole.

"Better get that bump checked out," the senator said to Pete. Then to Paula, "You take care of yourself, young lady. And be careful about making wrongful accusations against people." He smiled and patted her on the shoulder, then, with a dignified and purposeful walk, returned to his seat.

Pete leaned down and hissed in her ear. "You're fired."

She nodded, but didn't move. Her humiliation was paralyzing, even though all she wanted in that moment was to disappear.

"Now," Pete said through clenched teeth.

Paula nodded again. "I'm going," she said, and she did.

Mayree

Mayree heard the phone ringing from within a dream in which she was oversleeping. The phone became the alarm clock her father used, a heavy, German-made torture device with twin bells that he'd brought home when he was discharged from the army. After he'd lost his sense of humor, the kindness her mother swore he'd once had, and most of his high-frequency hearing in the trenches, the alarm clock was the only way to reliably pull him out of his hungover stupors. The problem was that it was loud and shrill enough to also rouse everyone within a quarter-mile radius, and so Mayree jolted abruptly awake nearly every morning of her childhood with a sense of impending doom.

"What!" she said after snatching the handset off the cradle. According to the digital clock next to it, it was 5:16 a.m.

"Is this Mrs. Mary Baker?"

"No," she said, pushing her hair out of her eyes. "It's Mrs. Mayree Baker. May-*ree*. Who the hell is this?"

"This is Officer Hackett with the Austin Police Department. Do you have a daughter, Paula Baker?"

"Paula?" She sat up. "What's going on?"

"Is Paula Baker your daughter?"

"Yes. What do you want with her? It's not even light out yet."

"She was picked up for public intoxication this morning. We have her in custody now."

"What the hell are you talking about? She's here. Asleep in her bed."

"No, ma'am. She's here at the Travis County jail in downtown Austin," he said. "One of our patrol officers encountered her passed out in her car on the 2700 block of Exposition Boulevard, in the Casis Elementary School parking lot at about two this morning. She's just sobered up enough now to give us your phone number."

"Jesus Christ." Mayree patted the nightstand for her cigarettes. "Like father, like daughter."

"Bond is set at five hundred dollars. Do you want to pick her up or should I let her know she'll be our guest for a few days?"

"I'll get her. Soon as the bank opens." It was bad enough Paula was in jail, now she had to spend $500 to get her out—a small fortune that should be going toward her tuition instead.

"Do you need the address?"

"Unfortunately, I do not." She hung up before he could respond.

~

When the officer led Paula out of the cell, red-eyed and still wearing her guac-stained black uniform skirt, oxford cloth button-down, torn pantyhose, and filthy shoes, Mayree gasped. "Who did this to you?" she hissed. She turned to the officer. "Is this what you do to baby drunks? You shave their heads?" She snatched Paula by the arm and looked around. "Who's in charge here? This is an outrage!"

"Settle down, ma'am," the officer said, deliberately calm. "She came in like that."

"Don't you settle-down *me*!" Mayree said. "How old are you, anyway? Fifteen? She did not come here like that. Look at her! She's in her work uniform. I want to talk to your commander, or whatever you call him."

"Mom, he's right."

"He most certainly is not! There are laws against this kind of thing."

"Ma'am, I'll ask the sergeant to speak with you, but you've got to lower your voice." He put his hand on her shoulder and turned her toward the hall. "Second door on the right. Have a seat and someone will be right with you."

Mayree gave a self-satisfied sniff and led Paula into the small office. Sissy was right—something *was* going on with Paula. She'd never acted out like this before. Mayree had known Paula hadn't told her the whole story about Saturday night. This behavior seemed like proof. Why, why, why hadn't Paula paid attention to her when she'd warned her about the kind of trouble she'd find if she went looking for it? God knew she wished her own mother had thought to tell her about men before she'd had to learn the hard way.

Glancing back and forth to be certain they were alone, she sat down next to her daughter and whispered through clenched teeth, "Are you trying to kill me? Huh? Are you trying to give me a heart attack and watch me drop dead? Is that what you want?"

Paula's eyes welled and she dropped her head into her hands.

"I mean it. I really cannot understand what's gotten into you. Staying out all hours of the night, getting drunk, fraternizing with low-lifes, telling me half stories about attempted murder, and now spending the night in the drunk tank and having your head shaved? What's next, huh? Tell me: What wonderful surprise awaits?"

"A barber cut my hair, not the cops."

Mayree leaned back and stared at her for a hard moment. "You mean to tell me you did this to yourself?" She flicked her hand as though swatting a fly. "Why on god's green earth would you do that?"

"You wouldn't understand."

Mayree paused. The expression on Paula's face reminded Mayree of a time long ago when she'd said the exact same thing to her own mother. She started to reply, then closed her mouth. For once she didn't know what to say. She wanted to tell her, *Yes, I understand. I understand more than you know and here's why.* But she didn't know how to talk about something that she'd never, ever talked about.

Instead, she looked down at her hands, which were clenched into fists on her lap. Spreading her fingers, she was unsettled by their resemblance to Irene's, the thick veins like tree roots pushing up from underground. Her mother's hands had been leathery and tan from five decades of ranch sun, lye soap, endless chores. The mortician had put makeup on them to make them look less worn, then crossed them over her heart, left hand—with its plain, dull wedding band—on top of the right. Mayree flipped hers over, but didn't like how they looked palms-up either, like a supplicant or a televangelist. She crossed her arms across her chest so she wouldn't have to look at them at all.

"And I didn't tell you a *half story* about attempted murder, Mom. I told you what happened."

"Good morning, ladies." A severe-looking officer entered the small room, removed his hat, and sat down heavily behind the desk. "I'm Sergeant Henderson. What's this about attempted murder?"

"It's none of your concern, Sergeant Henderson," Mayree said primly. "What I *would* like to talk to you about is . . ." *Was . . . what?* Paula just said she'd shaved her own head. Or had it shaved. Evidently, the cops didn't wrangle her into a cell and buzz it off as punishment after all. So what did Mayree want to talk about? That something terrible may or may not have happened to her daughter? That she was widowed and lonesome and friendless and broke and had no idea how to talk to her child and what she was going to do with the rest of her miserable life?

"Actually, ma'am, murder is one of my main concerns." His chair groaned as he leaned back and clasped his hands over his abundant belly. "Why don't you fill me in?"

"It's nothing," Mayree said.

The officer turned to Paula. "Doesn't sound like nothing." He winked at her, and she looked down. "You look pretty tough, but I wouldn't peg you for a murderer. Am I wrong about that?"

Paula moved her mouth like she was deciding what to say. "I—"

"Of course she's not a murderer!" Mayree started to rise from her chair, but the chief stopped her with a raised hand.

"I'm talking to Miss Paula here." His voice was still friendly in the way of old cowboys, but the expression on his face hardened. "I'm going to need you to sit down before things get out of hand." Mayree sat back down. "Let's hear it."

"My mom's right. It's nothing."

"I said, *let's hear it.*"

Paula must've known he wasn't fooling around, because she took a deep breath and, without looking at either of them, told a brief but far more detailed version of the story she'd told Mayree two days earlier. When she repeated what the guy had allegedly told her—*I'm gonna cut your throat and then I'm gonna fuck you in it. You hear me? I'm gonna fuck you in the neck*—Mayree sucked in a sharp breath. Before, Paula's story had seemed like an unpleasant but not quite death-defying experience, one that might even teach her the lessons about men that Mayree apparently hadn't been able to. The specificity of this graphic new information, the violence and vulgarity, as well as her daughter's shorn head and the dull, unfocused look in her eyes, like those of a dead animal, made something in Mayree catch. She closed her eyes, as if she could shut out the image of her little girl, a knife against her neck. Those awful words. Then, the unspeakable thing she'd spent the past thirty-two years trying to forget, the one that had permanently changed her, that had been awakened by Paula's story and had been clawing its way back into her conscious awareness over the past few days, was back.

~

On an otherwise beautiful May afternoon a week after her high school graduation, Mayree had been in her family's barn, mucking the stall of her favorite mare, humming along to Sam Cooke on the transistor radio, and thinking about the cute boy she'd met earlier that day at the feed store. Her daddy had always been strict about dating, but she liked the idea of having a secret summer romance. She was looking forward to moving to Austin in a few months to start classes at the University of Texas, excited about living in a city for the first time, going to parties and making friends and experiencing a world beyond the perimeter of a thousand-acre ranch. But until then, she planned on enjoying her almost-adulthood as much as she could. Her mother was making chicken-fried steak for dinner that night—her favorite—then she and her friend Sue were going to see a movie at the Blanco Theatre. Maybe the cute boy would be there.

One of her father's ranch hands—a leathery-faced man named Bobby Cox she'd known for half her life, came up behind her. "You startled me," Mayree had said, laughing as she took up the dropped pitchfork.

He stepped up close to her and said shyly, "I been waitin' 'til you graduated high school to show you somethin'."

"What's that?" she asked, still smiling.

He leaned in, grabbed her by the arms, and bared his crooked, tobacco-stained teeth. "It's time you learnt what it's like to ride a *real* stallion."

"What?" she whispered, not understanding.

"You heard me." He squeezed her arms hard, like he was handling cattle, and pushed his groin against her. She could feel his wet tongue on her neck, hear his panting in her ear.

"No!" she screamed, and he clamped a foul-tasting hand over her open mouth, hard enough to make her lip bleed.

"Don't you scream again, you hear me?"

He let go with one hand so he could undo his buckle. He could've let go with both hands; she was paralyzed with shock and fear. She stared at that buckle as he worked it, which she'd seen on his belt every day since he started working for her family, as if staring at it might get it stuck, might stop him. It was big and silver, engraved with CALF ROPING CHAMPION—BEXAR COUNTY, TEXAS—1953, and it unleashed the leather of his belt like a whip about to swing up and back, and she saw in slow motion how it opened the way a roper throws a whip forward, reversing its direction and creating a loop that starts rolling down, generating speed as the end gets thinner and lighter, reaching the tip as he follows through with his throw, when it accelerates so fast it breaks the sound barrier. They call it a *cattleman's crack*. But that was just the beginning. And it was only in her mind, where she stayed, escaping to a rodeo in her imagination while everything else was happening to her body. She was seventeen years, seven months, three weeks, and three days old.

After it was done—minutes or hours later, she didn't know—he flicked open his pocketknife and pressed the flat side against her cheek, then slid it down and held it against the soft flesh of her neck. "You tell anybody about this, I'll kill you. And then maybe I'll fuck you again," he said. "Besides, it's your fault. Pretty girl like you struttin' around in them tight dungarees all the time. You're a cocktease all right."

So she never told—not her parents, not Sue, not her brothers, not her future college roommate. And later, not Frank, not Sissy, not anyone. Nor did she tell anyone when she missed her next period, or when she began vomiting in the mornings, or felt a painful tenderness in her small breasts, or when she found some blue cohosh and brewed a strong tea with the roots and ate or drank nothing but that for several days, or—when the tea didn't work—she went out one afternoon and rode her father's gelding as hard as she could, bareback, around the Blanco River valley until she felt a gushing sensation and looked down to see blood seeping through the crotch of her jeans. When her mother had finally asked what was the matter with her, Mayree had shaken her head. *You wouldn't understand.*

~

Mayree, her whole body clenched like a fist, listened to the rest of Paula's account with new attentiveness.

When she finished, Sergeant Henderson leaned forward and picked up a pen. "How'd you get away from him?"

At this, Paula hesitated, like she was trying to decide what to say. "We were inside the car and I just . . . sort of fought him off, I guess. Then he chased me for a while."

"And he just stopped?"

Again she paused, her face flushed. She bit her bottom lip and nodded. Paula hadn't ever been a very good liar. Mayree wondered what she wasn't saying.

"This is a sensitive question," the sergeant said. "Did he rape you?"

Paula shook her head. "No. I mean, with what he said, I think he would have if I hadn't gotten away."

Her daughter had fought for her safety, thank god. How Paula had found the strength or the will, Mayree didn't know. She hadn't been able to when it happened to her. Mayree wanted to reach over and take her hand, but Paula pressed her palms against her thighs, curling into herself like her stomach hurt.

"Then what happened?"

"I . . . ran. I ran back to where the car was and I drove it back to the lake. I didn't see him again after that. I left his car there and went home. I don't know if he tried to follow me or anything, but I don't think so."

"And you didn't see him again?"

"No, sir." She looked miserable as she spoke. Mayree ached for her; she well understood how hard it must be for her to talk about this.

"Well, all that sounds terrible," he said, shaking his head as he wrote a few notes on his pad. He looked back up at her. "Is there anyone who can corroborate your story? Anyone who might've seen you with him?"

Paula looked down and slowly shook her head. Mayree thought about how she'd been alone in the barn back then, her father and brothers and all the other hands out working cattle. Then Bobby showed up and she knew there was no point in screaming; he'd known to find her when nobody else was nearby. It would've been her word against his. Nobody would've believed her.

"But you were at a party with a friend."

"She was the only one I knew there. And she was off with . . . other people. Before it happened, I was sitting by myself."

"What can you tell me about the car? Make, model?"

"I don't remember anything."

"Let's see. You'd been drinking, and judging by your current state, I'm guessing it was more than a beer or two, correct?"

Paula nodded again.

"And you can't give a description of the suspect or the car he was driving. You can't remember all the details. There's nobody who saw you leave the party with him. You weren't raped, and besides a small cut, you have no other evidence that an attack actually took place."

"I have my clothes. Maybe there's some of his hair or something on them."

Mayree shot her a wide-eyed look; she'd forced Paula to get rid of the bag.

Paula looked back at her. "No, wait. I forgot. I threw them away."

He shook his head. "In that case, I'm sorry—there's really nothing else we can do."

Mayree was surprised by the anger rising within her. The force of it helped, she noted, to cover an uneasy, emerging sense of guilt about how she'd handled things with Paula. "What do you mean, nothing you can do? Did you not hear my daughter? A man tried to kill and rape her. Apparently in that order."

Paula looked at her open-mouthed, obviously also surprised at Mayree's reaction.

"Like I said, Mrs. Baker, it sounds like it was an awful event," he said. "But as far as bringing a case, there's no proof."

"Are you saying if we had the clothes, you could do something?"

"What would you expect us to do?"

"I don't know, I'm not the detective here. Can't you put out an APB or something?"

The officer laughed, a head-back, deep-throated laugh that made Mayree furious with humiliation. "No, ma'am," he said, wiping the corners of his eyes. "It doesn't work like that, I'm afraid. Now if somebody else shows up to report a similar experience and they've got some better information to go along with it, then we might be able to pursue a lead. But that's a long shot. We don't get a lot of almost-rapes or almost-murders."

"This is ridiculous," Mayree snapped. But she couldn't offer a reason to continue arguing with him beyond the fact that not only was her seventeen-year-old self suddenly present and afraid, but her maternal instinct tingled with indignation. "Aren't you going to at least file a report?"

"Mom, it's fine."

"It is *not* fine!" Mayree banged her fist once on the desk.

Slowly, Sergeant Henderson pressed his meaty hands flat in front of Mayree's and spread his fingers wide. "Ma'am, I'm going to write up a report, because I have to. But you need to consider yourself lucky that I'm going to get up here in a minute and let y'all finish processing Miss Paula's bail for her Class C misdemeanor and walk out of jail free and clear. You don't want to keep pushing this or else we'll be looking at a citation for assault or interference of public duty." Then he turned to Paula. "Little lady, you might want to clean up your act. If we pick you up again for public intoxication or being a minor in possession, you're going to be in a world of trouble. And next time you go out, be more careful with what you drink and the company you keep." Then he pushed himself up, put his hat back on, tipped it at them, and left.

Mayree and Paula sat in silence for a long moment, not looking at each other.

For a long time after it happened, Mayree had refused to think about that day with Bobby Cox, or the days that followed. She put up her guard, and kept it up for so long, it became who she was. She never rode her favorite mare again, or any other horse. Never went back to the stalls or the barn. Never went anywhere where Bobby might catch her alone. If she could avoid thinking about it, then she could almost pretend that it had never happened. But on the rare occasion when it did come back to her, Mayree mostly got mad at herself for not fighting Bobby off. She should've tried at least. She should've been more like her daughter. Not just stood there like a ninny staring at his belt, waiting for him to ruin her.

Finally, another officer poked his head in and summoned them. "We just need the cash and a signature, then you can go."

"Mom," Paula said. "Mom. Did you hear him?"

Mayree looked at her. "What?"

"He said we can go."

March 3, 1989

Dear Mama,

I know I say this every time when I write you a letter, but it's been real hard being without you while I've been inside. I've had a lot of time to think about everything that's happened to you and me, and things I maybe could of done better. I'm getting out soon and there's things I've been thinking about doing to make things right. OK, maybe it's too late to make them exactly right, because we both know nothing except a time machine would fix everything. I keep having this same dream where I'm standing in front of one of the big washing machines at the washateria and looking into that big round door like I'm trying to look through the wrong end of a telescope and the clothes and soapy water are churning around and around until I start to feel dizzy like I'm about to fall into the machine and get sucked into a swirl of dirty water. I kind of want to go in because I can see you in the glass, like you're standing behind me but also inside. It wakes me up feeling like I'm drowning every time. You're the only person in this whole world I don't hate. I can hide it when I need to, but mostly I want to kill everyone who ever crossed me. When I get angry, I pretend you're standing next to me saying, breathe. I don't know how you never got mad. You had a right to be mad at all the injustices done to you by God and my father, plus the ones I probably don't even know about. You said you forgive everyone who trespassed against us, but I can't. This pastor who comes here every week trying to save our souls, which is bullshit, says the same thing. I've been trying to but I can't. Anyway, I've been trying to do what you told me—stay out of trouble, don't get in fights, don't talk back. I taught myself how to keep my outside smooth as a glass door on a washing machine, only mine isn't see-through. Nobody can see the dirty water churning inside, which is a good thing. They're letting me out early for good behavior.

 Love,

 Your son

Paula

Paula and her mother drove home in such thick silence that the ten-minute ride felt at least twice that long. Even though it was cloudy and what sun there was fell behind them, Mayree kept her sunglasses on, so when Paula stole a few sideways glances, she couldn't read her mother's expression. Not that she needed to see anything to know what was there. If she had to someday bail a daughter out of jail, Paula figured she'd be furious, too. The night in jail had been miserable, and the interview with the cops terrifying. What if they found out she'd left the guy for dead in the park? She wished Mayree could be more generous with her feelings, like her father had been; it was awful trying to deal with this on her own.

It wasn't so much that Mayree was angry—she'd get over that eventually—it was that the baseline unhappiness between them seemed to drop a little bit lower each time Paula frustrated her. Worse, Paula knew she'd always been something of a disappointment to her mother, even when she got perfect grades or kept her room clean or stayed mostly out of Mayree's way. It was like living with a constant, low-level sigh, just below the threshold of awareness, the way a refrigerator thrummed in the background of a family's existence.

Still, the way the muscles in Mayree's neck had gathered into tight cords and the ferocity of her grip on the steering wheel were unnerving. She'd seemed shocked by what Paula had told the officer, but apparently not enough to soften toward her.

"Say something," Paula said. She didn't want to sound pleading, but nor did she intend for it to sound as much like a challenge as it did.

Mayree said nothing, but the skin stretched tighter over her knuckles. She flipped on the right blinker as she approached Pease Road from Enfield. In all the years Paula had been driving with her mother, she'd never seen her turn on the blinker at that particular intersection. In fact, when Paula had her learner's permit and had to practice signaling each turn or lane change, coming to a complete stop three feet before each stop sign, and looking each way twice before proceeding, Mayree used to clap at her from the passenger seat. "Don't be such a Goody Two-shoes. Nobody follows those rules anyway, so giddyup."

"I know you're mad. I mean, obviously you'd be mad. So just yell at me or whatever you're going to do. Please."

Mayree turned onto Pease, drove exactly the speed limit past the old governor's mansion, then signaled again to turn onto their street. Unheard of.

"Were you lying to the sergeant?" Mayree asked.

"What? No!" She lied now.

"You left something out, I could tell. You certainly left plenty out when you described the events to me on Monday."

Paula was afraid of what Mayree would do if she knew the full story. Would she take her back to the station and force her to tell the sergeant?

"I'm waiting." Mayree took off her sunglasses and shot her a glare.

Paula wiped her palms on her filthy uniform skirt. "When he was chasing me, I accidentally tripped him and he fell. He didn't move. I don't know if he got knocked out or something worse." Saying it aloud amplified her dread. "I might've killed him."

Mayree's silence was agonizing.

"Are you going to kick me out?" Paula asked. A month ago, when she and Will had been working together at Mamacita's, sneaking kisses in the kitchen, tearing off each other's fajita-stinking uniforms in his little shack after their weekend shifts, Paula might've welcomed the idea of being thrown out of her house. She'd have been offended, sure, but that would only have galvanized her efforts to make a real life with Will. "Your loss," she'd have said, or at least thought, as she packed her clothes and CDs and books. She'd have walked out of her childhood bedroom for the last time, good riddance, finally feeling like the adult she deserved to be as she and Kelly and Will stuffed the last boxes into her car.

But now, the idea of having to leave home terrified her. She had no job, no Will. Of course, Sissy wouldn't turn her away, but it would be awkward. She and Kelly hadn't spoken in two days, which was the longest they'd gone in more than a decade. She wasn't close with her uncles on her mother's side, and all her grandparents were gone. Felicia and her husband, Kenny, would take her in, but Mayree might fire Felicia for it, and Paula knew Felicia needed the income. Plus, they didn't have a spare room and apparently her nephew, Curtis, who was often there, used the couch for a bed. He was being released from juvenile detention soon, if he hadn't been already, and would probably end up at Felicia's.

Mayree pulled into the driveway and parked.

"Mom?" She felt a desperate, rising panic.

Mayree pushed her sunglasses onto the top of her head and looked at Paula. "No," she said, and Paula felt such relief it made her nauseated. "Of course I'm not going to kick you out. Also, I doubt you killed a man by tripping him, but if he is dead, then he probably deserved it." Then she got out of the car, slammed the door, and walked into the house with the posture and pace of someone leading a funeral procession.

~

Paula took a shower, standing under the water until it came out cold, trying to wash off the stink of Mamacita's and tequila and jail and fear. Right now, she couldn't imagine the latter would ever come off no matter how long or hard she tried. Worse, her hangover was beginning to kick in.

After the fiasco with Senator Huribe and the humiliation of being fired in the middle of her shift, she hadn't been able to bear the idea of going home right away. Instead, she went to the convenience store where she and Kelly had been buying alcohol since before they could even reasonably pass for the legal age. Paula had bought a seven-dollar bottle of tequila and driven to her old elementary school, because that was the last place she could remember feeling genuinely carefree. The tequila was almost gone by the time the police cruiser turned into the school parking lot with its blue and red lights flashing.

Now, as she pulled on a clean pair of jeans behind her closed bedroom door, Paula heard the back door slam. Her mother must've left for her usual two-hour volunteer shift at the animal shelter. Aside from grocery shopping on Mondays, this Wednesday outing was Mayree's only other regular activity anymore. Paula opened the curtain an inch to watch for her car to go down the street. After it was out of view, Paula let the fabric fall back into place.

A moment later, she heard the door open and close again, quieter this time. Had Mayree returned? Maybe she'd forgotten her purse. Or was it her attacker? She sucked in and held her breath. She hadn't been able to stop thinking that if the guy wasn't dead, then he would come back for her.

Now panicked, she crept to her closet and groped for something to use as a weapon. She grabbed her old tennis racket and moved to her door, holding the racket aloft, trying to decide if she should go out and surprise the intruder or wait for him to find her. She glanced over her shoulder—maybe she could shimmy down the trellis the way she and Kelly used to—then there was a soft knock on her door before it opened. Paula screamed.

"Sweet baby Jesus," Felicia said, bending over with one hand on the doorjamb and the other pressed to her stomach.

"Felicia!"

"Girl, put that thing down. You gonna brain me with a tennis racket after you scare me half to death?"

"You scared *me*!"

Felicia softened her voice. "Well, now, that was not my intention." She stepped forward and gently pried the weapon from Paula's grip, then led her to the bed and sat down. She passed her warm hand over Paula's shaved head and down her cheek, then cupped her chin so Paula would look at her. "What's all this about?" she asked, lifting her eyes to Paula's hairline.

Paula looked at Felicia's eyes, as familiar as any she'd known. They were such deep brown Paula used to stare at them trying to find the edge between pupil and iris. She never could, but she saw wisdom and kindness there before she'd had the vocabulary to describe them. They didn't mist up easily, but Paula could read Felicia's emotion from the slightest twitch. She leaned into Felicia's shoulder and sobbed. She let out all the held breath, fear, tension, shame, and uncertainty that had plagued her, especially since the party, but that which had also been building up since well before that—Will, her father's death, her mother's caustic moods, her tenuous grasp of her own place in the world. Felicia rocked her slowly side to side, like she had almost all of Paula's life, shushing and whisper-singing hymns in her ear until Paula was cried out and her eyes stung and she took a final heaving, stuttering breath and sat up. Then she told Felicia everything that happened Saturday night and after, including the fact that nobody, including her mother, seemed to think it was that big a deal.

"You've had a real time of it," she said, nodding, after Paula finished. "Speaking of." She looked at her watch. "I know your mama went to do her animal thing, but no telling if she'll come back early and I don't want her to know I'm here. She's been struggling, too, you know."

Paula considered it, then shrugged. Yes, her mother had been widowed and was on the outs with her best friend, but it was hard to be sympathetic after the way she'd been treating Paula all week.

Felicia dipped her head and held Paula with a serious gaze. "She has." Then she took a deep breath and picked a speck of lint off Paula's sleeve. "But that's not what I want to talk about. I want to tell you that you're stronger than whatever happened at that party. You're stronger than that boy, Will. You're stronger than all the bad things and bad people that are ever going to enter your life. You're even stronger than your mama, and she's a fighter. I knew it since you were a year and a half old, running around this house like a wild animal." She laughed, probably at the memory of the day she'd started working for the Bakers, which she'd shared with Paula many times over the years, always with a shake of her head and a smile that went all the way up to her eyes. She drew her thumb across Paula's right eyebrow. "You remember when you cut your eye here?"

Paula shook her head. "Just that it was on my third birthday."

"You were on a sugar high, tearing around, jumping up and hitting all the balloons. Mayree filled the living room with balloons, by the way. You shoulda seen her working that rented helium tank, cussing like a sailor every time one of them got away from her. Anyway, before I know it, you come crashing down face-first on the edge of the coffee table. Blood starts gushing everywhere and I scoop you up and all you said was, 'Ow.' It was your mama who did all the screaming that day. She never could stand the sight of blood, especially yours."

"She can't stand a lot of things."

"Baby girl, someday you'll understand your mama. Maybe not all the way, but better than you do now. It's hard raising children. Nobody ever tells you that going into it. They just throw you a little party and give you some diapers and then when the baby comes, they send you on home and expect you to know how to take care of her. Sometimes it comes natural and sometimes it doesn't. It didn't come natural to your mama, and she didn't have much in the way of help—least not until I showed up." At that she smiled and leaned her shoulder against Paula's with a gentle bump. "But even then, you gotta figure out how to feed and clean the baby and get her to go to sleep when she doesn't want to. You gotta teach her things and keep her safe and ride out her crying, knowing you're making mistakes every single day, all while still trying to take care of your own self and your husband if you got one. And lord, you are *tired*. All-the-time kind of tired. Now, you know I never had my own kids, not if you don't count you and Curtis, but I watched my mother and my aunties and my sisters and my sister-in-law and your mama, and it's all the same. All of them going through different kinds of the same thing."

It occurred to Paula that she hadn't ever thought about her mother in that regard. Mayree didn't talk much about her own childhood—or even Paula's for that matter. Mayree's parents both died before Paula was born, and even though she was her uncles' only niece, her family had only visited the family ranch in Blanco once that she could recall. Her paternal grandparents were long gone, too. It was as though both her parents had been delivered by stork and abandoned to their own devices, and so Paula had no frame of reference for how either of them had navigated their ways into adult- or parenthood. They just were there, often either engaged in some subsurface psychological battle, or about to be. That her mother suffered Paula's existence was a given—but she'd never before wondered exactly why.

She leaned away and looked at Felicia. "Wait. Why did you say you didn't want her to know you were here?"

Felicia slapped her thighs and stood. From the hallway, she retrieved the green swim bag that Paula had thrown away two days earlier and carried it back to Paula's bed.

"Something about this whole thing didn't set well with me," she said. "So I didn't go home straightaway on Monday after we were talking at the table. You know I've watched Curtis go through his share of troubles and then some, so I decided to wait in the car for a minute, just to think about things a little bit deeper. Then I saw you come out and dump this in the can—and now you listen, I know your mama's heart and I know she's trying to protect you—but I figured throwing this bag out was her idea and I thought it was foolhardy."

Paula touched the zipper tab, then pulled her hand away, as if it were hot to the touch. "She'd be so pissed if she knew you took it out," Paula said. "Like I told you, it's like she's mad at me for getting myself into a bad situation. She just wants things to go back to normal, whatever that is."

"For what it's worth, I don't think any of this is your fault," Felicia said. "I know your mama would be upset with me for going against her. That's why I snuck over here and why I gotta leave pretty quick." She grabbed Paula's hand and squeezed it. "I don't know what you should do with these clothes. Put them in your closet for now. You might need to show them to somebody at some point. What happened to you was terrible, but you're gonna be okay."

For some reason, Paula thought of Senator Huribe and his ominous warning: *Be careful about making wrongful accusations against people.* She pushed the bag back toward Felicia. "No. Mom was right. It's nothing to worry about anymore."

Felicia picked it up and shoved it back into the dark corner of Paula's closet, where she'd found it. "I'm not saying you have to do anything with it now. You just keep on going with your life. You're a woman. Women bear this awful stuff all the time, sweeping hard things under the rug just to get them outta our sight." Felicia gave her a hard look that Paula took to mean that Felicia, too, had borne things she'd never spoken about. She didn't want to think about what Felicia or Mayree or any other woman in her life had gone through that might resemble Saturday night. It was like being initiated into a sorority she didn't want to be a member of. Felicia squeezed her hand again. "But that doesn't mean we don't deserve justice if we can get it."

Paula, looking at her feet, shook her head.

"Don't think about it now. Call Kelly. Give yourself a manicure, something. Just remember what I said: you're stronger than all this. We all are, even if we don't think so." Felicia kissed Paula's shorn head and slipped out.

Paula sat still for several minutes, thinking. In the distance, she heard Herb Walker's lawn mower start up. Her father once told her that when people started mowing their lawns in the middle of the week it meant spring had unofficially sprung, whether the vernal equinox had passed or not. It was a hopeful time of year. She didn't know how she felt about having the bag back in her closet, but she liked that Felicia had scavenged it from the trash can, and that she believed her and believed in her. It was like she'd pulled a discarded superhero costume out of the trash and bestowed its unknown powers on Paula. She still felt dirty and sad and sick—but a tiny bit less so.

She picked up her phone, hesitating a moment as she stared at the illuminated buttons. Then she dialed Kelly's number.

Mayree

Still thinking about the morning at the police station and the memories it brought back, Mayree transferred a load of tattered, second-
hand towels from the animal shelter's washer to the dryer. She preferred
the tasks that didn't require her to interact very much with either the
people or the animals. It was Sissy's idea to start volunteering at the
Paw-stin Pet Shelter two and a half months before Frank's death, saying
they needed to do more to "give back" to the community. Mayree didn't
think the community deserved anything she had to offer, but Sissy said
that it would make them and their husbands look like better citizens
and also give them something to talk about at parties besides recipes.
"Everyone who's anyone volunteers for something, Mayree. Besides,
Stan won't let me get a puppy, so at least I can get my fix this way."

The irony was that two weeks after their first shift, during which
Sissy eagerly played with, groomed, and baby-talked to all the dogs,
Stan moved out, and she took home a schnauzer puppy she named
Chico, and that was the end of her work at the shelter. Or maybe the
irony was that Mayree, who wasn't fond of animals, even though she'd
grown up on a ranch, and hadn't wanted to be part of the animal rescue
enterprise at all, was the one who still showed up every Wednesday at
1:00 p.m. for her two-hour shift. She still didn't particularly like it, but

continuing after Sissy quit made her feel a tiny bit superior. Maybe that's what Sissy had meant about the volunteering: it wouldn't make them look better than they were before, it would make them look better than other people.

Anyway, she was probably going to have to find a job soon, and it would at least be something to put on her otherwise empty résumé.

After starting another load of soiled towels, she went into the storeroom to check the inventory of cleaning and medical supplies, food, treats, and toys. She noted on a checklist what the director needed to buy or request more of, then went into the hall to organize the leashes by length so that volunteers could easily find one when they took a dog out to pee or to the playroom to interact with an adoption candidate.

Over the barking and general chatter coming from the main area in front, Mayree heard a small whimper. Normally, she tried not to pay attention to the dogs' noises: the growling, barking, whining, licking— lord, how she hated the sound of an animal licking itself—but after seven months at the shelter, seventeen years on a ranch, and forty-nine years of living, she couldn't help but notice the sounds of affliction.

She looked down at a crate that was draped with a dark sheet. That wasn't uncommon; especially when the shelter was full, they tried to keep the dogs settled by draping makeshift curtains between the cages. Whatever was inside fell silent. Mayree went back to hanging leashes on hooks.

The dog whimpered again, quieter and more desolate this time, as if it expected no acknowledgment, no assistance, but was just coexisting with its misery. Mayree sighed. She set down the unsorted leashes on a bench and went over to the crate. A handwritten tag with the name BUDDY was clipped to the handle.

"Jesus, Mary, and Joseph," she said when she lifted the sheet and saw the pathetic creature inside. "What the hell happened to you?"

Buddy dropped his head onto his front paws and looked up at her with one eye. Mayree crouched down to get a better look. He was the ugliest thing she'd ever laid eyes on. Scrawny, with patches missing from his wiry, gray fur, a single, sad-looking eye, and a freshly healed wound where the other one had been. He looked like a little old man, but the information sheet taped to the crate said he was only three months old. She read the summary of his background: he'd wriggled under someone's fence and was attacked by the dog who lived there. The owner stopped the attack and took the puppy to an emergency vet where he was treated for his injuries. Nobody claimed him, and obviously the dog owner couldn't keep him, so he was delivered to the shelter in the hope of finding a forever home.

They looked at each other through the grille, and as Mayree took stock of his shortcomings, he began to wag his stumpy tail.

"Don't look at me like that," Mayree said. "No way in hell I'm taking you home, so don't even think about it." He wagged his tail a little harder. "Buddy. What a dumb name. You look like you've been through some deep shit; Buddy won't cut it. How about Cyclops? No, that's too obvious. You're too scrawny for a big name anyway. I hate it when people name their dogs Zeus and Thor and ironic crap like that. Unless it's something giant like a Saint Bernard or a mastiff, but even then it sounds stupid and pretentious. What about Hector? Isn't he the one who fought Achilles? He did a pretty good job, if I remember my Trojan War history correctly. Defending his homeland, that is. Achilles killed him in the end. Stabbed him in the neck or something. Or maybe the eye? Then dragged his body around until it got pretty ragged, kind of how you are." She tilted her head and regarded him. "Hector. I like it."

By now, the newly named Hector was practically writhing with pleasure at Mayree's attention. He made a few hopeful whining sounds and inched forward, which made Mayree self-conscious. She pressed on her knees and stood. "Look. Just because I gave you a decent name doesn't mean I like you, because I don't. The last thing I need in my life is a damn dog." She found a marker and crossed out BUDDY and wrote HECTOR on his tag, then dropped the sheet back over the side.

Hector whimpered again. "Cut it out," she said, more sharply than she intended, and once again he was quiet.

For the rest of her shift, Mayree spent as much time as she could in the storeroom, tidying things that were already organized, and checking her watch. When she had only fifteen minutes left, she couldn't hold her bladder any longer and stepped out to use the restroom, refusing to look at Hector as she passed. Just as she was wondering if she could hide in there until three o'clock, someone knocked on the door. She sighed. "Just a minute," she said, pulling up her pants.

A little girl about six years old with Coke-bottle glasses caught her attention when she emerged from the restroom. She was gripping her mother's hand tightly—or at least Mayree assumed it was her mother. They were wearing matching embroidered dresses, the kind artisans made by hand in Oaxaca. Frank had taken Mayree to Oaxaca in the fall of 1971, an apology trip of sorts after Mayree found some suspicious receipts in his desk. He didn't admit outright that he'd been seeing someone. He didn't have to; the trip—their first and only out of the country—was evidence enough. But Mayree, who'd already dealt with what she'd assumed was his first affair the year before, chose to pretend that everything was fine, that nothing bad had happened.

They'd stayed in a wonderful hotel that had once been a convent, and Frank was so attentive, it was like they'd only just met. They ate and drank and made love at least once a day. He bought her a heavy silver necklace that she rarely wore afterward, because the reality of life at home was never again as happy as they'd been on that trip. She bought Paula a tiny embroidered dress for her upcoming second birthday from an old woman selling them on the street that looked just like the one this little girl looking at stray dogs had on now.

The mother stopped at the cage of an adolescent German shepherd that immediately started barking. The little girl dashed behind her mother, clinging to her. They moved down the row to the next cage, then the next, each dog barking at the girl as she passed.

"Mommy, let's go," she said. "I don't like them."

"But you said it's all you wanted for your birthday," the mother answered, not unkindly. "Maybe we just haven't found the right one."

"I want to go home."

She gave you an out, you ninny, Mayree thought. *Go! You won't have to deal with fur or shit or barking or walking in the heat—and it won't even be your fault.* But she didn't say that. Instead, she found herself approaching the terrified-looking girl and her saintly mother, whom Mayree simultaneously loathed and envied.

"There's a puppy in the hallway down there that just got dropped off," Mayree said, slipping into the kindergarten-teacher voice she used for only the first week of her one fated school year. "His name's Hector. Maybe you'd like to see him?"

The little girl's hugely magnified blue eyes looked skeptical, but the mother said, "That would be great, wouldn't it, Paige?"

"Paige, huh?" Mayree said. "I have a daughter named Paula. With a pair of names like that, you could be twins. But she's much older than you." Mayree led them down the hall, thinking about Paula and what a mess she'd become, and her face burned with a confusing combination of anger, melancholy, and guilt. Of all the children in the world, the last one she'd have thought would end up in jail was hers. But maybe that was just willful ignorance on her part. What the hell did she know about anything in this wretched world? If she'd given birth to the child she'd briefly carried when she was seventeen, it would be thirty-one years old by now. She stopped at Hector's cage and closed her eyes for a moment to calm her galloping heart.

"Here he is." She bent down and opened the door.

Warily, Paige peered inside, and upon seeing Hector, she dashed back behind her mother. "He's ugly!"

"Ugly?" Mayree said. "No, no, he's wonderful. He fought in a mighty battle and barely made it out alive. He's very, very brave." She reached in and dragged him out, then held him like a baby. Even as he squirmed into an upright position, she felt a tingling in her chest, realizing that she hadn't embraced any living thing in longer than she could remember. It could've been years since she'd held anyone so close. She blinked hard a few times, then put her teacher voice back on. "Let's take him into the viewing room and you can see for yourself."

They followed her into a room with a Dutch door. She closed the bottom portion behind them and gently set Hector down on a blanket in the middle of the floor. "He was attacked by another dog," she said. "A vicious, older male." Hector tried to retreat under a chair, but Mayree pulled him back out and began stroking his wiry fur. "He lost his eye, but look how strong he is." After a moment, he began to wag his tail. Mayree looked up at Paige, who was pressed against a wall, staring at Hector. "Do you want to pet him?"

In slow motion, the little girl sank down to the floor and crawled toward him. She reached out a tentative finger, touched his paw, then yanked her hand back.

"Turn your hand over and let him smell you. Like this," Mayree said. "He just needs a minute to get adjusted. After what he's been through, he doesn't trust people easily."

Paige did as she was told, and Hector licked her fingers. She giggled. Hector inched toward her. She tickled him under his chin and he thumped his tail against the blanket. Within minutes, he was in the girl's lap and she was rubbing his belly and making cooing sounds at him. He pumped his hind leg in the air in time with her scratches and she laughed. He jumped up and licked her on the face and she squealed. The mother clapped.

"Well," Mayree said eventually. "What do you think? He seems to like you a lot."

Paige turned to her mother, her smile revealing a few missing teeth. "Can I have him?"

"Of course you can!" She looked at Mayree and mouthed, *Thank you.*

Mayree couldn't imagine why this woman was so grateful to be taking home a hideous-looking, half-blind puppy, but she smiled at her anyway. "Let me get Janet, the director, and she'll help you do the adoption paperwork. It shouldn't take long."

When Mayree tapped Janet on the shoulder and told her that she'd found someone to adopt Buddy-turned-Hector, the director raised her eyebrows. "Well, well," she said. "I can't say I was expecting that. Nice job." In the viewing room, she introduced herself to the mother and Paige, and said how happy she was they were going to take the dog home. The mother swiped beneath her eye with a quick motion. Was she really that happy about having an animal? Janet turned to Mayree. "Would you mind staying in here with Paige and Hector for a moment while we fill out the forms?"

Mayree looked up at the clock. "It's already past three."

"I'm sure Mrs. Benson here would appreciate having a few minutes to do the paperwork without distraction."

Mayree looked at Paige's mother—Mrs. Benson—and noticed the dark circles under her watery eyes. Maybe she was already regretting her decision and Janet was going to talk her out of it in private. She sighed. "Fine."

The two women stepped out of the viewing room and Mayree sat down in a chair, watching Paige play with Hector.

"You know, maybe you shouldn't get too attached to him," she said.

Paige lifted her head, pushed her glasses up higher on her nose. Her eyes, Mayree noted, matched the blue of her dress. "Why not?"

"Just in case the adoption doesn't go through, I guess."

"But why wouldn't it?"

Mayree shrugged. "Sometimes things just don't work out how we want them to."

Hector scrambled over Paige's crossed legs in pursuit of the ball she was rolling. "My baby brother died," she said flatly.

"Oh my," Mayree said. Hector seemed to misjudge the position of the ball and bumped into the door. Paige slid over and helped him up. An uncomfortable moment—for Mayree, at least—passed. "How did he die?"

"He drownded."

"Drowned."

"Drowned."

"I'm sorry."

"It's okay, I forget how to say it."

"No, I mean, I'm sorry he died."

"Yeah."

Mayree wanted to know how old he was, how long ago he died, and where it'd happened. She wanted to know what his name was and what color his hair was and if he would've needed glasses like his sister. She wanted to know if Mrs. Benson lay awake at night, thinking about him, and how she got through her days. She wondered how her own would-be child might've turned out. Whether it had been a boy or a girl. What color its eyes would've been. If it would've been more like its father or her—and which would've been worse. She wanted to know what she could've done better for the daughter she did have.

Eventually, Janet and Mrs. Benson returned, both of them smiling. "You're all set!" Janet said. "Hector is officially yours!"

Paige squealed and hugged her new puppy. "We're attached," she said.

Mrs. Benson scrunched her eyebrows and smiled.

"Yes," Mayree said, standing abruptly up. "Like I said, you're attached. He loves you already."

After they were out the door, clutching their paperwork and Hector with his new-old leash, Janet turned to Mayree. "I'm impressed."

"Don't be," Mayree said, still waving through the glass door, even though she could no longer see them.

March 10, 1989

Dear Mama,

I can hardly sleep knowing I'll be free in two weeks. Plus I'm also pissed off because I should've gotten out a long time ago. Sometimes I feel so trapped I think I'm gonna go fucking crazy. Like really fucking nuts. This guy who's a sorta friend of mine in here left today and all I could think about was how it was gonna feel to walk through those locked doors out into Freedom. It's the only thing that keeps me from ripping somebody's head off. Plus writing these letters to you, which helps. I turned in my library books and already packed up a lot of my stuff. Some of it I never want to see again, so I trashed it and maybe it'll help me forget some of my bad memories. But I kept that picture of you and me from when I was about five, which was my favorite. I was wearing the Batman costume you made me from old clothes you got from the lost and found at the washateria. Remember you made me a mask by cutting holes in some old dude's black sock and I didn't want to put it on my face and you said don't worry, it was clean? I can still remember it stunk like vinegar up close like that. Maybe some things don't ever come out clean, even if they get washed a million times. I remember you stayed up late after work sewing that stupid costume so I could go trick or treating like the other kids. You called me the Caped Confectioner instead of the Caped Crusader, and I was so mad because I didn't get it. You laughed and I thought I was so dumb, but I know you didn't mean anything by it. I finally learned what c-o-n-f-e-c-t-i-o-n meant thanks to reading Charlie and the Chocolate Factory, which I got from the library, and now it makes me think of how smart you are. I bet you're smart about a lot of things I never knew about, except maybe men, but I know you tried.

Love,

Your son

P.S. You're the only person in this shitty world I could never hate.

Paula

After English—the only class she didn't share with Kelly—Paula waited for her on the shaded side of the natural sciences building so they could walk together to biology. She'd noticed a few stares and surprised looks from people, hers being a stark contrast to the big, permed hairstyles that so many UT girls wore, but several had made positive comments, calling her buzz *rad* and *bitchin'* as they passed. After two days, she was already used to and even starting to like it—especially because she had to spend exactly zero minutes getting ready—and the affirmation was nice. She wondered what Will would think if he saw her.

After talking to Felicia the day before, she'd told Kelly on the phone about the haircut and getting fired and going to jail so there wouldn't be any surprises when they saw each other. It was weird—they hadn't spoken for a couple of days, their conjoined schedules had been disrupted, but Kelly acted like nothing had happened. She told her about the biology lecture Paula had missed the previous day, and that she'd gotten asked out by the guy who'd sat next to her in Paula's absence, and that she was going to go on a starvation diet because she'd gained two pounds. When Paula said she wasn't feeling up to going to their five o'clock macroeconomics class that evening, Kelly said not to worry, she'd take notes for them both. But she didn't ask Paula how she was doing in the aftermath of Saturday night, or how she felt after cutting off her hair, or if she'd made up her missed exam, or if she was going to look for another job, or if her offense was going on her permanent record. She did, however, ask if it was true that the jailhouse only had a hole in the floor to pee in to keep the drunks from falling and knocking themselves out against a real toilet. Paula said she couldn't remember; she'd been too drunk to notice.

Kelly jogged up the steps and after rubbing Paula's head, stood looking at her with her hands on her hips. "I don't know, Paul. I definitely think you should grow it back out."

"Hi to you, too."

"I'm just saying you're too pretty to go butch." Kelly took Paula's chin and turned her head side to side, examining her.

Paula twisted out of her grasp. "I'm not *butch*, but so what if I was?"

"If all else fails, you could join the army," she said.

"Gee, thanks."

"I'm serious. It suits you."

"Suits me how?"

"You know—*fall in* and all that."

"Because I'm such a rule follower?" If anything, Paula felt like she'd become an outlaw. Especially if she'd murdered someone. She frowned. Kelly had seemed sympathetic on the phone yesterday, and now she sounded like an asshole.

"God, you're so sensitive! I meant it as a compliment."

"I don't see how it's a compliment."

"You *are* a rule follower—usually. It's part of your charm. And part of why you're going to be good for my law firm."

"*Your* law firm? Since when did it stop being *our* law firm?"

"Yours, mine, ours, whatever. You know what I mean," she said with a dismissive gesture. "Just promise you'll grow your hair by then at least. In the meantime, maybe you should get one of those dog collars with spikes that the punkers wear. You know, like a choker." She put both her hands around Paula's neck and smiled, leaning so close in that her breath was hot on Paula's face.

Paula froze. *I'm gonna cut your throat and then I'm gonna fuck you in it. You hear me? I'm gonna fuck you in the neck.* She felt her pelvic floor muscles relax. If she hadn't recently emptied her bladder, she'd have wet herself. "Stop," she whispered. "Stop."

Kelly dropped her hands and waved at a guy who smiled as he passed them on his way into the building. "Come on, or we'll be late," she said, and grabbed Paula's hand.

"I hate you," Paula said under her breath.

"Hate you, too!" Kelly sang as she tugged her along.

~

"This is deoxyribose," the teaching assistant said, pointing to an illustration on the overhead. "And so are these. So that obviously tells us we have two strands of deoxyribonucleic acid, or DNA. This part of the chain is derived from a deoxyribose being attached to phosphate groups and a nitrogenous base . . ."

Paula stared at the colorful image projected behind the TA but was unable to focus. She stopped taking notes and instead closed her eyes.

She felt a tap on her arm and jolted in her seat. Kelly passed her a folded piece of notebook paper, smiled, then went back to taking notes.

> *I'm sorry for teasing you about your hair. It does actually look cool (but I still think you should grow it out). :) Want to hang out after class? LYLAS.*

Ever since she'd started seeing Will, Paula had become increasingly offended by Kelly's push-pull affection, her bossy attitude and often demeaning treatment of her, but now—as throughout the history of their friendship—she was always happy and relieved when Kelly made amends. In the past, Paula let herself believe that Kelly's occasional apologies indicated not only genuine remorse but a permanent, positive shift between them. It took years of these ups and downs for Paula to realize that theirs would eventually slide back into an uneven power dynamic. Still, Paula had been feeling so fragile and had endured so much emotional upheaval in the past four days that having Kelly back, even temporarily, made her want to weep with gratitude. *Love you like a sister.* It even soothed her enough that she could pay attention to the TA's lecture on biosynthesis and degradation of nucleotides.

~

They drove separately from campus to Paula's house, Paula following behind Kelly in her Probe, shielding her eyes from the sunlight glinting off Kelly's rear windshield. Paula felt like she was a supporting actor in a movie about someone else—Kelly, no doubt—learning her lines as she went along. *Okay, pull in behind her. That's it. Let her exit her car first. She'll remove her sunglasses and cast a glance around the place as if it's familiar but different. Now, Paula, you follow.*

Kelly walked up to the front door and let herself in as she had a thousand times before. If she was on her own, she would ring the bell and wait for someone to answer. But since Paula was with her, she marched in like she owned the place. "Hey, Mama B!" she yelled.

Mayree called from upstairs. "Kelly, sweetie, is that you?"

"It's me and Paula!"

Mayree descended the stairs to greet her. "You mean Paula and I," she said with a smile.

Kelly rolled her eyes. "It's Paula and I." She went to Mayree for a hug. It hurt Paula's feelings that her mother still called Kelly by terms of endearment, like sugar or sweetie, and that she seemed to enjoy it when Kelly hugged her. She hated feeling jealous of her mother's ease with her best friend, but she did.

"It's good to see you girls together again."

Kelly glanced at Paula, then back at Mayree. "It's only been a couple of days. No biggie."

"No biggie," Mayree said with a smile that Paula could tell was forced. She ran her fingers through her hair. "You'll have to forgive me, I haven't had a chance to put my face on yet."

"She's been busy," Paula said.

Mayree's face turned red, but she raised an eyebrow in spite of it. "Don't sass me, young lady. May I remind you that I hauled your ass out of jail yesterday at the crack of dawn? I'm still recovering."

Now Paula's face turned red. She turned to Kelly. "Let's get something to eat."

~

They made sandwiches and took them up to Paula's room along with a bag of chips, a box of cookies, and two diet sodas.

"Did you skip breakfast or something?" Paula asked when Kelly reached for yet another cookie.

"I'm on my period. I'm starving."

"So that's what you mean by going on a starvation diet."

Kelly threw a cookie at her and they laughed.

"You don't need to go on a diet, anyway," Paula said, as she always did when Kelly complained about her nonexistent weight problem.

It was, on the surface, like old times. How many meals and snacks and giggles had they shared sitting across from each other on their bedroom floors? And of course Paula knew that Kelly was on her period, because she was, too; their cycles had been synced practically since the beginning of puberty. But there was an undercurrent of something running between them now. A kind of wariness or guardedness that Paula was subtly aware of feeling that kept her from fully enjoying Kelly's company. She ate half her sandwich and pushed her plate away.

"You're done?"

Paula nodded. "You can have it."

Kelly pulled the plate toward her. "What's the matter?"

"I'm just not that hungry."

"You still upset about Saturday and stuff?"

"Yeah, sure. Of course," she said. "But I'm trying to put it out of my mind."

Kelly nodded. "How about Will?"

Good lord, had she really sat in her car just two days before and watched his house like a groupie, hoping to see him—even from afar? Even after everything else she'd been through? It seemed so ridiculous now, like she'd aged an order of magnitude faster since then. She shook her head.

"Really? That's great," she said, chewing. "'Cause I saw him yesterday, and like I told you, he's totally not worthy of you."

In defiance of her rational thinking, her heart rate shot up. "You saw him?" She heard the eagerness in her own voice and forced herself to calm down. Casually—she hoped—she reached for a handful of chips. "Did he say anything?"

"He was walking his bike past the Tower and acted like he didn't see me at first, but I totally wasn't going to let him get away with that. I called his name and went over to him. The girl he was with looked pissed but who cares, right? I even gave him a hug for show, which I would never do otherwise. Honestly, I don't know what you saw in him. He smelled like that hideous hippie stuff—patchouli or whatever—and looked like he hadn't taken a shower in a few days. Gag me. Anyway, I said hi and asked how he'd been. He looked really uncomfortable and I had to stop myself from laughing at him. Then the girl sticks her hand out and goes, 'Hi, I'm Amber.' Then he goes"—Kelly moved her voice into a mockingly low register—"'Oh yeah, sorry. Amber, this is Kelly. She's, uh, a friend of a friend.'"

"A friend of a friend?"

"Yeah. But I called him out. I go, 'Actually, I'm his recent ex-girlfriend Paula's best friend.' His face got all red and she just looked down. Then I go, 'I'll tell her you said hi!' and jogged off."

Looking smug with her report, Kelly bit into the last half of Paula's sandwich. Paula thought she might be sick. She could taste the copper of a dozen questions under her tongue and was instantly disgusted with herself when the first one slipped out. "What did she look like?"

"I mean, she was fine. Maybe even a little pretty. Longish strawberry-blonde hair, light eyes."

"Long hair?"

Kelly swallowed and her face shifted. "Sorry, I shouldn't have mentioned that. But don't worry, it looked greasy. And her outfit was totally wrinkled. Now that I think about it, she was actually kinda gross. Like a total step down from you."

Three minutes ago, Paula thought she might finally be over Will. This unwelcome information proved she wasn't. At least it made her slightly more angry than sad, which was probably a good thing. Maybe not. She didn't know. She'd never truly been in love before him, so all of this was new. She reached for a cookie but didn't eat it; she broke it into smaller and smaller pieces, relishing the minor destruction piling up on her plate.

"So there's another party this weekend. Want to go?" Kelly poured the chip crumbs directly from the bag into her open mouth.

Paula watched her. She looked like a bass taking bait. Did she really think Paula would want to go to another party a week after she was almost murdered by a stranger? Was she that dense? "Kelly."

"What?"

"Are you serious? After what happened?"

Kelly rolled her eyes. "There's going to be a band—that cool dance one, The Crush or maybe The Crutch, I can't remember. Come on, don't be so boring. It'll be fun!" She reached over and slapped Paula on the thigh. "Look, I know last time was a weird night, but you're fine. So some dude came on too hard. You've proven you can handle it, right? And you know what they say: you get bucked off, you need to get right back on the horse. Show 'em who's boss."

Paula pictured the fraternity guys she'd seen on campus. Packs of rich white guys reveling in privilege and power, lust and liquor. Their carefree laughter, their confident swagger, the way they all wore smug grins and thick, white T-shirts under their starched button-downs like a uniform. Cowboy boots even if they'd never worked a day in the fields. They looked like how she imagined her father had been when he was young, and they terrified her. She'd have been terrified of her father, too, if he hadn't loved her so much. She'd seen the fights between her parents, had heard him on the phone when he was angry. And these frat guys—who knew if they loved anything other than themselves and each other. Or if they knew what love was at all.

"I'm not ready for another party. Honestly, I don't know if I ever will be."

"You can't hide out for the rest of your life. It's not even at the lake. It's close by, at the Sigma Nu house."

There were rumors about the Sigma Nu house. They had a dirt basement called The Pit where all kinds of crap allegedly took place. Why would Kelly want to go there? Why would she trust them not to hurt her? And why should Paula? What if the guy who'd taken her showed up?

"Oh shit, I just thought of something," Paula said. "Remember when Will and I went to that party right before Valentine's Day and that weird guy from high school, Kevin Atwood, came up to me?"

"Oh right, that freakazoid from swim team who had a thing for you. Didn't he get mad at you about not going out with him?"

147

"Yeah, he asked me to winter formal senior year and I said no. Remember the next day he gave me a mix tape and then sent me letters off and on for months?" Paula said.

"Like a hot senior girl was really going to date a junior," Kelly said, rolling her eyes. "Especially a goober like him."

"It was totally creepy. He was drunk at this party and started yelling at me in front of Will, calling me a rich bitch and a cocktease and stuff. It's been like three years and he was still pissed that I blew him off. I'd totally forgotten about him until that night."

"That was so fucked up. He really was weird. Remember when he got in trouble for keeping a machete in his locker?"

Paula nodded. "I didn't even know he went to UT." She thought about how Kevin had yelled at her at the party, how drunk and angry he'd been. How he'd kept pushing his dark hair out of his eyes so he could glare at her. Will had finally shoved him away and taken her home. "Kel, what if he was the guy who attacked me?"

"If what you said is true about him being all over you and stuff, you'd have known if it was Kevin," Kelly said dismissively.

"It *was* true," Paula said, irritated again by Kelly's insensitivity. "God, I can't believe you sometimes."

"Anyway," Kelly said, flicking her hand. "It wasn't him."

"How do you know that?"

Paula thought she saw a tiny flash of surprise on Kelly's face before she smiled and reached for the chips. "Kevin Atwood is so gross, I totally would've noticed if he was there." After a moment of consideration, Paula shrugged. It was true; Kelly always noticed guys.

"JESUS FUCKING CHRIST!"

Paula and Kelly looked at each other for half a second and then bolted out of Paula's room and outside toward Mayree's voice.

~

On the side of the house next to the driveway, where the row of box-woods stopped, Mayree stood with her hands on her hips looking down at something in the dirt.

"Mom, what is it?" Paula yelled as she and Kelly turned the corner. Mayree pointed. "Possum."

It was a young opossum, or at least a small one, lying prone with its eyes closed inside one of those huge, old, steel-jaw traps. Its back leg was caught between the teeth and bleeding. One of its ears—fragile and nearly translucent—seemed to twitch. Paula bent down to see if it was breathing but she couldn't tell.

"I wouldn't even have known it was there if I hadn't been standing by the sink." Mayree flicked her cigarette toward the kitchen window. "I heard that thing snap shut and it damn near scared the shit out of me."

"We have to get it out," Paula said, frantically looking for something nearby that could help her unclench the jaws. There was a hose coiled on the ground. A rusty shovel leaning against the side of the house. "It might still be alive." She couldn't bear the sight of that inno-cent creature trapped and injured.

"Oh hell no," Mayree said. "Possums are rodents. They can carry rabies. Besides, that one's dead."

"Dad told me possums play dead even when they're not. It might just be hurt."

"What I don't understand is where that nasty trap came from," Mayree said. "I sure as hell didn't set it."

"Maybe Uncle Frank put it out before he died," Kelly said.

"I doubt it," Mayree said. "This looks homemade, or at least old as hell. Even back home we didn't use contraptions like that."

Distraught, Paula took the shovel and tried to use the flat edge to wedge the trap open. The animal's front paws were splayed out on either side of its head. Its fur looked incredibly soft. "What if its mother is looking for it?"

In her mind, she was being chased, running through the woods, the moon barely lighting a path between the trees, her abrupt stop accidentally tripping the guy, him lying face down in the dirt, hands splayed out, not moving. Maybe not breathing. She didn't know; she hadn't checked. *Find the road.*

Mayree grabbed the shovel from Paula's hands. "Stop it," she said. "Mama possums never come back for their babies." With both hands, Mayree hoisted the shovel and brought it down on the opossum's neck like a guillotine. "There. If it wasn't dead before, it is now. Kelly, honey, do me a favor. Call your daddy and ask him to come give us a hand. I just don't feel like dealing with this mess right now." She leaned the shovel against the house and went inside.

Paula dropped to her knees and stared at the blood seeping slowly into the dirt.

Mayree

Mayree went inside the kitchen and leaned against the sink. She stared out the window at the street until her cold sweat passed. It had been a while since she'd dispatched an animal.

On the ranch, there'd always been animal problems to deal with. There were the horses and dogs to care for, and the wild hogs, mice, rats, and other vermin to get rid of. Rodents were forever chewing into containers and bins, contaminating feed, damaging crops. They'd had a fierce old barn cat named Beans who took care of many of them, but even he couldn't eliminate the all-you-can-eat buffet of ranch pests. Running cattle had its own set of issues, everything from feeding, breeding, processing, culling, selling, and more. Mayree didn't like any of it except for the horses, and for the most part dragged her feet on any chores that didn't have to do with them.

The winter she was fourteen, when the cows were calving, her father had some business in San Antonio and told her to stay in the barn overnight with her brothers to help look after the herd. She balked, complaining that it was cold and wondering why all three of them had to stay out there. "Because I said so, first off. And second, if you're ever going to be worth your weight around here, you need to get through a calving season without whining about it."

In the middle of the night, freezing in her sleeping bag, surrounded by moaning cows and their calves, she thought, *What the hell am I doing*, and slipped back inside the house and into her own bed. She couldn't wait to see the ranch a final time from some future rearview mirror, so she decided she didn't need to sleep with her brothers and a bunch of animals for no reason. When Ray came home and heard what she'd done, he disagreed. He called her some unflattering names at high volume, told her she wasn't allowed to go to the winter dance, and when a calf got separated from its mother and severed a tendon trying to break through a barbed wire fence to get back to her, he drove them out to the cow graveyard, handed her his Remington, and told her to take care of it. "She can't walk. She won't be able to nurse or move with the herd."

Mayree had never shot a calf before. Nor any other animal. Only cans and only to prove that she could. The whole drive out to the farthest pasture, with the injured calf bawling in the truck bed, she begged her father not to kill it, promised to sleep in the barn as long as it took, said she'd nurse the calf back to health herself. "Please don't make me do it."

He pulled over near the bone pile and took the calf out of the bed, then drove a little farther and parked by the river. "Come on."

"Don't make me do it," she said, even as she climbed out of the truck. There was only so much disobedience she could get away with.

He put a single bullet in the rifle, pushed the bolt forward and down, then thrust it back at her. "Do it," he said. "Now."

She shouldered the Remington, but between her trembling and her tears, she couldn't aim it.

He kicked the side of her boot with his. "You shoulda done what I said. Now quit your bawling and shoot."

She closed her eyes and squeezed the trigger, hoping the rifle would jam or she'd miss by a mile, that she could spare the calf's life for a few more minutes, maybe long enough for Ray to change his mind. Or, barring that, to do it himself.

The shot rang out, low and concussive, loud enough to drown out everything else, and her ears started ringing immediately. When she opened her eyes, the calf was slumped and bleeding from the neck, eyes bulging and tongue hanging out.

Her father took the gun from her and patted her once, hard, on the shoulder. "You always were a natural," he said. "Shame you're not a boy."

She stood still, her mind simultaneously frenetic and numb, watching the blood bubble out of the calf's delicate white neck until Ray yelled at her to get her ass back in the truck.

It was true what she'd told Paula about the opossum. A mama carries her young around on her back until they're grown enough to survive without her. If one falls off, well, she just goes on about her business, figuring it was ready to strike out on its own—if she thinks about it at all. That baby was more likely carrying ticks or fleas than rabies, but it was too young and too injured to survive. Mayree was doing it a favor, putting it out of its misery. Still, she wasn't as natural a killer as Ray might've once thought.

~

Paula retreated upstairs, and Mayree settled in her chair in the living room with her crocheting on her lap. These days, Mayree reflexively picked up whatever partially finished blanket was in her sewing basket, vaguely intending to work on it when she sat down, though more often she ended up just holding it and staring at nothing while she smoked. When the doorbell rang an hour or so later, she stubbed out her cigarette and went to the door. Stan Cagle was there, silhouetted by the glaring midafternoon sunlight. She hadn't seen him since Frank's funeral.

"Look what the cat dragged in," she said, stepping aside.

"More like a possum, from what I hear." He took off his hat and hung it on the rack, like he'd done a thousand times before. Stan was as confident and arrogant as Frank had been, but whereas those qualities came off her late husband like an aggressive stink, Stan wore his like a subtle cologne that you had to get close in to notice. Once you did, though, you never forgot it was there.

"You just missed Kelly. She said she had some homework to do. And I think Paula's asleep already. Coffee?"

"Sure. But add a shot of whiskey."

Mayree raised an eyebrow at him.

"Yeah, forget the coffee. I'll just have the whiskey."

"Thought so," she said.

He followed her into the kitchen, where she pulled down a couple of highball glasses and put three cubes of ice into each. Meanwhile, he opened the cabinet above the refrigerator and rummaged around in the back for the top-shelf stuff he preferred. Mayree watched as he lifted his arm up, noticed how his dress shirt stretched over a newly slim torso. His arm, too, looked more muscular. She let her gaze stroll from his biceps over his broad shoulder, down the width of his back to a narrower waist, over his sturdy-looking backside, and down his legs, hidden beneath well-fitting slacks. He was tall as ever, of course, but she'd never noticed before that he didn't have to stand on his toes to reach the whiskey. She smoothed her hair even as she chastised herself for thinking impure thoughts about her former best friend's estranged husband. That she felt any desire at all—especially a misplaced one— was unexpected. That factory had been closed for a long time, and she'd assumed it was permanent.

"You look different," she said.

He poured three fingers' worth into each of their glasses. "Different—good?" He winked at her as he clinked his glass against hers.

"Don't fuck with me, Stan. I'm in a reduced state."

As he sank into the chair across from her, grooved frown lines bunching up his receding hairline, the momentary infatuation dissipated. He was dumpy old Stan again—inside if not as much out.

"Maybe you should start pumping iron with me at the Y."

"No thanks," she said. "How much longer are you going to be there?"

"'Til Sissy decides if she'll take me back, I guess."

"What makes you think she'll take you back after you leave her for a 'break,' which anybody with a brain knows is a euphemism for *fucking your way through Travis County*?"

"Look, I was wrong, okay? I never should've done what I did."

Mayree made a harrumphing noise. "Says you and every other heterogametic asshole on the planet."

"What?"

"The Y chromosome," Mayree said, tapping out a cigarette. "Never mind. Speaking of *Y*s, though, how is it there?"

"Not too bad. There's mostly a bunch of ne'er-do-wells, drunks and ex-cons and the like. I don't mind the convicts too much, as long as they stay out of my business, but I try to avoid the drunks. They tend to be a bad influence." He raised his glass and took a drink. "So, I started lifting weights at night. I'm not turning into an evangelist or anything, clearly, but I feel better lifting more than a few ounces at a time."

Mayree nodded. She leaned across the table and felt his biceps, which he instantly flexed. Thankfully, it was no more titillating than touching the arm of one of her brothers. An imbroglio like that was the last thing she needed. "Good for you," she said, sitting back down. "Sissy'll be impressed."

His face brightened. "You think so?"

"Probably. You'd know better than me."

"Y'all still aren't talking?"

She waved his comment away. "Oh sure, you know, here and there."
The mention of Sissy brought up more negative feelings she didn't want
to deal with. "So, can you get rid of that possum for me?"

~

He got a pair of workman's gloves and a heavy-duty trash bag from the
garage. Mayree hadn't known they owned those gloves. In fact, she had
no idea what all was in the garage, given that she never went inside it.
She hadn't thought Frank did either, but what did she know. Maybe
Felicia had brought them over. Stan crouched down and pried open
the trap's jaws, then lifted the opossum by the tail and dropped it into
the bag.

He picked up the trap and held it away from his body. "Who'd set
a trap like this? Y'all have a rodent problem?"

"Not that I know of. And you got me. No telling how long it's
been there."

"Well, if you do need to get rid of possums or squirrels or whatever,
they make traps that just catch 'em, not cut their legs off. This thing
looks like something from a bygone era."

"If I had an infestation, I'd call pest control—or you."

"Aw, you could do it. You're tough as an armadillo."

"That may be true, but I've already dealt with enough dead animals
in my life."

Stan shrugged. "Well, since I'm here, you got anything else needs
doing? Any light bulbs out? Stuck windows? Leaky faucets?"

Mayree looked up at the siding and the roofline, and thought
about the general state of her home. It was an elegant, formal estate
on a picture-perfect street. The neighborhood was so grand that when
Frank had first brought her to see it, she couldn't even imagine herself
living there. It took years for her to feel truly at home. Now there
were leaves poking out of the gutters, which hadn't been cleaned out

since long before Frank died, and the fence was starting to rot. The foundation had shifted, veining certain walls and ceilings with cracks. The garage housed an unknown menagerie that probably should be gone through. And there was, in fact, a slow leak in her bathroom sink. She'd gotten used to it, however, and besides that, she didn't think it was a great idea to invite Stan into a space so close to her lonesome bed, even if he was fit-though-dumpy and off-limits. If not for her restraint, the depths of his loneliness might lead them both into temptation. At least that's what she'd like to think.

"Have you been able to figure out who else Frank owes money to?"

"I'm still working on it. He wasn't exactly careful with his recordkeeping."

"What about his little whore secretary? Wasn't she supposed to be taking care of that?"

"Come on now, don't get worked up about all that. I'm getting things settled. And anyway, she's already moved on."

"Well, that's comforting. Whose marriage is she wrecking these days?"

"I heard she went back home to Arkansas. I don't know anything else. And it's not really that important anymore, is it?"

Mayree flicked her hand. "Never was." She picked his empty glass up off the brick windowsill. "Want a roadie before you head out?"

"Nah, I'm good. Thanks, though." He smiled warmly at her.

"No, thank *you*," she said, momentarily wistful. It was nice to have a man offer her help, especially after having gone without for so long, even when Frank was still alive. She thought briefly of the boy in the grocery store parking lot who'd tried to help her after nearly killing her with his shopping cart. Maybe she should've been nicer to him. She thought about asking Stan to stay, confiding in him about Paula, letting someone else share her load of worries. But she decided against it. It was embarrassing enough to be the lonely, jilted widow with money troubles. She didn't want to invite even more pity. "It's good to see you."

He smiled and opened his arms as if to take her into an embrace, something they'd done countless times in the past and to which she'd never before given a second thought. Instead, she stuck her hand out into the space between them.

He looked down at it and, after a moment, began to laugh and laugh, so hard that he started coughing and pressed a hand to his chest to try to stop. Then he grabbed her and hugged her anyway, her arms dangling by her sides, highball glass dropping to the soft ground. He kissed her on the top of her head, then released her and said, "Mayree Baker, I love you with all my heart. But in a thousand years, I'd never try to sleep with you."

~

That night, Mayree lay in bed, smoking and counting cracks in the ceiling. Sleep wouldn't rescue her from her thoughts, which swirled and danced to the tune of Stan's laughter.

Paula

Watching Mayree behead the opossum was a shock to Paula, especially after having suffered such an anguishing series of events the past five days. She'd knelt by the poor animal until Kelly finally helped her up and led her upstairs to her room. Kelly filled a glass from the bathroom tap, and asked Paula if she should stay. "No, I'm okay," Paula said, as much to herself as to Kelly. "I'm okay."

After Kelly left, Paula buried herself in her bedcovers, shivering as though she had a fever, overlaying the ghastly scene by the hedges with the one from deep in the woods. She wanted some form of comfort, but she didn't know what. Even if she'd been able to identify what might make her feel better, she instinctively knew Kelly wasn't the one to provide it. Nor was Mayree.

She wished Felicia were there. When Paula was little, Felicia took care of her whenever she got sick because Mayree claimed that her system couldn't handle a contagion. Felicia would put damp washcloths on her forehead, rub her back, bring her chicken noodle soup and oyster crackers on a tray, sing hymns and lullabies. She'd hold Paula's hand, close her eyes, and thank Jesus for His glory and grace and ask Him to use His powers to heal Paula's sickness. Once, Mayree had overheard Felicia praying over Paula, and she said from the doorway, "Felicia, if that horseshit actually worked, the world wouldn't be such a fucking mess," and walked away.

Paula dialed Felicia's number. After six rings, she was about to hang up when someone answered.

"Hello?"

"May I speak to Felicia?"

"Who's calling?"

"It's Paula," she said. "Baker. Wait, is this Curtis?"

"Yeah."

"Oh." Paula didn't know what to say. They'd met only once when they were younger. She couldn't even remember what he looked like. Felicia had brought him to their house one time because his mother was out of town. He'd been angry at his aunt for not letting him go swimming with his friends instead, but Felicia told him he was too young to go without adult supervision. Refusing Mayree's invitation to watch television with Paula, he stayed in the backyard all morning, breaking sticks and kicking the live oaks and occasionally cussing. When Paula went into her parents' bedroom to look out the window at him, he reached down and grabbed a fistful of dirt and flung it toward the glass. If it had been a rock, the window would've broken. Paula ran back to her own room and didn't leave until Felicia finished for the day and took him home. That was the last time she'd seen him.

"This an emergency or something?"

"No." She felt like she should apologize, though she'd done nothing wrong. "Everything's fine. She doesn't need to call me back. Sorry for bothering you." Heart pounding, she hung up before he could reply.

She took her last high school yearbook off her bookshelf and flipped to the index. Kevin Atwood. She looked at each of the pages on which he appeared: his junior portrait; the JV swim team; the technology club; and a random page of party pictures, one in which he had a classmate in a choke hold, smiling maniacally. He looked the part, but hard as she tried, she couldn't reconcile her memory of the guy from Saturday with Kevin's image. Kelly was probably right that she'd have known if Kevin was at the party.

Paula burrowed deeper into her bed, even covering her head with her pillow, as if by blocking out the world she might be able to also block out her own thoughts. She concentrated on the sound of the air wheezing out of the register above her, and eventually she fell asleep.

Sometime later, she woke from a nightmare in which she was being chased. The faster she tried to get away, the slower her body seemed to move. Just as she was about to give in, let the villain do with her what he would, she woke up. Heart pounding, she opened her eyes and scanned her room, trying to reorient and calm herself down. She hated that realistic feeling of not being able to call out for help.

She wished she could go back in time—far, far back to when she was young and the worst thing that had happened to her was a bump or a bruise. Back when her father was still alive and Felicia was there every day and she didn't yet realize that her mother loved her but didn't like her, not really.

She got out of bed and took off her clothes, which she'd sweated through during her nap. Judging by the lack of light at the edges of her curtained window, she could tell it was dark outside already. She pressed her hand against her bare stomach, felt how her ribs exaggerated the concavity of her belly. Since Saturday night, she'd barely eaten. Her appetite had vanished. She rummaged around in her closet for her favorite sweatpants and shirt, and found them on the floor—next to the green swim bag that Felicia had returned. She withdrew her hand like she'd touched fire. Then more of the missing chunks of time from Saturday night appeared in her mind's lost and found.

~

"I know where there's a pay phone nearby," the guy sitting next to her had said. "I could take you there if you want. We could walk."

She'd perked up. All she'd wanted that night was to talk to Will. If she could talk to him, then maybe he'd forgive her for whatever she'd done, and they could get back together. Everything would be okay if she could just talk to him. "Yeah?"

"Yeah, it's not far. Maybe two minutes."

She leaned away to look at him, but his image was doubled and offset just enough that she couldn't make out any of his features. She closed one eye and tried again. Dark hair. Eyes. Too dark outside to tell the color. Face. Regular looking. He seemed young for a college student but so did she. He smelled good. Where was Kelly? "Do I know you?" she asked.

He laughed. "Do you want to go?" She accepted his help standing up. "Careful your step."

She looked around. There seemed to be more people than before. The fire was bigger. The music louder. The moonlight brighter. "Okay," Paula said, and followed him as he walked away from the group by the fire, toward the parking area. She stumbled and pitched forward, dropping her beverage.

The guy caught and righted her before she fell. "Let's take my car instead," he told her. He gripped her hand, tugging her along.

She pulled away. "I'm not a dog," she said, sharp beneath her slurred words.

He lifted his hands. "Hey, I'm the one doing you a favor here. You don't want to use the phone? Fine."

The phone. Will. She thought of him cupping her cheek and looking at her deeply, so deeply, his eyes switching back and forth between her own as though he was trying to memorize her. His crooked smile, the weight of him moving on top of her. She started to cry. Now this guy, a stand-in. The frustration in his voice was her fault. Maybe she hadn't been a good enough girlfriend. She had done something wrong. Was that it? Had she wanted too much? Been too demanding or loud? Maybe she was a disappointment in bed. The guy started to walk away.

"Don't go," she called after him. "I'm sorry."

"Okay, then."

A short walk among the parked vehicles. He opened the passenger door of one of them and guided her into the seat. Once inside, his scent—a familiar, musky, powdery smell—seemed more intense. She closed her eyes, lulled.

Something, though, pulled her back to the moment. Some part of her brain that recognized a wrongness of time and distance. She sat up and squinted through the windshield. "I thought you said we could walk there."

He didn't look at her. "I misjudged how long it would take, I guess."

She heard the door locks click into position. A moment later, they were driving. It looked like they were still in the park, but she couldn't tell. She'd never driven around there in the dark. "Where are we?"

He didn't speak. A moment later, he turned off the headlights and increased their speed.

"What are you doing?" She looked at him, but in the moonlit dark, she couldn't make out his expression. He let out a sound like a short bark, something between a laugh and a growl.

It was then that Paula, even drunk, knew that she had made a very big mistake.

"Please stop. Let me get out."

His voice was a sneer. "You said you wanted to make a phone call."

"I don't want to anymore. Please."

"Should've thought about that before." He bark-laughed again.

"Please, please stop the car," she said. He hit the gas, and her head slammed back against the seat rest. She knew: he wasn't playing around. She knew: he was going to hurt her. Fear and bile surged upward. "Stop—I'm going to be sick."

"You better fucking not. I borrowed this car."

She leaned forward and threw up on the floor between her feet, hard. She was still spitting when he slammed on the brakes and they skidded off the road onto the gravel shoulder, barely missing a clump of mesquite trees. He threw the car into park, then backhanded her across the jaw with his left fist, driving her head against the window.

She'd been hit in the face only once before: by a slow-moving foul ball in a middle school softball game. She'd thought that hurt. It was nothing compared to a fist.

He swatted her hands away from her cheek, grabbed her by the hair, and yanked her head back. She was too stunned to speak, to scream. Things were happening too fast. Something cold against her throat. She sucked in air, reached up again to pull it away, felt the sharp edge. He pressed harder.

"You asked for this," he yelled in her ear. "I was being nice and you fucked it up." He clambered into a crouch and threw a leg onto the passenger side, straddling the console and crushing his bulk against her.

"I'm gonna cut your throat and then I'm gonna fuck you in it. You hear me? I'm gonna fuck you in the neck." He smiled as he said it, his lips curling back like an animal baring its teeth. His breath was hot on her face. His voice was a scream. What he was saying didn't make sense, but the way he was screaming it, so loud, so close, made her release her bladder, the urine hot like a burn.

She had never been physically threatened before. She had never hit or been hit by anyone. She didn't know how to defend herself, but she knew: if she didn't fight, she would die.

With her eyes closed, she flailed at him, swatting, striking wildly. He dropped the knife. She bucked in her seat, knees making contact with the glove box, her own arms, his body. She felt no pain, made no vocal sounds that she was aware of. It was as though she'd left her body to do this on its own without her. She was somehow only vaguely aware of him screaming and screaming and hitting her back.

Their bodies collided over and over for seconds or minutes or hours, she didn't know. He found the knife, raised his hand—if the moon hadn't been bright enough to cast a glint, she might not have seen it— and she flung her arm out to block him. She didn't feel the slice through her forearm until later.

She wedged her back against the door and kicked and kicked at him, and he grunted when she landed one to his stomach. Her hand thrashed around behind her, grasping at the door, trying to open it, and she was kicking, kicking, and then there was nothing against her back and she was falling out of the car headfirst. She landed with a thud and right away he was on her again, trying to pin her down. She bucked and twisted her hips, rolled onto one side, and knocked him into the doorframe.

As soon as he was off her, she launched herself away from him. She felt nearly sober now from all the adrenaline, running over rocks and roots, crashing through mesquite trees, him right behind her. All she could hear was the rustle of underbrush and their panting breath; then his hand grabbed at her shirt.

She heard a voice as clear as a bell: *Stop.* She did.

Coming up behind her, he tripped over her left foot and went down hard. Like that baby opossum caught in the trap, he lay there, unmoving. She should've checked to make sure he was breathing, but the voice inside her head was louder: *Find the road.*

～

Paula yanked on her sweatpants and shirt. She couldn't be alone in her room, not with the swim bag full of soiled clothes in her closet, all the violent memories spilling out. Even if Mayree wouldn't comfort her the way Paula wished she would, being with her was better than being alone. Hesitating only briefly, she grabbed the bag.

"Mom?" she called out as she hurried downstairs to the living room. "Are you there?"

"In here," Mayree said. She tapped her cigarette into the ashtray next to her. "I've been thinking," she said on an exhale of smoke. "There's something fishy about that trap we found. I wonder if somebody set it to send a message."

March 17, 1989

Dear Mama,
I can't believe I'm finally getting out next week. A year and a half and then some, even though I wasn't supposed to be in more than a year. I never did drugs before juvie. Don't believe anybody no matter what they say. Every ten days going in to court for the judge to decide if I was a flight risk or a danger to myself or others saying, Let's see how you're doing, and every time told I had to stay because there was no other place for me to go. (I know if you could you'd take me home.) You know how it is in here because I already told you a million times, but I like writing it down so I can remember, 'cause I never want to come back. You know my PO, Jazzy? (I know that's not his real name.) He left. He was cool, always bringing me comic books and candy and stuff. He used to say every time just before we went into the courtroom Don't blow it, but then with a wink because he knew I wouldn't. His wife had a baby and they moved to Indiana to be near her folks. He gave me this journal to write in when he left. He said I deserved more than a spiral notebook to write out my feelings, but I don't know about that. I like writing to you even though you wouldn't even get my letters, so I just keep them in here. The first thing I'm going to do when I leave here is come see you. I know you've been missing me a lot. Then I've got some other stuff to do. I have to see some people. I know

you don't want me to say this, but there's people who owe us stuff and I want to clean up the accounts, so to speak. Those motherfuckers deserve whatever they get. Don't worry about me, though, because I'm going to be fine. I'll be careful. I've learned a lot here, and I know what I need to do to make a complete life for myself. Maybe complete isn't the word you would use, but I think you know what I mean.

Love,

Your son

Mayree

Mayree looked at Paula, who was standing like a hobo at the threshold of the living room, sweatshirt askew, eyes wild, hair . . . gone. Then she noticed what Paula was holding.

"Jesus, Mary, and Joseph," she said, her voice rising. "Did you not throw that thing away like I told you?"

"I did!"

"Then what the hell is it doing back in here?"

"I . . ." Mayree could tell by the way Paula's face flushed that she was searching for a story. "I got it back out."

"That's horseshit and you know it."

"Fine." Paula hesitated. "Felicia found it."

"Found it?" Mayree shoved the blanket off her lap and stood up. "Damn that woman. Sometimes she seems to forget who pays who around here." She tried to take the bag, but Paula snatched it away.

"Don't get mad at her. She was trying to help me," she said. "Unlike you."

Mayree felt like she'd been slapped. She looked at her daughter, who in that moment could've been four or eight or nineteen, could've been Mayree at that age, until her frustration found its footing again, though she wasn't sure which of them she was actually angry at.

"I was protecting you by getting rid of that pile of filth. What the hell good does it do to have it? It's a foul reminder of a bad night."

"Wait a minute. Yesterday at the police station, he said they couldn't do anything without evidence. Now we have it."

Mayree's voice went up a notch. "Did you hear what I just said? It wouldn't change anything."

"But it's proof of what happened to me."

Mayree paused. These past few days, the memory of Bobby Cox was always at the periphery of her thoughts, like his hot breath against her neck. "Which *happened* because you were drunk. Even the police said so." She cringed even as she said it. She hadn't been drunk when Bobby Cox did what he did, but she'd tempted him somehow. Made it easier for him. She'd never forgiven herself for giving that man the opportunity to destroy her. "Trust me, you'll feel better if you just try to put it behind you."

Paula sank down onto the edge of the couch and leaned forward with a pleading expression on her face. "But what if it wasn't because I was drunk? Or wasn't just that?"

Mayree held firm to her belief in letting sleeping dogs lie; the alternative was far too disruptive. "The sergeant already said they couldn't do anything."

Paula took a deep breath, set the bag down by her feet, then clasped her hands together as if beginning an interview. "What did you mean just now, that someone set that trap to send a message?"

Mayree recognized that conversational gambit. Frank used to use it on her all the time. He'd say or do something infuriating—usually because he was guilty of something—and Mayree would become incandescent with fury. Her voice would go up an octave, her face would burn red hot, she might throw something in his direction—a glass of whiskey, an ashtray, a fist. From there, he would become calm and aloof, which only enraged her further. Back and forth they'd go, tables predictably turned, until he'd announce that he was going to bed, that she was being hysterical, that they'd talk again when she could get her emotions under control. Even after she figured out the pattern, years after she stopped giving a shit what he thought, she still had a hard time avoiding his psychological warfare, and it pissed her off every time. She refused to let Paula use it on her, too. She regretted mentioning the trap; it only seemed to keep the incident in the forefront of their minds. It was time for them both to move on.

She sat back down in her chair, crossed her legs, lit another cigarette, and lied. "What I meant was that this neighborhood has no shortage of snobs who probably think I'm not keeping up enough with the Joneses. I bet some old biddy who's worried about the garden club put that trap out there with the opossum already in it," she said. "So, fine. I'm going to hire the handyman to take care of a few things. That's all."

That's not at all what she'd been thinking, but it sounded reasonable, even to her, and was vastly preferable to the unsettling thought she'd been turning over and over since Stan left: that the opossum in the trap was a metaphor. What if the attack against Paula, as she'd just suggested, was in fact more than some boy taking advantage of an innocent girl and then turning violent? What if Paula's attacker had chosen her specifically? Had she done something to invite that kind of trouble? Shaken, Mayree pulled the blanket in her lap up higher as she narrowed her eyes at Paula and drew a long inhale on her cigarette.

Paula looked down. "Do you really think it was my fault?" she asked, as if she'd read her mother's thoughts.

Mayree smashed out her cigarette, then jutted her chin at the bag. Who was she to decide the fault of things?

"Just put it down there and I'll deal with it," she said. "I'm sure you've got some studying to do, don't you?"

After a moment, Paula nodded. "Are you going to throw it away again?"

"Probably."

"Pickup isn't until Tuesday."

"Then it doesn't really matter."

Paula shrugged. "I guess not."

Mayree watched Paula bite her fingernail for a moment, the silence between them becoming uncomfortable. Mayree thought back to when Paula was a toddler, how hard she'd thought parenting was then. The questions, the demands, the messes. If she could go back in time, she'd slap some sense into herself. She'd tell young Mayree to quit being such a ninny, that it was going to get so much harder later on.

"Do you want me to order a pizza?" Mayree asked.

"Yes, please."

Mayree nodded. No matter how badly she'd failed as a mother, at least she'd raised Paula to be polite. "I might go to bed, so I'll put some money on the banister. You listen for the bell." She picked up the phone and dialed the number to the pizza place, which she'd memorized after calling it so many times in the months since Frank died.

Paula stood to go, then turned and looked at Mayree. "Mom?"

With the receiver pressed against her ear, Mayree raised her eyebrows at Paula.

"Never mind," she said, and patted the doorframe on her way out of the living room. "'Night."

~

After placing the order, Mayree poured herself another drink, then sat thinking about the bag Paula had left on the floor. What would Frank have done with it, if he were alive? What would he do about any of this? If he'd been at home when he had a heart attack, screwing her like he should've been doing instead of another woman, maybe he wouldn't have died. At least Mayree would have called an ambulance right away; who knew how long that whore spent worrying about her own hide before she decided to call one? On his death certificate, the medical examiner had noted the cause as "cardiac arrest occurring during sexual

171

intercourse" and the place as his secretary's address. Mayree had been humiliated anew each time she'd handed over a copy to a banker or creditor.

"Fuck you, Frank," she said, but without as much rancor as usual. She was tired.

The clock on the wall ticked off the empty minutes.

Maybe Frank had actually put out that stupid trap at some point, thinking, in some fleeting moment of domesticity, that he was solving a rodent problem before one occurred. In occasional, guilt-fueled bursts, he'd done things like that to reassure himself that he wasn't a complete asshole. She hoped there was an afterlife just so Frank could know that he was, in fact, a complete asshole who'd left her to deal with the embarrassing aftermath of his infidelity and raise their wild child all alone. It was exhausting.

Disgusted, she picked up the bag and carried it at arm's length out to the garage. Maybe Stan would have an idea of what she should do with it, but for now, she didn't want it inside the house. The remote to the overhead door was dead, so she tried the regular entrance instead. The lock was stuck. She jiggled the key back and forth, silently cursing Stan for having somehow broken the mechanism. She tried again, and feeling the lock release, shouldered the door open. If she could find some spray lubricant, then she'd oil the hinges. Otherwise, that would be one more thing she'd have to add to her hypothetical handyman's to-do list. She couldn't actually afford to hire him.

The fluorescent light flickered on, revealing a light coating of dust over a generally haphazard array of items: Paula's old banana-seat bike, a lawn mower that hadn't been used in a decade, a tool chest that Mayree had given Frank early in their marriage and which he'd never used, mostly empty cans of paint that were so old they probably wouldn't match their corresponding wall colors, and more. She didn't see any lubricant on the disheveled shelves, so the door would have to stay as it was. Oh well. It's not like it mattered much anyway. She dropped

Paula's bag near a collection of flowerpots she couldn't remember buying, locked the door, and went back upstairs to bed.

~

Sometime later, Mayree woke with a start, her heart pounding with the sensation of being under some kind of duress. The clock read 1:14 a.m. Reflexively, she reached for her cigarettes and lighter, but stopped when she heard a noise. It sounded like a rustling or rattling on wood. She turned her ear toward the door, trying to discern its direction and source.

"Paula?" she called out. She waited a moment, then grabbed the knife she'd always kept on her nightstand—even when Frank was still alive—and went into the hall. "Paula?" she said again, opening the door to her room. "Did you hear something?"

Paula moved the pillow off her head. "What?"

"Nothing," Mayree said. "Go back to sleep."

She went downstairs, avoiding the creaky steps, listening for movement. She released the blade with her thumb. She crept into the living room, Frank's office, the kitchen. Nothing, and no sign of entry. Then she leaned over the sink and looked out the window, above which the opossum had been trapped earlier that day. From there, she could see that the door to the garage was standing open.

She knew she'd closed and locked that door after leaving it earlier, particularly because it had been so hard to handle. There's no way it could've opened by itself. Her stomach dropped as she tightened her grip on the knife. The light in the garage was off, so she couldn't see much inside. She waited, trying to decide what to do next. Call Stan? The police? What would Frank have done in her place? He'd have barged out there in his boxer shorts, brandishing whatever he picked up on the way as a weapon, demanding to know who was out there and what the hell did they think they were doing on his property.

It was probably nothing. She'd worked hard to shove the door open, yes, but maybe she only thought she remembered closing it. She'd been distracted, letting her mind wander as it was wont to do, and on top of that, she'd drunk more whiskey after Stan left. She'd been half-soused, if not completely so. Most likely the noise she heard was something in a dream; the door was ajar because she'd left it like that.

"Mom?"

Paula was standing behind her in a pair of baggy boxers, an old T-shirt, and holding a softball bat. She looked so much like Frank it was hard to believe, like she'd conjured him.

"What are you doing down here?"

"You said you heard something."

"It must've been a nightmare."

"Is something out there?"

"I don't think so."

"Want me to go check?"

"No, you go back to bed. I'm going to go close the garage door."

"I'll go with you."

Mayree regarded her, admired the fierceness of her grip on the bat. There was an odd comfort to it. She wondered if this display of bravery was new, a result of Saturday night, or if it had been there all along and she just hadn't noticed it. "If you insist."

Still, Mayree took the lead. Holding her knife out, she unlocked the back door and crept across the pebbled walkway to the garage.

"Hello?" she called. "Anybody out here?"

Mayree could feel Paula at her back. Heart pounding, she stepped into the garage and smacked the switch. The light flickered on.

"Hello?" she said again. There was nobody there. She looked around at the dust-covered menagerie she'd observed hours earlier. The dust was undisturbed; nothing appeared to have been touched. If there were footprints, she couldn't see any. Stan or she could've made some that afternoon, so it didn't matter. She and Paula maneuvered around the garage, lifting tarps and peering behind large objects, weapons at the ready. Then she came back to the flowerpots. There was a sack of mulch, a partially used bag of fertilizer, a small trowel, and a rake.

"Where's the bag?"

"What bag?"

"*The* bag. That had your filthy clothes from Saturday night in it. I brought it out here before I went to bed." She stabbed her finger toward the ground. "I put it right here."

"I don't know."

"You didn't come out here and take it back inside?"

"No. I didn't even know you moved it."

"It was right here."

"Are you sure?" Paula started wandering around, looking.

"I'm absolutely sure." Mayree felt her stomach lurch again. "I put it here. And now it's gone."

"I'll go look inside," Paula said.

"Jesus H. Christ, Paula," Mayree said. "I'm telling you, it was here. You know what that means? Someone was here, giving us a message. First with the opossum and now with the bag." She thought of what Paula had asked earlier, whether she'd been attacked just because she was inebriated or if she'd been specifically targeted for some reason. She shuddered, feeling the sickening presence of Bobby Cox. "I don't know if it's the boy you were with or somebody else, but now I'm thinking it's not an accident and it's not random." She lowered her voice to a whisper. "Somebody is fucking with us."

Paula

Paula hadn't thought the opossum was there to send a message to them, and she wasn't sure Mayree, who looked like a madwoman with her bedhead and switchblade, had actually moved the bag at all. Mayree insisted that she'd taken the swim bag to the garage, but Paula could tell from the stink on her mother's breath that she'd gone heavy on the booze that night. Paula could always tell, just like she had with her father when he was alive. There was a difference between alcohol breath and alcohol coming off the whole body, like the difference between the Chanel No. 5 perfume her mother used to wear and the cheap drugstore body spray she started using after she ran out, saying she didn't need nice things anymore.

"I don't know, Mom. Why me? I don't have any enemies that I know of. Do you?"

"I have no idea if you have enemies or not!"

"I mean, do *you* have enemies?"

Mayree looked thoughtful, as if running down a mental list. "None who would attack you, I don't think."

How was Paula supposed to forget about what had happened to her now that her mother was convinced someone—including possibly her attacker—was messing with them? Until she was reminded of Kevin, whom she'd apparently snubbed in high school, Paula had assumed that the guy who'd attacked her had been just a drunk and angry opportunist. But now that she thought about it, the idea of them being targeted didn't seem entirely implausible. "Did . . . Dad?"

"Oh sweet Jesus, your father probably had as many enemies as friends," she said, shaking her head. "Maybe more. But he was a charmer, I'm telling you. If somebody was ever fool enough to show up here or somewhere else with his iron out, hell-bent on being the last person your father ever laid eyes on, somehow he'd end up your father's best friend, and leave drunk and smiling a few hours later with his pistol forgotten on the coffee table. So no, I don't think this has anything to do with him."

"Who, then?"

"How the hell am I supposed to know?" Mayree replied. "What about jealous boys? Or girls, for that matter. Someone connected to Will?"

Paula shook her head. There was no way Will had anything to do with it. "I saw a guy from my old swim team at a party and he yelled at me, but that's it."

"Yelled about what?"

"Nothing. He was wasted," she said. "Besides, Kelly said he wasn't even there Saturday."

"Maybe it's one of those break-ins they've been reporting on the news lately. Somebody's going around making hits on houses in nice neighborhoods. I saw something about it on the news this week, in Tarrytown. Homeowner said they took all her family heirlooms and lord knows what else."

"But"—Paula looked around at the abandoned-looking garage—"nothing's missing."

"The *bag* is missing."

Paula sighed. "Okay, Mom, let's just go back inside. It's late. If you really think it's missing, we can look again in the morning." She took her mother's arm and pulled her along the pebbled walkway between the garage and the back door.

"Paula Lee Baker, you sound like you're talking to a senile old woman and I do not appreciate it."

"Fine," Paula said.

"Much obliged."

"So what are we going to do now?"

"I'm going to make a phone call," Mayree said.

Paula tensed. *You said you wanted to make a phone call.*

"Why? To who? Not the police."

"Why not the police?" Mayree picked up the receiver. "Also, it's 'to whom.'"

Paula lunged at her and slammed it back down onto the cradle. "Because you sound drunk and they'll think we're crazy." She gasped after she heard the words come out of her mouth. There was a time—a very long time until not that long ago—when Paula wouldn't have dreamed of speaking to her mother like that. What had changed between them? She thought of what Felicia had said the day before, hinting that Mayree had been suffering, too. Yes, of course she had been suffering. But did that give her the right to treat her own daughter with such acrimony? Mayree was the mom. She was supposed to be taking care of her.

The summer she was eleven years old, Paula and Kelly went to a weeklong day camp at the zoo. It had bothered Paula that not only were the animals kept in pens and cages, but that the different species were separated by their enclosures. She'd raised her hand and asked the zookeeper leading them that day why the animals couldn't be together, like in nature. The zookeeper explained the concept of a food chain, and that it was necessary to keep predators and prey apart. Paula pressed her. "But what about humans and pets? They can live together." The zookeeper said that yes, some species have altruistic or symbiotic relationships (Paula had to look those words up later), like looking out for predators or sharing food, but that especially in the wild, it's more likely for animals to eat the young of another species than to protect them. It's far more common for animals to help their own kind, especially if they are closely related, to ensure their survival.

Then it dawned on Paula why it had become so easy to talk back to her mother. Mayree had never been the kind of mom who baked cookies for the class or went all out for birthdays, but Paula had always felt cared for. Yet ever since her father died and maybe even before then, so gradually Paula couldn't identify the moment it shifted, Mayree seemed to have grown resentful of her, the way she had been of Frank. Mayree had been treating Paula as if she were one of the dogs she visited once a week at the shelter, like she belonged to someone else.

"If the police think we're crazy, then it's because they picked your bald, drunk ass up off the street like some kind of vagrant. God only knows what kind of mother they think I am."

Not a very nurturing one, Paula wanted to say, but thought better of it and held her tongue.

"But I'm not sure I want to deal with them right now, anyway." Mayree snatched the receiver off the cradle again. "I need to talk to Stan." As she dialed the number he'd given her for his room at the YMCA, she glanced at Paula and said, "No need for you to stay up. I'll take it from here."

Paula sat down at the kitchen table.

"Suit yourself," Mayree said.

After she'd convinced Stan that he needed to come back to the house right away, that there'd been *developments*, Mayree got out the cheap whiskey and poured herself three fingers, which she downed in one shot. She poured some more, sat down wearily across from Paula, and lit a cigarette. Paula got a Tab out of the fridge, a glass from the cabinet, and sat back down.

"That has caffeine. It'll keep you up all night."

"I'm already going to be up all night."

Mayree nodded. They sat in silence as they had so often lately. They weren't the kind of family to sit around the table playing Monopoly or cards or even simply engage in comfortable conversation. If the Cagles were over, they might play a game of charades or something similar, and if Paula was alone with her father, they could talk and laugh. But when it had been the three of them, silence in its myriad forms—angry, bitter, jealous, lonesome—was often the loudest sound in the room, especially the last few years.

Paula regretted that she hadn't actually known her father very well. She knew the heft and scent of him, the boom of his voice, the vast envelopment of his bear hugs, the ease of his laughter when he was drunk or when the two of them were out for their occasional adventures camping or fishing or getting haircuts or ice cream. But she wasn't familiar with his business dealings, or his philosophies, or why he chose his path in life. She didn't know much about his childhood, or his dreams, or his shadow side, which she assumed he'd had because everyone did. She'd never thought to ask him about all of that before it was too late.

Mayree frequently commented how much Paula reminded her of him. Now that Paula knew about his cheating, she understood why Mayree would've been so angry with him—but she had no idea what about herself raised her mother's pique. What she was certain of, however, was that her father had loved her. He used to say that he loved her *and* he liked her. He thought she was smart and funny, ambitious and pretty. And regardless of whether he was sober or drunk, he always seemed happy to see her when he came home. In spite of his character flaws, Paula missed him so much it hurt.

"Mom, do you love me?"

Mayree squinted at her through an exhale. "Of course I do," she said.

"Do you like me?"

At that, Mayree took a deep inhale and slowly blew out what seemed like all the air in her diminished body. She stared at the ashtray in front of her. "I don't really like anybody much these days," she finally said.

Paula looked down and nodded slowly. At least her mother was honest. She reached over and poured some whiskey into her glass of Tab. When Mayree didn't say anything, she poured a little more.

Mayree slowly tapped the bottom of her glass against Paula's. "Cheers."

~

Stan arrived soon enough, looking like he'd been awakened from a dead sleep, which he had been. "Missed me, huh?"

"There's no time for horseshit, Stan. We got a problem."

"Another opossum?"

He followed Mayree into the kitchen for the second time that day. When he saw Paula, he said, "Whoa, now. Look at you."

"Yeah," Paula said, passing a hand over her head. She couldn't tell if he was displeased or just surprised. "I'm not sure it was such a great idea."

He pulled her up and into a hug. She pressed her face into his chest, surprised at how emotional it made her to see him. After Mayree had banished Sissy from their lives, it was as though she'd lost her father, her aunt, and her uncle practically all at the same time.

"If anyone can pull it off, it's you, sweet girl," he said, kissing her on the head. She hugged him harder. "I've missed you. I was sorry not to see you earlier. Your mama said you were napping—though she didn't mention your cool new hairstyle. You been studying hard?"

Paula didn't lift her cheek from his sweatshirt when she answered, and she could hear the echo of her own voice in the cotton. "Sort of."

"Sit," Mayree commanded, and they did. She pointed at her glass and raised her eyebrows at Stan. He frowned and shook his head once.

"So what's up?"

Mayree looked at Paula. "You want to tell him, or shall I?"

Paula recounted the events, including the vile threat, the chase, the escape, and her fear that she'd killed the guy.

"Clearly he's not dead if he came back for the evidence," Mayree interrupted, then shared her conviction that the bag had been stolen from the garage that night. "I heard a noise and went out to check. That's how I found out someone was here."

Stan had questions, lots of them, more than the cops had. Paula half expected him to lecture her the way her mother had on personal responsibility and not being the kind of girl that filthy men try to take advantage of, but instead, he squeezed her hand and searched her face when he asked her, "All that in less than a week? Are you sure you're okay?"

Paula fought back tears and nodded. He seemed to have more concern for her than everyone else but Felicia had thus far.

"Why didn't you tell me about any of this earlier?" he said to Mayree. "Seems a helluva lot more important than a dead animal."

"It didn't come up then," she said, a defiant look on her face. "Now it has."

"Shit," he said, pressing his fingertips into his forehead, then dragging his hands down his face. "I was afraid something like this might happen."

Mayree reared back in her chair. "What?" Then she leaned forward, pushing her midsection so hard against the table that her breasts bulged at the gap in her bathrobe. "Why would you think that?"

Stan stood and poured himself a drink. Paula knew that meant trouble since he'd said no to one before. Nobody said anything until he sat back down.

"Tonight, Paula asked me if Frank had any enemies," Mayree said. "Did he?"

Stan took a deep inhale, his pause long enough to turn Mayree's face bright red and to stir Paula's stomach into an angry knot.

"Did he?" Mayree's voice was loud and high.

"Jesus, Mayree, calm down."

"Don't tell me to calm down! You were his friend *and* his lawyer. You'd know more than anyone else."

Stan raised his hands. "I don't know. Maybe. Believe it or not, I wasn't involved in all his business."

Mayree stood up, lit another cigarette, and looked hard at Stan as she paced the length of the table. "I *don't* believe it, as a matter of fact. You two were thick as thieves. If he was up to something, you were either up to it with him or pulling him out of whatever shit he got into."

For as long as Paula could remember, Stan and her father had done everything together: business deals, social engagements, father-daughter outings, haircuts. She'd never thought about the intricacies of their relationship. The idea of him pulling Frank out of trouble was new and disconcerting information.

"Well, that's true enough, I guess," he said, leaning back. Mayree seemed to wait for him to continue, but he didn't.

"Is that it? Is that all you have to say?" Mayree swept her arm through the air. "Some maniac assaulted Paula and now he's come to the house to take the evidence. Who knows what he could do next? He might be planning to come kill us in our sleep."

Paula blanched. Mayree thinking someone had stolen a bag of dirty clothes was one thing, but her blunt suggestion that they might become victims of murder was quite another.

"Whoa, now, you're making some pretty big assumptions there." Stan looked at Paula. "And you're scaring the shit out of your daughter."

"I'm trying to connect the dots, Stan, which for some reason you don't seem inclined to help me with."

"It's two in the morning and I'm here, aren't I?"

"Don't be such a smart-ass," she said. "I think you know something you don't want to tell me."

"Damn right I don't want to tell you," he said. "Not until I think it through."

"Is that some horseshit lawyer tactic, Stan? If you know something, you need to tell me what it is."

Paula thought she could feel in her own body the electricity her mother was throwing off, and it made her even more anxious than she was. "Mom, please."

Mayree swatted the air in front of Paula, ignoring her. "What if it had been Kelly? If it was *your* daughter, would you still be sitting there like nothing's the matter? Or would you actually give a shit?"

Paula watched the color rise on Stan's face. He turned to her. "Honey, I'm sorry this happened to you. You *are* like my own kid." Then he stood and faced Mayree and his expression hardened. He opened his mouth as if to speak again, but no words came out. All Paula could hear was the ticking of the clock on the wall and the sound of all of them breathing like a small pack of dogs. Without farewell, Stan walked out, slamming the door behind him.

Less than a minute later, he was back. "Just so you know, there's a big fat opossum out by the garage. That's probably the noise you heard, her rooting around, looking for her joey." He left again, this time for good.

As if the fight had drained out of her, Mayree sank down into her chair. "Whoever put men in charge of women ought to have his horns clipped." She lit another cigarette with a tiny tremble in her hands.

Mayree

Mayree woke up for good to noise coming from Herb Walker's garage next door. She sighed. She'd gone to bed shortly after Stan left the night before—or rather, early that morning—but had lain awake for at least an hour. What little sleep she got was in fits, snatched awake as she was from strange dreams she couldn't remember, trips to the bathroom, cigarettes. Now it was barely nine on a Friday morning and Herb, who spent his days mowing his lawn and the Bakers' and tinkering, was already making a racket in his garage. He once called himself an inventor, which seemed to Mayree a wild exaggeration, since all he seemed to do was fix broken appliances or weld disparate metals together into machines that performed a single banal function or none at all. His wife looked as long-suffering and worn-down as an old mare and, whenever she happened to see Mayree, glared at her with an inscrutable emotion that might've been jealousy that Mayree most certainly didn't deserve. Though she didn't object to romantic gestures like free lawn care, she'd never reciprocate them with disgusting old Herb. The way he wore his once-office-appropriate trousers with sweat-stained undershirts and suspenders was bad enough, but up close, she could hardly bear the sight of the hair that had somehow migrated from the crown of his head into his ears and nostrils, or his breath, which smelled like he'd packed his cheek full of decaying matter rather than tobacco. No, Mayree would gladly take the lawn mowing, but Mrs. Walker had nothing at all to worry about on this side of the fence.

She lit a cigarette, pulled on her bathrobe, and went down to the kitchen, where Paula was eating a bowl of cereal. Sitting in the center of the table was the missing swim bag.

"Morning," Paula said.

Mayree looked at the bag, the glasses, and the empty whiskey bottle, and felt a twinge of nausea, which might've been the start of a hangover, or the crow she was about to eat, or both. "Where'd that come from?"

"It was in the living room, behind your chair."

Mayree poured a cup of leftover coffee and put it in the microwave, struggling to remember taking the bag out to the garage. She'd had trouble getting in, she knew; her shoulder hurt this morning from having used it to shove the door open. The garage had been dusty and full of forgotten detritus. How long had she stayed there? What had she been doing? She was absolutely sure she'd left the bag somewhere by a bike or maybe the Christmas decorations. But then again, she couldn't recall going back inside the house or to bed, only that she'd been awakened by a noise that she thought had come from outside. Was it possible she'd taken the bag out, intending to leave it, but brought it back and put it behind her chair? Or perhaps she hadn't even taken it out at all. Maybe after she ordered the pizza for Paula, she simply moved it, then went to the garage empty-handed. "Fuck," she said.

"Uh-huh," Paula mumbled.

"I swear I took it out there." She sat down across from her daughter.

Paula looked at her with dull eyes. "Sucks when you're sure something bad happened and other people don't think it's a big deal."

Mayree thought but refused to say aloud, *Touché*.

Paula carried her bowl and the whiskey glasses to the sink. "Kelly's picking me up soon. We have government at ten. I'll put this in the garbage can on my way out."

"No." Mayree slid the bag closer to her.

"What? Why not? You were the one who wanted to get rid of it—twice."

"Maybe I was mistaken." The urine stench had dissipated somewhat over the past five days but was still present. In spite of that and whatever filth it had acquired from already having been in the garbage can, Mayree pulled it onto her lap and hunched over it, in case Paula tried to grab it from her. "After last night, I'm thinking we should probably hang on to it."

"No, Mom, we shouldn't. This back-and-forth over a stupid bag is getting ridiculous. Look, the fact that it's still here proves that nobody came to steal it. The baby opossum got stuck in that trap by accident. Nobody's watching us. There's no message. We're fine. Or as fine as we can be, I guess." Paula shrugged and loaded the dirty dishes into the dishwasher.

Over the scent of day-old coffee, Mayree smelled hay and horse sweat and manure. She heard Bobby Cox's voice in her mind as clearly as she had heard it in her family's barn over three decades ago: *It's time you learnt what it's like to ride a* real *stallion.* She gripped the bag in her lap. "Even if someone didn't try to take it, I still think something's going on. I don't want anything like this to happen to you again."

Paula closed the dishwasher door and turned to her.

Mayree softened her voice. "It shouldn't have happened in the first place," she said.

Paula chewed the inside of her bottom lip, a habit Mayree had even enlisted the help of her dentist to break. But the habit persisted, and now it had become her tell. Mayree knew how hard her daughter was chewing on an idea by how hard she chewed on the soft tissue of her mouth. "Okay," she finally said. "Thanks."

"So we need to hang on to it. Or take it to the police. Just in case."

"Jesus, Mom." Paula threw the dish towel onto the counter. "Have you already started drinking again today?"

"Jesus yourself, Paula Lee. I just told you it shouldn't have happened. Isn't that what you wanted?"

Paula sighed. She gripped the chair back with both hands and closed her eyes for a moment. When she opened them, she looked so weary that Mayree could imagine her as a much older woman, worn down by the burden of unpleasant memories. It was, sadly, like looking in the mirror.

"Honestly," Paula said, "I wish all the bad stuff would just go away. I don't want to think about it anymore."

After a moment, Mayree nodded. She'd wanted the same thing back then.

Paula held out her hand. "Can I please just throw it out once and for all?"

Mayree didn't know whether to go back to urging Paula to forget about Saturday night or dig deeper into it. That she didn't know which would be better for Paula made her feel even more incompetent as a mother. That she didn't have anyone else to help her with what felt like such an important decision made her feel even more alone. She wondered what Sissy would do in her place. "What about what Stan said? He said he was afraid something like this was going to happen," she said after a moment. She squeezed the bag harder, releasing a puff of foul-smelling air. "He knows something."

"What difference would it make if he did?"

"You're a child, Paula. You don't even know what you don't know about life and men and the terrible mistakes they make."

"Uncle Stan would tell us if there was something to worry about." Paula sat down. "Look, I've been thinking about it. You were right. I fucked up. I drank too much and put myself in a bad situation. It was my fault. Even the cops said so. I learned my lesson, okay? Now I just want to forget about it." She held out her hand again. "Please?"

For a while, Mayree had worried that Bobby would try to corner her again, but she, too, had learned her lesson and stayed clear of him the rest of that summer until she left the ranch for college. A few times, she saw him looking at her, but she was always too far away to read the expression on his face. She got a job working in the cafeteria so she could stay on campus that first Christmas break. When she reluctantly returned to Blanco the summer after her freshman year, Bobby was gone. It took her a while to work up the nerve to ask one of her brothers where he'd gone and if he was coming back. Evidently, Bobby had been drinking on the job and gotten his hand crushed in the squeeze chute. *Mangled* was what her brother had said. If there was to be any justice for what he'd done to her, maybe that was it. When he tried to get their daddy to pay damages, Ray had told him he'd gotten what he deserved and ought to be glad it wasn't worse. She didn't know what else he'd done to make Ray say that. They never heard from him again.

She guessed Bobby had been around thirty-six or so back then, which would put him in his late sixties now if he was still alive. She'd never tried to find out where he went, so she had no idea what happened to him. She didn't really want to know. As time passed, she thought and dreamed about him less and less until the wound of him settled into a faint scar hidden within her body that she could almost forget existed. Until this week, she hadn't thought of him in years. Now she wondered what Ray would've done to Bobby if he'd known what Bobby had done to her. She wondered what her mother would've done.

She handed Paula the bag but didn't let go completely. "You sure?" she asked.

"Yes."

"Okay then."

Outside, a car honked. "Kelly's here." Paula shouldered her backpack and took the bag from Mayree. She held Mayree's gaze for an extra moment. "Thanks, Mom."

As soon as Paula was out the door, Mayree jumped up and stood at the sink to watch her. The trash cans were alongside the fence opposite the kitchen window; Mayree shifted so that she'd be mostly hidden if

Paula looked back. She didn't. She flipped open the lid and dropped the bag inside like she couldn't wait to be rid of it, then wiped her hand along the side of her jeans and jogged down the driveway to Kelly's car.

Mayree wondered if Bobby had left Texas in 1958 after he crushed his hand. What could he have done for work without the use of both? Not calf roping for sure. Not ranch work. One of his tasks had been the seemingly endless repair of fences to keep livestock in and, ironically, predators out. He couldn't have done that with only one functioning hand. He could barely do it with two.

Maybe he'd moved up north or out west, got a job long-hauling or something else that didn't require much dexterity or brainpower. Maybe he'd drunk himself to death.

Or maybe he'd stayed close by, close enough to keep tabs on her. To watch her and her daughter.

She gripped the edge of the sink as an ominous feeling overtook her, making her knees quiver and her mouth taste bad. She stood there for a long time, staring at the trash cans, jumpy and restless and aware of the emptiness inside the house, inside herself, until the need for a cigarette overshadowed all the other terrible needs she feared she'd never be able to satisfy.

She lit one and breathed.

March 25, 1989

Dear Mama,
I'm out. I'm free. I never thought about Freedom having a smell but it does. Just like how you smell, like laundry soap and these wildflowers that I picked on the side of the road like we used to. I'm leaving you this letter here, hoping you'll find it. I got some things to do but I'll be back.
    Love,
    Your son
    P.S. I hope you like the flowers.
    P.P.S. I wish you were here.

Paula

As she climbed into the car, with Kelly smiling and singing along loudly to a bouncy, shuffling hit song by a pop artist who shared her first name, Paula felt a faint but genuine sense of relief for the first time in almost a week. She was tired from being up so late last night with Mayree and Stan, but the sky was a crisp, clear blue, trees were showing new green leaves, and flowers were popping up all over. The stupid bag debacle was over, her mother seemed at least mildly placated for the time being, and she could feel the torment from the weekend before slipping away like a caught fish released back into a stream. Even the thought of Will was less an open wound than a tender, new scar.

What was the point of holding on to such unpleasant memories anyway? Reliving that night over and over hadn't changed the fact of it. She didn't want to live in fear. And why should she? It was even possible that she'd exaggerated the memory, given how drunk she'd been. She might not have actually been in as much danger as she'd thought after all. Her father had always said she had an active imagination, and it was possible that this was just a good example of that. All she could do was learn the lesson and not let herself get into a similar situation in the future.

She felt a twinge of guilt for not following Felicia's suggestion that she seek justice if she could, especially since she was supposedly planning on becoming a lawyer. But what could she do anyway, since her story was vague and unsupported, and the police hadn't been helpful or even concerned when she and Mayree told them about the incident. Without any hard evidence, it made more sense to just purge it from her mind so it wouldn't cause her or anyone else further distress. Besides, Felicia had also told her that's how women have always coped. Justice or no, it was the only reliable way to get on with things. Even her mother, who'd lost her husband and just about everybody else, was moving along. Sort of.

Paula hoped she could figure out how to at least be satisfied with her own life. She was envious of Kelly, to whom joyfulness came so naturally. No matter what was going on—a bad grade, a worse haircut, her dad living at the YMCA, whatever—Kelly lived in a perpetual state of good cheer. She'd had that foundation at home with a brother and the kind of parents who laughed and teased and enjoyed doing things together as a family, even if it was just watching football on TV. Maybe, if only through sheer determination, Paula could learn to cultivate her own happiness. Or earn it. She would focus on her inner strength and think more about her future. She'd double down on her studies and look for a new job. She wasn't afraid of hard work, though she wouldn't mind something less messy and demeaning than the restaurant. She'd be more social. Smile more. Have more fun.

"Oh, oh, oh," she and Kelly sang together when the chorus came on. By the time they got to campus, Paula was flush with forced optimism.

~

After Spanish class, Kelly suggested they go to El Viejo for lunch to celebrate the fact that they both got As on their most recent test. "I need enchiladas," Kelly said. "I haven't had any for days."

Paula laughed. "Me either. Not since I got fired from Mamacita's on Tuesday. Three days without enchiladas is practically torture." She was pleased to notice that she felt a bit removed from even that humiliation. "Let's go. I'm starving!"

Kelly grabbed Paula's arm and whispered, "Wait. There's Mike, that cute guy from macroeconomics class."

Paula followed Kelly's gaze. "Who?"

"Don't look! He'll know we're talking about him," she said. "Be cool. He's coming this way."

"I have no idea who you're talking about."

Kelly shifted her backpack and smiled, pretending not to notice the guy walking toward them. "He introduced himself after class Wednesday night. He just switched his schedule last week for some reason, which is why we haven't seen him before. Remember I told you about the Sigma Nu party? He's the one who invited me—or us. God, he's so fine."

Paula ducked her head and turned to see who Kelly was talking about. Indeed, a tall blond wearing a stiff white button-down with the collar turned up and jeans with a visible crease down the center of each leg was making his way down the sidewalk toward them.

"Hey," he said to Kelly as he ran his fingers through his hair.

"Hi," she said, clearly smitten. "Oh, Mike, this is Paula. She's in—"

"She's in the same class, too. Yeah, I know. I saw you once, but your hair was different." He smiled at Paula a fraction of a second too long—long enough for Paula's face to turn hot and Kelly's expression to change. "It looks cool like this, too."

The shift in mood was as immediate and palpable as a blast of wind. She tensed at Mike's unexpected attention. Not only was Kelly obviously hurt, it made Paula feel vulnerable again. "Thanks," she said without enthusiasm. She rolled her eyes at Kelly, hoping to convey her lack of interest in him. Kelly tilted her head toward her shoulder almost imperceptibly, which, because of their long history, Paula understood to mean that it was okay, she was disappointed but not mad, and furthermore, he was probably a dick and didn't deserve either of them. Still, Paula was unsettled by the whole situation.

"So," Mike said, turning back to Kelly. "You coming Saturday night? It's gonna be rad." He looked around, then tapped the side of his nose. "Especially if you like to party."

"Yeah, we're not really into that," Kelly said. "But maybe we'll come anyway if we're not doing something else. I hear there are some hot guys in your frat." She gave him a self-satisfied smile.

The doors to the building they were standing near opened, and a large group of students emerged, adding to the already heavy flow of pedestrians around them. Someone bumped into Paula, jostling her backpack and nearly causing her to lose her balance.

"Sorry," whoever it was mumbled in passing.

Paula glanced behind her, but the person who'd run into her hadn't stopped. She adjusted her straps, bothered by a lingering disorientation as the crowd pushed past and the volume of ambient noise increased. She inhaled deeply, trying to steady herself, and noticed a faint but distinctive odor: a musky, powdery aftershave. The kind her father used to use. The scent she smelled on her attacker. She grabbed Kelly's hand to keep her knees from buckling.

"We have to go," Paula said.

"In a sec."

"No, now."

"Wait, you mean me, right?" Mike said to Kelly. "I'm one of the hot guys?"

Kelly, smiling, let Paula pull her away. She looked over her shoulder at him and shrugged.

"See you tomorrow?" he called after them.

But Paula, with Kelly in tow, was already walking fast, and neither of them bothered to answer.

"What's the matter?" Kelly asked her, trying to keep up. "You have to go to the bathroom or something?"

"No, I just needed to get out of there."

Kelly stopped, forcing Paula to stop, too. "Talk to me," she said. "Everything was totally fine. I don't care about Mike. He's cute but after talking to him, he actually seems kinda stupid."

She took a breath. "I smelled that aftershave again. Or I thought I did."

"Paul, it's barbershop aftershave. It's not like it's rare."

She couldn't remember noticing it on anyone else besides her father and Uncle Stan before Saturday. "Maybe."

"You know how once you notice something specific, like a certain car or vocabulary word or whatever, you suddenly see it everywhere? It's like that."

Paula took a breath, trying to notice a different odor to hold on to. "I guess."

"So you're okay?" Kelly asked.

"The way Mike was looking at me was weird."

"Whatever. You're pretty, even with your army buzz. Guys are going to look at you." She fluffed her own teased coif, well cemented in place with Aqua Net. "Shit, maybe I ought to cut mine, too."

"It's not that. I don't know—it reminded me of . . . you know."

"Jeez, Paul. If you freak out every time a guy looks at you, you'll turn into one of those weirdos who never leaves the house. What is it, agrophobia?"

"Agoraphobia," Paula said. "Speaking of vocabulary words."

"Right. That's what I said."

"No, you said *agrophobia*. That would be a fear of farming." It sounded silly enough out loud to make Paula giggle.

"Smarty-pants." Kelly play-shoved her. "Come on, let's forget about stupid guys. I'm hungry. What's the fear of starving?"

"Ypositismosphobia."

Kelly laughed. "That's a load of crap."

"If you were afraid of that, it would be coprophobia."

"Stop it! Where did you even learn that?"

"Fifth grade, when we were studying for the spelling bee. Don't you remember? My dad got a list of all the phobias and made us study them. I think he was drunk." They both laughed at that.

"Oh yeah! And then my dad said we shouldn't waste our brain cells on stupid words and sent us to the liquor store for more alcohol," Kelly said. "I can't believe you still remember them."

"I can't believe the guy at the store actually let us buy whiskey," she said. "We were eleven!"

"Hey, my yposit-whatever is flaring up. If I don't get some food soon, I can't be responsible for what might happen." Kelly held out her hand, and Paula smiled and took it. She didn't want to think about anything negative at all.

~

They went to El Viejo, where they knew they wouldn't get carded, and Paula ate more in one sitting than she'd probably had all week: chips and queso, mole chicken enchiladas—a complex flavor with twenty-seven ingredients that her father had introduced her to and that she adored but that most of her peers thought was disgusting—and two frozen margaritas. Stuffed and pleasantly buzzed, she felt like she could go home and nap for hours, then wake up ready to start her life anew.

"So what do you think?" Kelly asked as they got into her car. "Should we go to the party tomorrow?"

"No way."

"Why? Because of Mike?" she asked. "It's a frat party. There'll be tons of people. We'll drink and meet people and have fun. Screw Mike."

Paula thought about her earlier exuberance, her determination to enjoy her life. Then she thought about Kevin Atwood, screaming in her face at a party the month before. What if he was planning to be at this one? Should she go and confront him? If he admitted to attacking her, she could press charges. But what if it wasn't him? Or it was, and he attacked her again?

"I really don't want to go," she said.

"Just think about it," Kelly said. "Okay? I'll be your bodyguard."

Reluctantly, Paula nodded. How did Kelly always manage to pull her into these things? Well, maybe it was for the best; without Kelly, she'd probably end up a recluse like her mother.

~

Mayree was, as usual, sitting in her chair, smoking, when Paula walked in. "Nice day?" her mother asked.

Paula noticed that her mother had gotten dressed and done her hair and makeup. "Yeah, it was, actually," she said, dropping her backpack on the couch. "How about you? You're all dolled up."

"Oh, not really." Mayree patted her hair, which hardly moved from the generous application of hair spray. "I just thought it would be nice to put on some real clothes."

Paula peered into the kitchen. "Is Uncle Stan coming over?"

"That beast? No, of course not. Besides, I don't need a reason to get dressed. I'm not doing it for anyone else's benefit but my own."

Judging by the indignant tone in her mother's voice, Paula assumed that she was, in fact, doing it for someone else's benefit, but she didn't know whose and didn't particularly care. It was a pleasant surprise to see her making an effort, even if she was still just sitting in her chair with her basket of crocheting and endless supply of cigarettes. Maybe they'd coincidentally both decided overnight to undertake some self-improvement. Sort of a simultaneous reinvention. "Well, you do look nice."

Mayree closed her eyes slowly and dipped her chin, a tiny bow of acknowledgment.

Paula picked up her backpack, hesitating a moment before heading upstairs. "What do you think . . . do you want to maybe go out to dinner or something? It's Friday night after all." How silly to feel butterflies as though she were asking a guy for a date instead of her own mother. Or perhaps less silly than sad.

"That's nice of you, but actually, I do have plans. Felicia's coming over."

"For dinner?" In all the years Felicia had been part of their family, Paula had never known her to come over for a social visit. "That's weird."

Mayree shrugged. "I invited her."

"Why?"

"Oh, she's worried about her nephew. He's having some trouble adjusting to regular life after being in juvenile detention. I told her I'd do the cooking, but she insisted on bringing dinner. Knowing her, it'll be enough to feed us all weekend."

The thought of seeing Felicia lifted Paula's spirits a notch higher, and she smiled. "Don't make her clean up afterward, at least."

"That woman is going to do whatever she wants, and you know it. She doesn't trust me to do it right, anyway. That's probably why she didn't want me to cook." Mayree shrugged. "I don't know how much help I can be about Curtis, though, seeing as I haven't exactly done an impressive job raising you."

Paula gaped at her as she processed the insult. "Gee, thanks."

"What? It's the truth, as much as I hate to admit it."

The warmth Paula had started to feel toward her mother a moment ago was gone. As much as she wanted to see Felicia, she didn't want to be anywhere near Mayree. "You mean because I'm such a disappointment? Or *you* are?" Paula turned and walked up the stairs to her room, then slammed the door behind her with a satisfying bang.

March 28, 1989

Dear Mama,
I got itchy feet. Not for real, but like you used to say
when I wanted to go somewhere or if I was excited
about something and couldn't stand still. I started
thinking about all the ways you and me have been
fucked over and treated so bad, like not having enough
money, and I got mad enough to punch the wall.
Don't worry, I won't get in trouble again. I'd rather
die than go back inside anyway. You know how you
said it all comes out in the wash? Let's see.
    Love,
    Your son
    P.S. I wish I knew where you are.

Mayree

When Felicia rang the doorbell, Mayree sighed with relief. She was surprised at how eager she was for some friendly conversation. She stubbed out her cigarette and pushed herself out of her chair. "You could've just let yourself in," she said.

"It's not a working day," Felicia answered. "And hello to you, too."

Formalities dispensed with, Felicia carried two heavy bags of food in insulated containers to the kitchen and began laying everything out on the table: chicken-fried steak, mashed potatoes, shrimp and okra soup, tomato pie, corn bread biscuits, and Mayree's favorite—apple-rutabaga cobbler.

"Did you invite the Texas Rangers to eat with us, too?"

Felicia raised an eyebrow as she appraised her. "By the looks of you, you need every bite. It's nice to see you out of your bathrobe at least."

"I had to put it in the wash. It was starting to smell a little funky."

Felicia got three plates out of the cabinet. "You sure you don't want me to come back more than just once a week?"

"Felicia, you know I can't afford it, at least not until I figure things out," she said as she took out two place mats from a drawer. "Put one of those back. Paula's in a snit about something. She can eat later."

Felicia did as she was told. "I'm going to start working Tuesdays through Thursdays for an old lady down the street next week. I could come here on Fridays just for half a day."

"Let me think about it."

"If it helps, you could keep a tab running and pay me later, when things turn around. Honestly, I'd be glad just to be out of the house, especially now that Curtis is staying with us full time."

"I appreciate the offer, but if you work, you'll get paid. I'm not taking charity."

"It's not charity if it serves me, too. Besides, I miss seeing Paula. And believe it or not, I even miss your cranky ass."

"That's hardly a proper way to speak to your employer, you know."

"It's not a working day; I can speak however I please."

"Touché." She served Felicia a helping of the tomato pie, then took some for herself.

"So to what do I owe the honor of this evening?" Felicia asked, eyeing her critically. "You're not going to try to fire me, are you?"

"You know I wouldn't do that." Mayree took a bite of the mashed potatoes. No matter how hard she'd tried over the years, she couldn't make that simple dish taste half as good as Felicia's.

"You're right," Felicia said. "If I really thought that, I wouldn't have brought you all this food. So what is it?"

Mayree shrugged. She'd told Paula that she was going to advise Felicia about her nephew, but what she really wanted was Felicia's advice on how to deal with Paula. But now that Felicia was here, she didn't even know where to begin. "Parenting is hard," she said, somber.

"Mm-hmm."

"Life is hard."

Felicia nodded, looking down at her plate. "It is."

"Not to you," Mayree said, fishing for some words of encouragement. Her pride kept her from asking for it outright.

"Ha!"

"What do you mean, *Ha*? You're the only one I know who's got it all together."

"Did I just hear a compliment come out your mouth?"

"Oh hush."

Felicia put down her fork and clasped her hands together beneath her chin. "Seriously, Mayree," she said, looking at her like she was an absolute fool. "What in the hell do you know about whether I've got it together or not?"

Mayree sat back in her chair, feeling like she'd been reprimanded by her grade-school teacher. "I just mean you always make everything seem easy."

Felicia looked at her with a calm intensity that made Mayree want to look away. "Maybe. But that doesn't mean it is."

"I don't remember you ever complaining about anything personal," Mayree said. "Except maybe me."

"I don't remember you ever asking."

Mayree realized then how little she'd ever wondered about Felicia's life outside the Bakers' home. She knew about her husband, Kenny, that he was a hard worker and good provider for Felicia. She knew their address but had never been to their house. She knew they hadn't had her own children, but never asked why. Yet Felicia knew practically everything about Mayree. In the measure of intimate knowledge between them, the scales were tipped precariously out of balance.

"I should have."

Felicia patted her on the hand. "I never expected you to. That wasn't the arrangement." She picked up her fork again.

Mayree looked at her for a moment. "Why have you put up with me all these years?"

Felicia took a bite of food and said nothing for so long Mayree wondered if she'd even heard her. Then Felicia dabbed the corners of her mouth, put her napkin in her lap, rested her chin on her clasped hands as though in prayer, and stared back across the table until Mayree looked away.

"You shall not see your brother's donkey or his ox fallen down by the way and ignore them. You shall help him to lift them up again," Felicia said. "I know you don't read Scripture, but that's Deuteronomy 22:4. It's one of the speeches Moses gave the Israelites on how to behave before they entered the Promised Land."

"Am I the brother or the ass?"

Felicia laughed. "Both."

"I don't deserve you," Mayree said.

"According to God, you do. That's good enough for me," Felicia said. "But listen, I want to know about Paula. She's the one we need to be worrying about, what with cutting off all her hair like she did."

Mayree, chagrined, stood to refill their glasses. She felt guilty for being so focused on her own troubles, for assuming Felicia would be happy to swoop in and save her from herself once again. "No need to worry. Paula said she wants to forget it ever happened, so that's what we're going to do."

"You sure?"

"Yes," she said emphatically. She didn't want to admit to Felicia how she'd reacted every step of the way. Nor did she want to discuss that Stan hadn't seemed entirely surprised to learn about Paula's attack. "Now. Do me a favor and change the subject. Tell me about your nephew."

"Do you really, or are you just feeling regretful?" Felicia winked at her.

"Yes and yes," Mayree said. "Now go on."

"Lord, that child," she said, shaking her head. "He's always been a handful, you know. Well, maybe you don't. I don't like to talk ugly about anybody, especially family." She sighed heavily, then continued, "His daddy, Ralph, is so different from my Kenny. They're only three years apart, but it's like they were from different families. Maybe because Kenny was the oldest, but he was so good, and smart, and always taking care of people. Signed up for the service before the draft started, just a year and a half after we got married, honorable discharge after the Paris Peace Accords, got a steady job when he got home. But Ralph—and of course I only know the stories from before I met him, but the way he acts now, I know the stories were true—he was just trouble. Started drinking early, dropped out of high school, didn't want to join the military, got by working odd jobs and living at home with their mama. Did some time for petty theft, that sort of thing. Then he meets Bonita at a bar. She's younger than him by eight years or so and not much of an upstanding member of society either, but they get together and pretty soon she gets pregnant with Curtis.

"They got married when she was about seven months along. I'd been working for you just about a year by then. Kenny practically dragged them both down the aisle, if you could call it that. Just a courthouse event to make sure Curtis had at least a chance at a normal family arrangement. Plus by then it was obvious Kenny and I couldn't have our own babies, so he wanted to make sure the family name got passed down somehow." Felicia took a sip of tea and leaned back. "Listen to me going on," she said with a wave of her hand. "You don't need to hear all this."

She put her hand on the table and looked at her. "I want to," she said. "Please."

Felicia nodded, indicating her trust that Mayree was being sincere. Also, she seemed glad to be talking about it. "It was hard trying to keep Ralph out of jail and Bonita from running off. He thought she'd been stepping out on him, even early on, and they fought a lot. Apparently, when he went looking for her, he usually found her at her drug dealer's house. As for Curtis, Ralph never did think the boy was his, and that made it hard for him to feel too parental toward him. Ralph's light-skinned like Kenny, but truth is, Curtis looks a little bit too much like Bonita's drug dealer, who was white, if you know what I mean."

Mayree nodded in agreement, even though she couldn't remember what Curtis looked like, having met him only once. All she knew of him was what Felicia had told her over the years—that except for his recent trouble, he'd always been a loving nephew, a good student with a passion for science, and wanted to be a veterinarian when he grew up.

"It was hard coming home after work, not knowing if we were gonna find baby Curtis in the playpen we kept for him, hungry, crying from sitting in his own filth. Bonita never bothered to call or leave a note; she'd just drop him off at our house whether Kenny and I were home or not. I guess I owe her credit for taking him somewhere safe at least, before going off and getting high."

"I'm sorry," Mayree said, surprised at how much she meant it. It occurred to her that all these years, when she'd been so easily over-whelmed by motherhood, Paula had actually been a relatively easy child to raise—the recent past notwithstanding. Meanwhile, Felicia, who had some real challenges at home, managed to handle them with such grace and still had enough energy, empathy, and attention left to give Paula five days a week for the past nearly eighteen years.

Felicia waved it away. "Don't be. It was the hand the good Lord dealt us," she said. "But I gotta say, I'm truly worried about that boy."

"What's he doing?"

"It's not so much what he's doing as what he's not. He stays out 'til all hours, then sleeps half the day. I can smell the marijuana on his clothes, even though he denies using drugs, of course. He's quiet and seems angry all the time. Cusses a blue streak. He won't enroll in school to finish out his year even though he was taking classes in juvie, because he says it'd be humiliating. So I say, then he needs to get a job, but he hasn't so much as looked at the want ads in the paper. I know I spoiled him some, trying to make up for what he didn't get from Ralph and Bonita. Maybe I did too much for him. Made too many excuses. Now I don't know what to do. How do you force somebody to get on the right track in life?"

How the hell was Mayree supposed to answer that? "What about his parents?"

"Ralph's back in prison for possession, and Bonita's . . . Bonita. She says she's working part time at Kmart, but Curtis says she's hardly ever home, especially nights. I'm sure she's up to no good."

It made her think of Paula, and by extension, Frank. How being up to no good could so easily get people into real trouble. "So all he's got is you and Kenny. Is he respectful to you for that at least?"

"As respectful as an angry teenage boy who's been locked up in juvenile detention can be, I guess. He knows it's his own fault he went to juvie, so he's mad at himself but he's also mad at his daddy, especially, and the system, and the whole damn world. It's like he's got to start from scratch. Learn how to wash his own clothes, cook his own food, be a member of society, do the things he didn't do when he was inside. Needs to grow up and be a man."

"That sounds like a helluva mess."

"I can clean up almost any mess you put in front of me, but this one . . . I just don't know. I feel like I failed him."

"You're wrong there," Mayree said, quick and decisive as a declaration of love, followed immediately by a moment of shyness. She had no idea if Felicia had failed Curtis, but she knew damn well Felicia hadn't failed anyone in the Baker household, least of all herself. She wasn't good at saying it, but in most cases, she trusted Felicia's judgment even above her own. Even without having had biological children, Felicia had a maternal instinct and confidence that would've made Mayree jealous if she hadn't relied on it so much over the past two decades. She didn't know why the good Lord hadn't seen fit to share some of Felicia's mothering skills with Mayree, but at least He'd had the sense to make her a beneficiary of it.

"And why are you so sure about that?"

Mayree leaned forward, looking Felicia directly in the eyes. "I just am," she said.

~

They ate the rest of their dinner in companionable silence, offering each other second helpings and refills of iced tea. After they finished, Felicia started to clear the plates, but Mayree stopped her. There was no way she'd let Felicia clean anything that night, even if Paula hadn't already suggested as much. "You can check my work after I'm done," she said. Then, knowing which of them her daughter would probably rather see, she asked, "Will you make a plate, take it up to Paula?"

Felicia smiled. "Of course."

Paula

Paula was sitting on her bed with her notebook and a mimeographed copy of the 1917 short story "A Jury of Her Peers." It was an early-feminist work by the playwright Susan Glaspell that she was writing an essay about for her English class. Even though it wasn't due until Monday, she figured she might as well get a head start on it. Maybe it was the leftover buzz from lunch or the leftover annoyance from the exchange with her mother, but as soon as she started writing, she entered a flow state where the ideas and words just poured out of her. By the time there was a soft knock on her bedroom door, she'd just written the concluding paragraph:

Glaspell communicates to her reader that in a society where the law favors men, justice cannot always be served to women. Through the use of dialogue, symbolism, and the actions of the characters, Glaspell suggests that the only way Minnie can get the justice she deserves is if she is judged not by men but by her female peers: Mrs. Peters and Mrs. Hale.

"Come in," Paula said. She leaned back against the wall, feeling a rush of satisfaction with her work.

Felicia brought in a tray loaded with food and set it down on Paula's nightstand. "How you doing, honey girl?"

She scooted over and gathered her papers into a pile to give Felicia room to sit down. "Good," she said, happy that it was Felicia and not Mayree.

"Well, I'm glad to hear that. Your mama said you were upset about something. I wanted to check on you, see if there was anything you wanted to talk about."

"Not really," she said. She was actively trying to get on with her life, in spite of Mayree's fretting and the uncomfortable encounter earlier that day with the guy from her macroeconomics class. "Oh, but I want to show you something!" She dumped the remaining contents of her backpack out onto her bed between them, looking for the Spanish test. She could imagine that Mayree would've been dismissive, saying something along the lines of how she expected nothing less from a Texan who'd been taking Spanish since the sixth grade.

"What's all this mess?" Felicia said, picking up a candy bar wrapper and empty carton of gum from among the papers and notebooks. She began unfolding miscellaneous pages and sorting out trash.

"I've just been busy," Paula said, flipping through a notebook. "I was going to organize it, I promise. Here." She held out the two-page persuasive essay she'd written on why the Bush administration's silence on human rights in Mexico contributed to election-related violence in the country. She'd made only three grammatical errors.

But Felicia had picked up a rumpled, folded piece of paper from the pile and was reading it, her eyebrows drawn together in a manner suggesting alarm.

"What?" Paula asked. She moved closer, and read the brief, type-written letter Felicia was holding:

HEY YOU LITTLE TRUST FUND BITCH I WASN'T TRYING TO KILL YOU. I ONLY NEEDED TO USE YOU FOR A WHILE. I WAS BEING NICE EVEN GONNA LET YOU MAKE

YOUR STUPID PHONE CALL BUT THEN YOU FUCKED EVERYTHING UP. YOU OWE ME AND NOW YOU'RE GONNA PAY. YOU DON'T DO WHAT I SAY I REALLY WILL KILL YOU THIS TIME. DON'T TALK TO ANYBODY ABOUT THIS. THERE WILL BE MORE INSTRUCTIONS.

Felicia and Paula looked at each other, then Paula answered Felicia's silent question. "I don't know," she said. "I have no idea." Her scalp tingled as more questions with no answers raced through her mind. She felt sick to her stomach.

"When was the last time you cleaned out your bag?"

"I don't know. Days."

"I don't suppose there's any question this was meant for you? Is this the person who hurt you?"

Paula nodded. "It has to be. He even mentioned the phone call." She recalled having been bumped into earlier that afternoon on campus, while she and Kelly were talking to Mike. That uneasy feeling. The ephemeral but distinctive scent of barbershop cologne. A literal shiver ran through her; he'd been following her after all.

"What phone call?"

"It doesn't matter." Since Saturday, she'd alternated between trying to put the events behind her and trying to squelch the fear that returned each time she heard the guy's voice in her head. The physical presence of this note brought a new level of terror: not only had she been attacked, she'd been targeted. And he wasn't finished. *I'm gonna cut—*

"We need to tell your mama. Now." Felicia stood and fixed her with a stern look.

Paula felt sick with fear and dread. It was like she was back in his car with him, the moment she realized she was probably going to die. "But it says not to talk about it to anyone. What if he finds out?"

"We have to, Paula. You can't keep something like this from her."

She couldn't go through that terror again. She reached for Felicia and pulled her back down, her grip so tight Felicia pried her fingers off. "Please. She'll tell Uncle Stan, the police, everybody."

"It's her job to protect you. What does this person even want? What does he mean, you owe him?"

"I don't know." She put her head in her hands and bent forward. "If he said something that night, I don't remember what it was."

"Let's go," Felicia said. She pinched the upper corner of the letter between her fingernails and was halfway down the stairs before Paula could try to stop her.

~

"Mayree, read this." Felicia dropped the letter on the kitchen table. Paula stood close, her arms wrapped tightly around herself. Mayree looked at them both, wiped her hands on a dish towel, then reached for the paper. "Don't touch it!" Felicia said. "It might have his fingerprints."

Nervously, Paula watched her mother's eyes travel back and forth over the page, then again before she asked the same questions of Paula that Felicia had. *You fucked everything up.* What could she possibly have done to deserve this?

"I told you someone was watching us. I could feel it," she said. "And Stan, that motherfucker. I knew he knew something, whatever this horseshit is about you owing somebody. Lord only knows what your father got us into, assuming it's got something to do with him." She untied the apron she'd put on and threw it on the counter. "And in case you're wondering, obviously no, you do not have a trust fund, so whoever wrote this is sorely mistaken. I'll be right back." As she marched toward the back door, she called, "Put your shoes on."

"Where are we going?" Paula called back, but Mayree had already gone outside. She turned to Felicia. "I'm scared."

Felicia pulled her close. "It's gonna be all right." To Paula, it sounded like she didn't believe that for a second.

Mayree returned, holding the omnipresent swim bag. "Good thing trash day's not 'til Tuesday," she said. "Felicia, thank you for a lovely dinner. We're going to the police station. I'll let you know what happens."

~

Paula followed Mayree up the steps to the modernist police station like the condemned walking to the gallows. She kept thinking of the warning not to talk to anyone about the letter. She'd tried, but there was no point in arguing with her mother that they shouldn't involve the cops—not when they'd been directly threatened, and especially not when Mayree was walking with the kind of heel-clacking purpose that she embodied as she strode through the lobby to the reception, nearly knocking into a very obviously drunk man being escorted down the hall. Paula didn't want to be back at the jailhouse with every ounce of her being. Once in a lifetime was bad enough. On the other hand, at least while she was there, the guy, wherever he was, couldn't hurt her. The main door locks buzzed behind them; for now at least, they were secure. Hopefully the police would be willing to help them this time.

"May I please speak with Sergeant Henderson?" Mayree tapped her unpolished fingernails on the grubby countertop.

The female officer behind the desk looked wearily up at Paula's mother. It wasn't even nine thirty, but this Friday night was already buzzing with activity. Nevertheless, the officer was drinking a Coke and watching *Miami Vice* on TV. "May I ask what this is regarding?" she said in a faux-formal voice, subtly mocking Mayree's. Paula didn't blame her; it was probably a terrible job.

Mayree put the letter, which she'd slipped into a plastic food storage bag, on the counter. "My daughter received a threatening letter after being violently attacked. We have reason to fear for her safety. For *our* safety." Paula knew she should be glad that her mother was taking the letter seriously, but she also felt like Mayree had put her emotions through a spin cycle.

The officer scanned the letter without expression. Paula wondered if maintaining nonchalance was part of their training. Even if it was, even if her lack of alarm was only affect, Paula found her detachment reassuring. As was, oddly, the loud and tangible presence of drunkards and complainants and detainees of all sorts, the ringing phones, the commanding voices of people in authority.

The officer handed the letter back to Mayree. "Do you have a case number?"

"Maybe, I don't know. He didn't give me one."

"But you've spoken to him about this before?"

"Well, not this letter, but yes, a situation it relates to."

"And he didn't file a report?"

"I'm not sure."

"If he didn't file a report, he probably didn't think there was a case."

Paula watched the color rise on her mother's cheeks and her eyes squint into predatory slits. "There is a goddamn case," she said in a voice like a growl.

The officer sighed. "Have a seat," she said, jutting her chin toward a row of chairs. "I'll see if he's available."

Mayree thanked her. She gathered her things and chose a seat directly in front of the desk, as if to ensure the officer was reminded of their presence. She sat rigidly on the edge, expectant. Despite being upset with her mother for taking her there, and terrified of what it could mean later, Paula was glad to have her support. She leaned a little closer to Mayree.

"Well, well, Mrs. Baker. What brings you back so soon?"

They'd been waiting for just under half an hour, during which Mayree had gone back to the officer at the front desk no fewer than three times, first hissing at and then ignoring Paula's protests. Mayree stood as soon as she saw Sergeant Henderson approach.

"We have a problem," Mayree said, holding up the swim bag and the letter.

"Let's hear it," he said, hooking his thumbs in his belt, looking not at all concerned.

"Right here in the hall?" she asked, shooting a look at the officer at the desk. "This is very serious. We've been threatened."

He took the letter from her, read it, then gave it back. "Did this come in the mail?"

Paula answered. "No, sir. I found it in my backpack after class today."

"You found it. How did it get there?" He spoke to her in a patronizing manner, clearly prepared to dismiss what he probably thought was a silly waste of his time.

"Someone bumped into me on campus today. I think he must've slipped it in there while I was distracted."

"Like a reverse pickpocket?" He gave them a bored-looking smirk.

"Yeah," she said, feeling stupid. "I guess."

"What's in there?" he asked, tipping his chin toward Mayree's other hand.

"The soiled clothes my daughter was wearing Saturday night. Proof that she was attacked. They weren't thrown out after all. Now, can we please go somewhere private to discuss what we're going to do next?"

The officer rocked back on his bootheels and sighed. "Mrs. Baker, technically, I'm off duty. The only reason I'm still here is because I had a dozen reports to update. It's been a long day. I missed my kid's basketball game. I'm hungry and I'm ready for a cold beer. I can tell you right where we're standing that there's nothing for us to *do next*."

"Wednesday, you said without her clothes there was nothing else you could do. But now we have them." She held the bag up again, shook it vigorously in his direction.

He leaned in, sniffed, then recoiled. "And all that'll prove is that she pissed her pants."

Even as she felt her cheeks burn, Paula lifted her chin and straightened her posture. "What about DNA testing? Yesterday, my biology professor said that two years ago, a rapist in Florida was the first person to be convicted using DNA evidence from biological evidence. What if some of his hair or blood got on my clothes when we were fighting? Couldn't you test that?"

"DNA testing is expensive and unreliable," he said, dragging his palm down his face. "And unless you didn't give us the whole story the other day, you weren't raped."

"This is horseshit!" Mayree threw the bag onto the floor.

"Mom." Paula picked it up. She couldn't imagine how this day could get any worse, but her mother seemed intent on trying.

"Mrs. Baker, I feel for you. I have kids, too. I'd do anything in my power to keep them safe," he said.

Paula glanced at her mother's face, looking for an affirmative reaction to Sergeant Henderson's comment, but her enraged expression didn't change.

"You found a note in your backpack and you don't know how it got there. It's not addressed to or signed by anyone. It's typed, so no handwriting to check out." He continued, "What proof do you have that any of this is real? And even if it was, what would you want us to do? Go looking for a guy with a typewriter and a telephone?"

"This is a direct threat. Put a patrol car in front of our house."

"Look around." He gestured at the entirety of the lobby. "It's Friday night and things are just getting started. My officers can't sit around in front of people's houses like they've got nothing better to do."

"There was a dead opossum, too. We found it yesterday in a trap." Mayree's voice went up an octave, and Paula felt her panic rise along with it. They weren't going to protect her after all. Quietly, she reached for her mother's hand, which Mayree pulled away.

Sergeant Henderson shook his head. "Are you nuts, lady?" he asked. "Look. This letter's a prank. Not a very nice one, I'll admit. But some wise guy out there probably thought it would be funny to scare a pretty girl."

"And if it's not? It says there'll be further instructions."

He shrugged. "Well, we'll just have to wait for them then." He tipped his hat. "Have a good night, ladies."

Mayree

The next morning, Saturday, Mayree shot out of bed even before having her first cigarette of the day. After worrying all night about the letter, she realized that if the cops weren't going to offer any support, then she'd have to come up with a plan on her own. The only information they had at that point was Stan's hint that someone from Frank's past could be behind both Paula's attack and the new threat against her. However, since she'd thoroughly pissed Stan off, she had to recruit an assistant. The best—and only—candidate for the job was Sissy.

Mayree hurried downstairs to bake a tray of sticky buns. It was an easy recipe, using ingredients she always had in the kitchen, as long as they hadn't expired: canned biscuit dough, store-bought caramel sauce, pecans, sugar, and cinnamon. Growing up, Irene had made everything from scratch. Bread for every meal—including those for the ranch hands, whom she served twice a day—every sauce, every jar and can of preserves, every dessert, even ice cream. Mayree had never questioned her mother's homemaking tics until she was a homemaker herself. When she discovered that just about anything could be purchased at a grocery store and thrown together with minimal effort and still be considered homemade, she decided Irene was a martyr and vowed never to make anything harder for herself than it needed to be.

She tried to open the can of dough the normal way, by peeling the little tab of paper that would make it pop open, but it wasn't working. "Dammit," she said after the third try, then grabbed her switchblade to pry off the end. She fumbled around, unable to jam the blade into the right spot, cutting her finger in the process. The cut was deep and started to bleed, spurting out with each beat of her heart. "Dammit," she said again. There were drops of blood on the counter, on her pants, on the floor. She wiped it down quickly, then rinsed and bandaged her finger. After giving herself a minute to calm down, she was finally able to open the can and make the dough.

No wonder she was frazzled; she was worn out from worry and exhaustion. She'd gotten up several times throughout the night to make sure everything was locked, moving stealthily through the darkened house with her switchblade at the ready. In the three decades since her own attack, she'd occasionally questioned her decision not to tell anyone what had happened, thinking maybe if the sheriff had gotten involved, Bobby Cox might've been arrested and punished. Nothing would've felt like enough justice; what he did caused permanent and unforgettable damage. But it might've kept him from hurting someone else, might've kept her from spending years looking over her shoulder with a sense of dread. However, if the authorities could so easily dismiss Paula's case now, reporting Bobby probably wouldn't have made much of a difference for her back then either. Maybe things hadn't actually changed as much for women since she was a teenager as she'd thought.

She saw her reflection in the oven door as she closed it; her eyelids were sagging from strain and fatigue. There was probably not enough concealer in her makeup drawer to hide the puffy, dark skin that bagged beneath her eyes. Oh well. She didn't have to look good; she only needed to show up with something far too sweet for normal humans in order to woo Sissy back.

While the sticky buns baked, Mayree wrote Paula a note telling her where she was going and slipped it underneath her door.

She'd been so distraught after leaving the station the night before, she went straight up to her room and closed herself inside. Mayree worried that if Paula woke up while she was gone, she'd be terrified. She thought about waking her up, but decided she needed the rest. She also thought about calling Sissy and inviting her over instead of going to her house, but considering how Mayree had behaved when Sissy brought over the casserole on Tuesday, there was a good chance Sissy would refuse. She'd just have to be quick.

Then she wrote a different note and left it on the kitchen table, just in case the letter-writer decided to break in while she was gone:

> Dear Paula,
> That giant nutria that's been digging in our back-yard got inside the house. He's big as a dog, so get out of here fast. If he finds you, he'll bite—and these rodents carry some terrible infections and parasites. You could end up with tularemia, tuberculosis, septicemia, or that god-awful nutria itch that causes oozing lesions that you can hardly ever get rid of. I'll be back in a minute with the sheriff and the people from pest control.
> Love,
> Mom

As soon as the treat was done, Mayree wrapped the tray in foil and settled it inside her casserole carrier—only ever used in her twenty-four-year marriage to cart food back and forth between her and Sissy's houses. Then she checked the locks a final time, scanning the grounds through each of the windows, then hurried to her car.

～

"Well, this is quite a surprise," Sissy said when she opened the door. She was already dressed for the day, wearing a teal-blue knit vest over a starched button-down with the collar up, a sleek pair of khakis, and penny loafers. The teal was a good color on her—it highlighted her eyes—and depending on how well things went, Mayree decided she might even tell her so.

"I'm here on emergency business."

Sissy crossed her arms. "It must not have been too urgent an emergency if you had time to bake."

Mayree sighed. After Sergeant Henderson's condescension the night before, she didn't need any more of it from Sissy. "This is hot, so step aside; I'm coming in." She walked through Sissy's irritatingly bright and clean living room, taking delight in disturbing the vacuum pattern on the peach-colored carpeting. How Sissy had trained her rescue schnauzer not to walk in there was beyond her imagination. But Mayree did know that the second she left, Sissy would get out her Kenmore and re-create the perfect vacuum lines. Mayree had teased her about it mercilessly over the years, demanding to know why Sissy wanted a living room that didn't look lived in, but even though she'd laugh along with Mayree at the time, she never modified what Mayree considered to be a compulsive cleaning habit.

Mayree unpacked the sticky buns while Sissy poured them each a cup of coffee from the thermal carafe she kept on the counter. Her domestic compulsions did have an upside; Sissy could reliably offer hot coffee on demand damn near any time of the day.

"What on earth happened?" Sissy said, finally noticing the blood on Mayree's pants and the bandage on her finger.

"Oh, nothing. A little kitchen accident."

"Well, here." Sissy opened her junk drawer, which of course was perfectly organized, and offered Mayree a fresh bandage.

Mayree accepted it even though she didn't need a new one. She was going to do her best to be nice. Not only did she need Sissy's help, she needed her friendship—though it was easier to admit the former than the latter. "Thank you."

"These look delicious," Sissy said. Chico trotted in from wherever he'd been and made a beeline for the table. Sissy shooed him away, then got out two of her fancy china plates, which Mayree took as strong indication that she wouldn't have to work too hard to be forgiven, which felt like a gift. Considering that their estrangement was mostly her fault, it was hard for Mayree to show up hat in hand like this. But right now, she had bigger problems than her pride to think about.

Sissy served them each a bun. "So tell me," she said with her mouth full. "What's the emergency?"

"Remember when you said on Tuesday that Kelly had been worried about Paula?"

Sissy nodded. She fed bites of sticky bun to Chico, who was shockingly ill-mannered, standing with his front paws on her knees, begging.

"Well, turns out she had reason to be." Mayree then told Sissy the whole story up to that point: the attack against Paula; her shaved head, because that would be impossible to hide; her being fired and spending the night in jail, all of which Kelly had probably told her mother already anyway; finding the opossum, though she didn't mention Stan's first visit or her impure thoughts about his new physique as he dug through the liquor cabinet; Paula's discovery of the letter; Stan's (second) visit, which she made sure was conveyed as being strictly business; and their trip to and dismissal from the police station the night before.

"Sweet Jesus, that's just awful. Just *awful*. Poor girl, she must be out of her mind with terror. I knew about some of it, but not everything. I don't know about Paula, but Kelly doesn't talk to me like she used to. I can still coax her into a conversation, especially if we're in the car together, but these days it takes *work*."

Mayree nodded, although she hadn't really thought about it. She took a deep breath. "Sissy, I need your help."

Sissy wiped caramel sauce off her lip, put down her napkin, and sat forward with an earnest expression. For all her faults—well, she really didn't have too many, if Mayree was being honest—Sissy was always ready and eager to offer assistance whether called upon or not. Mayree had neither the temperament nor the energy for volunteerism the way Sissy did. Sissy was usually the first one to deliver a casserole to anyone sick or grieving, the one to organize clothing drives for hurricane victims and food drives for the homeless during the holidays. She, of course, was the one who'd roped Mayree into working at the animal shelter, even though she'd quit and gone on to a much more sanitary position pricing donated clothing at the women's shelter boutique once a week. She'd even talked about adopting a child from Pripyat in Soviet Ukraine after the Chernobyl disaster, but Stan said he didn't want any more dependents, especially irradiated ones. "Of course," she said. "What is it?"

"I think Stan knows something he's not telling me. I told him as much and he got huffy and stormed out, which could either be because I was wrong or I was right. But I think I'm right, Sissy. I think Frank did something to piss somebody off bad, and Stan knows who it is."

Sissy's face brightened. "And you want me to see if I can find out?"

Mayree nodded. "Will you?"

"Of course I will!"

Her quick offer to help made Mayree feel both relieved and remorseful. She knew she didn't deserve to be let off the hook so easily. She knew she ought to admit it, but right now it was more important to focus on Sissy's relationship with Stan. "Honestly, Sissy, I didn't think it would be so easy to convince you. When you said you stopped putting mushrooms in your King Ranch casserole, it sounded like you were glad to be done with him."

Sissy jabbed her fork into the tray and speared another sticky bun, which she silently offered to Mayree. Mayree shook her head, so Sissy put it on her own plate. "I thought I was, too," she said. "It was fun at first not having him around. I started sleeping in the middle of the bed, not worrying if I wiggled too much or snored, having all the covers to myself. Not having to pick up after him constantly or take his suits to the cleaners or look at his stubble all over the bathroom counter. After Dean went to Lackland, it's just been Kelly and me, so I don't have to cook a big dinner every night. I mean, sometimes I do, but if I don't feel like it, we can eat TV dinners or just have cookies and ice cream if we want." She looked at Mayree with a forlorn expression.

"Same here," Mayree said, nodding in joyless agreement. Frank died two weeks after Sissy's son, Dean, left for Air Force Officer Training School in San Antonio in October, so she well understood the abrupt transition to an all-female household. "Especially the ice cream."

"I don't know if I miss Stan so much as I miss the idea of him, but either way, the truth is I'm lonely."

Mayree nodded again, but she wasn't ready to admit that she felt the same way—not so much because Frank was dead, but because she'd missed Sissy so dearly.

"Doesn't help that I don't have you anymore. Remember how we used to fantasize about running off together and living like old spinster sisters?"

"Our house would be pristine." Mayree gave her a wry smile. "Especially the carpet lines."

"Very funny." Sissy gave her the bird.

Mayree kept the smile on her lips, but didn't laugh, didn't say what Sissy probably expected her to, which was that she was there now, all was forgiven and forgotten, they'd go back to how things were immediately and never look back. It's not that Mayree didn't want those things; she just didn't know how to cross back over that bridge. If she was a better, happier person, maybe it wouldn't be so hard. She felt like a completely different person than she was even a week ago. Old, miserable, incapable of fun, and scared for Paula's and her safety. Trying to slip back into the once-easy friendship she and Sissy'd had seemed almost frivolous now, and she felt a sagging in her insides at the loss.

Sissy, clearly feeling rejected, took another bite of sticky bun. "Anyway, I've been thinking that maybe a little stubble on the bathroom counter isn't such a bad thing."

"Maybe not," Mayree said. Nor was homemade King Ranch casserole.

"So, I'd been considering inviting Stan home for dinner one night soon, just to see where things stand. He takes Kelly out to dinner once a week, but I haven't seen him in almost two months." Mayree almost blurted out that she might be surprised at how good he looked, but then thought better of it and stayed quiet. "If he agreed to come, then I could also ask him about Frank. I might have to get him drunk so he'll spill any secrets he might be holding on to. And if he's drunk, maybe he'll get sentimental and beg me to take him back, which I'd seriously consider doing if he apologized for being such an ass and promised never to cheat on me again. I can kill two birds with one bottle." She winked at Mayree.

"Thank you, Sissy." Mayree reached out and took her hand, which was warm and soft. "I don't know what else to do. I'm scared to let Paula leave the house."

"I'll call him right now." She got the phone and dialed his number.

Mayree's heart pumped in her ears as she waited, watching Sissy twirl the cord around her manicured finger.

Sissy's face brightened as she gave Mayree a thumbs-up. Then she obviously tried to calm her voice into something soothing and seductive. "Hi there. It's me . . . No, everything's fine, it's just been a while since we talked. You've been on my mind . . . Oh yeah? . . . Well, that's nice to hear." She flashed a smile at Mayree, her cheeks pinking. "So I was thinking about making oyster pie, you know, before the season ends, and I know how much you love it. What do you think about coming here for dinner tonight?" She crossed her fingers. Then a frown

225

darkened her face. "Is that right? . . . Well, do you think you could take a rain check? I mean, do any of those guys know how to make an oyster pie?" She rolled her eyes at Mayree, then forced a smile. "Of course Tito does, he's a chef. But you always said mine was your favorite. Besides, isn't the max for Texas Hold'em nine players? I'm sure they'll have enough if you skip . . . Well, of course, you know I do." Her face lit up again. "That would be lovely, yes . . . White, I think . . . No, it's Saturday--I'm sure she has plans. It'll just be the two of us . . . Champagne, really?" She flared her eyes at Mayree. "I'd love that." She laughed. "Sure, why not two? Let's celebrate . . . something . . . Seven's perfect . . . I'm looking forward to it, too. See you then!"

She put the peach-colored receiver back on the cradle and turned to Mayree. "We're on!"

"Thank baby Jesus."

"I know. When he said he had poker, my heart sank. But obviously he came around. And he's bringing champagne!" She leaned forward. "You know what? I think he misses me, too."

For many reasons, Mayree sent up a silent prayer of thanks to whoever might be listening that she didn't act on her silly, fleeting attraction to Stan. He may have said he didn't want to sleep with her, but she could've seduced him if she'd really wanted to. Of course he'd have slept with her; men were dogs. Besides, he wasn't that attractive, anyway. Sex with Stan probably wouldn't have even been that satisfying, and worse, it would've killed Sissy. No matter what had transpired between them, she didn't want to cause any more pain to her friend.

"I think he does, Sissy. I really do."

Paula

After returning home from the police station Friday night, Paula took to her bed like an invalid. She desperately wanted the escape of sleep, but her mind was too busy remembering the horrific scenes from Saturday night that she'd tried so hard to forget as well as imagining what her attacker might do to her next. Her mother was obviously shaken, too, because she spent half the night roaming around the house, checking locks on all the doors and windows, even Paula's. Mayree didn't even try not to wake Paula up; she walked in with her flashlight and little switchblade—as if that was going to do any good against an intruder—and scared Paula half to death. The first time Mayree barged in, Paula was still awake but jerked upright nonetheless. "Jesus, Mom! What the hell?"

"Oh hush, I'm not here to hurt *you*." Mayree had marched over to the window and rattled the lock, toggling it open and then closed again to be sure it was secure. "I'm just making sure we're locked up tight. Go back to sleep."

Paula was exhausted. That whole week had been exhausting. She hadn't had a solid night of rest since before the incident, she'd eaten poorly, and her nerves were like a tangle of live wires. It felt like the only thing keeping her alive right now was adrenaline.

She finally fell into a dreamless sleep around seven in the morning, and when she woke up four hours later, she still felt too scared and vulnerable to leave the cocoon of her own bed. She hoped she could convince her mother to bring her some coffee and, despite their being at odds, maybe even sit with her for a while.

"Mom?" she called out through the closed door. "Mom?" She couldn't hear any movement. Reluctantly, she got up. "Mom?" she called from the top of the stairs. Why didn't she answer? She checked Mayree's bedroom, then the bathroom. The bed was unmade but the shower was dry. "Mom?" She crept downstairs, her imagination conjuring images of a marauder waiting for her.

The kitchen was a mess. She peered through the window above the sink full of dirty cookware. Mayree's car was gone. She poured a cup of lukewarm coffee and took it to the table. There she saw a smear of blood and the note Mayree had written about the nutria. She screamed.

"Paula! What in the hell's the matter?" Mayree rushed inside, slamming the back door behind her.

"Nutria!" She leaped onto a chair and climbed onto the kitchen table.

"Oh, come down from there," Mayree said, holding out her hand to help. "There's no nutria. I wrote that in case someone broke in."

Paula let her mother help her down and when she did, she collapsed into Mayree's arms. The relief was overwhelming—not because there wasn't an enormous wild rodent, but because just having her mother close made her feel slightly less terrified and alone.

Mayree hugged her awkwardly, then extricated herself from Paula's clench. "Didn't you see the note I put under your door?"

She shook her head. "All I saw was blood everywhere and this note on the table. I thought you'd been bitten."

"I cut myself opening a can of biscuits." She held up her bandaged finger, then she pointed at the table. "And this piddly little smudge hardly counts as *blood everywhere*. I just didn't do a very good job of wiping it off. I was going to clean everything up when I got back." She softened her voice. "But I understand. With everything that's happened, it's easy to let your mind run off wild like that. I'm sorry."

Paula wiped her eyes with the back of her hand. She knew apologies didn't come easily to her mother. "It's okay. I'm glad nothing bad happened. No nutria itch or whatever." She gave her a shy smile.

Mayree let out a soft chuckle. "No, in fact, I have some good news. I went over to Sissy's. She's going to have Stan over for dinner tonight to try to get some information out of him."

"But he said he didn't know anything."

"Maybe he doesn't, maybe he does. But if the police aren't going to do anything, then it's up to us. And if that sonofabitch comes here looking for you, he's going to get something else instead." Mayree unsheathed her biggest kitchen knife from the block it was stored in and brandished it.

Paula was moved by her mother's bravado, especially since it seemed to be for her benefit, but she still felt a surge of panic when she thought about the guy coming after her. "Mom, we shouldn't stay here," Paula said.

Mayree tested the sharpness of the knife with her thumb, then pulled the sharpener out of the drawer and began to draw the blade smoothly against it from heel to tip.

"Did you hear me?"

"I heard you. I'm thinking."

Paula watched her mother glide the blade gently, firmly, again and again, testing it periodically. It was almost hypnotic. Paula had watched Mayree sharpen various knives many times over the years, but had never asked her how she learned to do it. For all Paula knew, little girls living out in the middle of nowhere whetted knives as a matter of course. It made sense, not having the benefit of neighbors or police to call in the event of an emergency. If Mayree had ever needed to use one, Paula wouldn't know; her mother rarely spoke about her childhood on the ranch. But somebody must've taught her the value of keeping a sharp edge handy, since she'd started carrying that switchblade of hers like it was an extension of her own body.

"Maybe you should spend the night with Kelly tonight. You could eavesdrop on Stan and Sissy like y'all used to when you were little. And don't try to deny it; I know y'all did it to Daddy and me, too. We thought it was funny."

"Then why'd you yell at us?"

"We had to, obviously. That's what parents do. Anyway, go hang out with Kelly."

Paula thought about the Sigma Nu party that night, and Mike with his creased jeans and smooth allure, and Kelly, so eager, always so eager to find some fun. "I can't. She's going to a frat party."

Mayree looked up at her. "Oh, the hell she is. Hand me the phone."

Paula did and watched as Mayree dialed the Cagles' number.

"It's me," she said by way of hello. "No way should Kelly go to some godforsaken fraternity party tonight with everything that's going on . . . Well, like you said, they don't tell us shit these days . . . That's a good idea . . . No, not here. They should stay at your house, it's safer. Just tell them to stay in Kelly's room . . . Okay, I'll tell her . . . Good luck with Stan and thanks again."

She hung up the phone with a definitive smack. "You're going to Kelly's."

"But what if Kelly doesn't want to stay home?" Paula heard the whine in her own voice; she felt like she was ten years old again, worried that Kelly would choose one of a multitude of invitations that Paula hadn't been included in instead of her. To Kelly's credit, she'd usually said she'd attend a birthday party or other event only if Paula could go, too, or else she'd decline and do something with Paula instead.

"Sissy draws the line when she needs to."

"What about you? I can't just leave you here alone."

"I'm not alone. I've got this." She held up the knife again.

"Mom, come on. No offense, but look at you. You're not exactly built like the Hulk. If someone tried to come in . . ." Paula shook her head, as though to banish the thought.

Mayree stepped over and cupped her daughter's chin. She looked back and forth into Paula's eyes with an alarming intensity. Paula didn't dare try to move away.

"Let him try," Mayree said.

~

Paula walked in with her overnight bag slung across her shoulder and went into the kitchen to say hello. She knew that Sissy, who loved food and feeding people, was going to insist she eat something right away.

"Hey, Aunt Sissy. I'm here."

Sissy, stirring something on the stove, hugged her with her free arm. "I'm glad, sweet girl. Look at you. No offense to your mama, but when was the last time you had a decent meal?"

Neither the smell of Sissy's cooking nor her predictable worry stirred Paula's appetite; she was concerned about Mayree being alone in the house, about the note, the threat, the future, everything. "It's not her fault. I just haven't been that hungry lately."

"Kelly's in her room. Uncle Stan'll be here soon. He'll want to see you both before he leaves, but I told him y'all were studying so he and I can have some time down here alone." She winked. "I made y'all a picnic to eat upstairs, okay? Promise me you'll eat something."

Paula nodded and went up to Kelly's room. The door was open, and she paused before entering. Kelly was lying on her bed, listening to something on her Walkman, one foot tapping to the beat. How blithe she looked. How unaffected. Paula wondered if she'd ever be able to lie in such calm repose again, listening to music and thinking, ostensibly, of nothing but the lyrics to a song. It made her feel alien—even more than usual—that she now lived with a pervasive feeling of uncertainty and fear. She felt so alone with it. Exactly one week ago, she'd experienced something that bisected her life into a before and an after. Since then, her reality had fallen out of sync with everyone else's. Kelly, lying on her bed, still existed in the Before. Kelly knew what had happened, but she didn't *know*. Paula, on the other hand, her strap digging into her shoulder, realized at that moment that she would hereafter exist in the After, a state that would be intimately known only to her.

"Hiya," Kelly said, sitting up. "Why are you just standing there, weirdo? Come in."

~

At seven o'clock on the dot, the doorbell rang. Paula and Kelly looked at each other as they listened to the soft, affectionate sounds exchanged between Kelly's parents. "Do you think they'll get back together?" Kelly asked.

Paula shrugged. She'd borne witness to Stan's angry response to Mayree's accusations that he was keeping information from them. He looked harder than he used to, and not just because he was more muscular. "He seemed happier when he lived here than he does now," she said.

"My mom said that widows live like ten years longer than widowers do, because men get used to having someone do everything for them, and so when their wives die, they fall apart. But women finally get a break when their husbands kick the bucket. They get to hang out with their friends all the time, travel wherever they want, eat whatever they want, watch whatever they want on TV," Kelly said. "I don't know if it works the same way with divorces or separations or whatever, though. I think my mom was happier when he lived here, too."

"Let's go listen," Paula said. She was, in fact, as eager as Mayree to learn if Stan knew something that might help them figure out who'd written the letter and what they wanted. She wondered if it could be connected somehow to her father's mistress. Or one of the ones before her. An angry husband or son, maybe? Or a business associate her father might have crossed? She still could hardly believe that he'd failed her mother—and her—so miserably.

They crept down the stairs, the carpeting muffling their footsteps, and tiptoed into the darkened room that had been—and ostensibly still was—Stan's study. All his legal texts were still on the shelves, his diploma from UT School of Law and a photo of him shaking hands with Governor Bill Clements still hung on the wall, and the desk was still littered with various awards and filled, presumably, with his files. He once counseled Kelly and Paula to always keep backups of important documents at home or in a safe-deposit box in case something happened to the ones at their future firm. "You can't be too careful," he'd told them. "Somebody leaves a cigarette burning and—poof. Or you get subpoenaed. Robbed. You never know."

They could hear typical kitchen sounds—the oven door opening and closing, the tapping of salad tongs, a clink of glasses, vague conversation punctuated by an occasional laugh or giggle. "Sounds like they're getting along," Paula said.

Kelly nodded. "Let's get closer."

They slipped out of the study and into the hall, sliding down onto the floor just outside the kitchen door.

Stan and Sissy's talk was calm as they exchanged little bits of uninteresting information, caught each other up on their various recent observations and happenings. He complimented her on the oyster pie, and she topped off his glass of wine. Paula closed her eyes for a moment, lulled by the sense of being transported back in time. She and Kelly used to think they were so clever, hiding in the hallways when they were younger, listening. But more often than not, they fell asleep to the sounds of their parents' conversations—whether it was just one of the couples or all four of them together—their attempts at spying thwarted by fatigue. Eventually, the owners of those voices on the other side of the wall would find them and put them to bed.

"Honey," Sissy said now in her sweetest voice. "There's something I wanted to ask you."

"Hmm?"

"Do you know who might've tried to hurt Paula?"

Paula and Kelly flared their eyes at each other, the temporary spell of comfort broken by the sound of Stan dropping his fork onto his plate.

"Shit, Sissy. Is that what this is about? Here I thought you'd finally forgiven me, but you're just running some kind of reconnaissance mission."

"No, no, honey. It's not just that, I swear. I really did want to see you." Paula could imagine Sissy reaching over to smooth Stan's wrinkled forehead or touch him on the arm. "It's just that they're nervous, you know? And rightfully so, it sounds like. Paula got a nasty letter from whoever attacked her. If we can do something to help them, we should."

"What kind of letter?" Stan asked, his voice grave.

"I don't know exactly. But it scared them."

"Sissy, I know you like helping people, but you need to stay out of this one."

"This one? Why? What's going on?"

"Look, Mayree already asked me—you obviously know that—and . . ." There was a pause. "Jesus Christ, I can't believe I'm going to say this out loud."

Sissy's voice was serious. "What is it, Stan?"

Stan exhaled heavily. "Frank did some unscrupulous shit in his time. I'm sure Mayree knows most of it, or at least some of it."

"I'm not sure what she knows, but yes, some of it for sure," Sissy said. "Is this about his gambling? Is there someone after them for that?"

"It's possible." Stan was silent for a moment. Paula's heart raced in anticipation of whatever news he was about to deliver.

"Stan, talk to me."

Paula could hear him blow out a long breath. "Okay. There's this one thing he did, and I don't know if it's connected to what happened to Paula or not. I swore I'd never say anything about it, not even to you."

"Well, you have to tell me now."

"A year or so after Paula was born, Frank allegedly—and I mean *allegedly*—fathered a kid with another woman."

Paula's mouth fell open. Months after learning of his affairs, she was still processing the loathsome idea that her father was a cheater. But a kid? After a few silent seconds that seemed to stretch into minutes, during which time Paula's heart seemed to stop beating, Sissy said, "No."

Kelly took Paula's hand and leaned in close. "Call your mom and tell her to get over here," she whispered. "She needs to hear this."

March 31, 1989

Dear Mama,
Some people are so damn stupid.
     Love,
     Your son

Mayree

Mayree barged into the Cagles' house, breathless. She hadn't run that far or that fast since she was a little girl chasing cattle on the ranch. Still, she paused to lock the door behind her before rushing into the kitchen.

"Mayree, what are you doing here? Did something happen?" Sissy asked, standing up.

"First off, why wasn't your front door locked when somebody could be out there trying to kill Paula and maybe even the rest of us? And second, what in the goddamn hell is going on, Stanley Cagle, you fucking liar?"

"Whoa, now." Stan lifted his hands and stood up slowly, as though Mayree was going to shoot him.

"Don't try to weasel out of this one. The girls heard what you told Sissy just now about Frank having another kid."

Stan shot a look at Paula and Kelly, who now stood sheepishly in the doorway. Then he sat down and leaned his head all the way back until it rested on the top of the chair. Mayree looked at his neck, clean-shaven for Sissy's benefit, that Lothario, that rake, his Adam's apple protruding like a hillock from level ground. If she'd thought to bring her knife when she'd dashed out of the house after Paula's call, she might've been tempted to press the edge of it against that vulnerable flesh. As if sensing her intent, he lifted his head and looked at her.

"I don't know if it was really his," he said. "Or even if it's relevant right now. Are you sure you want Paula to hear this?"

Mayree glanced at Paula, whose face looked gaunt and bewildered. She'd sounded calm and slightly incredulous on the phone a few minutes before, but now she looked like she'd seen a ghost. "No, actually, I don't. But it's too late for that now."

"Fine." He looked at Paula, too. "Sorry for this, P."

Paula just stared at him.

"Frank had a thing with this woman—"

"Which woman?" Mayree interrupted.

Stan paused. "I don't remember her name."

"Horseshit."

"He had a thing with her for a few months. Maybe more. I don't know exactly."

"Horseshit," Mayree said again.

"Do you want to hear this or not?"

Mayree flicked her fingers at him in the *go-on* gesture her mother used to use with the chickens.

"This was two or three years before we even knew y'all, so I actually don't know the precise timeline," he said. "Frank told me about it much later—and I'm talking around two years ago—after this kid shows up at Frank's office and tells him he's his son."

Mayree's mind scrolled back two years to 1987. The perm Sissy talked her into getting that made her look like a poodle. Paula and Kelly's graduation from high school. That baby, Jessica somebody, who'd been rescued from a well in her backyard in Midland after being trapped for more than two days. The tornado that killed damn near everyone in Saragosa. And, according to Stan, a boy that showed up at Frank's office. She felt light-headed, so she lowered herself carefully into one of Sissy's kitchen chairs. One she might well have been sitting in when the aforementioned boy supposedly knocked on her husband's door.

"Frank said he remembered his mother, but there was no way he could've been his kid because of the timing. Plus, he didn't look anything like Frank."

Sissy asked, "Frank said he didn't look like him?"

"Yeah. But also . . . I didn't think so either."

"You were there?"

"No," he said. "Well, yes, but later, I mean. This kind of thing happens sometimes to men with money, though usually it's the woman who shows up."

"Oh my god, Dad. Has it happened to you?" Kelly asked, but Stan ignored her and continued.

"Frank told me what had happened, that this kid showed up and started making demands out of nowhere, and he asked me to help him . . . take care of it. So I did."

Mayree felt her stomach drop. "What the hell do you mean, *take care of it?*"

"Jesus, Stan, what did you do? Did you . . . hurt somebody?" Sissy asked.

"If by *hurt* you mean *kill*, then no," Stan said, shaking his head. "But I suppose I hurt someone, yeah. We had to teach him a lesson. Make sure he wouldn't come around again down the line."

Kelly and Paula both stared at him, aghast. "We?" Paula asked.

Mayree was aghast, too. "Do you mean you physically hurt him? Or something else?"

"That's not important."

"The hell it isn't," Mayree said. "You must not have done a very good job, whatever you did, if he's the one who attacked Paula."

"Look, I helped my best friend, something that all y'all ought to be able to understand," he said, pointing at the four of them. "He was full of himself, this kid, demanding Frank acknowledge him and give him money. He threatened to make a scene, to tell you and Paula, his business partners, everybody. It's hard to prove a negative, you know—that you *didn't* do something—and it would've been unnecessarily bad for Frank's reputation, not to mention his family life, if this kid was allowed to run around making false accusations."

Mayree couldn't believe what she was hearing. Or, more truthfully, she could, but she didn't want to. Knowing that Frank had been chronically unfaithful was bad enough, but the idea of him fathering a child—a sibling to Paula—was simply unthinkable. If she'd ever felt alone before, it wasn't worse than how she felt now, imagining her husband of twenty-four years as a father to a human being she didn't know existed. Had this ever happened to her own father? Did she have any half siblings out in the world? Had it happened to Bobby Cox? In the almost thirty-two years since he'd raped her, impregnated her, had he done the same to other women? If she'd given birth to Bobby's child, how many siblings would it have by now? Bobby, Frank. Bobby, Frank. BobbyFrank. BobbyFrankBobbyFrankBobbyFrank. "Lord, Sissy, I need to lie down."

Sissy rushed to her and helped her to the living room. She ran back to the kitchen to dampen a towel, which she placed on Mayree's forehead. "Girls, get," she said. Kelly and Paula disappeared as quickly as they had when they were children.

"I'm sorry, Mayree," Stan said. "This is exactly why I didn't want to tell you last night. It's awful business."

"But what does this have to do with Paula? Why would this kid hurt *her*?" Mayree asked. "It doesn't make sense."

"Stan, you have to go to the police," Sissy said, holding Mayree's hand. "You have to tell them everything."

"I can't do that. But I've already started making inquiries. After I left Mayree's last night, I called some people who might be able to help and I'm waiting to hear back."

"If it has something to do with that letter, we can't just wait around," Sissy said. "You know something Mayree and Paula don't and you have to tell."

He took Sissy's free hand in his and looked at her face as if Mayree wasn't even in the room. "God, it feels good to tell you the truth after carrying this around for so long. And by the way: no, it hasn't happened to me."

Sissy wrenched her hand away. "Confessing doesn't make it go away, Stan. You have to go to the police. If you don't, then any good you think you did before means nothing now."

"I told you, I already started looking into it. I'm going to figure it out."

"Stan, what the hell is going on? Why are you being so cagey about this?" Mayree asked, pushing herself upright.

"Because I got involved. Like I said, this kid was making threats. I have—*had*—a friend on the force who owed me a favor. This gets out and people find out I was part of it, I could get in serious trouble."

The idea of Stan "teaching somebody a lesson" was deeply disturbing, but not as disturbing as her daughter being targeted. "If this kid is after Paula, it doesn't matter what kind of trouble you could get into."

Stan shrugged. "There's a good chance the kid didn't have anything to do with this. It could be two totally unrelated threats. There's been a bunch of break-ins; maybe someone thought y'all had come into some money and decided to go after it. This was just the first possibility that came to mind."

"Fine, then let's just rule it out. Tell me what you know about him, and I'll talk to the police," Sissy said. "I won't say anything about you."

"You and I share a last name, Sissy. If you start poking around, it won't be too hard to trace what happened back to me."

"Kelly," Sissy called toward the hallway while pinning Stan with a glare. "I know you and Paula are still there, so don't try to scurry off. Go into Daddy's filing drawer and start digging."

"What are we looking for?" Kelly called back.

"I don't know," Sissy said.

Mayree could hear the girls clambering to their feet and whispering. She knew she didn't deserve the ferocity with which Sissy was standing up for her. She squeezed Sissy's hand.

"Girls, don't," Stan said. He tried to stand, but Sissy grabbed on to his arm and pulled him back. He regained his balance, shook off her grip, and flung the chair to the ground. He stormed into his study, Sissy and Mayree close behind, and stood over his daughter as she riffled through his files. Mayree thought he might physically remove Kelly— he was strong enough to do it—but he just stood there with his fists balled and his face turning an ugly shade of red.

"You won't find anything," he said in a growl. Then he turned to Mayree. "I did have a file, but after Frank died, I burned it. I didn't think I'd need it again. The kid threatened Frank, not you or Paula. When he was gone, I thought that was the end of it. Bygones."

Paula, who'd hardly uttered a word since Mayree arrived, said rather sweetly, "But, Uncle Stan, you told us we should always keep a backup of our files. Don't you have a backup somewhere?"

"P, if I did, I'd tell you. I swear. I got rid of both. Right outside, in fact. You know those aloe vera plants in the back in those big ceramic pots? I dumped one of them out and burned the files in it a few days after his funeral."

"What? You weren't even living here then," Sissy said. "Where was I?"

"Out somewhere. I waited down the street until you pulled away, then let myself in. You don't believe me? Go dump the plant out and check the pot. I didn't realize it was going to turn the inside black."

"This is ridiculous," Mayree said. "You have to tell me who these people are. Who's the mother? Where is she?" She wanted to hurt Stan somehow. To punch him in the chest and throat and face. To kick him in the groin. To scream obscenities and insults until he caved, until he cried. He was a good proxy for her late husband. Instead, it was she who

felt kicked and punched and screamed at, and she who felt utterly helpless and ruined, and she—who hadn't cried about anything in years, not
even after the deaths of Frank, her financial stability, or her friendship
with Sissy—who began to quietly sob.

"I can't tell you, because it might not be him and I'd get in trouble
anyway. But I'm going to get to the bottom of this, Mayree. I'll find this
kid and if it's him who sent that letter, I'll make sure that's the last thing
he does where you and Paula are concerned. I just have to be careful or
else I could lose my license. I'll lose everything."

Sissy held on to Mayree and said, "Stan, if you're not going to look
after my best friend and a child who is like our own, then fuck you. If
nothing else, you'll for sure lose me."

"Sissy, come on," Stan said.

"I mean it, Stan. Either tell us now what you know or we're done."

Mayree looked at Sissy, this unprecedented fury hardening her
lovely face. She didn't know if she'd ever felt more valued, more but-
tressed, by anyone in her life.

"Dad," Kelly said in a pleading voice.

Stan closed his eyes for a moment, and an expectant hush fell over
them all. Then he looked at Sissy, then at the rest of them. "Please don't
worry about this. I'm going to find him, I promise," he said. "And if I do
and it's not him, I'll figure out who it was. I have some other ideas, guys
Frank owed money to. Trust me, okay?" He hugged Kelly and kissed
her on top of the head, then grabbed his jacket and left.

Mayree wished she could trust Stan to fix everything. But trusting
men to do what they promised hadn't worked out too well for her thus far.

"I don't know what the hell is wrong with that man," Sissy said to
Mayree after they heard the front door close. She yanked a few tissues
from a nearby box and handed them to her.

"Thank you, Siss," Mayree said, shaking her head. "That was incred-
ible." Sissy smiled.

"What did he mean by 'teach him a lesson'? What do you think he did?" Paula asked, her face full of concern.

"Something stupid and illegal," Sissy said. "Who knows. I say we give him a day or so and see if he comes clean."

Kelly said, "I don't want him to get in trouble."

"Well, I don't either, but we also have to worry about Paula and Mayree."

Mayree turned to Paula. "Are you okay? This is an awful shock."

Paula nodded, though she didn't look okay. Kelly put her arm around her. "Let's go look through the rest of the files," Kelly said. "Maybe we'll find something." Paula nodded again.

Mayree pressed the towel against her eyes, then blew her nose. "I need a cigarette," she said to Sissy. "And a drink."

"Of course, honey. I'll get you something. In fact, I'll get us all something. You can smoke out back."

Mayree patted her pockets, realizing that she was wearing her bathrobe and pajamas. Yearning for some comfort, she'd changed out of her regular clothes just before Paula called. How far she'd fallen, she thought, that being in her old robe by sundown was her new definition of comfort. She probably looked as ragged as she felt, but at least she had a pack and a lighter handy when she needed them. And Sissy.

She and Sissy left the girls in Stan's office. While Sissy made them a drink, Mayree went out to the back porch and lit up. A cool, humid wind was ushering parcels of cloudy air across a low altitude, mostly obscuring the almost-full moon. As she took that first lusty inhale, she stared up at the sky, which looked like it was gathering up a storm, and thought about Frank and the kind of women he'd cheated on her with.

After she'd discovered his infidelity, she wondered if he'd ever really been attracted to her, except as a possible heiress to a lucrative ten-thousand-acre ranch. She'd resisted him, especially at first. She wasn't a knockout. Maybe it was just the chase that fascinated him. Once he caught her, like a roper handling livestock, she'd tried to meet his expectations. She performed sexual and social duties for him. Hosted dinner parties and indulged hangovers. Birthed a kid, albeit a girl—although not having a male heir didn't seem to bother him like it would have her father. She never met any of his other women, except for the secretary, but she imagined the rest of them looked like she did and nothing like Mayree: curvy and attentive, coiffed and soft-spoken. But who the fuck knew what turned men on when it came down to it? Maybe they were so base they could come thrusting inside anybody.

"Here you go," Sissy said, closing the sliding glass door behind her. She handed Mayree a glass of champagne. "Stan brought it, but we didn't get around to it. Just as well. Cheers."

Mayree lifted her glass, then drained it in a gulp. From underneath her arm, Sissy withdrew the bottle and poured. "I figured that was how you're feeling."

"I really thought he was going to give us something to go on," Mayree said after another gulp. "Now I don't know what the hell we're supposed to do. I'm not really of a mind to go back down to the police station for a third time this week."

"We're going to have to sleep on it. We'll figure something out."

Mayree exhaled a long breath. "Do you think—if Frank hadn't died when he did—do you think he'd have ever told me?"

"Oh, honey, I honestly don't know. I don't think Stan would've ever told me he'd cheated on me if I hadn't figured it out. As long as Frank figured you didn't know, what would've been the incentive to confess?"

She thought about it. Would Frank have eventually outgrown his philandering? Maybe once he was too fat or too tired to chase skirts? Would they have settled into a new commitment to one another, maybe even one in which they told each other the truths about themselves? Truths that they hadn't even known were relevant until they'd wormed into the crevices of their marriage and began to rot it from the inside out? There had been some tender moments early on, lying in bed together after making love, or sharing a look over Paula's head as she went about the business of growing into herself. Maybe, if they'd had enough time, after traveling their personal way of sorrows, enduring all the trials and tribulations, they could've finally found their way back to each other, like pilgrims on a marital quest. But then again, maybe this was just the way it would've been, regardless of whether Frank had died. Mayree shrugged.

"Well, it doesn't matter now, does it?" Sissy asked.

"No, I guess not," Mayree said. "But if he really did get somebody pregnant, what does that mean? Not for me, but for Paula?"

"I honestly don't know."

"If he's after an inheritance, he'll be sorely disappointed. Even if he could legally claim it, there's nothing to give him—at least I don't think there is," Mayree said. "Worse for her would be the sudden appearance of a half brother. How's she supposed to handle that?"

They were quiet for a moment, letting the question float around in the humid air.

"Listen, you're already dressed for bed," Sissy finally said. "Let's have a slumber party. I don't want you and Paula going back to your house alone."

Mayree refilled Sissy's glass, then her own. "You have any more of this?"

"Yep. Another whole bottle."

"Get it, will ya?"

"So you'll stay?"

"Sure," Mayree said. She didn't want to admit how good the idea of a slumber party actually sounded.

"Great!" Sissy put down her glass and started for the kitchen, then turned back. "Hey, I have a question."

"Shoot."

"You know what that useless piece of skin attached to a penis is called?"

Mayree could feel the giggle bubbling to the surface like the champagne in her glass. "A man," she said, and they both laughed so hard they nearly cried.

Paula

Paula and Kelly quickly devised a plan: they pulled all Stan's files out of the drawer and each took half. They flipped through each one, regardless of the handwritten title on the manila tabs, in case he'd devised a secret filing system in situations just like this one.

"That's actually a great idea," Kelly said. "We should come up with a code or something for our future firm. Or write the real names in invisible ink to put snoopers off the trail."

"Quidnuncs," Paula said. "Yentas."

"What's the matter with you? Did you hit your head on something?"

"No. Just remembering more vocabulary words. Snooper synonyms."

Paula couldn't reconcile the man who'd made her study for spelling bees and school exams, taken her fishing, taught her the constellations, snuggled her after nightmares, laughed at her dumb jokes, bought her ice cream, and provided a sense of security with the one her mother and Uncle Stan were arguing about. As she'd gotten older and understood more about relationships, she'd suspected that her father was unfaithful. The countless late nights, her mother's frustration, the fact that her parents didn't show much affection for one another were all banal clues, but the clincher was the time she'd picked up the phone to call Kelly and heard her father talking to a woman who was crying. *Come on, Cecile,* he'd said. *You know I care about you. But I can't do this anymore.* It was the month before Paula graduated from high school. She and Kelly were going to go shopping for outfits to wear to their joint graduation party. Paula couldn't remember hearing her father speak like that—intimate, soft, apologetic—with anyone but her. He didn't even talk that way with Mayree. It had made Paula vibrate with an emotion she couldn't name, as if she'd been walking along on solid ground and someone had tripped her and sent her falling into a heretofore-unknown abyss. She'd hung up the phone and tiptoed into her parents' bathroom, where Mayree was staring intently at herself in the mirror, putting her hair into soft rollers.

"You don't have to do that," she'd whispered to her mother. "You're beautiful just as you are."

Mayree had looked at Paula as she rolled a segment of frosted hair around a pink sponge. "If only it were so easy," she'd said, then returned her focus to her reflection.

Looking back at her family life after her mother confirmed Paula's suspicions helped explain why Mayree had always seemed so unhappy. Knowing this part of him was still new to Paula. She could only imagine what it was like for her mother, having lived with that knowledge for so long.

She and Kelly went through each file and found nothing. No hint of an illegitimate kid or a cover-up. She hoped that meant it wasn't true; she didn't think she could forgive her father for hiding something as significant as that.

"Want to go check the pot to see if he really burned something in it?" Kelly asked.

Paula thought about it. "I can't see what good it would do. He could've burned anything in it. Like he said, it's hard to prove a negative."

"I guess." Kelly began the process of returning the files in their original order to her father's drawer.

"I have to pee," Paula said, feeling suddenly overwhelmed. "Be right back."

But instead of the bathroom, Paula went to Kelly's room and sat down on the ecru-colored bed. All week, each time she'd thought about what happened on Saturday night, she'd wondered if the guy would've assaulted her if she hadn't been so desperate to call Will. Or if she hadn't been drunk. Or if Will hadn't broken up with her. Or if she hadn't dated him in the first place. Now there was this new information about a potential half brother who was seeking revenge for something. A half brother! All her life she'd wished for a sibling. Kelly had mostly made up for the lack of a real sister and Dean was like a brother, but nonetheless, she'd always felt a specific vacancy in her life where a blood relative might've been, like feeling homesick for a place that had never actually existed. But she certainly didn't want one under these circumstances, especially one who may have tried to kill her.

And if he'd tried to hurt her—or "only needed to use her for a while" as his note indicated—because he had a bone to pick with their father, then maybe it didn't matter that she'd been drunk and emotional about her wayward boyfriend. Maybe he'd have done the same thing at another time and place. Maybe it hadn't been her fault at all.

Thinking about her father awakened the same lonesome, needy desire to call Will that had started all this on Saturday night. She felt like an alcoholic sneaking a drink, knowing it was a bad choice but unable to stop herself all the same. She was already regretting it even as she punched in Will's number. It was Saturday; he was probably out somewhere. Probably with Amber, the girl with the long strawberry-blonde hair that Kelly had seen him with the day before yesterday. If he wasn't home, should she leave a message, as she had a few days ago? Her palms were clammy as she pressed the receiver against her ear. Each ring ratcheted up her heart rate another notch until finally, the machine: "You know what to do."

Cupping the mouthpiece to keep her voice from traveling, she whispered, "Hi. It's me. Paula. I don't really know why I'm calling. I guess it's because a lot of stuff's been going on lately and I—I don't know—I just miss you." Why had she thought calling him would allay her fears about the attacker coming back? Or help her sort out her feelings about her father's possible love child and what her uncle Stan may or may not have done to him? She wished that being with Kelly was enough to make her feel better. Or Mayree. "Never mind. Forget I called. Sorry." She pressed the switch to disconnect the call, then quietly returned the handset to the base. She sighed, hating herself for being so foolish. She flushed Kelly's toilet and went back downstairs.

～

Paula didn't get up until ten the next morning, having finally fallen asleep close to dawn. She'd lain awake, tormented by what she'd learned about her father along with all the other thoughts and fears she'd been suffering. Trying not to disturb her sleeping friend, she untangled herself from the covers on her side of Kelly's bed and peeked out the window behind the blackout curtains. Beyond the swaying oak branches, the sky was a cloudy, cozy gray. They'd heard on the news the night before that they were in for some storms the next few days despite the La Niña weather pattern that had given Austin a warmer, drier March than usual so far that year.

In the kitchen, she greeted Sissy with a kiss on the cheek, then poured herself a cup of coffee from the thermos. "Where's Mom?"

"Outside," she said, flipping a pancake on the stove. "Did you girls sleep okay?"

"Mm-hmm." She looked through the sliding glass door at Mayree, who was standing barefoot on the pebbled porch, one arm wrapped around herself and the other hovering a cigarette near her face. The way her mother was scowling at the sky made her wonder if she'd lain awake all night, too.

"Listen," Sissy said. "After breakfast, we need to go to your place to get some clothes and whatever you need so you and your mom can stay here for a few days. Your mom was right—it's not safe for y'all to be over there until we get to the bottom of this mess."

Paula nodded. "Did Uncle Stan call?"

"No. Or rather, not yet. I'm holding out hope, but I have to admit: it's waning." Sissy followed Paula's gaze through the glass at Mayree. Paula knew her mother had been hard on Sissy, basically cutting her out of their lives since her father's funeral. When she'd asked why Mayree had cut her off, she'd said only, "Some people don't know how to mind their own damn business." Yet here they were, Sissy as gracious and loyal as ever.

"Is Mom okay?"

Sissy winked at her. "She's a little salty this morning, so I guess she's good."

Sissy seemed to be in high spirits in spite of having announced to her husband that their marriage was over. She wondered if the prospect of having Mayree back in her life made up for Stan's permanent exile. Whatever it was, Paula hoped it would continue; with so little else to hold on to at that point, her mother and Sissy's friendship was like a personal flotation device in shark-infested waters. She felt the urge to protect it the same way she sometimes used to offer entertainment or distraction to her parents in the uncomfortable aftermath of one of their fights, hoping somehow it might coax them back to the same side of the room. She moved to the stove and put her arm around Sissy's waist. "I'm really glad we're here, Aunt Sissy. I don't know if Mom said it, but I know she's really missed you."

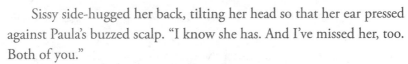

Sissy side-hugged her back, tilting her head so that her ear pressed against Paula's buzzed scalp. "I know she has. And I've missed her, too. Both of you."

Just then, Mayree slid open the door, bringing with her a waft of humid, smoky air. "Am I interrupting some kind of lovefest?"

"Yes!" Sissy said, reaching out a hand. "You want a turn?"

Mayree swatted her hand away. "Oh stop."

"It was nice hearing you laugh again last night, Mayree. You should do it more often," Sissy said.

Paula worried that Mayree's irritability would break the tentative spell between them, but was relieved to see her give Sissy an affectionate smile before Sissy turned back to the stove.

After Kelly woke up and everyone had eaten breakfast, the four of them set off on foot to the Bakers' house to gather clothes and other necessities and to pick up Paula's car. They decided to leave Mayree's in the Bakers' driveway, even though it was the more expensive one, in case the letter writer was watching the house to see whether or not Paula was home. They were barely past the Pease Mansion when Sissy, glancing side to side like a scared cat, said, "This is silly. Why are we walking? We should've taken my car."

"It's fine, Sissy," Mayree said. "I brought an extra weapon." She withdrew it from her bathrobe pocket and held it up.

"That's my good paring knife!"

"I'm not stealing it, for crying out loud. I'm only going to use it if someone jumps us."

A hush fell over them, as if they were all envisioning someone attacking them on the street. Without anyone verbalizing the directive to do so, they picked up their collective pace and finished the half-mile walk in anxious silence. When they reached the walkway leading to the Bakers' front door, Mayree put out her arm the way she used to while braking hard to keep Paula from being thrown into the dashboard.

"Wait a second," she said in a low voice. "I want to make sure everything looks okay before we go in."

Paula looked, too, scanning the bushes for signs of trampling and ensuring that none of the front windows were broken. Of course, they could only guess if anything was amiss on the two sides or back of the house. "Okay?" she asked.

But Mayree didn't answer; she'd opened their mailbox by the curb and was reading something she'd found inside. Her expression suggested it wasn't good news.

"Mom, what is it?"

"Get inside. Hurry," Mayree said, rushing to the front door. Once they were all in the house, she closed and locked it behind them. "Everyone, split up. Check the rooms and the window locks."

"Mayree, wait," Sissy said. "What's going on?"

Mayree handed her the letter, which Sissy scanned, then read aloud:

IT'S TIME FOR YOU TO PAY UP. PUT $100K IN A BAG AND TAKE IT TO THE WASHATERIA ON E. 12TH STREET BY 8:00 PM ON MONDAY NIGHT APRIL 3. PUT IT INSIDE THE DRYER CLOSEST TO THE FRONT DOOR. DO NOT TELL THE POLICE OR ANYBODY ABOUT THIS OR YOU WILL BE SORRY. IF YOU DON'T DO WHAT I SAY THEN YOU WON'T BE SORRY YOU'LL BE DEAD.

For several seconds that felt more like an eon, nobody said anything. They just looked at each other with dread until Paula, who felt strangely calm, as if she'd stepped outside her terrorized self and was watching everything from a sheltered distance, finally broke the silence. "We have to take this to Sergeant Henderson."

"But it says—" Kelly started to say.

"You weren't there," Paula said, her voice sharp. *You asked for this.* "This guy . . . this guy tried to kill me already. He had a knife at my throat. He said he was going to slit my neck and fuck me in it."

Sissy gasped.

"We already tried Sergeant Henderson and he didn't do shit to help us," Mayree said. She gripped the frayed lapels of her bathrobe and tightened it around herself. "I don't want to risk it going sideways. If it's money he wants, then I'll get it and we'll do what he says."

Paula shook her head. "We don't have the money."

"Oh my god, I can't believe this is happening," Kelly said, her mouth beginning to twitch.

Sissy wrapped her arm around Kelly's waist. "I have some savings," she said. "And Stan. We'll get him to pony up. After all, this is partly his fault."

Mayree squeezed Sissy's hand. "A hundred grand sounds like someone trying to collect a gambling debt, which is on Frank, not Stan. But thank you."

Paula picked up her bag and fished around inside it for her keys. After spending a week being tortured by scraps of memories and fearing more of the same, she was ready to find a way to end the nightmare. "How do we know he'll stop if he gets the money? He's probably going to try to kill me again whether I tell the cops about this or not, so we might as well try to get them to help us."

"I agree," Kelly said. "It's too dangerous to do it on our own."

"We're on our own," Mayree said. "Like it or not."

"We have each other," Sissy said. "We're going to be okay."

"Just give me a minute to think." Mayree sat down hard on her wingback chair and pressed her hands against her eyes. "I don't understand why this asshole is after Paula. She didn't do anything wrong."

Paula appreciated her mother's withdrawal of blame, but it didn't change the situation. "It doesn't matter who or why; right now I'm in danger," she said. "I'm going to the police station."

"I'm going with you," Kelly said.

"Mom?" Paula tried not to sound impatient. After all, it was Mayree who'd insisted on going to the police before. She couldn't understand why she wouldn't want to enlist their help now, with this new letter.

Mayree sighed. "I suppose I can't let you go alone. I'll drive."

Mayree

In spite of her initial reluctance, Mayree wasted no time marching to the front desk with Paula, Sissy, and Kelly in tow. It was a different officer from the one working there on Friday night, but apparently they shared the same attitude. When Mayree explained why they were there and insisted on speaking with Sergeant Henderson or someone else, the officer lazily picked up the phone and called the admin sergeant on duty. He summarized the situation without haste or urgency, as if Mayree had come in to complain about squirrels on her property. A moment later, he hung up.

"Detective Cervenka is going to talk to you upstairs. Just wait here a minute," he said, then went back to doing a great deal of nothing.

Sergeant Henderson appeared in the doorway and the desk officer buzzed it open. "Welcome back," he said, holding the door open for them.

"Further instructions," Mayree said, handing him the letter. She hadn't bothered to encase this one in a plastic bag.

He read the letter, then motioned for them to follow him to the staircase.

"It was in our mailbox this morning," Mayree, close at his heels, said before he could ask. "No envelope again."

"Did you—"

"Check the premises? Yes, before we went in. But not thoroughly; we came here as fast as we could."

Paula shot her a glance and Mayree knew what she was thinking. It's true, she hadn't wanted to talk to the police at first. Henderson was full of himself, condescending, and probably misogynistic—a word she'd only learned a few years ago but that felt like had been missing not only from her vocabulary but her entire life experience until then. But when Paula stated with such confidence, such authority, that they should take the letter to him, Mayree thought of how she'd reacted to her attack by Bobby Cox so long ago. Ashamed, she'd blamed and buried it inside herself. She'd stayed in her room, refusing to ride her horse or go to the barn or anywhere else outside. She hid from Bobby and waited until she could escape to her new college dorm, thinking that running away from the threat was the best—or only—course of action. Then she'd spent the next thirty years hardening herself around that terrible secret. She'd been passive then, but Paula's new determination inspired her to take charge now.

"I gotta admit, I wasn't expecting to hear any more about this," Sergeant Henderson said.

"You'll do something, right?"

He looked at each of them in succession. He breathed his signature sigh. "It seems we have no choice."

"Thanks for your concern," Mayree said, making no effort to hide her sarcasm. "Now what are you going to do?"

He led them to the third floor and introduced them to Detective Cervenka. "She's all yours." He tipped his hat at Mayree and left.

Detective Juan Cervenka was altogether a different breed of police officer. His hair was almost completely gray, yet his face was youthful and his smile genuine. He shook each of their hands, invited them to sit down around a conference table, and offered them coffee. Only Sissy asked for some—with cream and extra sugar—and as he handed her a

Styrofoam cup, he apologized for the sergeant's demeanor. "He's a good guy. Just a little gruff. Plus he hates doing intake reports."

Mayree harrumphed. She dragged a half-full ashtray closer and lit a cigarette.

Detective Cervenka flipped a pad of paper open to a clean sheet. He asked them to tell him everything from the beginning, and they did. He was very thorough, asking detailed questions about the party, the guy, his car, what Paula and Kelly had done moment by moment, what had happened afterward. He wrote down Kevin Atwood's name, even though Kelly insisted it wasn't him, and the detective said he wanted to collect as much information as possible, just in case.

He asked Mayree about Frank's previous business dealings, habits, and, delicately, his personal life. He even asked Sissy if, as such a close friend of the family, she'd ever observed anything unusual that might shed light on a motive. Sissy had glanced nervously at Mayree, who jumped in.

"We recently learned that my late husband may have fathered a child, but we don't know anything except that he denied it was true. Apparently, the boy approached Frank some time ago, but was turned away."

"Did your husband tell you that?"

"No," Mayree said, looking down. "His attorney did." Mayree struggled with whether to tell him what Stan had said. What was the point of asking for help if she didn't give him all the information they had? It was like lying to a psychiatrist. Not that Stan had given them anything definitive, not even a name. He'd even said he wasn't sure there was a connection, just that it had been the first thing that came to him. Still, couldn't "teaching someone a lesson" be a motive for revenge? In that case, why wouldn't the attacker have gone after Stan?

The detective seemed to sense her discomfort and embarrassment, and didn't ask anything else about Frank's alleged illegitimate son. "We may need to talk to his attorney if that's okay," he said.

"I don't think that would be necessary," Mayree said. "It's probably not even relevant." Stan was an asshole, but she didn't really want to get him in trouble with the law unless she had to; it would make things so much worse for Sissy and Kelly.

"Hopefully not," he said, smiling with such compassion that Mayree found herself relaxing into the moment as if it were a conversation with a concerned friend rather than a police interview. Even Paula appeared to be less fretful. For the first time in longer than she could remember, Mayree had the sensation of not just laying her troubles out, but actually putting them down. She glanced at the detective's ring finger and was disappointed to see a well-worn gold band on it.

"Are you sure you can't think of any details to help us identify the suspect besides dark hair?" he asked Paula.

"He was youngish, I think. Our age, give or take. But I really can't remember anything else." She shook her head. "I'm sorry."

Mayree thought about how long she'd known Bobby Cox before. Surely after so many years on the ranch, he'd made an impression on her—his features, gait, voice, mannerisms, something—but after he raped her, all she could recall with any clarity was his belt buckle, the foul heat of his breath on her neck, her own paralytic fear. If Detective Cervenka asked her to describe him now, she didn't think she'd be able to—and she hadn't even been drinking. It didn't surprise her that Paula, who'd only seen her attacker briefly that drunken night, couldn't remember anything.

The detective turned to Mayree. "Why the washateria? That's an unusual drop point. Does it mean anything to you?"

"No," Mayree said. She looked at Sissy, who shrugged.

Paula cocked her head. "Wait. East Twelfth. Is that the street Chapo's Barber Shop is on?"

Mayree stiffened. Chapo's always reminded her of when she first discovered Frank's extramarital activities. "That's where your father used to get his hair cut," Mayree said. "Stan, too."

"You're right," Sissy said.

"Let me get the Yellow Pages," Detective Cervenka said, standing.

"Don't bother," Mayree said as he left the room. "I'm sure of it. I can't believe I didn't recognize the address."

A moment later, the detective returned, flipping through the alphabetical listings. "Yep. Here it is." He tapped the entry. "It's 1917 East Twelfth Street."

"It was my husband's first big commercial real estate purchase," Mayree said. "He never developed it because he said nobody gave as good a shave as Chapo did."

"We were just talking about that place," Kelly said. "Remember? After . . . the party."

"You can say it," Paula said. "After I was attacked. The guy reminded me of how Daddy smelled after he went to the barbershop."

"The aftershave," Kelly said.

Mayree had liked the smell of that aftershave until she associated it with other women.

"I wonder what happened to Chapo," Sissy said.

"He's still there," Paula said, rubbing her head.

"Do you think that might be relevant to this case, Mrs. Baker?" said Detective Cervenka.

Mayree mashed the charred filter of her cigarette into the ashtray. "I can't see why it would be. Frank sold the property in eighty-seven when the market crashed."

"It is a strange coincidence, though," Sissy said.

The detective flipped through the Yellow Pages, looking at listings for washaterias in the area. "Maybe not. There are quite a few scattered around town, but this one is the most centrally located. The suspect might live nearby. You said he dropped a letter in your bag while you were on campus, right? It's only about a mile from there to the washateria. If he's around your age, then maybe he's a student."

"I think everyone at the party went to UT," Kelly said.

"You said you only knew one girl from English class." Paula's voice went up in pitch. "How do you know if everyone went to UT? He could've been anybody. And I'm not even sure about his age."

"It's okay," the detective said, nodding. His sincerity was such that Mayree thought he'd get up and hug Paula if it wouldn't have been wildly inappropriate. "Here's what we're going to do. I'm going to write this up and get approval for a proactive squad for tomorrow night. We'll have four, maybe five guys in street dress. One unit will be staged a few blocks away, ready to roll when the other guys see something."

"What about the money?" Paula asked.

"In a case like this, we'll use marked money from drug seizures." Then he leaned back and tapped his pen a few times against the table, looking at her as if considering something important. "Let me ask you something," he said. "How would you feel about doing the drop yourself?"

"What?" Paula asked. "What do you mean?"

"I'm saying, if you think you can handle it, and it's totally fine if you don't, it'd probably be more convincing if you were the one to put the money in the dryer. That way, if he's watching, he'll be more likely to move."

Paula stared at the detective. Mayree felt her stomach drop. The thought of her daughter deliberately going anywhere near the guy was almost unbearable. "No way," she said.

"She'd be protected the whole time, of course," he said. "All you'd have to do is put the bag into the dryer and leave. Then when he shows up to get the cash, we'll grab him."

"But how will you know if it's him?" Paula asked.

"Well, since we don't have a description to go on, we'll just have to judge by his behavior."

"Okay," Paula said, seemingly without hesitation. "I'll do it."

"Good girl," the detective said.

"No," Mayree said, also without hesitation. "She won't."

"Mom, it's fine. I can totally do it." Paula sat up straighter in her chair.

Mayree had to admire her bravery. She didn't think she'd have been able to do the same at her age. Still, she was wary. She turned to the detective. "You're absolutely sure she wouldn't be hurt?"

"I'd be lying if I said I could guarantee it," he said. "But I'll do my damnedest."

"We'll think about it," Mayree said.

"I understand."

Mayree sensed that the interview was over, but she didn't want to leave. The sparse conference room was hardly inviting with its fake-wood desk and uncomfortable chairs and industrial-gray walls. Yet Mayree wouldn't mind having another smoke and a cup of stale coffee, maybe asking for pillows and blankets so they could sleep on the floor. She didn't want to take Paula home. "So what do we do now?"

Detective Cervenka stood and smiled. "Go on home. Wait for my call. When it's time to make the drop tomorrow, either Paula will do it or someone on our team will. Given how little we have to go on, though, I still think it would be best if she were the one. I promise we'll stay close to her the whole time. Either way, try not to worry."

That would be like trying not to breathe.

Paula

A s they drove home, Paula leaned her head against the back seat window and looked out at the world scrolling by. The sky was overcast and the air damp, which made everything look monochromatic and run-down. The industrial brick buildings, the trash and debris along the curbs, the ugly bell tower on the corner of the Baptist church, the dry leaves on the trees at Waterloo Park, the dingy houses before they reached their neighborhood, Old Enfield, and even the really nice ones that looked dull in the insipid air. Paula wished it would hurry up and rain; it wouldn't improve the circumstances but it might make the mood less dreary.

"Did you hear about that guy, Mark Kilroy?" Kelly asked, breaking the silence in the car.

"Who?"

"He's a year ahead of us. Pre-med. Super cute."

Paula shook her head.

"He disappeared in Matamoros a couple weeks ago on spring break. I heard it could've been drug dealers who kidnapped and maybe even murdered him."

Paula made a sound as she sucked in a sharp breath of air.

Sissy spun around. "Kelly Ann Cagle! Why on earth are you talking about something so morbid at a time like this?"

"What, I'm just making conversation!" She crossed her arms and slumped against the seat back.

"Well, think of something more pleasant than kidnapping and murder. It's not very sensitive considering what Paula's just been through. We've got about"—she looked at her wristwatch—"twenty-eight hours until this maniac gets caught, so let's try to pass it as peacefully as we can. How about we stop at Blockbuster? We can have a movie marathon!"

"Sounds like a good idea to me," Mayree said. She did a U-turn in the middle of the street.

"I guess," Paula said, though it didn't matter what she thought, now that her mother had agreed.

"Let's get *Mystic Pizza*," Kelly said.

"I was thinking *Rain Man*," Sissy said.

"Or how about *Annie Hall*? I've never seen it," Kelly said.

"It's going to be a long night," Mayree said. "We'll get 'em all."

After an hour of browsing the video store aisles, they rented five movies, then stopped at the grocery store for frozen pizza, popcorn, ice cream, candy, Dr Pepper, and cigarettes. The four of them moved as tightly as a pack of animals, their heads constantly turning, checking for danger. When they were crammed into the open door of the freezer section, debating on ice cream flavors, Mayree noticed a single young man staring at them. She reached behind her and pinched Paula's arm, causing her to yelp. "Shh!" Mayree hissed. Without moving her mouth or dropping the man's stare, she whispered, "Do you recognize that guy?"

Paula pressed closer against the knot of female flesh and peered over Mayree's shoulder. He was dark-haired with a weak chin and slight overbite. She looked for anything that might trigger her memory, but his features were unremarkable, unfamiliar.

"No," she said, and they collectively exhaled their relief.

"We shouldn't even be here," Kelly said with a whine.

"It's fine, we're going home," Mayree said.

"Home to our house, not yours," Sissy said. "Right?"

Mayree sighed. "I wish you'd let me smoke inside."

"Two more nights won't kill you," Sissy said. "Once this guy's caught, you can go home and smoke your brains out."

~

Paula and Kelly stayed up long after their mothers went to bed, sitting unusually far apart on the old couch that Sissy had just re-covered in a floral chintz now that they were old enough not to make messes on it. They used to watch TV together there, sharing a blanket, dropping M&M'S between the cushions, wiping their hands on the brown corduroy cover.

For whatever reason, Kelly seemed awkward and formal now that they were alone, sitting upright with her feet on the floor instead of curled up and sprawled out. Paula didn't know if it was because of the new covering or if she was upset. Paula could feel something wrong in the air between them, but she wasn't really in the mood to pursue it. Instead, she sat—also formally—on the far end, half watching the movie and letting her mind wander along the string-thin grasp she had on her own life.

When the movie finally ended, they went upstairs and, without speaking, put on their pajamas and got into bed. Kelly turned off the light, plunging the room into darkness. It took a few minutes for Paula's eyes to adjust to the black. She looked at the clock; it was just past midnight. "It's Monday now," she said to Kelly as they wriggled their way into comfort under the covers. "It'll all be over soon." Paula didn't know if she believed it, but she wanted to cross the chasm that had opened up between the two of them, thinking perhaps it was the stress of the situation that made Kelly seem distant. She touched her socked foot to her friend's. Kelly didn't speak, and the silence stretched miserably. "You okay?"

"I have to tell you something," Kelly said. She turned onto her side, away from Paula.

When she didn't speak again for a few moments, Paula asked, "What?"

"You're going to hate me."

Paula thought quickly of the times that Kelly had said or done something that had disappointed her, knowing that it was equal to the number of times she'd forgiven her. Hate had never been part of the calculus.

"No, I won't."

"You promise?"

Paula hesitated. "Just tell me," she said.

Kelly rolled back and faced her. Paula didn't need to see her features to know she was about to cry. "I lied to you."

Paula felt a small, loud thing deep inside her as her mind fast-for-warded through a list of possible lies, the worst having something to do with Will. "About what?"

"At the party. I saw you with that guy."

"Which guy?"

"*The* guy. I saw you go with him to his car."

Paula sat up. She reached across Kelly's body and switched on the lamp. "What?"

"It's worse than that, though—I saw him looking at you and I told him he should go talk to you."

Paula stared at her, thinking she'd misheard. "You told him to talk to me?" She replayed that section of the night in her mind, trying to imagine when and how that could've happened.

"I know. I'm sorry." She covered her eyes with her hands.

"Are you fucking kidding me?" Her voice went up in pitch and volume.

"Please," Kelly said. "Don't wake up the moms."

"I don't fucking care if I wake up the dead!" Paula clambered over Kelly and off the bed. She didn't want to be anywhere close to her. "Let me get this straight. You told some random guy to talk to me, then after I told you I'd just been attacked, you told me you didn't believe me? You basically sent me off to get killed and then acted like I was making it up?"

"I didn't say I didn't believe you. I just . . . didn't tell you that I did. And obviously I didn't 'send you off to be killed.'"

Paula thought of the ride home from the lake, how Kelly had shamed her: *Why would you go off with a stranger like that?* And that she'd refused to go to the police with her right after it happened, insisting they'd get in trouble for underage drinking. "This makes no fucking sense. What kind of friend would do that? I doubted myself because you doubted me. You let me think that I was going crazy!"

Kelly pulled the covers up to her chin like a petulant child. "I told you you were going to hate me."

"I am totally and completely shocked." Paula pressed her hands against her head and squeezed, boiling beneath her skin. She turned away and paced the length of Kelly's room, darting her glace to the familiar posters on the walls, the furniture, the clothes in her open closet as though she'd never seen any of it before. She turned back to her. "Why would you do that to me? Seriously, I want to know."

Kelly sat up, her back against the headboard. "I didn't mean for anything bad to happen to you, I swear. I noticed this guy was looking at you like he was interested, but you were whining about Will so much and wanting to go home, so when you got another drink, I told him you'd just broken up with your boyfriend and he should go talk to you. I honestly was just trying to make you happy. I thought if some cute guy started talking to you, you'd feel better."

"What is wrong with you? Why couldn't you have told me that before?" Paula grabbed one of Kelly's decorative pillows off the floor and squeezed it as if she would wring the life out of it.

"Because I panicked. It was my fault you got hurt. I didn't want you to know because I didn't want you to be mad at me."

"What about the girl I was supposedly talking to? The one with boobs and dangly earrings? Was that true?"

Kelly looked down and shook her head.

Paula's anger seeped into every place where fear had been. "And this whole week, while I've been totally miserable, you still didn't admit any of this." She slammed her hand against the mattress, which made Kelly flinch. "Why?"

"Because I knew you'd react like this!"

"Which you totally deserve! I can't believe you're so selfish that you lied about really fucking important information just because you didn't want me to be mad at you. I shaved my head because of this!" Paula leaned in close, pointing at her head. Inside her, an abyss opened. If she thought she'd felt betrayed when Will dumped her, she was wrong. That was nothing compared to this.

"I know saying sorry won't undo it, but I really, truly am."

"You lied to me and my mom and your own parents! And the police! I told them I didn't know what he looks like because I was too drunk. But you talked to him so you must know. You should've told the detective—it might make a difference."

"I was drunk, too."

"You literally just told me that if *a cute guy* talked to me, I'd feel better. So you at least know he was cute."

"I remember thinking that but I wasn't really paying attention. He looked like any cute guy on campus. I can't even remember what the guy I was making out with looked like."

"Was it Kevin?"

"No," she said. "At least I don't think so."

"Goddamn it, Kelly, you have to remember something!"

"Why should I remember if you don't? You spent more time with him than I did."

Kelly's indignant tone was a lit match against the kindling of Paula's fury, and like a fiery explosion, she slapped the expression right off Kelly's face. "Go to hell," she said, and spun away. On her way out, she slammed the door, leaving both Kelly and their friendship behind.

Paula was too upset to cry, though her eyelids tingled as though she would. Her neck felt too small for the lump in her throat.

She wanted to go home. She didn't even care what might happen to her there. In fact, at that moment, she hoped the guy would try to come after her just so she could unleash herself onto him like a voracious animal going after its prey. She wanted to kick and punch and scratch and scream and spit, get out all this shit she'd been holding in, the fear and shame and grief and now, rage. She walked up and down the hallway, digging her fingernails into her palms until she couldn't stand it. To make things worse, Kelly didn't come after her.

She wouldn't go back into Kelly's room for her things, including her house key and shoes. It wouldn't bother her to walk home in the rain; she'd welcome the discomfort of the grainy asphalt on her bare feet. But with Mayree's obsessive window-locking, she wouldn't be able to climb in through her bedroom window even if she could shimmy up the trellis without slipping off. Instead, she stomped downstairs, thinking she'd pour a shot or three of something out of Sissy's liquor cabinet and try to sleep on the couch.

The rain was coming down hard, and far-off thunder growled. Through the sliding glass doors leading from the kitchen to the back patio, Paula could make out a single glowing ember. She followed it, stepping outside under the narrow awning. The rain ricocheted off the pebbled tiles, splashing the hem of Paula's pajama bottoms.

Paula stood next to her mother. Mayree's left arm hugged herself tightly, her right held her cigarette aloft. "Can I have one?" she asked.

"You don't smoke," Mayree said without looking at her.

"I do now."

After a moment, Mayree sniffed, then nodded. She reached into her pocket for the pack and handed it to Paula.

"What's the matter?"

Paula teased out a cigarette. "Kelly."

"Want to talk about it?" Mayree cupped the lighter and flicked it for Paula.

Paula coughed. Her first cigarette would also be her last. "Not really."

They smoked side by side, watching the sky. To Paula's surprise, standing next to her mother helped calm her down. "I've been thinking about what you said earlier, about being on our own," she said after a while. "We can't depend on anyone else to protect us. We have to protect ourselves."

Mayree

The springs on Sissy's guest bed squeaked, so Mayree had passed many dark hours trying not to toss and turn lest she wake her friend on the other side of the wall. Since she couldn't smoke inside, she fidgeted with her lighter, pinched a cigarette between her fingers until it broke. She counted bumps on the popcorn ceiling and cracks in the paint along the corners of the room. She stood to perform some deep knee bends, the popping both a relief and discomfort. She gripped the edge of the vanity and stared at her bladelike reflection in the mirror, all the while wrestling with the past and waiting for daylight to wash away the shadows.

She didn't like thinking of her childhood, but sometimes during an untroubled moment, a specific memory would float into her mind like a passing cloud: a late-spring afternoon, the sky breezy and crisp, wildflowers blooming on the low hills, bluebonnets and paintbrushes and daisies. She was on her mare, galloping along the riverbank in the gloaming time between chores and dinner, the sun spinning golden light over everything. More than the beauty of the terrain, she could remember how she felt rushing through it. Free. Joyful. Fearless.

She hated that memory, because after Bobby Cox taught her *how to ride a* real *stallion*, she never felt that way again.

Would Paula be affected the same way? Would she stagger, broken, along a crooked and rocky path into adulthood and beyond? She wondered if there was something she could do to keep her from such an unhappy fate. Was there anything her own mother could've done for her? She had no idea.

At least Mayree could try to solve the problem of the demand letter. She was having second thoughts about Detective Cervenka's plan with the stakeout team, especially since he wanted Paula to participate. She worried that involving the cops at all had been a bad idea that could get Paula killed. She even calculated how much she'd be able to take out of her diminished savings account without leaving them totally broke, and tried to figure out where she could get the rest of the money to meet the ransom demand on her own.

The morning sky was dark with storm clouds, as if reflecting Mayree's somber mood. After watching the rain for a while, she finally hauled herself up, causing the bedsprings to groan. She desperately needed a cigarette. If she could open the window, she'd blow the smoke out and hope Sissy wouldn't notice, but the sash was painted shut. Instead, she went downstairs, passing through the living room where Paula was asleep on the couch, into the kitchen. Sissy was there, making a huge platter of bacon and eggs.

"I can't take it anymore," Mayree said.

"I know, honey. But it's only a little while longer and then hopefully this will all be over."

"I'm not talking about that. I mean I can't take having to stand outside in the rain to smoke."

"Oh, Mayree."

"I appreciate your hospitality, Sissy, I do. And I thank you for letting us stay and worrying about us. You're a good friend. The best." She put her hand on Sissy's forearm. "But I gotta get the hell out of here."

"You can't go. It's not safe."

"It's mostly safe. We know for sure where he'll be at eight tonight, and if he really thinks we're going to leave a hundred thousand dollars in a dryer, he's probably not going to murder us before we have a chance to drop it off. Speaking of which, nothing against Detective Cervenka, but do you really think we should let the cops handle it?"

"As opposed to what?"

"I don't know. Paula said something last night that I couldn't get out of my head. She said we can't count on other people protecting us, and ultimately, we can only depend on ourselves."

"You don't really think that's true, do you?"

"Maybe. Look at what Frank and Stan did to us. We thought they were going to protect us, didn't we?" She wondered how many of their work dinners and business trips involved other women, how much money both of them spent courting their mistresses, if they ever felt guilty for the countless nights they left their wives home alone with their children. "What fools we were."

"They did for a while, I guess. Maybe they just weren't equipped to follow through until the end. But there are plenty of examples of people protecting each other. You just thanked me for doing it, right? Our parents protected us when we were growing up. And we protect our kids."

Ray had hired Bobby, probably without ever wondering if his daughter would be safe around him. Shouldn't he have been more watchful? And Paula. Mayree had depended on Felicia for so much all of Paula's life, she couldn't even say which of them had raised her. It felt inexcusable now that she'd outsourced such an essential job—the only one that actually mattered—especially after what she herself had experienced. What if she'd failed her daughter in some way that led to her being attacked? If she could go back in time, she'd do so many things over again. She hadn't intended to care about this daughter she ended up with, but in spite of herself, she did. She pulled the lighter out of her pocket and flicked it a few times. "If I'd done a better job protecting my kid, she wouldn't be in this mess."

Sissy served a heaping plate of food and guided Mayree to the table. "I think you're being too hard on yourself, Mayree. Even if we tried, we couldn't prevent every bad thing from happening to the people we love. We're doing the best we can."

~

While Sissy was busy with the dishes, Mayree shook Paula gently awake. "Hey, let's go home," she whispered.

Paula pushed herself up, scrubbed at her eyes like she did when she was a little girl, an insignificant gesture that flooded Mayree with a cocktail of nostalgia and regret. She wished she could travel back in time and do everything over again, better.

"Can we?"

"You bet. We're the bosses."

"Isn't it dangerous?"

"Probably." Mayree held up her switchblade. "But so am I."

Paula smiled. "Is Kelly up?"

"I don't think so. Do you want to say goodbye?"

"No. I just want to go. Can you go up there and get my stuff?"

Paula's expression told her something unpleasant had happened between them, but she knew now wasn't the time to discuss it. "Sure."

Once Mayree returned with Paula's things, Sissy walked them to the door. "I don't know about this, Mayree. I'd feel so much better if you stayed."

"We'll be fine. I'll keep the doors locked. Besides, Detective Cervenka told us he'd call us at our house."

"Okay. I'll call to check on you later. And if anything happens, you let me know." She pulled Mayree into an embrace. Mayree leaned against her friend and closed her eyes for a grateful moment before pulling away.

"Sissy, you're strangling me. This isn't goodbye. You know damn well I'm too mean to die."

"Well, that's probably true," Sissy said. She hugged Paula as tight as she could. "Y'all take care of each other."

"We will, Aunt Sissy."

"I assume you're not going to class today, so I'll have Kelly let you know what you missed."

Paula stole a glance at Mayree. "Oh, that's okay. I'll just go in early on Wednesday and figure it out."

"Love you both," Sissy said as she opened the door.

~

At home, they dashed through the rain and into the house. Felicia was in the kitchen, sitting at the table with a cup of coffee. She looked exhausted in a way Mayree had never seen her before, and she realized it was her fault. She hadn't talked to Felicia since Friday night.

"Oh shit, Felicia," Mayree said. "I'm so sorry. I should've called you."

"Thank you, Jesus," Felicia said, scraping her chair back and reaching for Paula. "I've been worried sick about the two of you."

"We're okay," Paula said, hugging her back.

"Didn't you get my messages? I must've left twenty on the machine."

"I didn't even think to check. We've been staying at Sissy's. You wouldn't believe what's been going on."

"I can only imagine. After finding that note in Paula's bag and y'all running off to the police, then I come in here and there's some crazy note about a nutria on the loose. I've been scared out of my mind. I called Kenny and told him if I didn't hear something soon, I was going to call the police. I couldn't even drink my coffee—it's gone cold."

"I'll make another pot," Mayree said. "I'm sure we could all use some."

After Felicia called Kenny back, the three of them sat down and Mayree filled her in on everything that happened over the weekend, including Stan's admission about Frank's possibly having another child, the second note, and Detective Cervenka's plan to send a special unit to the washateria that night to arrest the suspect.

"Lord have mercy," Felicia said, shaking her head.

"Maybe you should head home," Mayree said.

"I'm scared." Paula took Felicia's hand. "Please don't leave me."

Mayree felt a sting of fresh regret that she wasn't the one Paula wanted for comfort. It was either Frank or Felicia. Even now that Frank was gone, Mayree still hadn't been able to garner her favor. Then again, maybe she hadn't deserved to.

"Paula, stop that. It's bad enough you're here. The detective said we'd be safe, but what if he's wrong? If push comes to shove, I don't know if I could protect both of you. Felicia needs to get home to her family."

Felicia didn't protest. "You want me to ask Kenny to come over here? Having a man in the house might not hurt."

"No, no. We'll be fine," Mayree said, though she wasn't at all sure about that. What she did know was that she'd been depending on Felicia to take care of them all these years without ever wondering what kind of toll it might take on her. She'd cleaned and cooked and nurtured, and all along, Mayree took her generosity for granted. She absolutely wouldn't put her or her husband at risk now. "I mean it. You have Kenny and Curtis to worry about."

"All right," she said. "I'll just put the load into the dryer and then go."

"Oh lord, even I can put clothes into the machine and turn it on," Mayree said.

"Yes, but you won't. You're under a strain and you'll forget and then I'll have to deal with it next week."

"Fine," Mayree said, squeezing her hand. "But don't open any windows."

"I'm gonna assume you're worn out and ignore that. Why would I open the windows in weather like this and with some fool running crazy? Maybe you ought to go take a nap."

Mayree harrumphed.

Felicia nodded and headed up the stairs. When she came back down, she hugged first Paula, then Mayree. "You call me the second you hear something."

"I will," Mayree said.

Once Felicia was gone, Paula sat back down in her chair, picking at her fingernails. After a few minutes of silence, Mayree knew there was more than nerves going on with her.

"What is it?"

"Do you remember this one Friday night last year, you and Aunt Sissy were here having cocktails?"

"Well, before your father died, that could've been damn near any Friday night. Which one are you talking about?"

"I remember it because it was just a few days after Uncle Stan moved out."

"Okay." Mayree felt an uneasiness. She didn't know what Paula was talking about, but whatever it was, she was clearly upset by it.

"I overheard you say something," she said, looking down. "You said you never should've been a mother."

Mayree felt her face go hot. She did remember that night. She and Sissy had been complaining to each other about their various disappointments and fantasizing about a time in the near future when the girls would've graduated and they could take long trips together, close as a pair of shoes, not worrying about cooking or cleaning for their husbands. Sissy had said it was strange not having Stan around, but at least she had her kids and Chico and someday, she hoped, she'd have grandchildren to dote on. Mayree responded that she didn't even want the responsibility of a pet, much less a grandchild. She'd told Sissy that, in fact, she'd never intended to have children at all, that the only reason for her to have had children was if she was going to have to take over her daddy's ranch, and that when it was clear her brothers planned on running things and Frank wasn't going to send her back to

Blanco with a divorce certificate in hand, she should've had her tubes tied. She remembered clearly how Sissy had gasped and told her, "You don't mean it."

Now Mayree told Paula, "I shouldn't have said that."

"But you meant it."

Mayree took in a deep breath and held it, thinking. She tapped out a fresh cigarette. "There are things I never told you about. One thing in particular. I've never told anybody about it, in fact."

Paula leaned forward, waiting as the smoke rose up toward the ceiling.

"You weren't my first pregnancy." The words sounded like a foreign language coming out of her mouth. She'd never imagined actually speaking them—especially to Paula—and the fact of having done so made her light-headed. Mayree watched her daughter's expression change from curiosity to concern. "There was a ranch hand who worked for my daddy. I don't want to say his name. When I was seventeen, he took advantage of me."

"Oh, Mom." Paula moved her chair closer to Mayree's. She tried to hug her, but Mayree gently held her off.

"I'm fine, really. It was a long time ago."

"Did you . . . have it?" Paula looked afraid of knowing the answer, and Mayree felt terrible for her. She couldn't imagine finding out that she might have not just one but two unknown half siblings.

"No." Mayree shook her head. "No." She wasn't sure how much she wanted to tell, because talking about it made her remember it too clearly. But maybe Paula deserved to know, especially having just experienced her own traumatic attack. "I had a miscarriage," she said. "But if that hadn't happened, I don't know what I'd have done."

"Oh my god," Paula said.

"It's okay. Mostly," Mayree said. She took a thoughtful drag. The reasons she had for keeping her life story to herself, not telling even Sissy the truth of her secrets after their many years of friendship, seemed illogical now. Maybe it was the gentleness of Paula's expression, or maybe she was just so damn tired of holding everything in so tight, but it felt strangely relieving to tell Paula the truth. "Your uncles and I grew up in a different time. Life on the ranch was hard. We were expected to pull our weight, never complain, never talk back. We almost never had family or friends over, and I suppose I didn't ever develop a romantic notion of getting married and having babies the way other girls did. Then, after what happened, I felt like maybe I wasn't meant to have children. But I did get married and then had you, and I don't know how to explain it except I was overwhelmed. I was unprepared—emotionally, I mean. It was hard. But it wasn't your fault. It was never your fault."

Mayree stubbed out her cigarette. She felt like she'd just laid down a very heavy object.

Paula bent forward and put her head on Mayree's lap, crying quietly. Mayree put her hand on Paula's back, felt the bony ridges of her spine, the warmth coming off her. She remembered suddenly what it had felt like to hold her when she was a toddler, a child. To sit with her in the rocking chair and feel her little body as she cried or squirmed, and rub her warm back until she began to relax. She wished she could take back all the bad things she'd ever said.

$\sim$

Many uneventful hours later, the phone rang. Mayree jumped, dropping her crocheting to the floor. Before she could reach the phone next to her chair, Paula came in, holding the handset. "It's the detective."

Mayree sat up straighter, smoothing her hair as if he were in the room. Trying to orient herself, she glanced at the clock on the wall: six thirty. And out the window: dark but no longer raining. "Hello?"

Paula stood in front of her, eyes wide, hands clasped.

At the end of their brief conversation, Mayree said, "Okay then. I'm leaving now."

"Well?" Paula asked before Mayree had even hung up.

"I'm going to the washateria."

"What? Why?"

"It'll look better if it's one of us," Mayree said. "In case the guy's watching."

"But I was going to do it."

Mayree cupped Paula's cheek. "Not on my watch," she said. "He said the squad's in place. They're sending a car to follow me there and back. It'll be quick. They already told the woman working there what we're doing. They're going to have a patrol car parked in front of the house so you'll be safe. Then all we have to do is wait."

"Mom, please don't do this."

Mayree put her hand on Paula's head, touching her velveteen buzz for the first time. "I don't want what you went through to affect you the way my situation did me. If I could, I'd like to kill that son of a bitch," she said, feeling her anger bloom. "Both of them."

~

Mayree met her police escort at the park midway between Old Enfield and the washateria. He gave her a canvas laundry bag filled with money. For a nanosecond, Mayree imagined taking the hundred thousand, going back for Paula, and running off to Mexico to start over. Then she chastised herself for her selfish—and illegal—impulse. That's all Paula needed: a dead father and a felon for a mother.

Instead, she followed the officer's instructions: she drove to the washateria and parked in front. She stood outside and looked around, making herself visible to anyone watching. After a moment, she went inside. The woman working there watched her. Mayree gave her a tiny nod and the woman blinked slowly as if in response. The dryer closest to the front door. There was a load in it, still drying. Mayree looked at the woman and tilted her head at the dryer. The woman shrugged. Did that mean she knew what was going on? Was she going to inspect the bag and ruin everything? Well, it was too late to worry about that now.

"Fuck," she whispered. Looking around, she didn't see anyone watching her. She transferred the damp laundry into the next dryer over and fished a quarter out of her purse to start the cycle. Then she tossed the bag of money into the correct unit, closed the door, and hurried back to her car.

Back home, she locked the door and leaned against it, her heart pounding.

"Are you okay?" Paula rushed to her and pulled her into the living room. "Here, sit. I'll get you a drink."

"No, no. I can't sit," Mayree said.

"What happened?" Paula asked.

"Exactly what they told me." The drop may have been done, but Mayree was beside herself worrying about whether it was going to work. She peeked out the window. The patrol car that had been there was pulling away. She still wondered if she'd done the right thing by involving Detective Cervenka and his team. "Help me check the locks, will you?"

While Paula went through the downstairs, Mayree got Frank's shotgun out of the gun safe in his office and loaded it. She put extra shells in her pocket. Then, to pass the anxious time, she whetted her already-sharp switchblade again until the blade could slice through a piece of Frank's old stationery without any force at all.

In spite of the countdown to eight o'clock, the pervasive threat of danger, Mayree was exhausted. She sat down in her wing chair with her knife and a cigarette—she could smoke in the house, thank god—and turned on the television. Paula sat on the couch, both of them alternating between watching the television, the clock, and the phone. Mayree grew increasingly nervous as the appointed hour passed, then another fifteen minutes, then thirty.

The phone rang just after eight thirty.

Mayree grabbed it. "Yes?" she said in an urgent voice. "You did? Thank the lord. So you've got him, it's over." She slumped back heavily, exhaled her relief.

Paula gave her a thumbs-up along with a weary smile.

Then Mayree shot forward in her chair. "His name is *what*? But that's a common enough name. How do you know it's the same one?" She looked over at her daughter, who looked back at her with alarm. "You've got to be fucking kidding me. That's not possible!" After a moment, she nodded. "Okay, we'll be here. Thank you, Detective." She hung up and closed her eyes. "Sweet Mary, mother of God," she whispered.

"What, Mom? What did he say?"

Mayree shook her head. "I have to make a call." She dialed a number.

Paula watched her. "Why?"

Mayree started to speak, but her mouth was suddenly dry, and she couldn't find the words. Her mind went back to her conversation with Stan, how he'd said he was afraid something like this would happen. In a thousand years, she never would've imagined this.

"They got him," she said to Paula as she listened to the ring, waiting for someone to pick up. "He went to the washateria carrying an empty laundry bag. He went straight to the dryer and took the money out. There was a plainclothes cop watching and he immediately arrested him."

"That's good, isn't it?" Paula asked. "Why are you so upset? Who are you calling?"

Mayree held on to the precious silence for just a moment. She knew as soon as the call connected, everything was going to change.

"Hello?"

"Felicia," Mayree said. "It was Curtis. They arrested him for extortion and aggravated assault."

Paula

As Mayree repeated to Felicia what the detective had told her, Paula pressed "Talk" on the remote handset so she could hear Felicia's side of the conversation.

"No," Felicia whispered. "It can't be."

"That's what I said. But then he told me his birthday. Friday you told me Curtis was born after you'd been with us a year or so, right? That would've been 1972."

"August the eighth," she said. "He was born August the eighth, 1972."

"I'm so sorry, Felicia. They picked him up. They're taking him downtown now." Mayree's face registered apparent disbelief.

"Oh lord, Mayree," Felicia said. "Oh no. I can't believe it. It's not true."

Paula couldn't believe it either. Not Curtis. Not someone who was in any way related to this gentle, pious, principled woman who'd helped raise her. It wasn't possible. Besides, even though she didn't know Curtis and she'd been drunk the night she was attacked, she was sure she'd have recognized him somehow. "Maybe it was a mistake," Paula said.

"Which washateria was it?" Felicia asked.

"The one on East Twelfth."

"That's the one I've been sending him to. Remember I told you I've been making him do his own laundry?" Felicia paused. "I know I said he's been nothing but trouble since he got out of juvie, but there's no way he'd do something like this."

Paula wished she could hug Felicia. Of course Felicia wouldn't want to believe Curtis had done it. She knew how much Felicia loved her and Curtis both, so it would crush her to hear that one of them may have hurt the other. It crushed Paula, too, because she didn't know if it meant she might somehow lose Felicia because of it.

"It's not your fault, Felicia," Mayree said softly. "You've done everything you could for Curtis."

Felicia's voice went up in pitch. "Including not thinking for one second he could hurt Paula."

"I'm just telling you what they told me," Mayree said. "I'm so sorry."

"You there, Paula?" Felicia asked, her voice cracking.

"I'm here." Her heart ached at the sadness in Felicia's voice. She'd seen Felicia cry countless times—she was never shy about showing her emotions—but this situation was different.

"I'm so sorry for what you've been through, baby girl. I do think there was some kind of mistake, but if it was him, I'll never forgive myself."

"Felicia," Mayree said, "you're not responsible for him."

"Of course I am."

"The whole world can't be on your shoulders. That's too much for anyone."

"I'm not saying the whole world. But the people in it I love. I bear responsibility for them whether I want to or not."

Paula closed her eyes as they filled with tears.

"Kenny's outside, grilling," Felicia said. "This is going to break his heart. I can't call Ralph, him being in prison. Lord, who even knows where Bonita is."

"Do you want me to meet you at the station?" Mayree asked.

"No. Kenny and I'll go. I can hardly think what's gonna happen after this, even if it was a mistake, with Curtis just out of detention."

"Felicia," Paula said. It came out like a plea, but for what, she didn't know. She didn't know what to feel, much less to say. She couldn't feel the relief she was entitled to because of what it meant for Felicia. The problem hadn't been resolved after all; it had just been shifted to another person. "I'm sorry."

"You don't be sorry for one thing, you hear me?" Felicia said.

But it was too late for that; Paula was sorry for more things than she could count.

~

After saying goodbye to Felicia, Paula lay back on the couch, her thoughts in a tangle. She watched Mayree, who was staring at the phone in her hand like it was a grenade. "I need to call Sissy," she said, dialing her number. "Sissy, call me back when you can. It's over. You're never going to believe who it was. Even I can't believe it."

"Poor Felicia," Mayree said after she hung up. "As much as she's done for everybody else, she doesn't deserve this. Her own nephew. How is that possible?"

Paula moved to the floor near her mother, hugging a throw pillow. "I can't either." She thought of how he'd sounded on the phone when she'd called the Johnsons' house on Thursday: rude, yes. Angry. But not familiar. She wondered why she hadn't felt something hearing his voice. She really had been wasted on Saturday.

"Are you okay?" Mayree fumbled with her lighter. It took a few tries before she lit her cigarette.

Paula watched the tendrils rise up and dissipate into the air, feeling overcome by some emotion she couldn't identify. "I guess. I'm glad it's over," Paula said. The threat was gone. Nobody was going to break in and hurt them. She felt relief, but also sadness. "Everything feels upside down, you know? Like losing Dad, then Will. And then hearing what Uncle Stan said about that kid." She didn't know how to share with her mother that she also mourned her sense of safety, her job, her hair, her relationship with Kelly—at least how it used to be—and Mayree herself, whom she felt like she'd lost a long time ago. Instead, she asked, "Are you going to fire Felicia?"

"Lord, no. Never." She exhaled loudly. "I don't know if I'll be able to convince her not to quit, though."

"Good," Paula said. She hated that her life, upside down as it was, could go on now that Curtis had been caught, but Felicia's wouldn't be the same. She'd be hurting for a long, long time. "How about you?"

"I'm not sure yet," Mayree said with a weary half smile. "I've got a lot to think about. This, of course, and everything else."

Paula considered what Mayree had been through, too, that week. And before. "You mean about Dad and his . . . ?"

"Dad and his . . . legacy, yes. And Felicia. Sissy, Stan. You," she said. "Me."

Paula wanted so much to crawl into her mother's lap and rest her head against her shoulder. But she also wanted to stay where she was and let this more adult conversation continue. Based on their uneasy history, she couldn't be certain it would ever happen again.

The tentative calm that had settled over the room was interrupted by an abrupt, high-pitched, feral-sounding scream coming from outside that made Paula's heart race. "What was that?" she said to Mayree, whose eyes were wide. "Some kind of animal?"

The screaming continued, louder and with more anguish. "That's not an animal," Mayree said, flinging the blanket off her lap.

"Mom, don't!"

Mayree ignored her. She grabbed her switchblade from the table next to her ashtray and headed for the door. She picked up the shotgun that was propped against the wall in the foyer like it was an extension of herself, and ran, barefoot, out into the drizzling darkness with Paula on her heels.

"Mom, stop!"

The yard was drenched, and because the spring grass was still thin, it was a slippery, muddy mess. Mayree tripped over a protruding oak tree root and dropped the shotgun in a puddle. She righted herself and kept running. Paula was too worried about her mother to stop and pick it up. They rounded the corner to the east side of the house just as they heard the scream turn into a screeching plea for help.

There, directly beneath the trellis leading up to Paula's bedroom window, someone was lying on the ground, shrieking in pain. "What is it?" Mayree asked, her voice loud and urgent above the noise.

"Help me!" the voice said. It was a man's voice. "What's this fucking thing on my leg?"

Paula's mind hadn't caught up with her breathless body. Why was a man on the ground by their house, screaming? In the dark, they could barely see what the matter was. Paula bent closer and saw that the man's leg was caught in a trap—the same kind that they'd found on the other side of the house a few days before with the baby opossum in it. She let out her own scream as she reared away from him, her stomach lurching at the sight of the man writhing there with blood gushing from his wound.

Mayree hooked Paula with her arm and pulled her daughter behind her. "What the hell is going on?"

"Get it off!" he screamed.

"Mrs. Baker!" came another voice. "Mrs. Baker, are you all right?" The light from a handheld spotlight bounced toward them from next door, and then Herb Walker was there, out of breath and heaving.

"It's not me, Herb. Someone's caught in a trap! Help me get him out."

Herb flashed his light on the victim, who covered his face with his arm against the high-lumen light. "He's caught all right. Look at that—clear to the bone," he said. "I'm sorry, young fella. These were supposed to catch vermin, not people. Mrs. Baker, you hold this light for me while I spring him loose."

The man screamed again. Paula stood helplessly by, horrified. She could almost feel the pain in her own body as she watched him gasping and squirming on the ground. "Hurry," she said to Mr. Walker.

"*You* put these out?" Mayree asked.

"I sure did. Made 'em in my garage. I noticed things here had gotten a little overgrown lately, no offense. I was going to prune the trees myself after my back healed up, but in the meantime, I set out some traps to make sure nothing got inside the house. Here, hold this, will ya?" Mayree took the light. "Shine it down here where I can see the latch."

Mayree did as she was told, while the trapped man continued to struggle. He must've caught his foot in the trap and fallen. He was on his side in the mud, flailing at his trapped leg, which was bent underneath him. It just then dawned on Paula that this person, whoever he was, wasn't just on their property—he was beneath her window.

"Hold still, son, or it'll hurt worse."

"Mom, what if he's a burglar?"

Without the light directly on his head, Mayree leaned in and looked at the man's face. "You look familiar," she said. "Who are you?"

He responded with noises of agony.

Moving closer, Mayree shined the light in his face, then pointed it down to where his leg was caught. From her puzzled expression, Paula could see her mother's thoughts churning. Then Mayree snapped her fingers and pointed at him. "Wait a minute," she said. "I recognize you! You're that kid from the grocery store. You damn near killed me with a shopping cart."

"Get me out!" he cried.

"You said your shopping cart got away from you in the wind and you came running over to help me," Mayree said, shining the light on his face. "What the fuck are you doing here? Did you follow me home?"

Paula could feel her heart pounding in her throat. She wanted to grab her mother by the shoulders and pull her away from him. He shouldn't be there, this close to their house. Nobody should be. Whatever he'd been doing there wasn't good.

"Mrs. Baker, I need the light down here."

"Shut the fuck up, Herb." She glared at him until he seemed convinced of her sincerity. Herb pressed on both knees to heave himself upright.

In the distance, Lena Walker, Herb's wife, called out, "Herb? What's going on over there?"

Herb called back, "I'm not quite sure, Lena, but you better go ahead and call the police."

Mayree turned to the guy. "Who the fuck are you?"

"Off!" he cried.

Stepping nervously forward, Paula could now clearly see the man's face. She felt her stomach drop. *You asked for this.* She stumbled backward, her breath coming in short gasps. It seemed impossible with the rain and dirt, but she swore she could smell the powdery scent of aftershave. The man—the guy—groaned. Paula bumped against Herb, and she clutched on to him to keep herself from falling.

"Oh, hey there," Herb said. "Are you okay?"

Paula couldn't speak. Seeing the guy again filled her with abject, paralyzing terror. She stared at his face as the scene in the car played in her mind, recognizing the features she'd forgotten until now, his angry scowl just as it had been when he was screaming at her: *I'm gonna cut your throat and then I'm gonna fuck you in it. You hear me? I'm gonna fuck you in the neck.*

Mayree turned the flashlight toward Paula's midsection. "Paula, what is it?" she asked.

Paula's entire body was shaking violently as she pointed at the guy who'd taken her, attacked her, tried to kill her. "It's him," she said, her voice a gargle. "It's him."

Mayree

Mayree hadn't been able to fathom what was happening on her lawn, but seeing her daughter so upset with recognition was enough. She didn't need to hear a confession or confirmation; in that moment, Mayree knew in her gut that the police had caught the wrong person, that Paula's attacker was this guy lying beneath her window in a trap.

"Get back," she said to Paula, nearly growling. Herb and Paula shuffled backward a few steps.

Mayree knelt slowly down on one knee, putting the full weight of her fury on the guy's chest. The force against his torso caused his leg to twist inside the sharp jaws of the trap and he screamed, rolling his head back and forth, his dark hair and face smeared with mud.

"Get off!" He coughed as Mayree leaned her weight harder on his chest. "Goddamn it, off!" The guy took a swing at Mayree, landing it on her shoulder.

Mayree barely registered it. The need to protect Paula, compounded by decades' worth of rage, made her invulnerable. He struck her again, even harder this time, and Mayree slapped him across the face as hard as she could, sending drops of mud flying. "You little shit! Who the fuck are you?"

"Bitch! Whore!" He spit at her and screamed again. "It hurts!"

Mayree set down the light so that it shone on his face, then opened her switchblade and held it in front of him. "You're hurt?" she said. "You're *hurt?*" She pressed the flat side of the blade against his throat.

He tried to pull her arm away, and she pressed down harder. "Do that again and I'll kill you right where you're lying."

"Now, Mrs. Baker, I think things are getting a little out of control here," Herb said.

Without taking her eyes off the guy, she said, "Herb, get your fat ass off my property right now or you'll be next."

"Mom," Paula said, pleading. "Don't."

"What's your name? Michael? Isn't that what you told me at the grocery store? That shopping cart thing wasn't an accident, was it? What the fuck did you want? And why did you attack my daughter?"

"Fuck you!" he screamed.

Mayree slapped him again and he thrashed until she jammed the blade against his Adam's apple hard enough to choke him. "Listen, Michael. You hurt my daughter last Saturday night. You used a knife on her, didn't you? You told her you were going to cut her neck. And you said some other nasty things, didn't you? You know what? Somebody once used a knife on me, too. Pressed it right there." She pushed down harder and Michael coughed again. "Doesn't feel very good, does it?"

"Stop!" he said.

"Why should I?" Mayree hissed.

He stopped thrashing long enough to glare at her. "I'm Frank's son."

For a moment, she felt like she had the one time she'd smoked pot: like she was falling even though she was standing still. Mayree searched his face, looking for Frank's features even as she retained her grip on the abalone handle of her knife. Between the mud and darkness, she didn't see any resemblance, except possibly the crookedness of his eyeteeth when he bared them at her.

"Well, if that's true, then your mother fucked a married man. That makes her the whore, not me."

Michael stopped resisting and closed his eyes, whether in defiance or pain, she couldn't tell. She thought of him holding his own knife against her daughter's throat. She thought of how, long ago, Bobby had done it to her. If she wanted to hurt Michael now, she'd certainly be justified. All she'd have to do was change the angle of the blade just slightly so that the sharp edge would meet his soft flesh.

"Go ahead." He looked up at her with the sad and angry eyes of an abused dog. "I don't even fucking care."

Mayree had seen eyes like that in the shelter. It gave her pause, even as she imagined slicing into his neck and letting him bleed out on the ground. She glanced at Paula, who was leaning pitifully against Herb Walker, looking horrified. Herb was wide-eyed, his mouth sagging open.

Mayree felt a sinkhole opening up inside her, her wrath and sense of invincibility vanishing into it. The idea of hurting Michael had been briefly satisfying, but now that she had the opportunity, she didn't actually want that kind of vengeance. She wouldn't do that to Paula, especially after what her daughter had already endured. Mayree pulled the blade off Michael and folded it back into its handle. Knowing he couldn't go anywhere unless released, she got off him and stood back. She put her arm around her daughter, who let go of Herb and clung to her. "Where's your mother?" she asked Michael. "I want to talk to her."

"She's dead!" he screamed. Then he began to cry. Mayree saw him then for what he was beneath the vitriol and brutality: a child. He was just a child.

Police sirens blared in the distance, getting louder as they got closer. Three patrol cars screeched to a halt in front of the Bakers' house, and six officers came running toward them with their pistols out. "Put your hands up!" one of them shouted. Mayree, Paula, and Herb all did as they were told.

Paula

After they were released by the police, Paula asked Mayree, "I know it's late, but can we drive over to Felicia's?"

Mayree looked at her. "Do you want to take a shower first?"

Paula looked down; she was splattered with mud. She was not only filthy but also exhausted, hungry, and deeply rattled. "No. I just want to give her a hug."

"Let's go," Mayree said, picking up her purse.

As Paula slid into the passenger seat of her mother's car, which of course had been her father's, she shuddered. "Mom," she said. Then, as the wild reality of the day's events settled into her, she began to cry.

Mayree put the car into park, and they idled in the driveway. "It's okay," she said, patting Paula on the forearm. "Go ahead and let it out."

Paula didn't even know where to begin. She was overwhelmed by the fact that her attacker—Michael—had come back for her, as he'd threatened. Overwhelmed by watching her mother fight him, simultaneously avenging and defending her, and learning who he was—or claimed to be. "Do you think he really is Dad's?"

Mayree let her head drop back onto the headrest. "I honestly don't know. If he is, I guess we'll have to figure out how to deal with it.

Though after what he did to you, I hope the last time we ever have to lay eyes on him is in a courtroom before they haul his ass off to prison."

"I just can't believe it," Paula said. "I mean, he's probably my age. Or close to it." She pressed her fingertips to her eyes. "Dad's secretary was the only one you told me about, even though I figured it was more than just her. I guess it didn't really register until Uncle Stan was talking about it that Dad had been cheating on you for basically my whole life."

Paula had adored her father. Idolized him. If she was being honest, it had made her proud that, between her and Mayree, he'd always seemed to love her best. She'd never questioned it before; she'd just felt vindicated that he loved *and* liked her even if Mayree didn't. But now she had to wonder how much about her parents' relationship she hadn't understood, and how her own devotion to him may have affected her mother.

"It's not something a child should have to deal with," Mayree said after a moment.

"But you shouldn't have had to deal with it either," Paula said. "Why didn't you leave him?"

Mayree sighed and looked at her. "For a lot of reasons, I guess. You, for one. Money, or lack of it. Plus, I didn't want to admit defeat. I was embarrassed. I still am," she said, then gave a small chuffing laugh. "It's embarrassing for me to even say that."

"But it wasn't your fault he cheated on you."

"For a long time, I thought it was."

Paula thought about how she'd blamed herself for not being enough for Will after he broke up with her. She thought of her desperate longing for his affection, how willing she was to accept mere crumbs, because she didn't think she deserved more. She wondered if that's how her mother had felt about Frank. She'd witnessed how dismissive her father had been to Mayree over the years, how casually he insulted her, how infrequently he offered her any overt affection or kindness. Paula wished she'd stood up for her mother back then, instead of pridefully accepting the crumbs he offered to her instead. "No, Mom. You deserved better."

"Well, thank you for saying that," Mayree said, clearly uncomfortable. She reached across Paula to get a package of tissues out of the glove box and handed them to her. Paula wondered if Mayree didn't take compliments well because she didn't get them very often.

"It makes me hate him. Like, my whole life feels like a lie." She'd like to go back in time and confront him, force him to explain himself. Tell him that he wasn't the good man she'd always believed him to be.

Mayree turned to her. "Now listen. He's still your father. He was a flawed person, but who isn't? Except me, of course. I'm perfect." She kept a deadpan expression for a beat, then cracked a smile. Paula laughed, releasing some of her built-up tension. "Seriously, though. When you think about assigning blame, make sure you spread it out a little. I definitely wasn't perfect and never will be. And no matter what he did, your daddy loved you. That was real. You don't need to go back and revise that history."

Paula nodded, although she wasn't sure she wouldn't. It was gutting to learn all this about him. Not only because of how he'd treated her mother, but—if it was true that Michael was her half brother and her father and Uncle Stan had done something to him—then because of Michael and his mother, too.

"Let's go check on Felicia," Mayree said.

To get to Felicia's in East Austin, Paula consulted the map for directions. She realized that the Johnsons' house wasn't terribly far from Will's. She gave her mother directions that yielded a wider than necessary berth around his place. Crumbs of love were no longer enough. She thought about Kelly and realized that she'd also been accepting scraps from her. Paula knew she deserved better from a best friend, too.

They pulled up to what they hoped was the correct address and walked quietly to the front door. The porch light was on, but otherwise the house was dark. Just as Mayree was about to knock, Felicia opened the door wearing her robe and slippers. Paula rushed into her arms.

"I saw y'all pull up," Felicia said in a whisper. "I'm so glad you're okay. When we picked Curtis up, the detective told us what happened at your house. I was so worried. I called but nobody answered."

Mayree looked at Paula. "We're okay. We came because we were worried about *you*. And Curtis, of course. It wasn't right."

"He's inside, sleeping. I don't want to disturb him."

"Of course not," Mayree said. She stepped forward and gave Felicia a fierce hug. "I want to apologize for what happened. It's partly my fault; I moved what must've been Curtis's clothes into another dryer to put the money in the one mentioned in the letter."

"You don't need to be sorry. It was a mistake. A bad one, sure, but it also shocked some sense into him. He doesn't want to go through anything like that again."

"Why was he even there?" Paula asked.

"He was doing laundry is all. He was across the street having some ice cream while his clothes were drying; then he went back to get them. He was the only customer in the place, and the cops assumed it was him. Guilty until proven innocent. It happens to Black folks all the time."

"Shit, Felicia, I'm sorry," Mayree said.

None of them spoke for a moment, all of them thinking their own thoughts. Paula became aware of the sounds of cars in the distance, a dog barking, the wind rushing through the tree next to Felicia's front door. When Felicia had talked to her about women's struggles, that they bear awful stuff all the time, Paula hadn't known what awful stuff had happened to her. She'd assumed it was some form of violence against her as a woman. She hadn't considered how different it might be for a Black woman. She hadn't realized until now that Felicia's whole family had to deal with things hers never would.

"It's a shame for sure. You coming here means a lot to me, though." She hugged them both again. "It's late. I'm going to go sit with Curtis in case he wakes up. Y'all drive home safe."

Mayree leaned in and kissed her on the cheek.

"I love you," Paula told Felicia.

"I love you, too, baby girl," Felicia said. She clasped hands with Mayree. "Both of you."

Mayree

When they got home, Sissy was waiting for them in the living room, a plate of sandwiches and a bottle of wine laid out on the coffee table. "After I got your message, I figured you needed some sustenance," she said. "Hope you don't mind me letting myself in. I'm dying to know what happened."

"Of course not," Mayree said. She put her handbag down like it held the weight of the entire week. "That was nice of you."

"Thanks, Aunt Sissy," Paula said. "I'm starving."

"Where's Kelly?" Mayree asked, glancing at Paula, who gave a small shake of her head. She still didn't know what happened between the girls, but when things settled down, she'd ask her about it.

"She came home after y'all's economics class and crashed. I know she'd be here otherwise," Sissy said. "Listen, I know you must be exhausted so I'm not going to stay long, but can you fill me in? Who was it?"

Mayree poured them each a glass and told Sissy everything that had happened since they left the Bakers' house earlier that morning. Listening to herself talk about it, it was as if they'd lived three lifetimes between nine in the morning and eleven thirty that night. Sissy sat on the edge of the couch the whole time, eyes wide, her hand covering her mouth.

"That sounds like a horror movie," Sissy said when Mayree finished. "Poor Curtis. I'm so glad it wasn't him. And Felicia! She must be a wreck."

"She's doing pretty well considering," Mayree said. "But it was awful for her."

"And for y'all."

Mayree and Paula looked at each other and nodded.

"Well, now knowing who Paula's attacker was makes *this* even more interesting." She bent down to pull a manila file folder out of her purse and handed it to Mayree. "Stan didn't burn the backup file. I found it in a box in his closet. I went over to talk to him, and you were right about him knowing more than he admitted." She took a bite of her sandwich as Mayree flipped the folder open. "Also, I told him I want a divorce."

"Oh shit, Sissy," Mayree said, closing the file. "Are you sure? That's a big step."

Sighing, Sissy wiped some crumbs from her chest onto her plate and leaned back. "It is, but I can't get past what he did. Not the cheating, I probably could've forgiven him for that, but this business." She jutted her chin at the folder in Mayree's lap. "You can read it yourself but basically, this boy—Michael—did go to Frank and ask for money. Stan said he *fixed* the problem by planting drugs on him and reporting him to a friend on the force. Michael went to juvenile detention for more than a year for it."

"But he didn't do anything?" Paula asked.

Sissy shook her head. "Nothing but ask for money to help his mother, who was dying of cancer."

"You're shitting me," Mayree said. She thought of Michael writhing in the mud—the same boy who'd attacked Paula—crying for his mother. Her fury at what he'd done to her daughter remained, but now she couldn't help but also feel a little bit sorry for him. She took a breath, preparing herself for what Sissy might say. "Was Frank his father?" she asked.

"Stan says he doesn't know for sure," Sissy said. "He said that Frank met Michael's mother right after he bought the property we were talking about—where Chapo's is. She was managing the washateria back then. Apparently when she told Frank she was pregnant, he denied it was his and ran her off."

"Honestly, it wouldn't surprise me if he knocked her up and abandoned her," Mayree said. She felt a grim solidarity with this unknown woman, even if she did have an affair with her husband. "That explains why Michael picked the washateria at least. Frank probably met her when he was collecting rent or something, and the kid was trying to make a point by choosing that place."

"Could be why he smelled like Daddy, too," Paula said, sounding crestfallen. "If he went to Chapo's."

Mayree turned to her daughter. "I'm sorry, Paula. This is all too much at once."

Paula shook her head. "I need to hear it."

"It's possible he really wasn't the father," Sissy offered. "Stan said he did some digging after Michael showed up at Frank's office and couldn't find any records, any proof that it's true. His name's not even on the birth certificate."

"I don't know if that makes it better or worse," Mayree said.

"Either way, it's sad what they did to him," Sissy said. "That doesn't excuse what he did to you, though, Paula."

"Hell no, it does not," Mayree said. "Who his father is doesn't change that. He made the choice to hurt you—not Dad, not Stan."

"I can't believe Stan would stoop so low," Sissy said. She finished her wine in one long sip, then refilled their glasses. "I'll never look at him the same way again."

Mayree realized that Sissy wouldn't be in this position if she hadn't so adamantly stood up for her. She'd sacrificed her marriage for her friendship with Mayree. The tight knot of emotion she'd carried around inside herself for so long seemed to loosen. Her own life had been dominated by the specter of two men, first Bobby and then Frank. Paula had already had to grieve her father, her first love, and her innocence. Now Sissy was going to lose Stan. But they still had each other. She'd been so focused on the men in her life—their lives—that she'd forgotten to cherish the women.

"What will you do?" Mayree asked. "Are you going to tell the police what he did?"

Sissy sighed. "I don't know. I'm really struggling with what to do about it all. I feel like I have an ethical responsibility to tell, but at the same time, I have to think about what it would do to Kelly and Dean. I probably will, but I just need some time to think it through."

Mayree took her hand. "I'm here. We can figure it out together. You can even stay here if you want or need to."

"Oh, honey," she said, shaking her head. "I couldn't bear the smoke."

Mayree thought of everything Sissy had done for her that week, how gracefully she'd taken her back as a friend, even without an apology. She took her open pack out of her pocket and set it down on the coffee table. "Don't worry about that," she said. "For you, I might even quit."

$\sim$

Sissy left just before midnight and Mayree locked the door behind her. "Help me carry these dishes into the kitchen, will you?" she asked Paula.

As Paula put the leftover sandwiches away and Mayree rinsed their plates, Paula asked, "What's going to happen now? With Michael."

Mayree took a deep breath and turned off the water. "I suppose he'll go to trial. As for the rest of it, including Stan, I have no idea."

Paula leaned against the counter. "What do we do next? Like, how do we just go on after all this?"

Mayree thought for a moment, then resumed putting dishes into the dishwasher. "We just do. We'll go to bed and then get up in the morning. You'll go to class. I'll go to the grocery store. And I'm going to get a job."

"What kind of job?"

Mayree shrugged. "I was thinking I might apply for a paid position at the shelter. At least for now until I can figure something else out. If I'm going to be there, I might as well get paid for it, right?"

Paula cocked her head and looked at her with a penetrating gaze. "You're kind of a badass, you know."

"Ha!" Mayree said.

"I mean it. What you did outside tonight was awesome."

Paula's flattery embarrassed her, but Mayree was pleased nonetheless. "You're my kid," she said by way of explanation. Mayree wished she knew how to say what she really wanted to, which was that in spite of her many flaws as a person and as a mother, she loved Paula deeply. She loved her more than she'd ever loved anything or anyone, even if she hadn't intended to, even if she didn't show it very well. That she would do anything to protect and prepare her for whatever might happen down the line. That she wanted her daughter to have a better life than the one she herself had modeled so far.

She wanted to say all that and she knew that Paula wanted to hear it. She could see Paula's disappointment in the way she nodded and turned away.

"There are a bunch of messages on the machine," she said. "Want me to clear them out?"

"Sure," Mayree said, frustrated with herself for letting the moment pass.

Mayree heard Paula press the "Play" button on the answering machine. As Felicia had said, there were a dozen or more from her, and two from Sissy, asking for updates. Then there was the sound of a male voice: "Hey, Paula, it's Will. I got your—"

Paula pressed "Delete" before the rest of the message played.

Mayree turned. "Didn't you want to hear what he had to say?"

"No," Paula said.

"Really?"

Paula shrugged. "I deserve better."

"Yeah," Mayree said. "You sure do."

Paula patted the counter twice, a note of finality. "I think I'm going to go take a shower. I'm wiped. And I have class in the morning."

As Paula turned to go, Mayree felt something essential between them slipping away. She reached out and grabbed her by the arm. She pulled her daughter into a tight embrace, which Paula returned, briefly, before trying to step away. But Mayree held on. She held on and held on and held on—waiting until Paula finally relaxed—determined to make up for lost time.

ACKNOWLEDGMENTS

My sincerest thanks to the experts who helped me with the technical aspects of this story. Jill Mata, chief juvenile probation officer, Bexar County Juvenile Probation Department; Fred Hackett, corporal, Harris County Constable Precinct 1; and especially Scott Cervenka, detective (retired), Houston Police Department, Major Offenders Division. Their insights were generous and invaluable. Any mistakes relating to the crimes and punishments of my characters are mine alone.

To my beloved early readers for their brainstorming help, feedback, and encouragement, I offer endless gratitude: Mark Haber, Charlie Baxter, Sara Huffman, Jenny Johnson, Kristi Foye, Lee Ann Grimes, Shana Halvorsen, Julia Brown, Laura Moser, Tobey Forney, Mimi Vance, and especially Heather Montoya and Louise Marburg. I couldn't have done this without you. Nor would I have wanted to.

I'm beyond grateful to my literary agent, Jesseca Salky, for her unwavering faith in me. It's a lucky writer who has such unconditional support over the course of her career. I'm equally fortunate to have the support of my badass publishing team. To my keen-eyed editors, Carmen Johnson and Tiffany Yates Martin; copyeditor, Tara Whitaker; production editor, Lauren Grange; proofreader, Sarah Vostok; cold reader, Steve Schul; cultural research reader, Malika Whitley; and the entire team at Little A, thank you not only for making this book possible but for helping me make it the best it could possibly be.

This novel was inspired by a traumatic attack that occurred the summer of 1989, while I was studying abroad. As is true in many cases, the terrifying details of that central event are vividly encoded in my memory, while the peripheral ones are gone. However, I remember one positive moment of that awful night: when I finally made it back to the terraza I'd been taken from, long after it had closed, the friend I'd been with was still there. Afterward, along with so much else, my mind erased her last name. I looked for her for years to tell her how much that meant to me, but only after finishing this manuscript did I find her. Kelly Robinson de Schaun, thank you for waiting for me.

ABOUT THE AUTHOR

Photo © 2023 Paula N. Luu

Chris Cander is the *USA Today* bestselling author of the novels *A Gracious Neighbor*, *The Weight of a Piano*, *Whisper Hollow*, and *11 Stories*, and the children's picture book *The Word Burglar*. Her fiction has been published in twelve languages. A former firefighter, Cander holds a fourth dan in tae kwon do and is a certified women's defensive tactics instructor. She lives in Houston with her husband and two children. For more information, visit www.chriscander.com.